**Anne O'Brien** was born in the West Riding of Yorkshire. After gaining a BA Honours degree at Manchester University and a Master's at Hull, she lived in the East Riding for many years as a teacher of history. After leaving teaching, Anne decided to turn to novel writing and give voice to the women in history who fascinated her the most. Today Anne lives in an eighteenth-century cottage in Herefordshire, an area full of inspiration for her work.

Visit Anne online at www.anneobrienbooks.com. Find Anne on Facebook and follow her on Twitter @anne_obrien

ANNE O'BRIEN

The KING'S CONCUBINE

HARLEQUIN®MIRA®

This edition published in Great Britain 2015
by Harlequin MIRA, an imprint of Harlequin (UK) Limited,
Eton House, 18-24 Paradise Road,
Richmond, Surrey, TW9 1SR

Fleur Adcock, Poems 1960-2000 (Bloodaxe Books, 2000) reprinted with kind permission of the publisher on behalf of the author

Map and Family Tree acknowledgement Orphans Press Ltd

ISBN 978-1-848-45384-5

56-0115

Harlequin (UK) Limited's policy is to use papers that are natural, renewable and recyclable products and made from wood grown in sustainable forests. The logging and manufacturing processes conform to the legal environmental regulations of the country of origin.

Printed and bound by
CPI Group (UK) Ltd, Croydon, CR0 4YY

Royal Palaces &
Alice's Manors

Descendants of Edward III (simplified)

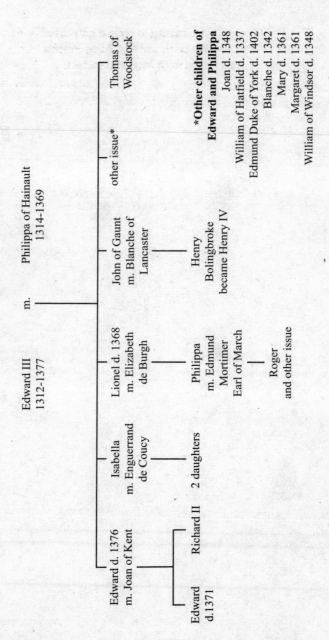

Edward III
1312–1377

m.

Philippa of Hainault
1314–1369

Edward d. 1376
m. Joan of Kent

Isabella
m. Enguerrand
de Coucy

Lionel d. 1368
m. Elizabeth
de Burgh

John of Gaunt
m. Blanche of
Lancaster

other issue*

Thomas of
Woodstock

Richard II

Edward
d. 1371

2 daughters

Philippa
m. Edmund
Mortimer
Earl of March

Henry
Bolingbroke
became Henry IV

Roger
and other issue

***Other children of
Edward and Philippa**
Joan d. 1348
William of Hatfield d. 1337
Edmund Duke of York d. 1402
Blanche d. 1342
Mary d. 1361
Margaret d. 1361
William of Windsor d. 1348

For George, who managed to live comfortably for
a year with both me and Alice Perrers.
As ever, with love and thanks.

'There was…in England a shameless woman and wanton harlot called Ales Peres, of base kindred… being neither beautiful nor fair, she knew how to cover these defects with her flattering tongue…'

—*A historical relation of certain passages about the end of King Edward the Third and of his death*

'It is not fitting that all the keys should hang from the belt of one woman.'

—*The Bishop of Rochester*

'…no one dared to go against her…'

—*Thomas Walsingham, a monk of St Albans*

Prologue

'*Today you will be my Lady of the Sun,*' King Edward says as he approaches to settle me into my chariot. '*My Queen of Ceremonies.*'

And not before time.

I don't say the words, of course—I am, after all, a woman of percipience—but I think them. I have waited too many years for this acclaim. Twelve years as Edward's whore.

'*Thank you, my lord,*' *I murmur, curtseying deeply, my smile as sweet as honey.*

I sit, a cloak of shimmering gold tissue spread around me, to show a lining of scarlet taffeta. My gown is red, lined with white silk and edged in ermine: Edward's colours, royal fur fit for a Queen. Over all glitters a myriad of precious stones refracting the light—rubies as red as blood, sapphires dark and mysterious, strange beryls capable of destroying the power of poison. Everyone knows that I wear Queen Philippa's jewels.

I sit at my ease, alone in my pre-eminence, my hands loose in my bejewelled lap. This is my right.

I look around to see if I might catch sight of the black scowl of the Princess Joan. No sign of her, my sworn enemy. She'll be tucked away in her chamber at Kennington, wishing me ill. Joan the Fair. Joan the Fat! An adversary to be wary of, with the sensitivity and morals of a feral cat in heat.

My gaze slides to Edward as he mounts his stallion and my smile softens. He is tall and strong and good to look on. What a pair we make, he and I. The years have not yet pressed too heavily on him while I am in my prime. An ugly woman, by all accounts, but not without talent.

I am Alice. Royal Concubine. Edward's beloved Lady of the Sun.

Ah…!

I blink as a swooping pigeon smashes the scene in my mind, flinging reality back at me with cruel exactitude. Sitting in my orchard, far from Court and my King, I am forced to accept the truth. How low have I fallen. I am caged in impotent loneliness, like Edward's long-dead lion, powerless, isolated, stripped of everything I had made for myself.

I am nothing. Alice Perrers is no more.

Chapter One

Where do I start? It's difficult to know. My beginnings as I recall them were not moments marked by joy or happiness. So I will start with what I do recall. My very first memory.

I was a child, still far too young to have much understanding of who or what I was, kneeling with the sisters in the great Abbey church of St Mary's in the town of Barking. It was the eighth day of December and the air so cold it hurt my lungs. The stone paving was rough beneath my knees but even then I knew better than to shuffle. The statue on its plinth in the Lady Chapel was clothed in a new blue gown, her veil and wimple made from costly silk that glowed startlingly white in the dark shadows. The nuns sang the office of Compline and round the feet of the statue a pool of candles had been lit. The light flickered over the deep blue folds so that the figure appeared to move, to breathe.

'Who is she?' I asked, voice too loud. I was still very ignorant.

Sister Goda, novice mistress when there were novices to teach, hushed me. 'The Blessed Virgin.'

'What is she called?'

'She is the Blessed Virgin Mary.'

'Is this a special day?'

'It is the feast of the Immaculate Conception. Now, hush!'

It meant nothing to me then but I fell in love with her. The Blessed Mary's face was fair, her eyes downcast, but there was a little smile on her painted lips and her hands were raised as if to beckon me forward. But what took my eye was the crown of stars that had been placed for the occasion on her brow. The gold gleamed in the candlelight, the jewels reflected the flames in their depths. And I was dazzled. After the service, when the nuns had filed out, I stood before her, my feet small in the shimmer of candles.

'Come away, Alice.' Sister Goda took my arm, not gently.

I was stubborn and planted my feet.

'Come on!'

'Why does she wear a crown of stars?' I asked.

'Because she is the Queen of Heaven. Now will you…?'

The sharp slap on my arm made me obey, yet still I reached up, although I was too small to touch it, and smiled.

'I would like a crown like that.'

My second memory followed fast on my first. Despite the late hour, Sister Goda, small and frail but with a strong right arm, struck my hand with a leather strap until my skin was red and blistered. Punishment for the sin of vanity and covetousness, she hissed. Who was I to look at a crown and desire it for myself? Who was I to approach the Blessed Virgin, the Queen of Heaven? I was of less importance than the pigeons that found their way into the high reaches of the chancel. I would not eat for the whole of the next day. I would rise and go to bed with an empty belly. I would learn humility. And as my belly growled and my hand stung, I learned, and not for the last time, that it was not in the nature of women to get what they desired.

'You are a bad child,' Sister Goda stated unequivocally.

I lay awake until the Abbey bell summoned us at two of the clock for Matins. I did not weep. I think I must have accepted her judgement on me, or was too young to understand its implications.

And my third memory?

Ah, vanity! Sister Goda failed to beat it out of me. She eyed me dispassionately over some misdemeanour that I cannot now recall.

'What a trial you are to me, girl! And most probably a bastard, born out of holy wedlock. An ugly one at that. Though you are undoubtedly a creature of God's creation, I see no redeeming features in you.'

So I was ugly and a bastard. I wasn't sure which was the worse of the two, to my twelve-year-old mind. Was I ugly? Plain, Sister Goda might have said if there was any charity in her, but ugly was another world. Forbidden as we were the ownership of a looking glass in the Abbey—such an item was far too venal and precious to be owned by a nun—which of the sisters had never peered into a bowl of still water to catch an image? Or sought a distorted reflection in one of the polished silver ewers used in the Abbey church? I did the same and saw what Sister Goda saw.

That night I looked into my basin of icy water before my candle was doused. The reflection shimmered, but it was enough. My hair, close cut against my skull, to deter lice as much as vanity, was dark and coarse and straight. My eyes were as dark as sloes, like empty holes eaten in wool by the moth. As for the rest—my cheeks were hollow, my nose prominent, my mouth large. It was one thing to be told that I was ugly; quite another to see it for myself. Even accepting the rippling flaws in the reflection, I had no beauty. I was old enough and female enough to understand, and be hurt by it. Horrified by my heavy brows, black as smudges of charcoal, I dropped my candle into the water, obliterating the image.

Lonely in the dark in my cold, narrow cell, the walls pressing in on me in my solitary existence, I wept. The dark, and being alone, frightened me—then as now.

The rest of my young days merged into a grey lumpen pottage of misery and resentment, stirred and salted by Sister Goda's admonitions.

'You were late again for Matins, Alice. Don't think I didn't see you slinking into the church like the sly child you are!' Yes, I was late.

'Alice, your veil is a disgrace in the sight of God. Have you dragged it across the floor?' No, I had not, but against every good intention my veil collected burrs and finger-prints and ash from the hearth.

'Why can you not remember the simplest of texts, Alice? Your mind is as empty as a beggar's purse.' No, not empty, but engaged with something of more moment. Perhaps the soft fur of the Abbey cat as it curled against my feet in a patch of sunlight.

'Alice, why do you persist in this ungodly slouch?' My growing limbs were ignorant of elegance.

'A vocation is given to us by God as a blessing,' Mother Sybil, our Abbess, admonished the sinners in her care from her seat of authority every morning in Chapter House. 'A vocation is a blessing that allows us to worship God through prayer, and through good works to the poor in our midst. We must honour our vocation and submit to the Rules of St Benedict, our most revered founder.'

Mother Abbess was quick with a scourge against those who did not submit. I remember its sting well. And that of her tongue. I felt the lash of both when, determined to be on my knees at Sister Goda's side *before* the bell for Compline was silenced, I failed to shut away the Abbey's red chickens against the predations of the fox. The result next morning for the hens was bloody. So was the skin on my back, in righteous punishment, Mother Abbess informed me as she wielded the strap that hung from her girdle. It did not seem to me to be fair that by observing one rule I had broken another. Having not yet learnt the wisdom of concealing my thoughts, I said so. Mother Sybil's arm rose and fell with even more weight.

I was set to collect up the poor ravaged bodies. Not that the flesh went to waste. The nuns ate chicken with their bread at noon the following day as they listened to the reading of the parable of the good Samaritan. My plate saw nothing but bread, and that a day old. Why should I benefit from my sins?

A vocation? God most assuredly had not blessed me with a vocation, if that meant to accept, obey and be grateful for my lot in life. And yet I knew no other life, neither would I. When I reached my fifteenth year, so I was informed by Sister Goda, I would take my vows and, no longer a novice, be clothed as a nun. I would be a nun for ever until God called me to the heavenly comfort of His bosom—or to answer for my sins in some dire place of heat and torment. From my fifteenth year I would not speak, except for an hour after the noon meal when I would be allowed to converse on serious matters. Which seemed to me little better than perpetual silence.

Silent for the rest of my life, except for the singing of the offices.

Holy Mother, save me! Was this all I could hope for? It was not my choice to take the veil. How could I bear it? It was beyond my understanding that any woman would choose this life enclosed behind walls, the windows shuttered, the doors locked. Why would any woman choose this degree of imprisonment rather than taste the freedom of life outside?

To my mind there was only one door that might open for me. To offer me an escape.

'Who is my father?' I asked Sister Goda. If I had a father, surely he would not be deaf to my entreaties.

'God in Heaven is your Father.' Sister Goda's flat response dared me to pursue the matter as she turned the page of a psalter. 'Now, if you will pay attention, my child, we have here a passage to study...'

'But who is my father *here*—out *there*?' I gestured towards the window that allowed the noise of the town to encroach, its inhabitants gathering vociferously for market.

The novice mistress looked at me, faintly puzzled. 'I don't know, Alice, and that's the truth.' She clicked her tongue against her teeth. 'They said when you were brought here there was a purse of gold coins.' She shook her head, her veil hanging as limp as a shroud around her seamed face. 'But it's not important.' She shuffled across the room to search in the depths of a coffer for some dusty manuscript.

But it was important. A purse of gold? Suddenly it was very important. I knew nothing other than that I was Alice. Alice—with no family, no dowry. Unlike more fortunate sisters, no one came to visit me at Easter or Christmas. No one brought me gifts. When I took the veil, there would be no one to hold a celebration for me to mark my elevation. Even my habit would be passed down to me from some dead nun who, if fate smiled on me, resembled me in height and girth; if not, my new garment would enclose me in a vast pavilion of cloth, or exhibit my ankles to the world.

Resentment bloomed at the enormity of it. The question beat against my mind: Who is my father? What have I done to deserve to be so thoroughly abandoned? It hurt my heart.

'Who brought me here, Sister Goda?' I persisted.

'I don't recall. How would I?' Sister Goda was brusque. 'You were left in the Abbey porch, I believe. Sister Agnes brought you in—but she's been dead these last five years. As far as I know, there is no trace of your parentage. It was not uncommon for unwanted infants to be abandoned at a church door, what with the plague... Although it was always said that...'

'What was said?'

Sister Goda looked down at the old parchment. 'Sister Agnes always said it was not what it seemed...'

'*What* wasn't?'

Sister Goda clapped her hands sharply, her gaze once more narrowing on my face. 'She was very old and not always clear in her head. Mother Abbess says you're most likely the child of some labourer—a maker of tiles—got on a whore of a tavern without the blessing of marriage. Now—enough of this! Set your mind on higher things. Let us repeat the *Paternoster.*'

So I *was* a bastard.

As I duly mouthed the words of the *Paternoster*, my mind remained fixed on my parentage, or lack of it, and what Sister Agnes might or might not have said about it. I was just one of many unwanted infants and should be grateful that I had not been left to die.

But it did not quite ring true. If I was the child of a tavern whore, why had I been taken in and given teaching? Why was I not set to work as one of the *conversa*, the lay sisters, employed to undertake the heavy toil on the Abbey's lands or in the kitchens and bakehouse? True, I was clothed in the most worn garments, passed down from the sick and the dead, I was treated with no care or affection, yet I was taught to read and even to write, however poorly I attended to the lessons.

It was meant that I would become a nun. Not a lay sister.

'Sister Goda—' I tried again.

'I have nothing to tell you,' she snapped. There *is* nothing to tell! You will learn this text!' Her cane cracked across my knuckles but without any real force. Perhaps she had already decided I was a lost cause, her impatience increasingly re-placed by indifference. 'And you will stay here until you do! Why do you resist? What else is there for you? Thank God on your knees every day that you are not forced to find your bread in the gutters of London. And by what means I can only guess!' Her voice fell to a harsh whisper. 'Do you want to be a whore? A fallen woman?'

I lifted a shoulder in what was undoubtedly vulgar in-solence. 'I am not made to be a nun,' I replied with mis-guided courage.

'What choice do you have? Where else would you go? Who would take you in?'

I had no answer. But as Sister Goda's cane thwacked once more like a thunderclap on the wooden desk, indig-nation burned hot in my mind, firing the only thought that remained to me. *If you do not help yourself, Alice, no one else will.*

Even then I had a sharp precocity. Product, no doubt, of a wily labourer who tumbled a sluttish tavern whore after a surfeit of sour ale.

Chapter Two

When I achieved my escape from the Abbey, it was not by my own instigation. Fate took a hand when I reached the age of fifteen years and it came as a lightning bolt from heaven.

'Put this on. And this. Take this. Be at the Abbey gate in half an hour.'

The garments were thrust into my arms by Sister Matilda, Mother Abbess's chaplain.

'Why, Sister?'

'Do as you're told!'

I had been given a woollen kirtle, thin, its colour unrecognisable from much washing, and a long sleeveless overgown in a dense brown, reminiscent of the sludge that collected on the river bank after stormy weather. It too had seen better days on someone else's back, and was far too short, exhibiting, as I had feared, my ankles. When I scratched indelicately, an immediate fear bloomed. I had inherited the fleas as well as the garments. A hood of an indeterminate grey completed the whole.

But why? Was I being sent on an errand? A feverish

excitement danced over my skin. A lively fear as well—after all, life in the Abbey was all I knew—but not for long. If I was to escape the walls for only a day, it would be worth it. I was fifteen years old and the days of my transformation from novice to nun loomed, like the noxious overflowing contents of the town drain after heavy rainfall.

'Where am I going?' I asked the wagon master to whom I was directed, a dour man with a bad head cold and an overpowering smell of rancid wool. Sister Faith, keeper of the Abbey gate, had done nothing but point in his direction and close the door against me. The soft snick of the latch, with me on the outside, was far sweeter than any singing of the *Angelus*.

'London. Master Janyn Perrers's household,' he growled, spitting into the gutter already swimming with filth and detritus from the day's market dealings.

'Pull me up, then,' I ordered.

'Tha's a feisty moppet, and no mistake!' But he grasped my hand in his enormous one and hauled me up onto the bales where I settled myself as well as I could. 'God help th'man who weds you, mistress!'

'I'm not going to be married,' I retorted. 'Not ever.'

'And why's that, then?'

'Too ugly!' Had I not seen it for myself? Since the day I had peered into my water bowl I had been shown the undisputable truth of my unlovely features in a looking glass belonging to a countess, no less. How would any man look at me and want me for his wife?

'A man don't need to look too often at the wench he weds!'

I did not care. I tossed my head. *London!* The wagon master cracked his whip over the heads of the oxen to end the conversation, leaving me to try to fill in the spaces. To

my mind there was only one possible reason for my joining the household of this Janyn Perrers. My services as a
maidservant had been bought, enough gold changing hands
to encourage Mother Abbess to part with her impoverished
novice who would bring nothing of fame or monetary value
to the Abbey. As the wagon jolted and swayed, I imagined
the request that had been made. *A strong, hard-working girl
to help to run the house. A biddable girl...* I hoped Mother
Abbess had not perjured herself.

I twitched and shuffled, impatient with every slow step
of the oxen. *London.* The name bubbled through my blood
as I clung to the lumbering wagon. Freedom was as seductive and heady as fine wine.

The noisome overcrowded squalor of London shocked
me. The environs of Barking Abbey, bustling as they might
be on market day, had not prepared me for the crowds, the
perpetual racket, the stench of humanity packed so close together. I did not know where to look next. At close-packed
houses in streets barely wider than the wagon, where upper
storeys leaned drunkenly to embrace each other, blocking
out the sky. At the wares on display in shop frontages, at
women who paraded in bright colours. At scruffy urchins
and bold prostitutes who carried on a different business in
the rank courts and passageways. A new world, both frightening and seductive: I stared, gawped, as naive as any child
from the country.

'Here's where you get off.'

The wagon lurched and I was set down, directed by a
filthy finger that pointed at my destination, a narrow house
taking up no space at all, but rising above my head in three
storeys. I picked my way through the mess of offal and waste

in the gutters to the door. Was this the one? It did not seem to be the house of a man of means. I knocked.

The woman who opened the door was far taller than I and as thin as a willow lath, with her hair scraped into a pair of metallic cylindrical cauls on either side of her gaunt face, as if she were encased in a cage. 'Well?'

'Is this the house of Janyn Perres?'

'What's it to you?'

Her gaze flicked over me, briefly. She made to close the door. I could not blame her: I was not an attractive object. But this was where I had been sent, where I was expected. I would not have the door shut in my face.

'I have been sent,' I said, slapping my palm boldly against the wood.

'What do you want?'

'I am Alice,' I said, remembering, at last, to curtsey.

'If you're begging, I'll take my brush to you...'

'I'm sent by the nuns at the Abbey,' I stated.

The revulsion in her stare deepened, and the woman's lips twisted like a hank of rope. 'So you're the girl. Are you the best they could manage?' She flapped her hand when I opened my mouth to reply that, yes, I supposed I was the best they could offer, since I was the only novice. 'Never mind. You're here now so we'll make the best of it. But in future you'll use the door at the back beside the privy.'

And that was that.

I had become part of a new household.

And what an uneasy household it was. Even I, with no experience of such, was aware of the tensions from the moment I set my feet over the threshold.

Janyn Perrers—master of the house, pawnbroker, moneylender and bloodsucker. His appearance did not suggest a rapacious man but, then, as I rapidly learned, it was not his word that was the law within his four walls. Tall and stooped with not an ounce of spare flesh on his frame and a foreign slur to his speech, he spoke only when he had to, and then not greatly. In his business dealings he was painstaking. Totally absorbed, he lived and breathed the acquisition and lending at extortionate rates of gold and silver coin. His face might have been kindly, if not for the deep grooves and hollow cheeks more reminiscent of a death's head. His hair—or lack of—some few greasy wisps around his neck, gave him the appearance of a well-polished egg when he removed his felt cap. I could not guess his age but he seemed very old to me with his uneven gait and faded eyes. His fingers were always stained with ink, his mouth too when he chewed his pen.

He nodded to me when I served supper, placing the dishes carefully on the table before him: it was the only sign that he noted a new addition to his family. This was the man who now employed me and would govern my future.

The power in the house rested on the shoulders of Damiata Perrers, his sister, who had made it clear when I arrived that I was not welcome. The Signora. There was no kindness in her face. She was the strength, the firm grip on the reins, the imposer of punishment on those who displeased her. Nothing happened in that house without her knowledge or her permission.

There was a boy to haul and carry and clean the privy, a lad who said little and thought less. He led a miserable existence, gobbling his food with filthy fingers before bolting back to his own pursuits in the nether regions of the house. I never learned his name.

Then there was Master William de Greseley. He was a man who was and was not of the household since he spread

his services further afield, an interesting man who took my
attention but ignored me with a remarkable determination.
A clerk, a clever individual with black hair and brows, sharp
features much like a rat, and a pale face, as if he never saw
the light of day. A man with as little emotion about him
as one of the flounders brought home by Signora Damiata
from the market, his employment was to note down the
business of the day. Ink might stain Master Perrers's fingers
but I swore that it ran in Master Greseley's veins. He disre-
garded me to the same extent as he was deaf to the vermin
that scuttled across the floor of the room in which he kept
the books and ledgers of money lent and reclaimed. I was
wary of him. There was a coldness that I found unpalatable.

And then there was me. The maidservant who undertook
all the work not assigned to the boy. And some that was.

Thus my first introduction to the Perrers family. And
since it was a good score of miles away from Barking
Abbey, it was not beyond my tolerance.

'God help th'man who weds you, mistress!'
'I'm not going to be married!'

Holy Mother! My vigorous assertion returned to mock
me. Within a se'nnight I found myself exchanging marriage
vows at the church door.

Given the tone of her remonstration, Signora Damiata
was as astonished as I, and unpleasantly frank when I was
summoned to join brother and sister in the parlour at the
rear of the house, where, by the expression on the lady's
face, Master Perrers had just broken the news of his intent.

'Blessed Mary! Why marry?' she demanded. 'You have
a son, an heir, learning the family business in Lombardy. I
keep your house. Why would you want a wife at your age?'
Her accent grew stronger, the syllables hissing over each

other. 'If you must, then choose a girl from one of our merchant families. A girl with a dowry and a family with some standing. Jesu! Are you not listening?' She raised her fists as if she might strike him. 'She is not a suitable wife for a man of your importance.'

Did I think that Master Perrers did not rule the roost? He looked briefly at me as he continued leafing through the pages of a small ledger he had taken from his pocket.

'I will have this one. I will wed her. That is the end of the matter.'

I, of course, was not asked. I stood in this three-cornered dialogue yet not a part of it, the bone squabbled over by two dogs. Except that Master Perrers did not squabble. He simply stated his intention and held to it, until his sister closed her mouth and let it be. So I was wed in the soiled skirts in which I chopped the onions and gutted the fish: clearly there was no money earmarked to be spent on a new wife. Sullen and resentful, shocked into silence, certainly no joyful bride, I complied because I must. I was joined in matrimony with Janyn Perrers on the steps of the church with witnesses to attest the deed: Signora Damiata, grim-faced and silent; and Master Greseley, because he was available, with no expression at all. A few words muttered over us by a bored priest in an empty ritual, and I was a wife.

And afterwards?

No celebration, no festivity, no recognition of my change in position in the household. Not even a cup of ale and a bride cake. It was, I realised, nothing more than a business agreement, and since I had brought nothing to it, there was no need to celebrate it. All I recall was the rain soaking through my hood as we stood and exchanged vows and the shrill cries of lads who fought amongst themselves for the handful of coin that Master Perrers scattered as a reluctant sign of his goodwill. Oh, and I recall Master Perrers's fingers gripping hard on mine, the only reality in this ceremony that was otherwise not real at all to me.

Was it better than being a Bride of Christ? Was marriage better than servitude? To my mind there was little difference. After the ceremony I was directed to sweeping down the cobwebs that festooned the storerooms in the cellar. I took out my bad temper with my brush, making the spiders run for cover.

There was no cover for me. Where would I run?

And beneath my anger was a dark lurking fear, for the night, my wedding night, was ominously close, and Master Perrers was no handsome lover.

The Signora came to my room, which was hardly bigger than a large coffer, tucked high under the eaves, and gestured with a scowl. In shift and bare feet I followed her down the stairs. Opening the door to my husband's bedchamber, she thrust me inside and closed it at my back. I stood just within, not daring to move. My throat was so dry I could barely swallow. Apprehension was a rock in my belly and fear of my ignorance filled me to the brim. I did not want to be here. I did not want this. I could not imagine why Master Perrers would want me, plain and unfinished and undowered as I was. Silence closed round me—except for a persistent scratching like a mouse trapped behind the plastered wall.

In that moment I was a coward. I admit it. I closed my eyes.

Still nothing.

So I squinted, only to find my gaze resting on the large bed with its dust-laden hangings to shut out the night air. Holy Virgin! To preserve intimacy for the couple enclosed within. Closing my eyes again, I prayed for deliverance.

What, exactly, would he want me to do?

'You can open your eyes now. She's gone.'

There was humour in the gruff, accented voice. I obeyed and there was Janyn, in a chamber robe of astonishingly virulent yellow ochre that encased him from neck to bony ankles, seated at a table covered with piles of documents and heaped scrolls. At his right hand was a leather purse spilling out strips of wood, another smaller pouch containing silver coin. And to his left a branch of good-quality candles that lit the atmosphere with gold as the dust motes danced. But it was the pungent aroma, of dust and parchment and vellum, and perhaps the ink that he had been stirring, that made my nose wrinkle. Intuitively I knew that it was the smell of careful record-keeping and of wealth. It almost dispelled my fear.

'Come in. Come nearer to the fire.' I took a step, warily. At least he was not about to leap on me quite yet. There was no flesh in sight on either of us.

'Here.' He stretched toward the coffer at his side and scooped up the folds of a mantle. 'You'll be cold. Take it. It's yours.'

This was the first gift I had ever had, given honestly, and I wrapped the luxurious woollen length round my shoulders, marvelling at the quality of its weaving, its softness and warm russet colouring, wishing I had a pair of shoes. He must have seen me shuffling on the cold boards.

'Put these on.'

A pair of leather shoes of an incongruous red were pushed across the floor towards me. Enormous, but soft and warm from his own feet as I slid mine in with a sigh of pleasure.

'Are you a virgin?' he asked conversationally.

My pleasure dissipated like mist in morning sun, my blood running as icily cold as my feet, and I shivered. A goose walking over my grave. I did not want this old man to touch me. The last thing I wanted was to share a bed with him and have him fumble against my naked flesh with his ink-stained fingers, their untrimmed nails scraping and scratching.

'Yes,' I managed, hoping my abhorrence was not obvious, but Master Perrers was watching me with narrowed eyes. How could it not be obvious? I felt my face flame with humiliation.

'Of course you are,' my husband said with a laconic nod. 'Let me tell you something that might take that anxious look from your face. I'll not trouble you. It's many a year since I've found comfort in a woman.' I had never heard him string so many words together.

'Then why did you wed me?' I asked.

Since I had nothing else to give, I had thought it must be a desire for young flesh in his bed. So, if not that…? Master Perrers looked at me as if one of his ledgers had spoken, then grunted in what could have been amusement.

'Someone to tend my bones in old age. A wife to shut my sister up from nagging me to wed a merchant's daughter whose family would demand a weighty settlement.'

I sighed. I had asked for the truth, had I not? I would nurse him and demand nothing in return. It was not flattering.

'Marriage will give security to you,' he continued as if he read my thoughts. And then: 'Have you a young lover in mind?'

'No!' Such directness startled me. 'Well, not yet. I don't know any young men.'

He chuckled. 'Good. Then we shall rub along well enough, I expect. When you do know a young man you can set your fancy on, let me know. I'll make provision for you when I am dead,' he remarked.

He went back to his writing. I stood and watched, not knowing what to do or say now that he had told me what he did not want from me. Should I leave? His gnarled hand with its thick fingers moved up and down the columns, rows of figures growing from his pen, columns of marks in heavy black ink spreading from top to bottom. They intrigued me. The minutes passed. The fire settled. Well, I couldn't stand there for ever.

'What do I do now, Master Perrers?'

He looked up as if surprised that I was still there. 'Do you wish to sleep?'

'No.'

'I suppose we must do something. Let me…' He peered at me with his pale eyes. 'Pour two cups of ale and sit there.'

I poured and took the stool he pushed in my direction.

'You can write.'

'Yes.'

In my later years at the Abbey, driven by a boredom so intense that even study had offered some relief, I had applied myself to my lessons with some fervour, enough to cause Sister Goda to offer a rosary in gratitude to Saint Jude Thaddeus, a saint with a fine reputation for pursuing desperate causes. I could now write with a fair hand.

'The convents are good for something, then. Can you write and tally numbers?'

'No.'

'Then you will learn. There.' He reversed the ledger and pushed it toward me across the table. 'Copy that list there. I'll watch you.'

I sat, inveterate curiosity getting the better of me, and as I saw what it was that he wished me to do, I picked up one of his pens and began to mend the end with a sharp blade my new husband kept for the purpose. I had learned the skill, by chance—or perhaps by my own devising—from a woman of dramatic beauty and vicious pleasures, who had once honoured the Abbey with her presence. A woman who had an unfortunate habit of creeping into my mind when I least wished her to be there. This was no time or place to think of *her*, the much-lauded Countess of Kent.

'What are those?' I asked, pointing at the leather purse.

'Tally sticks.'

'What do they do? What are the notches for?'

'They record income, debts paid and debts owed,' he informed me, watching me to ensure I didn't destroy his pen. 'The wood is split down the middle, each party to the deal keeping half. They must match.'

'Clever,' I observed, picking up one of the tallies to inspect it. It was beautifully made out of a hazel stick, and its sole purpose to record ownership of money.

'Never mind those. Write the figures.'

And I did, under his eye for the first five minutes, and then he left me to it, satisfied.

The strangest night. My blood settled to a quiet hum of pleasure as the figures grew to record a vast accumulation of gold coin, and when we had finished the accounts of the week's business, my husband instructed me to get into the vast bed and go to sleep. I fell into it, and into sleep, to the sound of the scratching pen. Did my husband join me when his work was done? I think he did not. The bed linen was not disturbed, and neither was my shift, arranged neatly from chin to ankles, decorous as any virgin nun.

It was not what I expected but it could have been much worse.

* * *

Next morning I awoke abruptly to silence. Still very early, I presumed, and dark because the bed curtains had been drawn around me. When I peeped out it was to see that the fire had burnt itself out, the cups and ledgers tidied away and the room empty. I was at a loss, my role spectacularly unclear. Sitting back against the pillows, reluctant to leave the warmth of the bed, I looked at my hands, turning them, seeing the unfortunate results of proximity to icy cold water, hot dishes, grimy tasks. They were now the hands of Mistress Perrers. I grimaced in a moment of hard-edged humour. Was I now mistress of the household? If I was, I would have to usurp Signora Damiata's domain. I tried to imagine myself walking into the parlour and informing the Signora what I might wish to eat, the length of cloth I might wish to purchase to fashion a new gown. And then I imagined her response. I dared not!

But it is your right!

Undeniably. But not right at this moment. My sense of self-preservation was always keen. I redirected my thoughts, to a matter of more immediacy. What would I say to Master Perrers this morning? How would I address him? Was I truly his wife if I was still a virgin? Wrapping myself in my new mantle, I returned to my own room and dressed as the maidservant I still seemed to be, before descending the stairs to the kitchen to start the tasks for the new day. The fire would have to be laid, the oven heated. If I walked quickly and quietly I would not draw attention to myself from any quarter. Such was my plan, except that my clumsy shoes clattered on the stair, and a voice called out.

'Alice.'

I considered bolting, as if I had not heard.

'Come here, Alice. Close the door.'

I gripped hard on my courage. Had he not been kind last night? I redirected my footsteps, and there my husband of less than twenty-four hours sat behind his desk, head bent over his ledgers, pen in hand, in the room where he dealt with the endless stream of borrowers. No different from any other morning when I might bring him ale and bread. I curtseyed. Habits were very difficult to break.

He looked up. 'Did you sleep well?'

'No, sir.'

'Too much excitement, I expect.' I might have suspected him of laughing at me but there was no change of expression on his dolorous features. He held out a small leather pouch, the strings pulled tight. I looked at it—and then at him.

'Take it.'

'Do you wish for me to purchase something for you, sir?'

'It is yours.' Since I still did not move, he placed it on the desk and pushed it across the wood toward me.

'Mine...?'

It contained coin. And far more, as I could estimate, than was due to me as a maidservant. Planting his elbows on the desk, folding his hands and resting his chin on them, Janyn Perrers regarded me gravely, speaking slowly as if I might be a lackwit.

'It is a bride gift, Alice. A morning gift. Is that not the custom in this country?'

'I don't know.' How would I?

'It is, if you will, a gift in recompense for the bride's virginity.'

I frowned. 'I don't qualify for it, then. You did not want mine.'

'The fault was mine, not yours. You have earned a bride gift by tolerating the whims and weaknesses of an old man.' I think my cheeks were as scarlet as the seals on the documents before him, so astonished was I that he would thank me, regretful that my words had seemed to be so judgmental of him. 'Take it, Alice. You look bewildered.' At last what might have been a smile touched his mouth.

'I am, sir. I have done nothing to make me worthy of such a gift.'

'You are my wife and we will keep the custom.'

'Yes, sir.' I curtseyed.

'One thing…' He brushed the end of his quill pen uneasily over the mess of scrolls and lists. 'It would please me if you would not talk about…'

'About our night together,' I supplied for him, compassion stirred by his gentleness, even as my eye sought the bag with its burden of coin. 'That is between you and me, sir.'

'And our future nights.'

'I will not speak of them either.' After all, who would I tell?

'Thank you. If you would now fetch me ale. And tell the Signora that I will be going out in an hour.'

'Yes, sir.'

'And it will please me if you will call me Janyn.'

'Yes, sir,' I replied, though I could not imagine doing so.

I stood in the whitewashed passage outside the door and leaned back against the wall as if my legs needed the support. The purse was not a light one. It moved in my fingers, coins sliding with a comforting chink as I weighed it in my hand. I had never seen so much money all in one place in the whole of my life. And it was mine. Whatever I was or was not, I was no longer a penniless novice.

But what was I? It seemed I was neither flesh nor fowl. Here I stood in a house that was not mine, a wife but a virgin, with the knowledge that my marriage vows would make absolutely no difference to my role in the household. I would wager the whole of my sudden windfall on it. Signora Damiata would never retreat before my authority. I would never sit at the foot of the table.

A scuff of leather against stone made me look up.

I was not the only one occupying the narrow space. Detaching himself from a similar stance, further along in the shadows, Master Greseley walked softly towards me. Since there was an air of secrecy about him—of complicity almost—I hid the pouch in the folds of my skirt. Within an arm's length of me he stopped, and leaned his narrow shoulder blades on the wall beside me, arms folded across his chest, staring at the opposite plasterwork in a manner that was not companionable but neither was it hostile. Here was a man adept through long practice at masking his intentions. As for his thoughts—they were buried so deep beneath his impassivity that it would take an earthquake to dislodge them.

'You weren't going to hide it under your pillow, were you?' he enquired in a low voice.

'Hide what?' I replied, clutching the purse tightly.

'The morning gift he's just given you.'

'How do you—?'

'Of course I know. Who keeps the books in this household? It was no clever guesswork.' A sharp glance slid in my direction before fixing on the wall again. 'I would hazard that the sum was payment for something that was never bought.'

Annoyance sharpened my tongue. I would not be intimidated by a *clerk*. 'That is entirely between Master Perrers and myself.'

'Of course it is.' How smoothly unpleasant he was, like mutton fat floating on water after the roasting pans had been scoured.

'And nothing to do with you.'

He bowed his head. 'Absolutely nothing. I am here only to give you some good advice.'

Turning my head I looked directly at him. 'Why?'

He did not return my regard. 'I have no idea.'

'That makes no sense.'

'No. It doesn't. It's against all my tenets of business practice. But even so. Let's just say that I am drawn to advise you. Don't hide the money under your pillow or anywhere else in this house. She'll find it.'

'Who?' Although I knew the answer well enough.

'The Signora. She has a nose for it, as keen as any mouse finding the cheese safe stored in a cupboard. And when she sniffs it out, you'll not see it again.'

I thought about this as well. 'I thought she didn't know.'

'Is that what Janyn told you? Of course she does. Nothing happens in this place without her knowledge. She knows you have money, and she doesn't agree with it. Any profits are the inheritance of her nephew, Janyn's son.'

The absent heir, learning the business in Lombardy. 'Since you're keen to offer advice, what do I do?' I asked crossly. 'Short of digging a hole in the garden?'

'Which she'd find.'

'A cranny in the eaves?'

'She'd find that too.'

'So?' His smugness irritated me.

'Give it to me.'

Which promptly dispersed my irritation. I laughed, disbelieving. 'Do you take me for a fool?'

'I take you for a sensible woman. Give it to me.' He actually held out his hand, palm up. His fingers were blotched with ink.

'I will not.'

He sighed as if his patience was strained. 'Give it to me and I'll use it to make you a rich woman.'

'Why would you?'

'Listen to me, Mistress Alice!' I was right about the patience. His voice fell to a low hiss on the syllables of my name. 'What keeps its value and lasts for ever?'

'Gold.'

'No. Gold can be stolen—and then you have nothing.'

'Jewels, then.'

'Same argument. Think about it.'

'Then since you are so clever…'

'Land!' The clerk's beady eyes gleamed. 'Property. That's the way to do it. It's a generous purse he gave you. Give it to me and I will buy you property.'

For a moment I listened to him, seduced by the glitter in his gaze that was now holding mine. His nose almost twitched with the prospect. And then sense took hold. 'But I cannot look after property! What would I do with it?'

'You don't have to *look after it*. There are ways and means. Give me your morning gift and I will show you how it's done.'

It deserved some consideration. 'What would you ask in return?' I asked sharply.

'Clever girl! I knew you had the makings of a business woman. I'll let you know. But it will not be too great a price.'

I looked at him. What a cold fish he was. 'Why are you doing this?'

'I think you have possibilities.'

'As a landowner?' It all seemed nonsense to me.

'Why not?'

I didn't have a reply. I stood in silence, the coins in my hand seemingly growing heavier as I slowly breathed, in and out. I tossed the little bag, and caught it.

'We don't have all day.' Greseley's admonition broke into my thoughts. 'That's my offer. Take it or leave it. But if you think to keep it safe within these walls, it will be gone before the end of the week.'

'And I should trust you.'

Trust had not figured highly in my life. This strange man with his love for figures and documents, seals and agreements, who had sought me out and made me this most tempting of offers—should I hand over to him all I owned in the world? It was a risk. A huge risk. The arguments, conflicting, destructive of each other, rattled back and forth in my brain.

Say no. Keep it for yourself. Hide it where no one can find it.

Take the risk! Become a landowner.

He'll take it and keep it for himself.

Trust him.

I can't!

Why not?

My exchange of views came to an abrupt halt when the clerk pushed himself upright and began to walk away. 'Don't say I didn't warn you.'

And there was the final blast of the voice in my head. *You can't do this on your own, Alice, but Greseley can. This clever little louse has the knowledge. Learn from him. Use it to your own advantage.*

Well, I would. 'Stop!' I called out.

He stopped, but he did not return; he simply stood there with his back to me.

'I'll do it,' I told him.

He spun on his heel. 'An excellent decision.'

'How long will it take?'

'A few days.'

I held up the pouch. Hesitated. Then dropped it into his outstretched palm. I was still wondering if I was an idiot. 'If you rob me...' I began.

'Yes, Mistress Perrers?' It caused me to laugh softly. It was the first time I had been addressed as such.

'If you rob me, Master Greseley,' I whispered, 'I advise you to employ a taster before you eat or drink in this house.'

'There'll be no need, mistress.' From his bland smugness, he thought I was making empty threats. I was not so sure. A good dose of wolfsbane masked by a cup of warmed ale would take out the strongest man. I would not care to be robbed.

The purse vanished into Greseley's sleeve, and Greseley vanished along the corridor.

Would I live to regret this rash business dealing? All I knew was that it created a strange, turbulent euphoria that swept through me from my crown to my ill-shod feet.

Fool! Idiot girl! I berated myself with increasing fury over the following days. *A sensible woman he called you. A business woman. And you let yourself be gulled! He knew how to wind you round his grubby fingers!*

By God, he did! By the end of the week I knew I had seen the last of my morning gift. Greseley was elusive, exchanging not one word with me and avoiding my attempts to catch his eye. And when my impatience overcame my discretion: 'What have you done with it?' I growled in his ear as he slid onto a stool to break his fast.

'Pass the jug of ale, if you please, mistress' was all I got by way of reply. With one gulp he emptied his cup, crammed bread into his mouth, and left the room before I could pester him more.

'Stir this pot,' Mistress Damiata ordered, handing over a spoon.

Later that day he was sent into the city on business that kept him away overnight. How could I have been so ingenuous, to trust a man I barely knew? I had lost it. I had lost it all! I would never see one of those coins again, and my misery festered, even though I was kept hopping from morning to night. My mind began to linger lovingly on the effect of that large spoonful of wolfsbane on the scrawny frame of the clerk.

And then Greseley returned. He wouldn't get away with ignoring me this time. Was he suffering from guilt? If he was, it did nothing to impair his appetite, as he chomped his way through slices of beef and half a flat bread, undisturbed by my scowling at him across the board.

'We need to talk!' I whispered, nudging him between his shoulder blades when I smacked a dish of herring in front of him.

His answering stare was cold and clear and without expression.

'Careful, girl!' snapped the Signora. 'That dish! We're not made of money!'

Greseley continued to eat with relish, but as I cleared the dishes, he produced a roll of a document from the breast of his tunic, like a coney from the sleeve of a second-rate *jongleur*, and tapped it against his fingertips before sliding it into an empty jug standing on the hearth, out of the Signora's line of sight. It was not out of mine. My fingers itched to take it. I could sense it, like a burning brand below my heart.

At last. The kitchen was empty. Janyn closed the door on himself and his ledgers, the Signora climbed the stairs to her chamber, and I took the scroll from its hiding place and carried it to my room. Unrolling it carefully, I read the black script. No easy task. The legal words meant nothing to me, the phrases hard on my understanding, the script small and close written. But there was no doubting it. He had done what he had promised. There was my name: Alice Perrers. I was the owner of property in Gracechurch Street in the city of London.

I held it in my hands, staring at it, as if it might vanish if I looked away. Mine. It was mine. But what was it? And, more important, what did I do with it?

I ran Greseley to ground early next morning in the kitchen with his feet up on a trestle and a pot of ale beside him.

'It's all very well—but what am I expected to do with it?'

He looked at me as if I were stupid. 'Nothing but enjoy the profits, mistress.'

'I don't understand.'

'It doesn't matter whether you do or not. It's yours.'

He was watching me closely, as if to test my reaction. I did not see why he should, so I said what I wanted to say.

'It does matter.' And in that moment it struck home how much it meant to me. 'It matters to me more than you'll ever know.' I glowered. 'You won't patronise me, Master Greseley. You will explain it all to me, and then I will understand. The property is mine and I want to know how it works.' He laughed. He actually laughed, a harsh bark of a noise. 'Now what?'

'I knew I was right.'

'About what?'

'*You*, Mistress Perrers. Sit down, and don't argue. I'm about to give you your first lesson.'

So I sat and Greseley explained to me the brilliance for a woman in my position of the legal device of 'enfeoffment to use'. 'The property is yours, and it remains yours,' he explained. 'But you allow others to administer it for you—for a fee, of course. You must choose wisely—a man with an interest in the property so that he will administer it well. Do you understand?' I nodded. 'You grant that man legal rights over the land, but you retain *de facto* control. See? You remain in ultimate ownership but need do nothing toward the day-to-day running of it.'

'And can I make the agreement between us as long or as short as I wish?'

'Yes.'

'And I suppose I need a man of law to oversee this for me?'

'It would be wise.'

'What is this property that I now own, but do not own?'

'Living accommodations—with shops below.'

'Can I look at it?'

'Of course.'

What else did I need to ask? 'Was there any money leftover from the transaction?'

'You don't miss much, do you?' He tipped out the contents of the purse at his belt and pushed across the board a small number of coins.

'You said I needed a man of law.' He regarded me without expression. 'I suppose you would be my man of law.'

'I certainly could. Next time, Mistress Perrers, we will work in partnership.'

'Will there be a next time?'

'Oh, I think so.' I thought the slide of his glance had a depth of craftiness.

'Is that good or bad—to work in partnership?'

Greseley's pointed nose sniffed at my ignorance. He knew I could not work alone. But it seemed good to me. What strides I had made. I was a wife of sorts, even if I spent my nights checking Janyn's tally sticks and columns of figures, and now I was a property owner. A little ripple of pleasure brushed along the skin of my forearms as the idea engaged my mind and my emotions. I liked it. And in my first deliberate business transaction, I pushed the coins back toward him.

'You are now my man of law, Master Greseley.'

'I am indeed, Mistress Perrers.'

The coins were swept into his purse with alacrity.

And where did I keep the evidence of my ownership? I kept it hidden on my person between shift and overgown, tied with a cord, except when I took it out and touched it, running my fingers over the wording that made it all official. There it was for my future. Security. Permanence. The words were like warm hands around mine on a winter's day. Comforting.

I did not dislike Greseley as much as I once had.

Plague returned. The same dreaded pestilence that had struck without mercy just before my birth came creeping stealthily into London. It was the only gossip to be had in the streets, the market, the alehouses. It was different this time, so they said in whispers. The plague of children, they called it, striking cruelly at infants but not the hale and hearty who had reached adult years.

But the pestilence, stepping over our threshold, proved to be a chancy creature.

Of us all it was Janyn who was struck down. He drew aside the sleeve of his tunic to reveal the whirls of red spots as we gathered for dinner on an ordinary day. The meal was abandoned. Without a word Janyn walked up the stairs and shut himself in his chamber. Terror, rank and loathsome, set its claws into the Perrers household.

The boy disappeared overnight. Greseley found work in other parts of the city. Mistress Damiata fled with disgraceful speed to stay with her cousin whose house was uncontaminated. Who nursed Janyn? I did. I was his wife, even if he had never touched me unless his calloused fingers grazed mine when he pointed out a mistake in my copying. I owed him at least this final service.

From that first red and purple pattern on his arms there was no recovery.

I bathed his face and body, holding my breath at the stench of putrefying flesh. I racked my brains for anything Sister Margery, the Infirmarian at the Abbey, had said of her experiences of the pestilence. It was not much but I acted on it, flinging the windows of Janyn's chamber wide to allow the escape of the corrupt air. For my own safety I washed my hands and face in vinegar, eating bread soaked in Janyn's best wine—how Signora Damiata would have ranted at the waste—but for Janyn nothing halted the terrifying, galloping progress of the disease. The empty house echoed around me, the only sound the harsh breathing from my stricken husband and the approaching footsteps of death.

Was I afraid for myself?

I was, but if the horror of the vile swellings could pass from Janyn to me, the damage was already done. If the pestilence had the ability to hop across the desk where we sat to keep the ledgers, I was already doomed. I would stay and weather the storm.

A note appeared under the bedchamber door. I watched it slide slowly, from my position slumped on a stool from sheer exhaustion as Janyn laboured with increasingly distressed breaths. The fever had him in its thrall. Stepping softly to the door, listening to someone walking quietly away, I picked up the note and unfolded the single page, curiosity overcoming my weariness. Ha! No mystery after all. I recognised Greseley's script with ease, and the note was written as a clerk might write a legal treatise. I sank back to the stool to read.

When you are a widow you have legal right to a dower—one third of the income of your husband's estate. You will not get it.

You have by law forty days in which to vacate the house to allow the heir to take his inheritance. You will be evicted within the day.

As your legal man my advice: take what you can. It is your right. You will get nothing else that is due to you.

A stark warning. A chilling one. Leaving Janyn in a restless sleep, I began to search.

Nothing! Absolutely nothing!

Signora Damiata had done a thorough job of it while her brother lay dying. His room of business, the whole house was empty of all items of value. There were no bags of gold in Janyn's coffers. There were no scrolls, the ledgers and tally sticks had gone. She had swept through the house, removing everything that might become an attraction for looters. Or for me. Everything from my own chamber had been removed. Even my new mantle—especially that—the only thing of value I owned.

I had nothing.

Above me in his bedchamber, Janyn shrieked in agony, and I returned to his side. I would do for him what I could, ruling my mind and my body to bathe and tend this man who was little more than a rotting corpse.

In the end it all happened so fast. I expect it was Janyn's wine that saved me, but the decoction of green sage—from the scrubby patch in Signora Damiata's yard—to dry and heal the ulcers and boils did nothing for him. Before the end of the second day he breathed no more. How could a man switch from rude health to rigid mortality within the time it took to pluck and boil a chicken? He never knew I was there with him.

Did I pray for him? Only if prayer was lancing the boils to free the foul-smelling pus. Now the house was truly silent around me, holding its breath, as I placed the linen gently over his face, catching a document that fell from the folds at the foot of the bed. And then I sat on the stool by Janyn's body, not daring to move for fear that death noticed me too.

It was the clatter of a rook falling down the chimney that brought me back to my senses. Death had no need of my soul, so I opened the document that I still held. It was a deed of ownership in Janyn's name, of a manor in West Peckham, somewhere in Kent. I read it over twice, a tiny seed of a plan beginning to unfurl in my mind. Now, here was a possibility. I did not know how to achieve what I envisaged, but of course I knew someone who would. How to find him?

I walked slowly down the stairs, halting halfway when I saw a figure below me.

'Is he dead?' Signora Damiata was waiting for me in the narrow hall.

'Yes.'

She made the sign of the cross on her bosom, a cursory acknowledgement. Then flung back the outer door and gestured for me to leave. 'I've arranged for his body to be collected. I'll return when the pestilence has gone.'

'What about me?'

'I'm sure you'll find some means of employment.' She barely acknowledged me. 'Plague does not quench men's appetites.'

'And my dower?'

'What dower?' She smirked.

'You can't do this,' I announced. 'I have legal rights. You can't leave me homeless and without money.'

But she could. 'Out!'

I was pushed through the doorway onto the street. With a flourish and rattle of the key, Signora Damiata locked the door and strode off, stepping through the waste and puddles.

It was a lesson to me in brutal cold-heartedness when dealing with matters of coin and survival. And there I was, sixteen years old to my reckoning, widowed after little more than a year of marriage, cast adrift, standing alone outside the house. It felt as if my feet were chained to the ground. Where would I go? Who would give me shelter? Reality was a bitter draught. London seethed around me but offered me no refuge.

'Mistress Perrers.'

'Master Greseley!'

For there he was—I hadn't had to find him after all—emerging from a rank alley to slouch beside me. Never had I been so relieved to see anyone, but not without a shade of rancour. He may have lost a master too, but he would never be short of employment or a bed for the night in some merchant's household. He eyed the locked door, and then me.

'What did the old besom give you?' he asked without preamble.

'Nothing,' I retorted. 'The old besom has stripped the

house.' And then I smiled, waving the document in front of his eyes. 'Except for this. She overlooked it. It's a manor.'

Those eyes gleamed. 'Is it, now? And what do you intend to do with it?'

'I intend *you* to arrange that it becomes *mine*, Master Greseley. Enfeoffment for use, I think you called it.' I could be a fast learner, and I had seen my chance. 'Can you do that?'

He ran his finger down his nose. 'Easy for those who know how. I can—if it suits me—have it made over to you as the widow of Master Perrers, and now *femme sole*.'

A woman alone. With property. A not unpleasing thought that made my smile widen.

'And will it suit you, Master Greseley?' I slid what I hoped was a persuasive glance at the clerk. 'Will you do it for me?'

His face flushed under my gaze as he considered.

I softened my voice, adding a plea. 'I cannot do this on my own, Master Greseley.'

He grinned, a quick slash of thin lips and discoloured teeth. 'Why not? We have, I believe, the basis of a partnership here, Mistress Perrers. I'll work for you, and you'll put business my way—when you can. I'll enfeoff the manor to the use of a local knight—and myself.'

So that was it. Master Greseley was not entirely altruistic, but willing with a little female enticement. How easily men could be seduced with a smile and outrageous flattery offered in sweet tones. He extended his hand. I looked at it: not over clean but with long, surprisingly elegant fingers that could work magic with figures far more ably than I. There on the doorstep of my erstwhile home, I handed over the document and we shook hands as I had seen Janyn do when confirming some transaction with a customer.

As I felt the grip of his rough clasp, I considered what I had just done. And how astonishing it was to me that an unpleasing face was no detriment to my achieving it. I had—as Greseley would say—a business partner.

'You'll not cheat me, will you?' I frowned and made my voice stern.

'Certainly not!' His outrage was amusing. And then his brows twitched together suspiciously. 'Where will you go?'

'There's only one place.' I had already made my decision. There really was no other to be made. It would be a roof over my head and food in my belly, and far preferable to life on the streets or docks as a common whore. 'Back to St Mary's,' I said. 'They'll take me in. I'll stay there and wait for better times. Something will turn up.'

Greseley nodded. 'Not a bad idea, all in all. But you'll need this. Here.' He rummaged in the purse at his belt and brought out two gold coins. 'I'll return these to you. They should persuade the Abbess to open the doors to you for a little time at least. Remember, though. You now owe me. I want it back.'

'Where do I find you?' I shouted, coarse as a fishwife, as he put distance between us, the proof of ownership of the manor at West Peckham stowed in his tunic.

'Try the Tabard. At Southwark.'

That was as much as I got.

So I went back, where I had vowed I would never return, wheedling a ride in a wagon empty of all but the rank whiff of fish. I might own a manor and a house in London—I left both precious documents in Greseley's care—but I was in debt to the tune of two gold nobles. Needs must. The coins did indeed open the doors of the Abbey to me, but they bought me no luxury. It was made clear to me that I must earn my keep and so I found myself joining the ranks of the *conversa*. A lay sister toiling for the benefit of the Brides of Christ. Perhaps it was the stink of salt cod clinging to my skirts that worked against me.

Why did I accept it?

Because the sanctuary it offered me was a temporary measure. I knew it, deep within me. I had supped in the outside world and found it to my taste. In those days of silent labour, a determination was born in me. I would never become a nun. I would never wed again at anyone's dictates. At some point in the future, in Greseley's clever hands, my land would bring me enough coin to allow me to live as a *femme sole* in my own house with my own bed and good clothing and servants at my beck and call.

I liked the image. It spurred me on as I scrubbed the nun's habits and beat the stains from their wimples to restore them to pristine whiteness. I would make something of my life beyond the governance of others, neither nun nor wife nor whore. I would amount to something in my own right. But for now I was safe in the familiar surroundings of the Abbey, accepting the unchanging routine of work and prayer.

I'll wait for better times, I had said to Greseley.

And I would wait with as much patience as I could muster. But not for too long, I prayed as my arms throbbed from wielding the heavy hoe amongst the Abbey cabbages.

I regretted the loss of my warm mantle.

Chapter Three

'She's here. She's come.' The whispers rustled like a brisk wind through a field of oats.

It was Vespers. We entered the Abbey church, the hush of habits and soft shoes a quiet sound against the paving, and we knelt, ranks of black veils and white wimples, I in a coarse fustian over-kirtle and hood with the rest of the *conversa*. Nothing out of the ordinary. The mind of every sister, choir or lay, centred on the need for God's grace in a world of transgression. But not tonight. The sin of self-indulgence was rife, bright as the candle flames. Excitement was tangible, shivering in the air. For in the bishop's own chair, placed to one side of the High Altar, sat the Queen of England.

From my lowly place in the choir stalls I could see nothing of Majesty, neither could I even hazard a guess as to why she would so honour us, the service proceeding as if that carved chair were unoccupied. The observance complete, the final blessing given, nuns and *conversa* stood as one, heads bowed, hands folded discreetly within sleeves.

Mother Sybil genuflected before the altar and Majesty, still outside my vision, moved slowly through our midst towards the transept.

Slowly. Very slowly. Unobtrusively, I glanced out of the corner of my eye, my anticipation keen. In my life I had had only one brief acquaintance with a lady of the royal court. The Countess of Kent was a woman of some brilliance, a woman difficult to forget. She had taught me to mend her pens, and she taught me much else besides, mostly to my personal humiliation. As the Queen approached, I considered how the Countess had arrived at St Mary's with dash and flair, announcing her arrival by courier and trumpet blast. How much more magnificent must be the Queen of England?

Even today I can recall my astonishment. I had envisaged a noble bearing, a gown in rich colours, sumptuous materials stitched with embroidery, with train and furred oversleeves. A crown, a gold chain, gold and silver rings heavy with jewels. A presence of authority. I looked at the Queen of England, and looked again. She was well nigh invisible in her anonymity.

Philippa of Hainault.

The years had not treated this woman with gentleness. All trace of youth, any beauty she might have had as that young bride who had come to England from the Low Countries to wed our vigorous King Edward, more than thirty years ago now, all were lost to her. And where was the expression of regal power? She was not elegant. She was not tall. She did not overawe. She wore no jewels. As for her hair, it was completely obscured, every wisp and curl, by a severe wimple and veil. Queen Philippa was neither a handsome woman nor a leader of fashion.

Who could admire this aging, shuffling woman?

Majesty halted. There was the faintest gasp for breath. The Queen must be even older than I had thought. I looked again—longer than a glance—and chided myself for my lack of compassion. There was a reason for the excruciatingly slow progress. She was ill. She was in pain. With a hand resting heavily on the arm of her attendant, the Queen continued to make her small halting steps because each one pained her beyond endurance. It seemed to me that she could barely move her head, her neck and shoulders were so rigid with a spasm of the muscles. The hand that clutched the arm of her woman was swollen, the flesh as tight and shiny as the skin of a drum. No wonder she wore no rings. How would she push them beyond her swollen knuckles without unbearable discomfort?

Her Majesty was nearly level with me when she paused to draw another breath, and we curtseyed. I saw the substantial bosom of her gown rise sharply on the inhalation, her nostrils narrow and a crease deepen between her brows. Then the royal feet moved on—only to stumble on the uneven paving so that she fell. Without her grip on the arm of the young woman at her side, it would have been a disaster. As it was, she sank to her knees with a cry of agonised distress. Horrified by her suffering, I was unable not to look.

'Help me,' she murmured, of no one in particular, eyes closed tight in agony, her free hand outstretched to snatch at some invisible aid. 'Dear God, help me!' And Queen Philippa dropped her rosary beads. They slid from her fingers to fall with a little clatter of pearls and carved bone on the stones before her.

'Help me to my feet...'

And because it seemed the obvious thing to do, the only thing to do, I stretched out my hand, and took hers in mine. I froze, my breath held hard. To take the hand of the Queen of England on sheer impulse? I would surely be punished for my presumption. I fell to my knees beside her as she gripped me as hard as she could. There was not much force in it, but she groaned as the skin covering her swollen flesh tightened with the effort.

'Blessed Virgin!' she murmured. 'The pain is too much!'

The tension around us, the shocked stillness, held for a moment. Then all was movement and sound: the lady-in-waiting lifting Her Majesty to her feet in a flutter of anxiety; the Queen's feverish clasp of my hand broken; the distress of her laboured breathing deepening. Looking up from where I was still on my knees, I discovered Queen Philippa in the midst of all the fuss regarding me. Once those eyes might have sparkled with happiness but now their rich brown hue was strained with years of suffering. I could not bear to see it, and lowered my gaze to where the rosary still lay on the floor. She was quite unable to stoop to recover the beads for herself, even if a woman of such rank would deem to pick up her own belongings.

So I picked it up for her.

I lifted the rosary and held it out, startled at my temerity, even without the sharp warning murmur of Mother Abbess, who was approaching, her habit billowing with the speed of her passage like a cloak in a gale, intent on snatching the rosary from me.

'Thank you. I am very clumsy today, and you are very kind.'

Incredibly, the Queen's words were for me. I felt the touch of her fingers on my hand. For a brief moment the devastation in her face was overlaid by a softness of gratitude.

'Accept my apologies, Majesty.' Mother Abbess directed toward me a look that boded ill for me in Chapter House the following day. 'She should not have pushed herself forward in this manner. She has no humility.'

'But she has come to my aid, like the good Samaritan to the traveller in distress,' the Queen observed. 'The Holy Virgin would honour such help to an old lady…' She cried out, more sharply than before, one hand spread across the damask folds over her abdomen. 'I need to sit down. My room, Isabella—take me to my room.'

And her attendant, with a fierce frown and a firm grip, lifted her to her feet.

'I am so sorry, Isabella.' The Queen's voice caught on a sob.

'You're tired, *Maman*. Did I not say this was too much for you? You should listen to me!'

'I am aware, Isabella. But some things needed to be done, and I could not wait.'

For the first time I did more than give passing cognisance to the Queen's companion. So this was her daughter, the Princess Isabella. A tall, fair young woman with a sprightly demeanour and a barely disguised expression of utter boredom. How could I have ever mistaken her for a mere attendant? The Queen might be clothed in muted colours, but the Princess proclaimed her position in every embroidered thread and jewel from her gold crispinettes to her gilded shoes.

'Some things could be left until you are recovered,' Princess Isabella remarked crisply. I watched with pity as the little group made their way along the nave. At the Abbey door the Princess looked back, briefly, over her shoulder. Her gaze landed on me.

'Don't just stand there. Bring the rosary, girl.'

'Something will turn up,' I had said to Greseley. I did not need telling twice.

* * *

In spite of her daughter's determination, the Queen refused to be put to bed.

'I'll be in my bed long enough when death takes hold of me.'

I stood inside the door of the Abbess's parlour as the Queen was made comfortable in a high-backed chair with sturdy arms that would give her body some support. I could have put the rosary down on the travelling coffer beside the door and left, invisible to all as Isabella issued orders for a cup of heated wine and a fur mantle to warm the Queen's trembling limbs. *Stay!* my instincts urged. So I stayed. If I stayed, perhaps the Queen would speak to me again. The kindness in her voice had stirred me, and now as I saw the woman behind the face of royalty, my heart hurt for her. She was ill, and her suffering was not only that of physical pain but also of grief. She was worn with it: black-cloaked death seemed to hover behind her shoulder. Never did I think to feel sorrow for a Queen, but on that evening I did.

'Don't tell the King, Isabella,' she ordered, her voice harsh with exhaustion.

'Why not?' Isabella took her mother's hand and pressed the wine cup into it.

'Don't speak of this. I forbid it. I do not wish him to be worried.'

Her eyes might still be closed, her voice a mere thread, but her will was strong. My admiration for her was profound, and my compassion. Did the King still love her? Had he ever loved her? Perhaps it was not expected between those of royal blood whose marriage had been contracted for political alliance. What must it be like to feel old and unwanted? And yet the Queen would protect her husband from concern over her pain.

It was as if she sensed the direction of my thoughts. Impatiently pushing aside Isabella's hand with the cup, she straightened herself in the chair. And there it was after all. There was royalty. There was authority. In spite of the pain she could give her attention to me and smile. Her face warmed, the harsh lines smoothing, until she became almost comely. Had I thought her broad features lacked charm and beauty? I had been wrong.

She stretched out her hand with difficulty. 'You have brought my rosary.'

'Yes, Majesty.'

'I told her to.' Isabella poured a second cup of wine and drank it herself. 'We were too busy with you to worry about a string of beads, if you recall, trying to prevent you from falling on the floor before a parcel of ignorant nuns.'

'Nevertheless, it was well done.' The Queen beckoned and I came to kneel before her. 'A *conversa*, I see. Tell me your name.'

'Alice.'

'You have no desire to become a nun?' Putting a hand beneath my chin, she lifted it and studied my face. 'You have no calling?'

No one had ever asked me that before, or addressed me in so gentle a manner. There was a world of understanding in her eyes. Unexpectedly, unsettlingly, tears stung beneath my eyelids.

'No, Majesty.' Since she seemed interested, I told her. 'Once I was a novice. And then a servant—who became a wife. Now I am a widow. And returned here as a lay sister.'

'And is that your ambition? To remain here?'

Well, I would not lie. 'No, Majesty. I will not stay longer than I must.'

'So you have plans. How old are you?'

'Almost seventeen years, I think. I am not a child, Majesty,' I felt compelled to add.

'You are to me!' Her smile deepened momentarily. 'Do you know how old I am?'

It seemed entirely presumptuous of me to even reply. 'No, Majesty.'

'Forty-eight years. I expect that seems ancient to you.' It did. It seemed to me a vast age, and suffering had added a dozen more years to the Queen's face. 'I was younger than you when I came to England as a bride. Yet it seems no time to me. Life flies past.'

'Take another drink, *Maman*.' Isabella replaced the cup into the Queen's hand, folding the swollen fingers gently around it. 'I think you should rest.'

I expected to be dismissed, but the Queen was not to be bullied.

'Soon, Isabella. Soon. But you, Alice. Have you no family?'

'No, Majesty.'

'And your father?'

'I don't know. A labourer in the town. A tiler, I think.'

'I understand.' And I felt that she did, despite the distance between us in years and rank. 'How sad. You remind me of my own daughters. Margaret and Mary. Both dead of the plague September last.'

Isabella sighed heavily. *'Maman...!'* How could I remind anyone of a Princess of the Blood?

'You are of a similar age,' she explained, as if I had spoken my doubt. 'You are young to be a widow. Would you seek to wed again?'

'Who would have me? I have no dowry,' I stated with little attempt to hide my dissatisfaction. 'All I can offer is...' I closed my mouth.

'What can you offer?' the Queen asked as if she were genuinely interested.

I considered the sum of my talents. 'I can read and write and figure, Majesty.' Since someone actually showed an interest, there was no stopping me. 'I can read French and Latin. I can keep accounts.' Ingenuously, I was carried away with my achievements.

'So much…' I had made her smile again. 'And how did you learn to keep accounts?'

'Janyn Perrers. A moneylender. He taught me.'

'And did you enjoy it? So tedious a task?'

'Yes. I understood what I saw.'

'You have a keen mind, Alice of the Accounts,' was all she said. Perhaps I amused her. I wished I had not boasted of my hard-won skills. She took hold of one of my hands, to my embarrassment running her fingers over the evidence of hard digging in the heavy soil. My nails were cracked, the skin broken and the aroma of onions was keen, but she made no comment. 'If you could choose your future path, Alice, what would it be?'

I replied without hesitation, thinking of Greseley, of the hopes that kept me from despair in the dark hours of the night. 'I would have my own house. I would buy land and property. I would be dependent on no one.'

'An unlikely ambition!' Isabella's remark interrupted, redolent of ridicule.

'But a commendable one for all that.' The Queen's voice trembled. Isabella was instantly beside her. 'Yes. I will rest now. Today is not a good day.' She allowed her daughter to help her to her feet and moved slowly toward the bedchamber. Then she stopped and despite the discomfort looked back at me.

'Alice, keep the rosary. It was a gift to me from the King

when I gave birth to Edward, our first son.' She must have read astonishment on my face. 'It is not very valuable. He had little money to spend on fripperies in those days. I would like you to keep it as a memento of the day when you rescued the Queen from falling in public!'

The rosary. It was still gripped in one hand, the gold-enamelled beads of the Aves clutched so tight that they left impressions in my palm. The pearls that marked the Paternosters and Glorias were warm and so smooth. The Queen would give this to me? A gift from her husband? I coveted it—who would not? I wanted it for my own.

'No…' I said. I could not. I was not courteous, but I knew what would happen if I kept it. 'We are not allowed possessions. We take a vow of poverty.' I tried to explain my refusal, knowing how crude it must seem.

'Not even a gift from a grateful Queen?'

'It would not be thought suitable.'

'And you would not be allowed to keep it?'

'No, Majesty.'

'No. I was thoughtless to offer it.' The tormenting pain gripped her again and I was forgotten. 'By the Virgin, I am tried beyond endurance today—take me to my bed, Isabella.'

Isabella manoeuvred the Queen through the doorway into the bedchamber, and I was left alone. Before I could change my mind I placed the rosary on the *prie dieu* and backed out of the room until I was standing outside the door. Quietly I closed it, leaning against it. I had refused a gift from a Queen. But what would be the good in my accepting what I would not be allowed to keep? The rosary, if I had it, would fall into the hands of Mother Abbess. I could see it in my mind's eye attached to her silver-decorated girdle. As I could imagine my mantle gracing the shoulders of Signora Damiata.

If ever I accepted anything of value in my life, I must be certain it remained mine.

Queen Philippa and her sharp-tongued daughter did not stay beyond the night. As soon as the service of Prime was sung next morning, they made ready to depart, the Queen helped into her well-cushioned travelling litter by Sister Margery, who had made up a draught of tender ash leaves distilled in wine against the agony of a bone-shaking journey. I knew what was in it. Had I not helped to make the infusion?

'Her Majesty suffers from dropsy,' Sister Margery had pronounced with certainty. 'I have seen it before. It is a terrible affliction. She will feel the effect of every rut and stumble.'

Sister Margery instructed Lady Isabella: too much would cripple the digestion; too little and the pain would remain intense. And here was a little pot of mutton fat pounded with vervain root. Smoothed on the swollen flesh of hands and feet, it would bring relief. I had done the work but it was not I who held the flask and offered the little pot. It was not I who received the Queen's thanks. I was not even there. I heard the departure from the cellar where I was engaged in counting hams and barrels of ale.

Take me with you. Let me serve you.

A silent plea that she did not hear.

Why would she remember me? It was an occasion of moment in *my* life, it had no bearing on what a Queen might remember. She would have forgotten about me within the quarter-hour of my returning the rosary. But I did not forget

Queen Philippa. She had the loving kindness in her homely face of the mother that I had never known.

I wondered what Greseley was doing, and if I would ever see him again. If he was taking care of the houses in Gracechurch Street and the little manor in West Peckham. Surely he could raise enough money from them for my own needs.

I prayed even more fervently over the hams than I had over the cabbages that it would be *soon* before my hopes died.

The hams and the cabbages were eaten, one with more relish than the other, the ale drunk and replaced by an inferior brew that brought down the ire of Mother Sybil on the brewer. Such tedious, unimportant events that barely ruffled my existence as high summer came and went, the early blossom on the gnarled trees in the orchard long gone. My patience ebbed and flowed, reaching painful depths in the nights when the silence closed around me like a shroud.

And then! Mother Abbess was in conversation with a tall, well-dressed man, perhaps a courier, to judge from his riding gear of fine wool and leather, accompanied by an elderly thick-set groom who held the reins of a fine gelding, and a small but well-armed escort, sword and bow very evident.

I took it all in at a glance. Barely had I considered why I had been summoned when the courier turned a penetrating stare toward me.

'You are Alice?'

'Yes, sir.' Conscious of my dishevelled state and the mud on my shoes—I had been kneeling beneath the low branches in the orchard to collect the fallen plums and damsons when I had been fetched—I made a desultory attempt to beat soil and grass from my skirts. The shoes were beyond remedy.

'You are to go with me, mistress.' He looked me up and down and from the narrowing of his eyes found me wanting. 'You will need a cloak.' And to the Abbess, 'Provide one for her, if you please.'

I looked to Abbess Sybil for instruction. Mother Abbess lifted a shoulder as if denying any complicity in what had been arranged. Had my labours been bought again? Holy Virgin! Not another marriage. The man continued to address me, impervious and uninformative.

'Can you ride, mistress?'

'No, sir.'

He motioned to the groom. 'She'll ride pillion behind you, Rob. She's no weight to speak of.'

Within minutes I was bundled into a coarsely woven cloak and hoisted onto the broad rump of the groom's mare, as if I were a cord of firewood.

'Hold tight, mistress,' growled the man called Rob.

I clutched the sides of his leather jerkin as the animal stamped and sidled. The ground seemed far away and my balance was awry. At a signal from the man who had so smoothly rearranged my future, the escort fell in and we rode through the streets of the town and into the open country without a further word.

'Sir?' I addressed the back of the courier, who was now riding a little way ahead of me. No reply, so I raised my voice. 'Sir? Where are we going?'

He did not turn his head. He might have addressed me as mistress, but it seemed I was not worthy of any further respect. 'To Havering-atte-Bower.'

It meant nothing to me. 'Why?'

'The Queen has sent for you.'

I could not believe it. What had caused her to remember me, when I had done nothing but pick up her rosary?

Nevertheless, the thrill of unknown adventure placed a cold hand on my nape and I shuddered. 'Is Havering-atte-Bower, then, a royal palace?' I asked.

The man slowed his horse and gestured the groom to pull alongside. On a level, he reined in his mount, allowing me to read his unspoken thoughts as clear as figures in a ledger. My kirtle and overgown bore the sticky remnants of the fallen fruit in St Mary's orchard, my hair was bound up in a length of coarse cloth, the borrowed cloak was far beyond respectability. Kicking his mount into a walk, we plodded on side by side as he considered what he thought of me, and what he would deign to tell me.

'Why would the Queen send for me?' I asked.

'I have no idea. Her Majesty will doubtless tell you.'

He shortened his reins as if to push on with more speed, our conversation finished. But I wanted more.

'Who are you, sir?'

He gave no reply, through choice, I decided, rather than because he had not heard me, so I took the time to appraise him. Nothing out of the way. He was neither young nor old, with regular features, a little stern, a little austere. He was certainly used to command but I thought he was not a soldier. Neither was he the courier I had first thought him. He had too much authority for that. His eyes were a mix of green and brown, sharp and bright, like those of a squirrel. I thought him rather pompous for a man who could not be considered old. So we would ride to Havering-atte-Bower in total silence, would we? I thought not. I held tight to Rob's tunic and leaned toward my reluctant companion.

'I have much to learn, sir,' I began. 'How far to Havering-atte-Bower?'

'About two hours. Three if you don't get a move on.'

I ignored the jibe. 'Time enough, then. You could help me. You could tell me some of the things I don't know.'

'Such as?'

'You could tell me how to behave when we arrive,' I suggested solemnly, at the same time widening my eyes in innocent enquiry. And I saw him waver. 'And how do I address you, sir?'

'I am William de Wykeham. And you, I suspect, are no wiser.'

I smiled deliberately. Winsomely, all demure insouciance, except for the tilt of my chin. How best to seduce information from a man than get him to talk of what was important to him? I had learnt that from both Janyn and Greseley. Talk about money and rates of interest and they would eat out of your hand. 'I am no wiser yet,' I replied. 'But I will be if you will be my informant. What do I call you? What do you do?'

'Wykeham will do. I serve His Majesty. And occasionally Her Majesty, Queen Philippa.' And I saw the pride in him. 'I am destined for the church—and to build palaces.'

'Oh.' It seemed a laudable occupation. 'Have you built many?'

And that was it. The door opened wide. For the rest of the journey Wykeham recounted to me his ambitions and achievements. Turrets and arches, buttresses and pillars. Curtain walls and superior heating methods. Holy Virgin! He was as dull as a meatless meal in Lent, as incapable of luring a nun from her vows as Janyn Perrers or Greseley. Perhaps all men in essence were as dry as dust. When I wanted to hear the minutiae of life in a royal palace, the food, the fashions, the important personages, all I got was a description of the new tower at Windsor, but I made no effort to deter him. Were all men so easy to encourage into conversation? Far easier than women, I thought. A smile, a question, an appeal to their achievements, their pride. I learnt very little about life at Havering during the journey, but a great deal about castle building. And then we were approaching an impressive array of towers, half-hidden in the trees.

'Your journey is at an end, Mistress Alice. And I forgot...' Transferring his reins into one hand, he fished in his saddlebag. 'Her Majesty sent you this. She thought you might like it—to give you God's comfort on the journey.' He dropped the rosary into my hand. 'Not that I think you need it. You can talk more than any woman I know.'

I was instantly torn between amazement at the gift of the rosary and the unfairness of the accusation: the unfairness won. 'You've done more talking than I have!'

'Nonsense.'

'Stop fussing, woman!' Rob gave a rough growl. 'You're as fret as a flea on a warm dog.'

I laughed. 'I ache!'

'Your arse'll recover soon enough. My sides are stripped raw with your clutchings!'

Even Wykeham laughed. The warmth of it—friendly and uncritical—helped to ease my growing apprehension of what awaited me.

'Why would she send me something so precious?' I held the rosary up so that the sun caught the beads, turning them into a rainbow of iridescence.

My companion surveyed me from my cloth-bound hair to my mud-smeared hem as if it was far beyond his comprehension. 'I really have no idea.'

Neither had I.

Chapter Four

Havering-atte-Bower

I knew nothing of royal palaces in those days when I arrived in Wykeham's dusty wake. Neither was the grandeur of the place my first priority. Every one of my muscles groaned at its ill usage. We could not come to a halt fast enough for me; all I wanted was to slide down from that lumbering creature and set my feet on solid ground. But once in the courtyard at Havering I simply sat and stared.

'Are you going to dismount today, mistress?' Wykeham asked brusquely. He was already dismounted and halfway up the steps to the huge iron-studded door.

'I've never seen…' He wasn't listening so I closed my mouth.

I have never seen anything so magnificent.

And yet it was strangely welcoming, with a seductive charm that St Mary's with its grey stone austerity lacked. It seemed vast to me yet I was to learn that for a royal palace it was small and intimate. The stonework of the building glowed in the afternoon sunshine, a haphazard arrangement of rooms and apartments, the arches of a chapel to the right, the bulk of the original Great Hall to my left, then further outbuildings, sprawling outwards from the courtyard. Roofs and walls jutted at strange angles as the whim had taken the builders over the years. And if that was not enough, the whole palace was hemmed about by pasture and lightly wooded stretches, like a length of green velvet wrapped round a precious jewel.

It filled me with awe.

'It's beautiful!'

My voice must have carried. 'It'll do, for now,' Wykeham growled. 'The King's grandfather built it—the first Edward. The Queen likes it—that's the main thing—it's her manor. It will be better when I've had my hands on it. I've a mind to put in new kitchens now that the King has his household here too.' He fisted his hands on his hips. 'For God's sake, woman. Get off that animal.'

I slid down from the rump, staggering when my feet hit the ground, grateful when Wykeham strode forward to grip my arm.

'Thank you, sir.' I held on tight for a moment as my muscles quivered in protest.

'I am at your disposal,' he replied wryly. 'Tell me when you can stand without falling over.'

Wykeham led the way up the shallow flight of steps, pushing open the door and stepping into the Great Hall. It was an echoing space, tables and trestles cleared away for the day except for the solid board on the dais at the far end. Cool after the heat of the sun, it was pleasant just to be there, the rafters above my head merging into deep shadows striped with soft bars of sunlight. Like the coat of a tabby cat. Servants moved quietly, replacing the wall sconces. A burst of laughter came from behind the screens at the far end that closed off the entrance to the kitchens. The tapestries on the walls glowed with rich colour, mirrored in the tiling beneath my feet.

I looked round in stark admiration. Was this where the Countess of Kent lived, that arrogant being who had left such an indelible impression on my younger self? I glanced at the shadows as if I might see her, watching me, judging me, before I chided myself for my foolishness. If the Countess had fulfilled her ambitions, she would be seated in the opulent splendour of the Queen's private apartments, sipping wine, while a servant brushed her magnificent hair. If the serving woman's comb happened to catch and drag on a tangle, the Countess would slap her without compunction.

A movement caught my interest. A maidservant crossed the room, busy with a tray of cups and a flagon, with a brief curtsey in Wykeham's direction. My eye followed her. Was this, then, to be my destiny? To work in the kitchens of the royal palace? But why? Did the Queen not have enough servants? If she needed more, would her steward not find enough willing girls from the neighbouring villages? I could not see why she would bring me all the way from the Abbey to be a serving wench. Perhaps she needed a tirewoman, one who could read and write, but I hardly had the breeding for it. So why, in the name of the Blessed Virgin, was I here? The Queen would hardly stand in need of my meagre talents.

'This way.' Wykeham was striding ahead.

Behind us in the doorway a commotion erupted. Wykeham and I, and everyone in the Hall, turned to look. A man had entered to stand under the door arch. He was silhouetted by the low rays of the afternoon sun so that it was impossible to see his features, only his stature and bearing. Tall, with the build of a soldier, a man of action.

Around his feet pushed and jostled a parcel of hounds and alaunts. On his gauntleted wrist rode a hooded goshawk. As the hawk shook its pinions, the man moved forward a step, into a direct sunbeam, so that he gleamed with a corona of light around head and shoulders, like one of the saints in the glazed windows of the Abbey. Crowned with gold.

Then, with another step, the moment passed. He was enclosed in soft shadow, an ordinary man again. And I was distracted when the hounds bounded forward, circling the Hall, sniffing at my skirts. Having no knowledge of such boisterous animals, I stepped back, wary of slavering mouths and formidable bodies. Wykeham bowed whilst I was engaged in pushing aside an inquisitive alaunt.

Wykeham cleared his throat.

'What is it?' I asked.

In reply Wykeham took hold of the ancient cloak that still enveloped me from chin to toe and twitched it off, letting it fall to the floor. I stiffened at this presumptuous action, took breath to remonstrate, when a voice, a strikingly beautiful voice, cut across the width of the Hall.

'Wykeham, by God! Where've you been? Why are you always impossible to find, man?'

It was a clear-timbred voice, filling the space from walls to rafters. And striding toward us was the owner. The man with the raptor.

Wykeham bowed again, with what could have been construed as a scowl in my direction, so I curtseyed. The newcomer looked to me like a huntsman strayed into the Hall after a day's exercise, looking to find a cup of ale or a heel of bread as he covered the ground with long loping strides, as lithe as the hound at his side.

And then he was standing within a few feet of me.

'Sire!' Wykeham bowed once more.

The King!

I sank to the floor, holding my skirts, my flushed face hidden. How naive I was. But how was I to know? He did not dress like a king. Then I looked up and saw him not a score of feet distant, and knew that he did not need clothing and jewels to proclaim his superiority. What a miraculous, god-like figure he was. A man of some age and experience, but he wore the years lightly. Handsome without doubt with a broad brow and a fine blade of a nose complemented by luxurious flaxen hair that shone as bright as silver. Here was no dry-as-dust dullard. The King shone like a diamond amongst worthless dross.

'It's the water supply!' the King announced.

'Yes, Sire. I have it in hand,' Wykeham replied calmly.

'The Queen needs heated water.'

The King's complexion might once have been fair but his skin was tanned and seamed from an outdoor life in sun and cold. What a remarkable face he was blessed with, with blue eyes as keen as those of the raptor on his fist, whose hood he was in the process of removing. And what fluidity and grace there was about his movements as he unclipped his cloak, one-handed, swung it from his shoulder and threw it to a page who had followed him across the Hall. How had I not known that this was King Edward? At his belt was a knife in a jewelled scabbard, in his hat a ruby brooch pinning a peacock feather into jaunty place. Even without the glitter of gems, I should have known. He had a presence, the habit of command, of demanding unquestioning obedience.

So this was Queen Philippa's magnificent husband. I was dazzled.

I stood, my heart beating fast, aware of nothing but my own unfortunate apparel, the heap of the disreputable mantle at my feet. But the King was not looking at me. Was I

not more poorly clad than any of the servants I had seen
in the palace? He would think—if he thought at all—that I
was a beggar come to receive alms from the palace kitchens. Even the raptor eyed me as if I might be vermin and
worth the eating.

The King swept his arm out in a grand gesture. 'Out! All
of you!' The dogs obediently vanished through the door in
a rush of excitement. 'Will—I've been looking at the site
for the bath house you proposed.' He was close enough to
clip Wykeham in an affectionate manner on his shoulder.
'Where've you been?'

I might as well not have been there.

'I've been to St Mary's at Barking, Sire.' Wykeham
smiled.

'Barking? Why in God's name?'

'Business for the Queen, Sire. A new chantry for the two
dead Princesses.'

The King nodded. 'Yes, yes. I'd forgotten. It gives her
comfort and—before God!—precious little does.' And at last
he cast a cursory eye over me. 'Who's this? Someone I employ?' Removing the beaver hat with its brooch and feather,
he inclined his head with grave courtesy, even though he
thought I was a serving wench. His gaze travelled over my
face in a cursory manner. I made another belated curtsey.
The King tilted his chin at Wykeham, having made some
judgement on me. 'St Mary's, you said. Have you helped
one of the sisters to escape, Will?'

Wykeham smiled dryly. 'The Queen sent for her.'

Those sharp blue eyes returned. 'One of her waifs and
strays perhaps. To be rescued for her own good. What's
your name, girl?'

'Alice, Sire.'

'Glad to escape?'

'Yes, Sire.' It was heartfelt, and must have sounded it.

And Edward laughed, a sound of great joy that made me smile too. 'So would I be. Serving God's all very well, but not every hour of every day. Do you have talents?' He frowned at me as if he could not imagine it. 'Play a lute?' I shook my head. 'Sing? My wife likes music.'

'No, Sire.'

'Well, I suppose she has her reasons.' He was already losing interest, turning away. 'And if it makes her happy… Come here!'

I started, thinking that he meant me, but he clicked his fingers at a rangy alaunt that had slunk back into the Hall and was following some scent along the edge of a tapestry. It obeyed to fawn and rub against him as he twisted his fingers into its collar. 'Tell Her Majesty, Will— No, on second thoughts, you come with me. You've completed your task for the Queen. I've demands on your time for my new bath house.' He raised his voice. 'Joscelyn! Joscelyn!'

A man approached from where he had been waiting discreetly beside the screen.

'Yes, Sire.'

'Take this girl to the Queen. She has sent for her. Now, Will…' They were already knee-deep in planning. 'I think there's the perfect site. Let me get rid of these dogs and birds…' Whistling softly to the raptor on his wrist, the King headed to the door. Wykeham followed. They left me without a second look. Why would they not?

Sir Joscelyn, who I was to learn was the royal steward, beckoned me to follow him but I hesitated and looked back over my shoulder. Wykeham was nodding, my last view of him gesturing with his hands as if describing the size and extent of the building he envisaged. They laughed together, the King's strong voice overlaying Wykeham's softer responses. And then he was gone with the King, as if my last friend on earth had deserted me. My only friend. And, of course, he wasn't, but who else did I know here? I would not forget his brusque kindness. As for the King, I had expected a crown or at least a chain of office. Not a pack of dogs and a hawk. But there was no denying the sovereignty that sat as lightly on his shoulders as a summer mantle.

'Come on, girl. I haven't got all day.'

I sighed and followed the steward to discover what would become of me as one of the Queen's habitual waifs and strays. I stuffed the rosary that I still clutched into the bosom of my overgown and followed as I had been bidden.

The Queen's apartments were silent. Finding no one in any of the antechambers to whom he could hand me over, Sir Joscelyn rapped on a door, was bidden to enter and did so, drawing me with him. I found myself on the threshold of a large sun-filled room so full of colour and activity and soft chatter, of feminine glamour, that it filled my whole vision, more than even the grandeur of the Great Hall. Here was every hue and tint I could imagine, creating butterflies of the women who inhabited the room. Ill-mannered certainly, but I stared at so beguiling a scene. There they were, chattering as they stitched, books and games to hand for those who wished, not an enshrouding wimple or brow-hugging veil amongst them. A whole world of which I had no knowledge to enchant ear and eye. The ladies talked and laughed; someone was singing to the clear notes of a lute. There was no silence here.

I could not see the Queen in their midst. Neither, to my relief, could I see the Countess of Kent.

The steward cast an eye and discovered the face he sought.

'My lady.' His bow was perfection. Learning fast, I curtseyed. 'I would speak with Her Majesty.'

Princess Isabella looked up from the lute she was playing but her fingers continued to strum idly over the strings. Now I knew the source of her beautiful fairness: she was her father's daughter in height and colouring.

'Her Majesty is indisposed, Joscelyn. Can it wait?'

'I was commanded to bring this person to Her Majesty.' He nudged me forward with haughty condescension. I curtseyed again.

'Why?' Her gaze remained on the lute strings. She was not the King's daughter in kindness.

'Wykeham brought her, my lady.'

The Princess's eye lifted to take in my person. 'Who are you?'

'Alice, my lady.' There was no welcome here. Not even a memory of who I was. 'From St Mary's Abbey at Barking, my lady.'

A line dug between Isabella's brows, then smoothed. 'I remember. The girl with the rosary—the one who worked in the kitchens or some such.'

'Yes, my lady.'

'Her Majesty sent for you?' Her fingers strummed over the lute strings again and her foot tapped impatiently. 'I suppose I must do something with you.' The glint in her eye, I decided, was not friendly.

One of the ladies approached to put her hand on the Princess's shoulder with the confidence of long acquaintance. 'Play for us, Isabella. We have a new song.'

'With pleasure. Take the girl to the kitchens, Joscelyn. Give her a bed and some food. Then put her to work. I expect that's what Her Majesty intended.'

'Yes, my lady.'

Isabella had already given her attention to the ladies and their new song. The steward bowed himself out, pushing me before him, the door closing on that magical scene. I had not managed to step beyond the threshold, and I was shaken by a desire to do so, to be part of the life that went on behind that closed door.

Sir Joscelyn strode off without a word, expecting me to follow, as I did. I should be grateful that I was being given food and a place to sleep. Would life as a kitchen wench at Havering-atte-Bower be better or worse than as a *conversa* in the Abbey at Barking? Would it be better than life as a drudge in the Perrers household?' I was about to find out, thanks to the effortless malice of Princess Isabella, for I knew, beyond doubt, that the Queen had not brought me all the way from Barking to pluck chickens in her kitchens. It was all Isabella's fault. I knew an enemy when I saw one.

'This girl, Master Humphrey...' The steward's expression spoke his contempt. 'Another of Her Majesty's gutter sweepings to live off our charity.'

A grunt was all the reply he got. Master Humphrey was wielding a cleaver on the carcass of a pig, splitting it down the backbone with much-practised skill.

'The Lady said to bring her to you.'

The cook stopped, in mid-chop, and looked up under grizzled brows. 'And what, may I ask, do I do with her?'

'Feed her. Give her a bed. Clothe her and put her to work.'

'Ha! Look around you, Jos! What do you see?'

I looked also. The kitchen was awash with activity: on all sides scullions, spit boys, pot boys, bottle washers applied themselves with a racket as if all hell had broken loose. The heat was overpowering from the ovens and open fires.

I could already feel sweat beginning to trickle down my spine and dampen my hair beneath my hood.

'What?' Sir Joscelyn growled. I thought he did not approve of the liberty taken with his name.

'I don't employ girls, Jos. They're not strong enough. Good enough for the dairy and serving the dishes—but not here.' The cook emphasised the final word with a downward sweep of his axe.

'Well, you do now. Princess Isabella's orders. Kitchens, she said.'

Another grunt. 'And what the Lady wants…!'

'Exactly.'

Sir Joscelyn duly abandoned me in the midst of the teaming life of Havering's kitchens. I recognised the activities—the cleaning, the scouring, the chopping and stirring—but my experience was a pale shadow to them. The noise was ear-shattering. Exhilarating. Shouts and laughter, hoots of ridicule, bellowed orders, followed inevitably by oaths and complaints. There seemed to be little respect from the kitchen lads, but the cook's orders were carried out with a promptness that suggested a heavy hand if they transgressed them. And the food. My belly rumbled at the sight of it. As for the scents of roasting meat, of succulent joints…

'Don't stand there like a bolt of cloth.'

The cook, throwing down his axe with a clatter, gave me no more than a passing look, but the scullions did, with insolent grins and earthy gestures. I might not have much experience of such signs with tongues and fingers—except occasionally in the market between a whore and a dissatisfied customer—but it did not take much imagination. They made my cheeks glow with a heat that was not from the fire.

'Sit there.' Master Humphrey pressed down on my shoulder with a giant hand, and so I did at the centre board, sharing it with the pig. A bowl of thick stew was dumped unceremoniously in front of me, a spoon pushed into my hand and a piece of stale wastel bread thrown down on the table within reach.

'Eat, then—and fast. There's work to be done.'

I ate, without stopping. I drank a cup of ale handed to me. I had not realised how hungry I was.

'Put this on.'

A large apron of stained linen was held out by Master Humphrey as he carried a tray of round loaves to thrust into one of the two ovens. It was intended for someone much larger, and I hitched it round my waist or I would have tripped on it. I was knotting the strings, cursing Isabella silently under my breath, when the cook returned.

'Now! Let me look at you!' I stood before him. 'What did you say your name was?'

'Alice.'

'Well, then, Alice, no need to keep your eyes on your feet here or you'll fall on your arse.' His expression was jaundiced. 'You're not very big.'

'She's big enough for what I've in mind!' shouted one of the scullions, a large lad with tow hair. A guffaw of crude laughter.

'Shut it, Sim. And keep your hands to yourself or...' Master Humphrey seized and wielded his meat cleaver with quick chopping movements. 'Pay them no heed.' He took my hands in his, turned them over. 'Hmm. What can you do?'

I did not think it mattered what I said, given the continuing obscenities from the two lads struggling to manhandle a side of venison onto a spit. I would be given the lowliest of tasks. I would be a butt of jokes and innuendo.

'Come on, girl! I've never yet met a woman with nothing to say for herself!'

So far I had been moved about like the bolt of cloth he had called me, but if this was to be my future I would not sink into invisibility. With Signora Damiata I had controlled my manner because to do otherwise would have called down retribution. Here I knew that I must stand up for myself and demand some respect.

'I can do that, Master Humphrey. And that.' I pointed at the washing and scouring going on in a tub of water. 'I can do that.' A small lad was piling logs on the fire.

'So could an imbecile!' The cook aimed a kick at the lad at the fire, who grinned back.

'I can make bread. I can kill those.' Chickens clucking unsuspectingly in an osier basket by the hearth. 'I can do that.' I pointed to an older man who was gutting a fish, scooping the innards into a basin with the flat of his hand. 'I can make a tincture to cure a cough. And I can make a—'

'My, my. What an addition to my kitchen.' Master Humphrey gripped his belt and made a mocking little bow. He did not believe half of what I said.

'I can keep an inventory of your food stuffs.' I was not going to shut up unless he ordered me to. 'I can tally your books and accounts.' If I was condemned to work here, I would make a place for myself. Until better times.

'A miracle, by the Holy Virgin.' The mockery went up by a notch. 'What is such a gifted mistress of all crafts doing in my kitchen?' The laughter at my expense expanded too. 'Let's start with this for now.'

I was put to work raking the hot ashes from the ovens and scouring the fat-encrusted baking trays. No different from the Abbey or the Perrers's household at all.

But it *was* different, and I relished it. Here was life at its most coarse and vivid, not a mean existence ruled by silence and obedience. This was no living death. Not that I enjoyed the work—it was hard and relentless and punishing under the eye of Master Humphrey and Sir Joscelyn—but here was no dour disapproval or use of a switch if I sullied the Rule of Saint Benedict. Or caught Damiata's caustic eye. Everyone had something to say about every event or rumour that touched on Master Humphrey's kitchen. I swear he could discuss the state of the realm as well as any great lord while slitting the gizzard of a peacock. It was a different world. I was now the owner of a straw pallet in a cramped attic room with two of the maids who strained the milk and made the rounds of cheese in the dairy. I was given a blanket, a new shift and kirtle—new to me at any event—a length of cloth to wrap round my hair and a pair of rough shoes.

Better than a lay sister at St Mary's? By the Virgin, it was!

I listened as I toiled. The scullions gossiped from morn till night, covering the whole range of the royal family. The Queen was ill, the King protective. The King was well past the days of his much-lauded victory on the battlefield of Crécy against the bloody French, but still a man to be admired. Whilst Isabella, a madam, refusing every sensible marriage put to her. The King should have taken a whip to her sides! As for the Countess of Kent—my ears instantly pricked up—who had married the Prince and would one day be Queen, well, she was little better than a whore, and an ill-mannered one at that when it suited her. Thank God she was in Aquitaine with her long-suffering husband. Unaware of my interest, the scurrilous gossip continued.

Gascony and Aquitaine, our possessions across the channel, were in revolt. Ireland was simmering like a pot of soup. Now the buildings of the man Wykeham! Water directed to the kitchens to run direct from a spigot into a bowl at Westminster! May it come to Havering soon, pray God.

Meanwhile I was sent to haul water from the well twenty times a day. Master Humphrey had no need for me to read or tally. I swept and scoured and chopped, burned my hands, singed my hair and emptied chamber pots. I lifted and carried and swept up. And I worked even harder to keep the lascivious scullions and pot boys at a distance. I learned fast. By God, I did!

Sim. The biggest lout of them all with his fair hair and leering smile.

I did not need any warning. I had seen Sim's version of romantic seduction when he trapped one of the serving wenches against the door of the woodstore. It had not been enjoyment on her face as he had grunted and laboured, his hose around his ankles. I did not want his greasy hands with their filthy nails on me. Or any other part of his body. The stamp of a foot on an unprotected instep, a sharp elbow to a gut kept the human vermin at bay for the most part. Unfortunately it was easy for Sim and his crowd to stalk me in the pantry or the cellar. If his arm clipped my waist once, it did so a dozen times within the first week.

'How about a kiss, Alice?' he wheedled, his foul breath hot against my neck.

I punched his chest with my fist, and not lightly. 'You'll get no kiss from me!'

'Who else will kiss you?' The usual chorus of appreciation from the crude, grinning mouths.

'Not you!'

'You're an ugly bitch, but you're better than a beef carcass.'

'You're not. I'd sooner kiss a carp from the pond. Now back off—and take your gargoyles with you.' I had discovered a talent for wordplay and a sharp tongue and used it indiscriminately, along with my elbows.

'You'll not get better than me.' He ground his groin, fierce with arousal, against my hip.

My knee slamming between his legs loosened his hold well enough. 'Keep your hands to yourself! Or I'll take Master Humphrey's boning knife to your balls and we'll roast them for supper with garlic and rosemary!'

I was not unhappy. But I was sorry not to be pretty, and that my talents were not used. How much skill did it take to empty the chamber pots onto the midden? And as I toiled, dipping coarse wicks in foul-smelling tallow to make candles for use in the kitchens and storerooms, all noise and bustle swirling around me, I allowed myself to step back into the days of my early novitiate. I allowed the Countess of Kent—indeed I invited her—to step imperiously into my mind. She might be in Aquitaine, but for those moments she lived again in the sweaty kitchen of Havering-atte-Bower.

How had such a lowly creature as I come to be noticed by so high-born a woman? What a spectacle she had provided for me, little more than a child that I had been. A travelling litter had swayed to a halt, marvellous with swags and gilded leather curtains and the softest of soft cushions, pulled by a team of six gleaming horses. Minions and outriders had filled the space. And so much luggage in an accompanying wagon to be unloaded. I had never seen such wealth. As I had watched, jewelled fingers had emerged and the curtains twitched back in a grand gesture.

Blessed Virgin! The sight had stopped my breath as a lady stepped from the palanquin, shaking out her silk damask skirts—a hint of deep patterned blue, of silver thread and luxuriant fur—and smoothing the folds of her mantle, the jewels on her fingers afire with a rainbow of light. She was not a young woman, but neither was she old, and she was breathtakingly beautiful. I could see nothing of her figure, shrouded as she was in the heavy cloak despite the warmth of the summer day, or of her hair, hidden beneath a crispinette and black veil, but I could see her face. It was a perfect oval of fair skin, and she was lovely. Her eyes, framed by the fine linen and undulating silk, were large and lustrous, the colour of new beech leaves.

This was Countess Joan of Kent, the ill-mannered whore of kitchen gossip.

From one of the wagons bounded a trio of little dogs that yapped and capered around her skirts. A hawk on a travelling perch eyed me balefully. And an animal such as I had never seen, all bright eyes and poking fingers, the colour of a horse chestnut with a ruff around its face and a long tail. Complete with a gold collar and chain, it leapt and clung to one of the carved side-struts of the litter. I could not look away. I was transfixed, entirely seduced by worldly glory, whilst the creature both charmed and repelled me in equal measure.

Then, without warning, with harsh cries and snatching hands, the exotic creature leapt to dart through the nuns, drawn up in ranks to welcome this visitor. The nuns flinched as one, their cries in counterpoint. The lap dogs yapped and gave chase. And as the animal scurried past me, I *knew*!

Stooping smartly, I snatched at the trailing end of its chain so that it came to a screaming, chattering halt at my feet, its sharp teeth very visible. I gave them no thought. Before it could struggle for release, I had lifted it into my arms. Light, fragile boned, its fur incredibly soft, it curled its fingers into my veil and held on, and I felt my face flush as a taut silence fell and all eyes turned on me.

Back in the kitchen, as the reek of hot tallow coated

my flesh, I shivered, almost able to feel the scratch of the creature's fingers as I cut and dipped. The rescue of Joan's monkey had been a selfishly calculated action, nothing like my impulsive gesture to grasp the hand of the Queen of England. Should I have regretted my boldness? I did not. I had seized the only chance I had ever had to make someone notice me. I did not regret it even when I discovered that the lady was perusing me as if I were a fat carp in the market. I tried a curtsey, unfortunately graceless, my arms full of shrieking fury.

'Well!' the lady remarked, her lips at last curved into the semblance of a smile, although her eyes were cool. 'How enterprising of you.' And the smile widened into one of blinding charm, sparkling like ice on a puddle on a winter's morn. 'I need someone to see to my needs. This girl will do.' And raising her hand in an authoritative gesture as if the matter was decided, 'Come with me. Keep hold of the Barbary.'

And so I followed her, my mouth dry, belly churning with a strange mix of shock and excitement. I was to become a maidservant. To fetch and carry and perform menial tasks for a woman who had chosen *me*. For only a short time, it was true, but I had recognised a chance to be noticed. To be *different*. And I had held it, by the scruff of its gold-collared neck. But not for long. As soon as I had stepped into the rooms set aside for our guest, it squirmed from my hold to scamper up the embroidered hangings of the bed, to worry at the damask with sharp teeth. I remained where I was, just within the door, ignorant of my tasks.

'Take these!' she ordered.

Holding out a pair of embroidered gauntlets, she dropped them to the floor, anticipating that I should retrieve them. Her veil and wimple followed in similar fashion, carelessly discarded with no thought for the expensive cloth. I leapt to obey. Thus I had my first lesson as a lady's waiting woman. The lady let the cloak fall into my arms, and I stood holding the weight of sumptuous cloth, not knowing what else to do. She gave me no direction, and the arrogance of her demeanour forbade me to ask.

'God's Bones!' she remarked with casual blasphemy that impressed me. 'Do I have to tolerate these drab accommodations? It's worse than a dungeon in the Tower. It's mean enough to make me repent!' Picking up a jewel casket, she opened it and trilled a laugh that was not entirely pleasant. 'You do not know who I am. Why should a novice in this backwater of a nunnery know of me? But by God! You will within a twelvemonth. The whole country will know of me.' The viciousness of the tone was incongruous with such lovely features. She tossed the box onto the bed so that the jewels spilled out in a sparkling stream and cast a cursory glance in my direction. 'I am Joan, Countess of Kent. For now at least. Soon I will be wife to Prince Edward. The future King of England.'

I knew nothing of her, or of the Prince who would be the next King. What I did know was that *I* had been chosen. She had chosen me to serve her. I think pride touched my heart. Mistakenly, as it turned out.

I became a willing slave to the Fair Maid of Kent whose grace and beauty were, she informed me, a matter for renown throughout the land. When she needed me, she rang a little silver bell that had remarkable carrying quality of sound. It rang with great frequency.

'Take this gown and brush the hem—so much dust. And treat it with care.'

I brushed. I was very careful.

'Fetch lavender—you do have lavender in your herb garden, I presume? Find some for my furs. I'll not wear them again for some months…'

I ravaged Sister Margery's herb patch for lavender, risking the sharp edge of the Infirmarian's tongue.

'Take that infernal monkey—' for so I learned it to be '—into the garth. Its chatter makes my head ache. And water. I need a basin of water. Hot water—not cold as last time. And when you've done that, bring me ink. And a pen.'

Countess Joan was an exacting mistress, but I never minded the summonses. A window into the exhilarating world of the royal Court had been unlatched and flung wide, through which I might peer and wonder.

'Comb out my hair,' she ordered me.

So I did, loosening the plaited ropes of red gold to free them of tangles with an ivory comb I wished was mine.

'Careful, girl!' She struck out, catching my hand with her nails, enough to draw blood. 'My head aches enough without your clumsy efforts!'

Countess Joan's head frequently ached. I learned to move smartly out of range, but as often as she repelled me she lured me back. And the most awe-inspiring revelation, to my naive gaze?

The Countess Joan bathed!

It was a ceremony. I held a freshly laundered chemise over my arm and a towel of coarse linen. Countess Joan stripped off all her clothes without modesty. For a moment embarrassed shock crept over my skin, as if I too were unclothed. I had had no exposure to nakedness. No nun removed her undershift. A nun slept in her chemise, washed beneath it with a cloth dipped in a bowl of water, would die in it. Nakedness was a sin in the eye of God. Countess Joan had no such inhibitions. Gloriously naked, she stepped into her tub of scented water, while I simply gaped as I waited to hand her the linen when her washing was complete.

'Now what's wrong, girl?' she asked with obvious amusement at my expense. 'Have you never seen a woman in the flesh before? I don't suppose you have, living with these old crones.' She laughed, an appealing sound that made me want to smile, until I read the lines of malice in her face. 'You'll not have seen a man either, I wager.' She yawned prettily in the heat, stretching her arms so that her breasts rose above the level of the scented water.

'Wash my hair for me.'

I did, of course.

Wrapped in a chamber robe with her damp hair loose over her shoulders, Countess Joan delved into one of her coffers, removed a looking glass and stepped to the light from the window to inspect her features. She smiled at what she saw. Why would she not? I simply stared at the object with its silver frame and gleaming surface, until the Countess tossed her head, sensing my gaze.

'What are you looking at?' I shook my head. 'I have no more need of you for now.' She cast the shining object onto the bed. 'Come back after Compline.'

But my fingers itched to touch it.

'Your looking glass, my lady...'

'Well?'

'May I look?' I asked.

She took me by surprise, and I was not fast enough. Countess Joan struck out with careless, casual violence, for no reason that I could see other than savage temper. An echoing slap made contact with my cheek so that I staggered, catching my breath.

'Don't be impertinent, girl!' For a moment she considered me. Then her brows rose in perfect arcs and her lips curved. 'But use the looking glass—if you really wish to.'

I took it from where it lay—and I looked. A reflection, a face that was more honest than anything I had seen in my water bowl, looked back at me. I was transfixed. Then without a word—for I could not find any to utter—I gently placed the glass face down on the bed.

'Do you like what you see?' Countess Joan enquired, enjoying my humiliation.

'No!' I managed through dry lips. My image in the water was no less than truth, and here it was proved beyond doubt. The dark eyes, depthless and without light like night water under a moonless sky. Even darker brows, as if drawn in ink with a clumsy hand. The strong jaw, the dominant nose and wide mouth. All so *forceful*! It was a blessing that my hair was covered. I was a grub, a worm, a nothing compared with this red-gold, pale-skinned beauty who smiled at her empty victory over me.

'What did you expect?' the Countess asked.

'I don't know,' I managed.

'You expected to see something that might make a man turn his head, didn't you? Of course you did. What woman doesn't? Much can be forgiven a woman who is beautiful. Not so an ugly one.'

How cruel an indictment, stated without passion, without any thought for my feelings. And it was at that moment, when she tilted her chin in satisfaction, that I saw the truth in her face. She was of a mind to be deliberately cruel, and as my heart fell with the weight of the evidence against me, I knew beyond doubt why she had chosen me to wait on her. I had had no part in the choosing. It had nothing to do with the antics of her perverse monkey, or my own foolish attempt to catch her attention, or my labours to be a good maidservant. She had chosen me because I was ugly, while in stark contrast this educated, sophisticated, highly polished Court beauty would shine as a warning beacon lit for all to wonder at on a hilltop. I was the perfect foil—too unlovely, too gauche, too ignorant to pose any threat to the splendour that was Joan of Kent.

I think, weighing the good against the bad, I truly detested her.

Without warning it all came to an end, of course. 'I am leaving,' the Countess announced after three weeks, the most exciting, exhilarating three weeks of my life. I had already seen the preparations—the litter had returned, the escort at that very moment cluttering up the courtyard—and I was sorry. 'God's Wounds! I'll be glad to rid myself of these stultifying walls. I could die here and no one would be any the wiser. You have been useful to me.' The Countess sat in the high-backed chair in her bedchamber, her feet neatly together in gilded leather shoes on a little stool, while the business of repacking her accoutrements went on around her. 'I suppose I should reward you, but I cannot think how.' She pointed as she stood with a swish of her damask skirts. 'Take that box and carry the Barbary.'

With difficulty, at the cost of a bite, I recovered the monkey, but my mind was not on the sharp nip. There was one piece of knowledge I wanted from her. If I did not ask now…

'My lady…'

'I haven't time.' She was already walking through the doorway.

'What gives a woman…?' I thought about the word I wanted. 'What gives a woman power?'

She stopped. She turned slowly, laughing softly, but her face was writ with a mockery so vivid that I flushed at my temerity. 'Power? What would a creature such as you know of true power? What would you do with it, even if it came to you?' The disdain for my ignorance was cruel in its sleek elegance.

'I mean—the power to determine my own path in life.'

'So! Is that what you seek?' She allowed me a complacent little smile. And I saw that beneath her carelessness ran a far deeper emotion. She actually despised me, as perhaps she despised all creatures of low birth. 'You'll not get power, my dear. That is, if you mean rank. Unless you can rise above your station and become Abbess of this place.' Her voice purred in derision. 'You'll not do it—but I'll give you an answer. If you have no breeding then you need beauty. Y*our* looks will get you nowhere. There is only one way left to you.' Her smile vanished and I thought she gave my question some weight of consideration. 'Knowledge.'

'How can knowledge be power?'

'It can, if what you know is of importance to someone else.'

What could I learn at the Abbey? To read the order of the day. To dig roots in the garden. To make simples in the Infirmary. To polish the silver vessels in the Abbey church.

'What would I do with such learning?' I asked in despair. How I loathed her in that moment of self-knowledge.

'How would I know that? But I would say this. It is important for a woman to have the duplicity to make good use of what gifts she might have, however valueless they might seem. Do you have that?'

Duplicity? Did I possess it? I had no idea. I shook my head.

'Guile! Cunning! Scheming!' she snapped, my ignorance an affront. 'Do you understand?' The Countess retraced her steps to murmur in my ear as if it were a kindness. 'You have to have the strength to pursue your goal, without caring how many enemies you make along the road. It is not easy. I have made enemies all my life, but on the day I wed the Prince they will be as chaff before the wind. I will laugh in their faces and care not what they say of me. Would you be willing to do that? I doubt it.' The mockery of concern came swiftly to an end. 'Set your mind to it, girl. All you have before you is your life in this cold tomb, until the day they clothe you in your death habit and sew you into your shroud.'

'No!' The terrible image drove me to cry out as if I had been pricked on the arm with one of Countess Joan's well-sharpened pens. 'I would escape from here.' I had never said it aloud before, never put it into words. How despairing it sounded. How hopeless, but in that moment I was overwhelmed by the enormity of all that I lacked, and all that I might become if I could only encompass it.

'Escape? And how would you live?' An echo of Sister Goda's words that were like a knife against my heart. 'Without resources you would need a husband. Unless you would be a whore. A chancy life, short and brutish. Not one I would recommend. Better to be a nun.' Sweeping me aside, she strode from the room and out into the courtyard, where she settled herself in her litter, and as I reached to deposit the monkey on the cushions and close the curtains, my services for her complete, I heard her final condemnation. 'You'll never be anything of value in life. So turn your mind from it.' Then with a glinting smile, 'I have decided how to reward you. Take the Barbary. I suppose it will give you some distraction—I begin to find it a nuisance.'

The creature was thrust out of the litter, back into my arms.

Thus in a cloud of dust Countess Joan was gone with

her dogs and hawk and all her unsettling influences. But I did not forget her. For Countess Joan had applied a flame to my imagination. When it burned so fiercely that it was almost a physical hurt, I wished with all my heart I could quench it, but the fire never left me. The venal hand of ambition had fallen on me, grasping my shoulder with lethal strength, and refused to release me.

I am worth more than this, I determined as I knelt with the sisters at Compline, young as I was. I *will* be of value! I *will* make something of my life.

And had I not done so, by one means or another? Now I smiled, even as the vile stench of tallow filled my nose and throat. Despite the Countess's judgement of me, here I was, by some miracle, at Havering-atte-Bower. Fate had snatched me up from the Abbey. I hummed tunelessly to myself. Why should fate not see a path to get me out of this hellish pit of heat and rank odours to where I might spread my wings? Especially if I gave it a helping hand.

As I dissuaded with the side of my foot one of the kitchen kittens from clawing at my skirts, I was distracted and my humming became a sharp hiss as the tallow dripped hotly onto my hand, pulling me back into the present.

When Princess Joan returned from Aquitaine, the frivolous royal Court would circle round the vivacious new Princess rather than the fading, unprepossessing Queen. Queen Philippa's virtues would count for nothing against the brilliance of Princess Joan. I felt sorry that the Queen would be so eclipsed by a woman who was not worthy of fastening her laces, but was that not the order of things?

'Well,' I announced to the kitten, which had latched its claws into my shoe, 'virtue or ambition? Goodness or worldliness? I would enjoy being able to choose between the two.'

Scooping it up, I shut the creature outside in the scullery, ignoring its plaintive mewing, as I went to answer an enraged bellow from Master Humphrey. Virtue was a fine thing—but could be as dull as a platter of day-old bread. Now, ambition was quite another matter—as succulent as the pheasants that Master Humphrey was simmering in spiced wine for the royal table.

And what happened to the monkey? Mother Abbess ordered it to be taken to the Infirmary and locked in a cellar. I never saw it again. Considering its propensity to bite, I was not sorry. Still I smiled. If I had the monkey now, I would set it loose on Sim with much malice and enjoyment.

Then all was danger, without warning. Two weeks of the whirlwind of kitchen life at Havering had lulled me into carelessness. And on that day I had been taken up with the noxious task of scrubbing down the chopping block where the joints of meat were dismembered.

'And when you've done that, fetch a basket of scallions from the storeroom—and see if you can find some sage in the garden. Can you recognise it?' Master Humphrey, shouting after me, still leaned toward the scathing.

'Yes, Master Humphrey.' *Any fool can recognise sage.* I wrung out the cloth, relieved to escape the heat and sickening stench of fresh blood.

'And bring some chives while you're at it, girl!'

I was barely out of the door when my wrist was seized in a hard grip and I was almost jolted off my feet—and into the loathsome arms of Sim.

'Well, if it isn't Mistress Alice with her good opinion of herself!'

I raised my hand to cuff his ear but he ducked and held on. This was just Sim trying to make trouble since I had deterred him from lifting my skirts with the point of a knife and the red punctures still stood proud on his hand.

'Get off me, you oaf!'

Sim thrust me back against the wall and I felt the familiar routine of his knee pushing between my legs.

'I'd have you gelded if I had my way!' I bit his hand.

Sim was far stronger than I. He laughed and wrenched the neck of my tunic. I felt it tear, and then the shoulder of my shift, and at the same time I felt the fragile string give way. Queen Philippa's rosary, the precious gift that I had worn around my neck out of sight, slithered under my shift to the floor. I squirmed, escaped and pounced. But not fast enough. Sim snatched it up.

'Well, well!' He held it up above my head.

'Give it back!'

'Let me fuck you and I will.'

'Not in this lifetime.' But my whole concentration was on my beads.

So was Sim's. He eyed the lovely strand where it swung in the light and I saw knowledge creep into his eyes. 'Now, this is worth a pretty penny, if I don't mistake.'

I snatched at it but he was running, dragging me with him. At that moment, as I almost tripped and fell, I knew. He would make trouble for me.

'What's this?' Master Humphrey looked up at the rumpus.

'We've a thief here, Master Humphrey!' Sim's eyes gleamed with malice.

'I know you are, my lad. Didn't I see you pick up a hunk of cheese and stuff it into your big gob not an hour ago?'

'This's more serious than cheese, Master Humphrey.' Sim's grin at me was an essay in slyness.

And in an instant we were surrounded. 'Robber! Pick-purse! Thief!' A chorus of idle scullions and mischief-making pot boys.

'I'm no thief!' I kicked Sim on the shin. 'Let go of me!'

'Bugger it, wench!' His hold tightened. 'Told you she wasn't to be trusted.' He addressed the room at large. 'Too high an opinion of herself by half! She's a thief!' And he raised one hand above his head, Philippa's gift gripped between his filthy fingers. The rosary glittered, its value evident to all. Rage shook me. How dared he take what was mine?

'Thief!'

'I am not!'

'Where did you get it?'

'She came from a convent.' One voice was raised on my behalf.

'I wager she owned nothing as fine as this, even in a convent.'

'Fetch Sir Jocelyn!' ordered Master Humphrey. 'I'm too busy to deal with this.'

And then it all happened very quickly. 'This belongs to Her Majesty.' Sir Joscelyn gave his judgement. All eyes were turned on me, wide with disgust. 'The Queen ill, and you would steal from her!'

'She gave it to me!' I was already pronounced guilty but my instinct was to fight.

'You stole it!'

'I did not.'

I tried to keep my denial even, my response calm, but I was not calm at all. Fear paralysed my mind. Much could be forgiven but not this. For the first time I learned the depth of respect for the Queen, even in the lowly kitchens and sculleries. I looked around the faces, full of condemnation and disgust. Sim and his cohort enjoying every minute of it.

'Where's the Marshall?'

'In the chapel,' one of the scullions piped up.

With the rosary in one hand and me gripped hard in the other Sir Joscelyn dragged me along and into the royal chapel, to the chancel where two labourers were lifting a wood and metal device of cogs and wheels from a handcart. There, keeping a close eye on operations, was Lord Herbert, the Marshall, whose word was law. And beside him stood the King himself. Despair was a physical pain in my chest.

'Your Majesty. Lord Herbert.'

'Not now, Sir Joscelyn.' King and Marshall were preoccupied. All eyes were on the careful lifting of the contraption. We stood in silence as it was positioned piece by piece on the floor. 'Good. Now…'

Edward turned to our importunate little group. So I was to be accused before the King himself, judged by those piercing eyes. I shivered as the evidence was produced, examined, the ownership confirmed, and I shivered even more as I was tried, condemned and sentenced by Lord Herbert to be shut in a cellar, all without listening to a word I said. And the King? He could barely snatch his concentration from the contraption at his feet, whilst I suffered for a crime I had not committed. Within the time it took to snap his fingers he would pass me over to the Marshall. It must not be! I would get his attention and keep it. And the flare of ambition and fiery resentment that I had felt under the tyranny of Countess Joan once more flickered over my skin.

I am worth more than this. I deserve more than this.

I wanted more than the half-life in the kitchens of Havering. I would *make* the King notice me.

'Sire!' I discovered a bold confidence. 'I am the woman the Queen sent for. And this lout…' I pointed a finger at

Sim '...who's fit only to be booted out of this palace onto the midden, calls me a thief!'

'Does he now!' The King's interest caught—but only mildly so.

I renewed my attack. 'I appeal to you, Your Majesty, for justice. No one will listen to me. Is it because I am a woman? I appeal to you, Sire.'

The royal eyes widened considerably. 'The King will always give justice.'

'Not in your kitchens, Sire. Justice is more like a clip round the ear or a grope in a dark corner from this turd!' I had absorbed a wealth of vocabulary during my time in the kitchens. I had the King's attention now right enough.

'Then I must remedy your criticisms of my kitchens.' The sardonic reply held out little hope. 'Did you steal this?'

'No!' Fear of close dark places, of being shut in the cellar, made me undaunted. 'It is rightfully come by. Wykeham knows I did not steal it. He'll tell you.'

Little good it did me. 'He might,' the King observed. 'Unfortunately he's not here but gone to Windsor.'

'Her Majesty knows I did not.' It was my last hope—but no hope at all.

'We'll not trouble Her Majesty.' The King's face was suddenly dark, contemptuous. 'You'll not disturb the Queen with this. Lord Herbert.' The dark cellar loomed.

'No!' I gasped.

'What is it that you will not trouble me with, Edward?'

And with that one question, the tiniest speck of hope began to grow in me.

A gentle voice, soft on the ear. Sir Joscelyn and Lord Herbert bowed. The King strode forward, so close to me that his tunic brushed against me, to take the Queen's hand and draw her towards one of the choir stalls. His face changed, the lines of irritation smoothing, his lips softening. There was a tenderness, as if they were alone together. The Queen smiled up into his face, enclosing his hand in both of her own. Simple gestures but so strong, so affectionate. There was no doubting it. Taken up as I was with my own miseries, I could still see it and marvel at it. The King gave her a tender kiss on her cheek.

'Philippa, my love. Are you strong enough to be here? You should be resting.'

'I have been resting for the past week. I wish to see the clock.'

'You don't look strong.'

'Don't fuss, Edward. I feel better.'

She did not look it. Rather she was drawn and grey.

'Sit down, my dear.' The King pushed her gently to the cushioned seat. 'Does your shoulder pain you?'

'Yes. But it is not fatal.' The Queen sat up straight, cradling her left elbow in her right palm, and surveyed what I realised was the makings of a clock. 'It is very fine. When will you get it working?' Then she noticed the number of people in the chapel. 'What's happening here?'

The Marshall cleared his throat. 'This girl, Majesty.' He glowered at me.

As the Queen looked at me, I saw the memory return, and with it recognition. Awkwardly she turned her whole body in her chair until she was facing me. 'Alice?'

'Yes, Majesty.' I curtseyed as best I could since my arm was still in the grip of Lord Herbert, as if I might make a bid for freedom.

'I sent Wykeham to fetch you.' Philippa's forehead was furrowed with the effort of recall, as if it were a long time ago. 'You must have arrived when I was ill.'

'Yes, Majesty.'

'What are you doing?'

'Working in your kitchens.'

'Are you?' She appeared astonished. Then gave a soft laugh. 'Who sent you there?'

'The Princess Isabella.' Sir Joscelyn was quick to apportion blame elsewhere. 'She thought that was your intent.'

'Did she? I doubt my daughter thought at all beyond her own desires. You should have known better, Sir Joscelyn.'

An uncomfortable silence lengthened until Lord Herbert pronounced, 'The girl is a thief, Your Majesty.'

'Are you?' the Queen asked.

'No, Majesty.'

Edward held out the rosary. 'I'm afraid she is. Is this yours, my love?'

'Yes. Or it was. You gave it to me.'

'I did? The girl was wearing it.'

'I expect she would. I gave it to her.'

'I told them that, my lady,' I appealed, 'but they would not believe me.'

'To a kitchen maid? Why would you do that?' The King spread his hands in disbelief.

The Queen sighed. 'Let go of her, Lord Herbert. She'll not run away. Come here, Alice. Let me look at you.'

I discovered that I had been holding my breath. When the Queen held out her hand I fell to my knees before her in gratitude, returning her regard when her tired eyes moved slowly, speculatively, over my face. As if she was trying to anchor some deep wayward thought that was not altogether pleasing to her. Then she nodded and touched my cheek.

'Who would have thought so simple a thing as a gift of a rosary would cause so much trouble?' she said, her smile wry. 'And why should it take the whole of the royal household to solve the matter?' Pushing herself to her feet, she drew me with her, taking everything in hand with a matri-archal authority. 'Thank you, Sir Joscelyn. Lord Herbert. I know you have my interests at heart. You are very assiduous, but I will deal with this. This girl is no thief, forsooth. Now, give me your arm, Alice. Let me put some things right.'

I helped her from the chapel, conscious of her weight as we descended the stair, and of the King's muttered comment that, thank God, I was no longer his concern. As we walked slowly towards the royal apartments, a warm expectancy began to dance through my blood. Maidservant? Tirewoman? I still could not imagine why she would want *me*, given the wealth of talent around her, but I knew there was something in her mind. Just as I sensed that from this point my life, with its humdrum drudgery and servitude, would never be the same again.

My immediate destiny was an empty bedchamber—unused, I assumed, from the lack of furnishings and the dust that swirled as our skirts created a little eddy of air. And in that room: a copper-bound tub, buckets of steaming water and the ministrations of two of the maids from the buttery. I was simply handed over.

With hot water and enthusiasm, buttressed by a remarkable degree of speculative interest, the maids got to work on me. I had never bathed before, totally immersed in water. I remembered Countess Joan, naked and arrogant, confident in her beauty, whereas I slid beneath the water to wallow up to my chin, like a trout in a summer pool, before my companions could actually look at me.

'Go away,' I remonstrated. 'I'm perfectly capable of scrubbing my own skin.'

'Queen's orders!' They simpered. 'No one disobeys the Queen.'

There was no arguing against such a declaration so I set myself to make the best of it. The maids were audacious enough to point out my deficiencies. Too thin. No curves, small breasts, lean hips. They gave no quarter, making me horribly conscious of the inadequacies in my unclothed body, despite my sharp observation that life in a convent did not encourage solid flesh. Rough hands, they pointed out. Neglected hair. As for my eyebrows… The litany unrolled. 'Fair is fashionable!' they informed me.

I sighed. 'Don't rub so hard!'

They ignored me. I was soaped and rinsed, dried with soft linen, and in the end I simply closed my eyes and allowed them to talk and gossip and put me in the clothes provided for me. And such garments. The sensuous glide on my skin forced me to open my eyes. They were like nothing I had ever seen, except in the coffers of Countess Joan. An undershift of fine linen that did not catch when I moved. An overgown, close-fitting to my hips, in the blue of the Virgin's cloak—a cotehardie, I was told, knowing no name for such fashionable niceties—with a sideless surcoat over all, sumptuous to my eyes with grey fur bands and an enamelled girdle. All made for someone else, of course, the fibres scuffed along hem and cuffs, but what did I care for that? They were a statement in feminine luxury I could never have dreamed of. And so shiny, so soft, fabrics that slid through my fingers. Silk and damask and fine wool. For the first time in my life I was clothed in a *colour*, glorious enough to assault my senses. I felt like a precious jewel, polished to a sparkle.

They exclaimed over my hair, of course.

'Too coarse. Too dark. Too short to braid. Too short for anything.'

'Better than when it was cropped for a novice nun,' I fired back.

They pushed it into the gilded mesh of a crispinette, and covered the whole with a veil of some diaphanous material that floated quite beautifully and a plaited filet to hold it firm, as if to hide all evidence of my past life. But no wimple. I vowed never to wear a wimple again.

'Put these on…' I donned the fine stockings, the woven garters. Soft shoes were slid onto my feet.

And I took stock, hardly daring to breathe unless the whole ensemble fell off around my feet. The skirts were full and heavy against my legs, moving with a soft hush as I walked inexpertly across the room. The bodice was laced tight against my ribs, the neckline low across my unimpressive bosom. I did not feel like myself at all, but rather as if I were dressed for a mummer's play I had once seen at Twelfth Night at the Abbey.

Did maidservants to the Queen really wear such splendour?

I was in the process of kicking the skirts behind me, experimentally, when the door opened to admit Isabella. The two maids curtseyed to the floor. I followed suit, with not a bad show of handling the damask folds, but not before I had seen the thin-lipped distaste. She walked round me, taking her time. Isabella, the agent of my kitchen humiliations.

'Not bad,' she commented, as I flushed. 'Look for yourself.' And she handed me the tiny looking glass that had been suspended from the chatelaine at her waist.

Oh, no! Remembering my last brush with vanity, I put my hands behind my back as if I were a child caught out in wrong doing. 'No, I will not.'

Her smile was deeply sardonic. 'Why not?'

'I think I'll not like what I see,' I said, refusing to allow my gaze to fall before hers.

'Well, that's true enough. There's only so much that can be done. Perhaps you're wise,' Isabella murmured, but the sympathy was tainted with scorn.

Peremptorily she gestured, and in a silence stretched taut I was led along the corridors to the solar where Philippa sat with her women.

'Well, you've washed her and dressed her, *Maman*. For what it's worth.'

'You are uncharitable, Isabella.' The Queen's reply was unexpectedly sharp.

Isabella was not cowed. 'What do we do with her now?'

'What I intended from the beginning, despite your meddling. She will be one of my damsels.'

A royal damsel? Isabella's brows climbed. I suspect mine did too. I was too shocked to consider how inappropriate my expression might be.

'You don't need *her*,' Isabella cried in disbelief. 'You have a dozen.'

'No?' A smile, a little sad to my mind, touched the Queen's face. 'Maybe I do need her.'

'Then choose a girl of birth. Before God, there are enough of them.'

'I know what I need, Isabella.' As the Queen waved her daughter away she handed the rosary back to me.

'My lady…'

What could I find to say? My fingers closed around the costly beads, whatever the Queen might say to the contrary. In the length of a heartbeat, in one firm command and one gesture of dismissal of her daughter's hostility, the Queen had turned my life on its head.

'Don't say I didn't warn you.' So Isabella had the last word.

She did not care that I heard her.

Why me? The one thought danced in my head when the ladies were gone about their customary affairs. A damsel— a lady in waiting to the Queen.

'Why me?' I asked aloud. 'What have I to offer, Majesty?'

Philippa perused me as if searching for an answer, her features uncommonly stern.

'Your Majesty?'

'Forgive me. I was distracted.' She closed her eyes: when she opened them there was a lingering vestige of sorrow, but her voice was kind enough. 'One day I'll tell you. But for now, let's see what we can do with you.'

So there it was. Decided on some chance whim, with some underlying purpose that the Queen kept to herself. I became a *domicella*. A lady in waiting. Not a *domina*, one of the highborn, but a *domicella*. I was the youngest, least skilled and least important of the Queen's ladies. But I was a part of her household. I was an inhabitant of her solar.

I could not believe my good fortune. When sent on some trivial errand through a succession of deserted antechambers, I lifted my skirts above my ankles and, fired by sheer exuberance, danced a measure of haphazard steps to the lingering echoes of the lute from the solar. Not well, you understand, for it was something I had yet to learn, but more than I had ever achieved in my life. It fascinated me what confidence a fine robe with fur edgings could bestow on a woman. When a passing maidservant, one I had brushed shoulders with in the hot squalor of the kitchens, dropped an open-mouthed, reluctant curtsey before rushing off to spread the news of the marvellous advancement of Alice Perrers, I danced again. This was more like it. Alice Perrers: a court lady, in such finery as she could never have imagined. It was all too much to believe, my transition from greasy servant to perfumed damsel, but if one of the kitchen sluts afforded me a sign of respect, then it must be so. I was so full of joy that I could barely restrain myself from shouting my good fortune to the still, watchful faces in the tapestries.

I would, if I had my way, never set foot in a kitchen again.

What would clerk Greseley say if he could see me now? Waste of good coin! I suspected. Better to put it into bricks and mortar! What remark would Wykeham find to make, other than an explanation of his ambitions to construct a royal bath house and garderobe? I laughed aloud. And the King? King Edward would only notice me if I had cogs and wheels that moved and slid and clicked against each other.

I tried a pirouette, awkward in the shoes that were too loose round the heel. One day, I vowed, I would wear shoes that were made for me and fitted perfectly.

As for what the Queen might want of me in return, it could not be so very serious, could it?

They tripped over their trailing skirts, the Queen's damsels, to transform me into a lady worthy of my new position. I was a pet. A creature to be cosseted and stroked, to relieve their boredom. It was not in my nature, neither was it a role I wished to play, but it was an exhilarating experience as they created the new Alice Perrers.

I absorbed it all: anointed and burnished, my hands smothered in perfumed lotions far headier than anything produced in Sister Margery's stillroom, my too-heavy brows plucked into what might pass for an elegant arch—if the observer squinted. Clothes, and even jewels, were handed over with casual kindness. A ring, a brooch to pin my mantle, a chain of gilt and gleaming stones to loop across my breast. Nothing of great value, but enough that I might exhibit myself in public as no less worthy of respect than the

ladies from high-blooded families. I spread my fingers—
now smooth with pared nails, to admire the ring with its
amethyst stone. It was as if I was wearing a new skin, like
a snake sloughing off the old in spring. And I was woman
enough to enjoy it. I wore the rosary fastened to my girdle, enhanced with silver finials even finer than those of
Abbess Sybil.

'Better!' Isabella remarked after sour contemplation. 'But
I still don't know why the Queen wanted *you*!'

It remained beyond my comprehension too.

The Queen's damsels were feminine, pretty, beautiful.
I was none of those. Their figures were flattered by the
new fashion, with gowns close-fitting from breast to hip.
The rich cloth hung on me like washing on a drying pole.
They were gifted in music for the Queen's pleasure. Any
attempt to teach me to sing was abandoned after the first
tuneless warble. Neither did my fingers ever master the lute
strings, much less the elegant gittern. They could stitch a
girdle with flowers and birds. I had no patience with it.
They conversed charmingly in French, with endless gossip, with shared knowledge of people of the Court. I knew
no one other than Wykeham, who deigned to speak with
me when he returned to Court, even noting my change of
fortune—'Well, here's an improvement, Mistress Perrers!
Have you learnt to ride yet?'—but his fixation with building arches was the subject of laughter. Master Wykeham
clearly did not flirt.

For the damsels, flirtation was an art in itself. I never
learned it. I was too forthright for that. Too critical of those
I met. Too self-aware to pretend what I did not feel. And if
that was a sin, I was guilty. I could not pretend an interest
or an affection where I had none.

Had I nothing to offer? What I had, I used to make myself useful, or noticed, or even indispensable. I had set my feet in the Queen's solar. I would not be cast off, as Princess Isabella cast off her old gowns. I worked hard.

I could play chess. The ordered rules of the little figures pleased me. I had no difficulty in remembering the measures of a knight against a bishop, the limitations of a queen against a castle. As for the foolish pastime of Fox and Geese, I found an unexpected fascination in manoeuvring the pieces to make the geese corner the fox before that wily creature could prey on the silly birds.

'I'll not play with you, Alice Perrers!' Isabella declared, abandoning the game. 'Your geese are too crafty by half.'

'Craftier than your fox, my lady.' Isabella's fox was tightly penned into a corner by my little flock of birds. 'Your fox is done for, my lady.'

'So it is!' Isabella laughed, more out of surprise than amusement, but she resisted a cutting rejoinder.

To please the damsels I made silly, harmless love charms and potions, gleaned from my memory of Sister Margery's manuscripts in the Abbey's Infirmary. A pinch of catnip, a handful of yarrow, a stem of vervain, all wrapped in a scrap of green silk and tied with a red cord. If they believed they were effective, I would not deny it, although Isabella swore I was more like to add the deadly hemlock in any sachet I made for her. I read to them endlessly when they wanted tales of courtly love, between a handsome knight and the object of his desire, to sigh over.

Not bad at all for a nameless, ill-bred girl from a convent. I would never be nameless and overlooked again. Pride might be a sin, but it filled my breast with gratification. Why should I not be proud of my advancement? I would be somebody worthy of a position at the royal court. I was Alice, Queen's damsel.

And Isabella was wrong. I would never use hemlock. I knew enough from Sister Margery's caustic warnings to be wary of such satanic works.

But what service could I offer Queen Philippa when the whole household was centred on fulfilling her wishes even before she expressed them? That was easy enough. I made draughts of white willow bark.

'You are a blessing to me, Alice.' The pain had been intense that day, but now, propped against her pillows, the willow tincture making her drowsy, she sighed heavily with relief. 'I am a burden to you.'

'It is not a burden to me to give you ease, my lady.'

I saw the lines beside her eyes begin to smooth out. She would sleep soon. The days of pain were increasing in number and her strength to withstand it was ebbing, but tonight she would have some measure of peace.

'You are a good girl.'

'I wasn't a good novice!' I responded smartly.

'Sit here. Tell me about those days when you were a bad novice.' Her eyelids drooped but she fought the strength of the drug.

So I did, because it pleased me to distract her. I told her of Mother Abbess and her penchant for red stockings. I told her of Sister Goda and her heavy hand, of the chickens that fell foul of the fox because of my carelessness and how I was punished. I knew enough by now not to speak of Countess Joan. Joan, the duplicitous daughter-in-law, far away in Aquitaine with her husband the Prince—she had entrapped him after all—was not a subject to give the Queen a restful night.

'It was good that I found you,' she murmured.

'Yes, my lady.' I smoothed a piercingly sweet unguent

into the tight skin of her wrist and hand. 'You have changed my life.'

A little silence fell but the Queen was not asleep. She was contemplating something beyond my sight that did not seem entirely to please her, gouging a deep cleft between her brows. Then she blinked and fixed me with an uncomfortable gaze. 'Yes, Alice. I am sure it was good that you fell into my path.'

I was certain it was not merely to smear her suffering flesh with ointments. A shiver of awareness assailed me in the overheated room, for her declamation suggested some deep uncertainty. Had I done something to lose her regard so soon? I cast my mind over what I might have said or done to cast her into doubt. Nothing came to mind. So I asked.

'Why did you choose me, my lady?'

When the Queen looked at me, her eyes were hooded. She closed her free hand tightly around the jewelled cross on her breast, and her reply held none of her essential compassion. Indeed, her voice was curt and bleak, and she drew her hand from my ministrations as if she could not bear my touch.

'I chose you because I have a role for you, Alice. A difficult one perhaps. And not too far distant. But not yet. Not quite yet…' She closed her eyes at last, as if she would shut me from her sight. 'I'm weary now. Send for my priest, if you will. I'll pray with him before I sleep.'

I left her, more perplexed than ever. Her words resurfaced as I lit my own candle and took myself to bed in the room I shared with two of the damsels. Sleep would not come.

I have a role for you. A difficult one perhaps. And not too far distant…

Chapter Five

It became my habit to keep a journal of sorts. I was not wishful to lose the skill I had learned with such painstaking effort. No one had a need of my ability to write in a palace where men of letters matched the vast number of huntsmen. Sometimes I wrote in French, sometimes in Latin, as the mood took me. I begged pieces of parchment, pen and ink from the palace clerks. They were not unwilling when I smiled, or slid a long-eyed glance. I was learning the ways of the Court, and the power of my own talents to attract.

And what did I write? A chronology of my days. What I wished to remember. I wrote, as I recall, for over a year.

Did I ever consider that the damsels might discover what I wrote? Not for a moment. They mocked my scribbling. And what I scribbled was excruciatingly dull. Once, to satisfy their curiosity, I read aloud…

'Today I joined the damsels in my first hunt. I had no enjoyment of it. The King celebrates his fiftieth year with a great tournament and jousting held at Smithfield. We all attend. I am learning to dance.'

'By the Virgin, Alice!' Isabella yawned behind her slender fingers. 'If you have nothing better to write about, what in heaven's name is the value of doing it? Better to return to scouring the pots in the kitchens.'

Dull? Infinitely. And quite deliberate, to ensure that no damsel was sufficiently interested to poke her sharp nose into what I might be doing. But what memories my writings evoked for me upon reading them again when my life was in danger and turmoil. There on the pages, in the briefest of record, the pattern of my life unfolded in that fateful year. What a miraculous, terrifying, life-changing year it proved to be.

Today I joined the damsels in my first hunt. I had no enjoyment. The gelding I was given was a mount from hell. I would never see the pleasure in being jolted and bounced for two hours, to come at the end to a baying pack of hounds and a bloody kill. Truth to tell, the kill happened without me, for I fell off with a shriek at the first breath-stopping gallop. Sitting on the ground, covered with leaf mould and twigs, beating the damp earth from my skirts, I raged in misery. My crispinettes and hood had become detached, the hunt had disappeared into the distance. So had my despicable mount. It would be a long walk home.

'A damsel in distress, by God!'

I had not registered the beat of hooves on the soft ground under the trees. I looked up to see two horses bearing down on me at speed, one large and threatening, the other small and wiry.

'Mistress Alice!' The King reined in, his stallion dancing within feet of me. 'Are you well down there?'

'No, I am not.' I was not as polite as I should have been.

'Who suggested you ride that brute that thundered past us?'

'It was the Lady Isabella. Then the misbegotten bag of bones deposited me here… I should never have come. I detest horses.'

'So why did you?'

I wasn't altogether sure, except that it was expected of me. It was the one joy in life remaining to the Queen when she was in health. The King swung down, threw his reins to the lad on the pony, and approached on foot. I raised a hand to shield my eyes from the sun where it glimmered through the new leaves.

'Thomas—go and fetch the lady's ride,' he ordered.

Thomas, the King's youngest son, abandoned the stallion and rode off like the wind on the pony. The King offered his hand.

'I can get to my feet alone, Sire.' Ungracious, I knew, but my humiliation was strong.

'I've no doubt, lady. Humour me.'

His eyes might be bright with amusement but his order was peremptory and not to be disobeyed. I held out my hand, and with a firm tug I was pulled to my feet, whereupon the King began to dislodge the debris from my skirts with long strokes of the flat of his hand. Shame coloured my cheeks.

'Indeed you should not, Sire!'

'I should indeed. You need to pin up your hair.'

'I can't. There's not enough to pin up and I need help to make it look respectable.'

'Then let me.'

'No, Sire!' To have the King pin up my hair? I would as soon ask Isabella to scrub my back.

He sighed. 'You must allow me, mistress, as a man of chivalry, to set your appearance to rights.'

And tucking my ill-used crispinettes into his belt he proceeded with astonishingly deft fingers to re-pin my simple hood, as if he were tying the jesses of his favourite goshawk. I stood still under his ministrations, barely breathing. The King stepped back and surveyed me.

'Passable. I've not lost my touch in all these years.' He cocked an ear to listen, and nodded his head. 'And now, lady, you'll have to get back on.'

He was laughing at me. 'I don't wish to.'

'You will, unless you intend to walk home.' Thomas had returned with my recalcitrant mount and before I could make any more fuss, I was boosted back into the saddle. For a moment, as he tightened my girths, the King looked up into my face, then abruptly stepped back.

'There you are, Mistress Alice. Hold tight!' A slap of the King's hand against the horse's wide rump set me in motion. 'Look after her, Thomas. The Queen will never forgive you if you allow her to fall into a blackberry thicket.' A pause, and the words followed me. 'And neither will I.'

And Thomas did. He was only seven years old and more skilled at riding than I would ever be. But it was the King's deft hands I remembered.

The King celebrates his fiftieth year with a great tournament and jousting. Magnificent! The King was superlative in his new armour. I could not find words, burnished as he was by the sun, sword and armour striking fire as his arm rose and fell, the plumes on his helmet nodding imperiously. And yet I feared for him, my loins liquid and cold with fear. I could not look away, but when blood glistened on his vambrace, dripping from his fingers, I closed my eyes.

No need of course. His energy always prodigious, he was touched with magic that day. Fighting in the *mêlée* with all the dash and finesse of a hero of the old tales, he had the grace at the end to heap praise on those whom he defeated.

Afterwards, when the combatants gathered in the banter much loved by men, the Queen's ladies threw flowers to the knight of their choice. I had no one. Neither did I care, for there was only one to fill my vision, whether in the lists or in the vicious cut and thrust of personal combat. And I was audacious enough to fling a rosebud when he approached the gallery in which we women sat with the Queen. He had removed his helm. He was so close to me, his face pale and drawn in the aftermath of his efforts, that I could detect the smear of blood on his cheek where he had wiped at the dust with his gauntlet. I was spellbound, so much so that the flower I flung ineptly struck the cheek of the King's stallion—a soft blow, but the high-blooded destrier instantly reared in the manner of its kind.

'Sweet Jesu!' Startled, the King dropped his helm, tightening his reins as he fought to bring the animal back under control.

'Have you no sense?' Isabella snapped.

I thought better of replying and steeled myself for the King's reproof. Without a word he snapped his fingers to his page to pick up the helm and the trampled flower. I looked at him in fear.

'My thanks, lady.'

He bowed his head solemnly to me as he tucked the crumpled petals into the gorget at his throat. My belly clenched, my face flamed to my hairline. Proud, haughty, confident, he was the King of England yet he would treat me with respect when I had almost unhorsed him.

'Our kitchen maid cannot yet be relied upon to act decorously in public!' Isabella remarked, setting up a chorus of laughter.

But the King did not sneer. Urging his horse closer to the

gilded canvas, the fire dying from his eyes as the energy of battle receded, he stretched out his hand, palm up.

'Mistress Alice, if you would honour me.'

And I placed mine there. The King kissed my fingers.

'The rose was a fine gesture, if a little wayward. My horse and I both thank you, Mistress Alice.'

There was the rustle of appreciative laughter, no longer at my expense. I felt the heat of his kiss against my skin, hotter than the beat of blood in my cheeks.

I am learning to dance. 'Holy Virgin!' I misstepped the insistent beat of the tabor and shawm for the twentieth time. How could I excel at tallying coins, yet be unable to count the steps in a simple processional dance? The King's hand tightened to give me balance as I lurched. He was a better dancer than I. It would be hard to be worse.

'You are allowed to look at me, Mistress Alice,' he announced when we came together again.

'If I do, I shall fall over my feet, Sire, or yours. I'll cripple you before the night is out.'

'I'll lead you in the right steps.' I must have looked askance. 'Do you not trust me, Alice?'

He had called me by my name, without formality. I looked up, to find his eyes quizzical on my face, and I missed the next simple movement.

'I dare not,' I managed.

'You would refuse your King?' He was amused again.

'I would when it would be to his benefit.'

'Then we must do our poor best, sweet Alice, and count the broken toes at the end of the evening.'

Sweet Alice? Was he flirting with me? But no. That was not possible. I exasperated him more than I entertained him.

'By God, Mistress Alice. You did not lie,' he stated ruefully as the procession wound to its end. 'You should issue a warning to any man who invites you.'

'Not every man is as brave as you, Sire.'

'Then I'll remember not to risk it again,' he said as he handed me back to sit at Philippa's side.

But he did. Even though I still fell over his feet.

The Queen did not forbid me to dance with the King, but she appeared to find little enjoyment in the occasion.

The Queen has given the King a lion. Ah, yes! The affair of the lion! Observing the damsels with scorn where they huddled, hiding their faces, retreating from its roars in mock fear, keen to find a comforting arm from one of the King's gallant knights, I walked towards the huge cage where I might inspect the beast at close quarters. I was not afraid, and would not pretend to be so. How could it harm me when it was imprisoned behind bars and locks? Its rough, tawny mane, its vast array of teeth fascinated me. I stepped closer as it settled on its haunches, tail twitching in impotent warning.

'You're not afraid, Mistress Alice?' Soft-footed, the King stood behind me.

'No, Sire. What need?' We had returned to formality and I was not sorry. Was he not the King? 'The girls are foolish, not afraid. They just wish to...'

'They wish to attract attention?'

'Yes, Sire.'

We looked across to where the fluttering damsels received assurance and flattery.

'And you do not, Mistress Alice? Does not some young knight take your critical eye? Is there no one you admire?'

I thought about this, giving his question more consideration than perhaps was intended, appraising the wealth of strength and beauty and high blood around me.

'No, Sire.' It was the truth.

'But you admire my lion.'

'Oh, I do.'

The lion watched us with impassive hatred. Were we not the cause of its imprisonment? I considered its state, and my own past experience. Both kept under duress, without freedom. Both existing on the whim of another. But I had escaped by miraculous means. There would be no miracle for this lion. This poor beast would remain in captivity until the day of its death.

'Does nothing fill you with terror? Other than horses, of course.'

He had unnerved me again. 'Yes,' I replied. 'But it's a fear *you'll* never know, Sire.'

'Tell me, then.'

Before I could collect my wits I found myself explaining, because he was regarding me as if he really cared about my fears. 'I am afraid of the future, Sire, where nothing is permanent, nothing is certain. Of a life without stability, without friends or family, without a home. Where I am nobody, without name or status.' I paused. 'I don't want to be dependent on the pity or charity of others—I have had enough of that. I want to make something of myself, for myself.'

Holy Mother! I looked fixedly at the lion. Had I really admitted to all that? To the King?

'It's a lot to ask,' he replied simply. 'For a young woman in your situation.'

Much as Countess Joan had observed, with far less courtesy. 'Is it impossible?'

'No. That was not my meaning. But it's a hard road for a woman alone to travel.'

'Must I then accept my fate, like this poor imprisoned beast?'

'Are we not all governed by fate, mistress?'

Aware that his attention was turned from lion to me, and that the conversation had taken a very personal turn, I sought for an innocuous reply. 'I don't intend ingratitude, Sire. I'm aware of how much I owe the Queen.'

'I didn't know that you saw your future in so bleak a light.'

'Why would you, Sire? You are the King. It is not necessary that you either know or care.' For that is how I saw it.

'Am I so selfish?' Startled, his fine brows met over the bridge of his nose and I wondered if I had displeased him. 'Or is it that you have a low opinion of all men?'

'I've no reason not to. My father, whoever he was, gave me no reason to think highly of them. Neither did my husband, who took me in a sham of a marriage to ward off his sister's nagging. I did not matter overmuch to either of them.'

For a moment the King looked astounded, as he might if one of his hounds dared to bite him on the ankle.

'You don't hold back with the truth, do you, mistress? It seems I must make amends for my sex.'

'You owe me nothing, Sire.'

'Perhaps it is not a matter of owing, Alice. Perhaps it is more of what I find I wish to do.'

The lion roared, lashing out with claws against the metal, interrupting whatever the King, or I, might have said next. He led me away as attendants from his menagerie came to transport the beast, and I thanked God for the timely intervention. I had said quite enough.

But the King was not done with me yet. 'You are not justified in your reading of my character, Mistress Alice,' he said with a wry twist of his lips as we came to the door. 'I know exactly what you fear. I lived through a time when my future hung on a thread, when I did not know friend from enemy and my authority as King was under attack. I know about rising every morning from my bed, not knowing what fate would bring me—whether good or evil.'

I must have shown my disbelief that a King should ever know such doubts.

'One day I will tell you.'

He walked away, leaving me dumbfounded.

I have a gift. From Edward himself. I frowned at my gift, all spirit with a mane and tail of silk, as neat as an illustration from a *Book of Hours*, as she fussed and tossed her head in the stableyard.

'You don't like her?'

'I don't know why you should give her to me, Sire.'

'Why should I not?'

'And why do you always ask me questions to which I have no answer?'

Edward laughed, not at all disturbed by my retort. 'You always seem to find one.'

'She's never short of a pert comment, that's for sure.' Isabella had arrived to stroke the pretty, dappled creature. 'When did you last give me a new horse, sir?'

'When you last asked me for one, as I recall. Two months ago.'

'So you did. I must think of something else, since you're generous today.'

'You have never had need to question my generosity, Isabella,' the King replied dryly.

'True,' she conceded, with a final pat to the mare. 'Get what you can, little Alice, since His Majesty is in the mood for giving. Here's your chance to make your fortune from the royal coffers!' And she wandered off, restless as ever.

'My daughter is free with her opinions.' He watched her go. 'I apologise for her lack of grace.'

It had been an unnerving interlude, leaving the King with less of his good humour, but still I asked, 'You have not told me why you have given me the mare, Sire.'

'I have given you the mare because you need a mount to take care of you when my son cannot. She will treat you very well, if you will be so good as to accept her.'

His reply was curt, giving me a taste of his latent power, his dislike of being questioned, his very masculine pride. I set myself to charm and amuse, as I knew I could. King or not, he did not deserve that his open-handed magnanimity to a servant be thrown in his face.

'I am not ungracious, Sire. It is just that no one has ever given me a gift before. Except for the Queen. And once I was given a monkey.' He began to smile. 'It was a detestable creature.'

Edward laughed. 'What happened to it? Do you still have it?'

'Fortunately not. I fear its fate was sealed at St Mary's.'

His laughter became a low growl. 'Then if you are so short of gifts, mistress, I must do what I can to remedy it.'

I considered this. 'The King does not give gifts to girls of no family.'

'This one does. He gives what he wishes, to whom he wishes. Or at least he gives a palfrey to you, Mistress Alice.'

'I can't, Sire...' I was not lacking in good sense. It would be indiscreet. The mare was far too valuable.

'What a prickly creature you are. It is nothing, you know.'

'Not to you.'

'I want you to enjoy her. Will you allow me to do that? If for no other reason than that you serve the Queen well.'

How could I refuse? When the mare pushed against my shoulder with her soft nose, I fell in love with her, because she was beautiful and she was the King's gift.

The Queen is ill. She cannot move from her bed and begs me to read to her. When the King visited I stood to curtsey, already closing the book and putting it aside, expecting to be dismissed. His time with his wife was precious. But he waved me on and sat with us until I had finished the tale.

It was a dolorous one in which the Queen found particular enjoyment. She wept for the tragedy of the ill-fated lovers, Tristan and Isolde. The King stroked her hand, chiding her gently for her foolishness, telling her that his love for her was far greater than that of Tristan for his lady, and that he had no intention of doing anything so spineless as turning his face to the wall to die. Only a sword in the gut would bring him to his knees. And was his dear Philippa intending to cast herself over his body and die too without cause but a broken heart? Were they not, after so many years of marriage, made of sterner stuff than that? For shame!

It made the Queen laugh through her tears. 'A foolish tale.' She gave a watery smile.

'But it was well read. With much feeling,' Edward observed.

He touched my shoulder as he left us, the softest of pressures. Did the Queen notice? I thought not, but she dismissed me brusquely, pleading a need for solitude. She covered her face with her hands.

Her voice stopped me as I reached the door.

'Forgive me, Alice. It is a grievous burden I have given myself, and sometimes it is beyond me to bear it well.'

I did not understand her.

The King has had his clock placed in a new tower. I stood and watched in awe. His shout of laughter was powerful, a thing of joy, for at last his precious clock was nearly ready. The tower to house it was complete and the pieces of the mechanism were assembled to the Italian craftsman's finicky satisfaction. Here was the day that it would be set into working order, and the Queen had expressed a desire to witness it. Had Edward not had it made for her, modelled on that of the Abbot of St Albans, with its miraculous shifting panels of sun and stars?

'I can't,' Philippa admitted, 'I really can't,' when she could not push her swollen feet into soft shoes. 'Go and watch for me, Alice. The King needs an audience.'

'Thank God!' Isabella remarked.

'For what precisely?' Philippa was peevish. 'I fail to see any need to thank Him this morning.'

'Because you didn't ask me to go to look at the monstrosity.'

'Well, I wouldn't. Alice will enjoy it. Alice can ask the King the right questions, and then tell us all about it. Can't you?'

'Yes, Majesty,' I replied.

'But not in great detail,' Isabella called after me as I left the room. 'We're not all fixated with ropes and pulleys and wheels.'

So I went alone. I *was* interested in ropes and pulleys and cogs with wooden teeth that locked as they revolved. I wanted to see what the Italian had achieved. Was that all I wanted?

Ah no!

I wanted to watch and understand what fascinated Edward when he didn't have a sword in his hand or a celebration to organise. I wanted to see what beguiled this complex man of action. So I watched the final preparations.

We were not alone. The King had his audience with or without my presence, the Italian and his assistant as well as a cluster of servants and a handful of men at arms to give the necessary strength. And there was Thomas, who could not be kept away from such a spectacle.

'We need to lift this into position, Sire.' The Italian gestured, arms flung wide. 'And then attach the weights and the ropes for the bell.'

The ropes were apportioned to the men at arms, the instructions issued to hoist the weights for the winding mechanism. Thomas was given the task of watching for the moment all was in place. I was waved ignominiously to one side.

'Pull!' the Italian bellowed. And they did. 'Pull!'

With each repetition, the pieces of the clock rose into position.

'Almost there!' Thomas capered in excitement.

'Pull!' ordered the Italian.

They pulled, and with a creak and a snap one of the ropes broke. The weight to which it was attached crashed down to the floor, sending up a shower of dust and stone chippings. Before I could react, the loose remnants of the rope flew in an arc, like a whiplash, snaking out across the stone paving, to strike my ankles with such force that my feet were taken out from under me.

I fell in an inelegant heap of skirts and frayed rope and dust.

'Signorina!' The Italian leapt to my side with horror.

'Alice!' The King was there too.

I sat up slowly, breathless from shock and surprise, my ankles sore, as the Italian proceeded to wipe dust from my face, before discreetly arranging my disordered skirts.

'*Signorina!* A thousand pardons!'

It all seemed to be happening at a distance: the cloud of dust settling; the soldiers lowering the still unfixed pieces of the clock, now forgotten in the chaos. Thomas staring at me with a mixture of horror and fascination.

My eyes fixed on the King's anxious face. 'Edward...' I said.

'You are quite safe now.' He enclosed my hands within his and lifted them to his lips.

And my senses returned.

'I am not hurt,' I stated.

Ignoring this, Edward sent Thomas at a run. 'Fetch my physician!'

'I am not hurt,' I repeated.

'I'll decide whether you are hurt or not,' Edward snapped back, and then to his Master of Clocks, who still fussed and wrung his hands, 'See to the mechanism. It's not your fault, man! I'll deal with Mistress Alice.'

Never had I been so aware of his presence, the proud flare of nostrils that gave him a hawkish air even when rank fear was imprinted in his face.

'Can you stand?' he asked abruptly.

'Yes.'

Gently, he lifted me and stood me on my feet. To my surprise I staggered and was forced to clutch at his arm—no artifice on my part but a momentary dizziness. Without a second thought Edward swept me up into his arms and carried me away from the dust and debris.

For the first time in my short existence I was enclosed

in the arms of a man. All the feelings I had imagined but never experienced flooded through me. The heat of his body against mine, the steady beat of his heart. The fine grain of his skin, the firmness of his hands holding me close. The pungency of sweat and dust. My throat was dry with an inexplicable need, my palms slick with it. Every inch of my skin seemed to be alive, shimmering in the bars of sunlight through the glazed and painted windows. I was alight, on fire, my heart thundering against the lacing of my gown...

Until I was brought back to reality.

'Put me down, Sire!' I ordered. 'You must not worry the Queen with this. She is ill today. Where are you taking me?'

He came to a sudden halt. 'I don't know.' He looked down at me, as jolted as I. How close his eyes were to mine, his breath warm against my temple. 'In faith, Alice, you frightened me beyond reason. Are you in pain?'

'No.' I was too aware, far too aware. 'Please put me down. Why are you carrying me when I can walk very well on my own?'

The lines that bracketed his mouth began to ease at last. 'Allow me to be gallant, if you will, and carry you to safety.'

I could hear the Italian tending lovingly to his mechanism and the voices of the soldiers. The proximity of the servants. 'Put me down, Sire,' I repeated. 'We shall be seen.'

'Why would that matter?' His brows winged upwards as if he had not considered it.

But I knew it would matter. All the Court would know of this within the hour. 'Put me down!' I abandoned any good manners.

Edward turned abruptly into the chancel, marched along its length and set me down in one of the choir stalls, allowing me some degree of privacy.

'Since you insist...'

And kneeling beside me, he kissed me. Not a gracious salute to my fingers. Not a brotherly caress to my cheek, as I imagined such a one to be. Not a chaste husbandly peck on the lips such as Janyn Perrers would have employed if he had ever come so close to me. Edward gripped my arms, hauled me against him, and his mouth descended on mine in a firm possession that lasted as long as a heartbeat, and more.

He lifted his head and I looked at him, stunned. My blood hummed, my thoughts scattered. 'You should not have done that,' I managed in a whisper.

'Would you lecture the King on his behaviour, Mistress Alice?'

He smiled ruefully, before he kissed me again. Just as forcefully. Just as recklessly. And when it was ended, 'You should not have looked at me so trustingly,' he said.

'So it was my fault?' My voice, I regret, was almost a squeak. 'That you kissed your wife's damsel?'

For a moment, Philippa's presence hovered. We felt her with us. I saw the recognition in Edward's eyes, as I was sure it was in mine. And I saw regret there as his voice and features chilled.

'No, Alice. It was not your fault. It was mine. You could have been injured and I should have been more careful with you.' It was difficult to keep my breathing even, and when I shivered with a sudden onset of nerves, Edward stood. 'You're cold.' He shrugged out of the sleeveless over-tunic he had worn in the church for warmth, and draped it around my shoulders. And when his hands rested there, heat built in me again, so that my temples throbbed with it.

'Sire...' I warned as footsteps approached. Edward stepped back, struggling to be tolerant of his physician's meaningless questions and orders for me to rest to allow my humours to settle.

'I'll return you to the Queen,' Edward said when the physician was done.

Yes, I thought. That would be best. To be away from this man who was all too compelling. And then a thought. 'How is the clock after the accident, Sire? The Queen will want to know.'

And he rounded on me, with a blaze of anger. 'To hell with the clock. I don't regret kissing you. I find you alluring, intoxicating...' He glared at me as if it was indeed my fault. 'Why is that?'

'A moment's fear, Sire. I doubt you will remember this interlude tomorrow when the danger is over and the clock restored.'

'This is not a sudden impulse. Do you feel nothing?' he demanded, the hawkishness very pronounced.

I dissembled. 'I don't know.'

'I think you do.'

'Would it matter whether I did or not? I am the Queen's damsel.'

'As I very well know, God save me.' His temper still simmering. 'Tell me your thoughts on this debacle, Alice.'

'Then I will. For it is a debacle. Yet I think you are the most amazing man I have ever met.' For was that not true?

'Is that all? I want more from you.' He was all authority, his hand strong on mine, his whole body as taut as a bow string. 'I want to see you again before tomorrow. I will arrange it. Come to me tonight, Alice.'

No permission. No soft promises. A Plantagenet order. I had no misconceptions of what would await me. I think for the first time in my life I had nothing to say, not even in my head.

I told the Queen that the clock was experiencing difficulties but that the King had it all in hand.

Did I know what I was doing? Had I seen it developing, unfurling, from the very beginning? Oh, I knew. I was never a fool. I saw what I had done. I saw when his attention was caught. I noted the first scratch of my pen in my puerile writings when I had called him *Edward* rather than *the King*, when he gave me the little mare, when I began to think of him as *Edward*, the man.

Did I enchant and entrap him, as the malicious tongues were to accuse many years later? Was I complicit in this seduction?

Complicit, yes. But when did any woman entrap a Plantagenet? Edward had his own mind and pursued his own path.

Was I malicious?

Not that either. I was too loyal to the Queen. Guilt was not unknown to me, whatever slanders held otherwise. Philippa had given me everything I had, and I was betraying her. Regret had teeth as sharp as those of Joan's ill-fated monkey.

Ambitious, then?

Without a doubt. For here was a certain remedy for obscure poverty. When a woman spent her young years with nothing of her own, why should she not seize the opportunity to remedy her lack, should the opportunity fall into her lap?

Ah! But could I have stopped the whole train of events before I became the royal whore? Who's to say? With Edward I could be myself, not a silly damsel without a thought in my head but gossip and chatter. Edward listened to me as if my opinions mattered. I found his authority, his dominance, his sheer maleness intoxicating, as would any woman. When his eyes turned to mine, it was as if I had just drunk a cup of finest Gascon wine. He was the King and I his subject. I was under his dominion as much as he was under mine.

Could I have prevented it? No, I could not. For at the eleventh hour it was taken out of my hands.

That night I waited, apprehension churning in my belly until nausea threatened to send me running to the garde-robe. Taking a sip of ale, I sat on the side of my bed, feigning interest in the gossip of two damsels as they plaited each other's hair for the night. I pretended to be unravelling a stubborn knot from a length of ribbon, except that I made it worse. Abandoning it, I took off my veil and folded it. Refolded it. Anything to keep my hands busy. I could not sit. I stood abruptly to prowl the room.

What division of loyalties was here in my mind, my heart. Commanded by the King, recipient of his kisses. Servant of the Queen, who honoured me with her confidences. This was a betrayal. A terrible riding roughshod over the Queen's trust, stealing from her what was rightfully hers. It was impossible to argue around it.

I looked around the room, at the damsels quietly occupied. What to do now? Was it all a mistake? Had I misunderstood? There would be no royal summons after all and my guilt could be laid aside.

A knock on the door. I jumped like a stag, and my hands were not steady as I opened the door to a page in royal insignia.

'It is the Queen, mistress. She cannot sleep. She has sent for you. Will you come?'

'I will come,' I replied quietly.

So this was how it was to be arranged. A royal stratagem. A clever, supremely realistic ploy to remove me from my room without rousing suspicion. Would I be waylaid in some dark corridor to be led to the King's apartments instead of the Queen's? I detested the thought of such secrecy, such underhand deceit. I did not want this—but I was trapped in a web that was partly of my own making.

While the page waited I wrapped a mantle around me and made to follow.

'I may not return before dawn,' I said, my hand on the latch, impressed that my voice was steady. 'If the Queen is ill and restless, I'll sleep on a pallet in the antechamber.'

They nodded, lost in their own concerns. It was so easy.

The King wants you in his bed.

I shivered.

I was not to be waylaid after all. Instead I was shown by the incurious page into the smallest of the antechambers with a second door leading into the Queen's accommodations. It was a room I knew well, often used for intimate conversation or to withdraw into if one felt the need for solitary contemplation. Had I not used it myself in the hour after the King had made his intentions plain? Built into one of the towers, the chamber had circular walls, the cold stone covered with tapestries, all flamboyant with birds and animals of the forest. As I stood uncertainly in the centre, deer stared out at me with carefully stitched eyes. Wherever I turned I seemed to be under observation. An owl fixed me unblinkingly with golden orbs, a hunting dog watched me. I turned my back on it to sit on one of the benches against the wall. I started at every sound. And strained in the silence when there was no sound.

What now? I could do nothing but wait. Whatever was to transpire within the next hour was not within my governance. What would I say? What would I do? The palms of my hands were clammy with sweat as my thoughts flew ahead. What if I displeased Edward? My knowledge of what passed between a man and a woman within the privacy of the bed curtains was so limited as to be laughable. My education with the nuns had not fitted me for the role of mistress, royal or otherwise. As for Janyn…I gripped the edge of the bench on either side of me until it hurt.

Holy Virgin, don't abandon me!

But how was I fit to call on the Queen of Heaven?

The door opened. I leapt to my feet.

In my anxiety I had not noticed that it was the door from the Queen's rooms, not the one from the corridor. I faced it, expecting another page to take me further along this treacherous journey.

Ah, no!

My blood froze. My feet became rooted to the spot. Fear was a stone in my belly.

The Queen stood there on the threshold.

She stepped slowly forward, as regal as if entering a state chamber, and closed the door behind her with the softest of clicks. She might be clad in a night shift beneath her loose robe, her hair might be plaited on her shoulder, but she was every inch a queen. Her face might be lined and pinched with long-suffered pain, but her innate dignity was superb. For a long moment we stood, alone in that little room except for the static gaze of hundreds of embroidered eyes, and regarded each other.

Philippa held herself stiffly, the elbow of her damaged arm supported by her opposite hand, yet still she had come here to see me, to remonstrate, to curse me for my presumption. It was as if she cried out to me in her agony.

And because I could not speak, I sank into a deep obeisance, hiding my face from her. Was I not stripping from her the duty and honour of her husband's body and name? Was I not about to create a scandal that would cloak her in humiliation? What I was about to do could destroy her.

At that moment I knew in my heart. I could not do this thing.

'Alice...' My name was little more than a sigh on her lips.

'My lady. Forgive me.'

'I knew you would be here.'

She *knew*. How would she not? Such an emotional tie as I had seen between them. Sometimes it seemed to me that Philippa knew Edward was present even before he entered the room. She must also know, through that same inner sense, that her husband, the one love of her life, intended to betray her.

I could not do this to her.

I fell to my knees before her. 'Forgive me. Forgive me, my lady.'

Without words she touched my hair and I looked up. Her face was wet with tears, so many that they dripped to leave dark spots on the damask of her robe. And so much sorrow, it struck at my heart. I lifted my hands to cover my face so that I could not witness such depths of grief. There were tears in my own eyes.

'I would never harm you, lady...'

'I know.'

'I'll go back to my room.' I heard my words muffled by my hands. 'I'll not do it. I promise I will not.'

Bending awkwardly, the Queen gripped my forearm and with a grunt of pain urged me to my feet.

'I'll tell the King that...' I continued, shame a bloody sword in my flesh. Tell him what? The words dried on my lips.

'What will you tell him, Alice?'

'I don't know. I'll leave Court if I must…' Anything to heal the wound of bitter betrayal. I turned my face away. I could not look at her.

'No, Alice.'

I shook my head. 'I don't deserve your forgiveness but…'

The grasp of Philippa's fingers, which must have hurt her as much as it did me, silenced me. 'No, Alice.' I heard as she took a breath. 'You will do as the King wishes. Do you understand?'

It made no sense. 'No.'

'You will go to the King. When the King's page comes, you will go with him.' How accepting her voice was.

'I can't. I can't be disloyal…' I protested.

'You are not disloyal. I *want* you to go to him.'

This confused me beyond reason. I covered her hand with mine even though she was Queen, as if I could force her to acknowledge what she was saying. 'You can't want that. Don't you see?' I could not put it into words.

The Queen raised her free hand to hold my chin so that I must look at her, and she at me. She gave an infinitesimal nod of her head. Then she released me and took a step away, creating a little space between us.

'Look at me, Alice,' she insisted. 'Not as the Queen but as a woman.' She lifted her hands so that I had no choice but to see the ravages of the disease that was slowly but inexorably engulfing her. 'I am almost fifty years old.' She smiled with her lips. 'I have worn my years less well than my lord. My body is wearing out. My fortitude might once have been great but the deaths of my children have robbed me of that too. I feel death treading on my hem, Alice.'

'I can make the pain less for you…' I urged

'I know you can. And you do. But sometimes it is so great. And I cannot bear to be touched.'

The Queen sighed and I took her meaning. The swollen flesh, the stretched skin, the displaced shoulder. Some days it took the Queen all her will-power to walk from bedchamber to solar. 'I know, my lady.'

'Of course you do. Edward is virile. He has needs, as all men. He needs a woman to warm his bed and pleasure his flesh. How can I do that? The weight of the bed linen is an agony to me. I have loved my lord. I have borne him eleven children and was honoured to do so. I still love him more than life itself—but I cannot be a wife to him in the flesh. It hurts my heart, but I cannot.'

'No…' There was nothing more to say.

'Once I could barely wait until he came to me at night. My skin warmed. My loins melted. Now I fear what he might demand from me—not that he is ever cruel or thoughtless, you understand. He does not demand what I cannot bear. I don't want fear to stand between Edward and I—so I must make my own remedy.'

How honest she was. How heart-breakingly transparent. I watched every stark emotion chase across her face and waited for her decision. And there it was.

'Do this, Alice. Do this for me. I thought I could stand back and allow it to happen without speaking to you. But I could not. You deserve to know what I have done. You are too intelligent to be treated as a cipher, your will to be disposed of at a whim in so personal a matter.' She ran her tongue over dry lips as if she had to screw up her courage before she could continue. But she did. 'I have told my lord to take a lover because such intimacy is beyond me.'

Oh, Philippa! I could imagine what it had taken her to do this. How she'd had to deny her pride and her position as Edward's wife.

'I want him to have you, Alice. Why do you think I have placed you into his way?'

A new emotion began to surface in my mind. 'So you have planned this.'

'Planned? Perhaps I have, although I do not like the word. It has been in my mind, let us say.'

'Does the King know?' I was suddenly aghast that it had been arranged between them, with me as the pawn to be moved on the chessboard at will, and I felt the ice of resentment in my belly.

'No.' Philippa's brief laughter was harsh. 'He is a man who has always made his own decisions, and he will do so in this. Would any Plantagenet Prince allow a woman to choose his lover?'

The crawling horror subsided a little. 'But with all the beautiful women at Court…'

'My husband is well aware of the beauty around him. If he wanted a particular woman as his lover, he would take her. But you have a strange charm, Alice. I have prayed he would see it and respond to it.'

'Is it not degrading to him for us to be speaking in this manner?' I found my voice had dropped to almost a whisper, as if the vividly embroidered creatures might hear. 'It is a dishonour to his manhood.'

'No, my dear girl. Never think that. It would be too much of a burden for him to embrace chastity—he is a high-blooded man—yet he has done so in recent months for my sake.' Her smile held a world of acceptance. 'This is my gift to him—and yours to me. I lifted you up from nothing, Alice. Now you can repay me.'

'My gift to you.' I let the words filter through my mind.

'Yes. You speak of humiliation. But think! How could I bear it if he were to take a common whore in the heat of frustrated passion? Or a titled woman of my own Court? A man in the throes of passion does not always discriminate. And I could not bear the scandal. The worst is always believed and I haven't the strength to hold up my head against it...'

Soft footsteps sounded in the distance, drawing nearer.

'Are you sure about this, my lady?' I asked. The moment had arrived. There would be no going back for either of us.

'More sure than I have ever been of anything.' She leaned forward, clumsy but determined, to place a kiss between my brows. 'I must go—I don't want us to be found here together. This is no plot, and Edward must not consider it as such. Give him what he wants, Alice, knowing it is with my blessing.'

She turned to go but I stopped her with my question.

'You once told me that you had a role for me to play. Is this it?'

'Yes.' She looked back. 'You will find that Edward is a magnificent lover.' The grief was almost her undoing; I heard the sob in her throat. 'I will make it as easy as I can for you.'

For the length of a breath, but which seemed an age, we regarded each other: Philippa with a certainty born of desperation; I with astonishment at her courage and a knowledge that it would not prove to be a simple role for her or for me. How could a loving wife accept her husband's whore as her own daily companion? It would be beyond my tolerance. Now I understood exactly what the Queen had meant by a grievous burden.

Then she was gone, and I was left in a quagmire of unbelief, mind racing. The door to the corridor opened as the one to Philippa's rooms closed. I raised my chin and prepared to become the King's mistress with the blessing of his wife. All I had to do was follow the royal page. This was a night for courage, and I suspected I had used all that was allotted to me.

There was Wykeham, regarding me as if I were a louse to be burned in the candle flame. He stepped aside with the most dismissive of gestures. Not once did his eyes meet mine, but stared somewhere over my left shoulder. It was as if he could not look at me, for fear of acknowledging the terrible transgression that was about to be branded on my soul.

'You are to come with me, Mistress Perrers.'

So Wykeham was to be Edward's minion on this sensitive mission. Yesterday he would have called me Alice. Yesterday he would have greeted me with a smile and asked after my health. Today he scorned me as the most despicable of creatures.

'This is a sin!' he growled in confirmation if I had needed it, as I walked past him from the room.

'It is the King's will.' The less I said, the better.

'You should not be part of this.'

I was brief but defiant. 'I am summoned.'

'By your own contriving, no doubt! What you do must disgust any man with an ounce of decency. The Queen has given you everything and this is how you repay her.' Wykeham's mouth shut like a trap.

'I think we should go,' I replied, and turned away so that I need not see the disgust of me glitter in his eye. What had passed between me and the Queen must remain locked away, and so I must be content to let this man I had called a friend think what he wished of me.

He led me through the deserted corridors. Had everyone been sent away deliberately? Not one of the royal household was about on that night that set my feet on a new and dangerous path. For the length of a single breath I stumbled almost to a halt. What if I didn't comply? Was this how I wished to lose my virginity, as a creature caught up in a scheme to benefit King and Queen?

My mind was clouded with uncertainty. How could I, an abandoned bastard, seek to become the King's mistress? I was a Queen's damsel—was that not enough for one of my base origins? Surely for me to slip into the King's bed, even at his invitation, would be an outrage when he had spent his whole life loyal to his beloved wife. What if I refused?

I shook my head to disperse that impotent line of thought. I could not refuse. Events had moved on too far and too fast. As I stood for that one moment in the echoing corridor, my lips curving into a smile, I acknowledged the need in my soul. I would be more than a damsel. I would be what Edward wanted me to be. And if that was his mistress, I would not deny him. What woman in her right mind would reject so great an honour, to be singled out by the King? I would not.

Quickly I pattered after Wykeham, until he came to a halt, so abruptly that I all but trod on his heel. Wheeling round, he forced me to retreat a step, but he seized my wrist.

'You should not be here!' His eyes were furious, his lips stretched in anger.

'Will you deny me to your King? Not even you could do that, Wykeham.' I put a sneer into my voice. 'You can build walls and arches, but you can't dictate to your King!'

Instantly he released me, thrusting me away so that I staggered against the wall.

'Wykeham...!' I gasped.

His mind was closed against me. And what could I have said without betraying the Queen's carefully crafted deceit? With a brush of his knuckles against a door, Wykeham opened it, stood back and gestured me to go through. I stepped into the room. The door closed at my back.

Chapter Six

It was Edward's private chamber, redolent of masculine luxury. Wood panelling hung with tapestry, a fireplace with burning logs and a favourite hound curled there. A *prie dieu* and a crucifix. A coffer, a standing table, a high-polished chair with carved arms and back—opulent, I decided as I took it all in at a glance, used as I now was to such magnificence. Edward may have spent most of his life engaged in the hardship of campaigning in France, but at Havering he enjoyed all that his consequence could bring him.

There were signs of recent habitation. A pole with a falcon that appeared to be asleep. A sumptuous damask and fur chamber robe in deep glowing red cast negligently over the coffer. A flagon for wine and cups and a platter of what remained of a meal. Books, one open, and a rosary cast on the bed; a bowl and ewer flanked by a candlestand, the fine quality of the candles casting a soft glow.

And a superlative bed.

My eye slid quickly away from its silk covers, its red and gold curtains. After the emotion of the past half-hour my control was compromised. I stood hesitantly with my back to the door, an animal, waiting for the predator to pounce. For surely the King of England was as much a predator as his hawk.

The hawk rustled its feathers and sank further into somnolence. The hound twitched and whined in the throes of a hunting dream.

And Edward walked towards me from where he had been sitting, perusing the pages of a book, hand outstretched in greeting. How beautiful he was. How carelessly he wore that beauty, how unselfconsciously, how unaware of the impression his fine-carved features and magnificent stature would make on the beholder. Would make on me.

'Alice.' His stern features softened into a vestige of a smile. 'You look as if you're considering that I might pounce and dismember you.'

'I think I am,' I replied.

Edward's laugh rumbled. 'I'll not do that.' His hand closed over mine. 'You're freezing—or frozen with fear. Come to the fire…' Pulling me gently forward, he placed me in his own chair, speaking all the time as if I were some flighty unbroken filly needing reassurance. Leaving me to look around, he poured two cups of ruby liquid. 'Here. It's from Gascony. The best wine we have.' He pushed the cup into my hand and sat on a low stool at my feet, lifting his own cup to his lips.

'Drink, Alice.' He nudged my forearm. I realised I had been staring at him, my thoughts paralysed with uncertainty. I still could not look at the bed. For sure the King had not invited me here to have me copy the nation's accounts into a ledger.

Edward drank, his eyes never leaving my face. Under that intense gaze my nerves faltered and I looked down at the chasing on the fine silver cup, inconsequentially following the outline of a tined stag with my finger.

'Would it please you to be my mistress?' he asked, as if enquiring about my health.

'I don't know.'

'That's honest, by God!'

'It has to be, Sire. I don't know how to answer you otherwise.'

I took a careless gulp of wine and coughed. One of the logs collapsed with a sigh. The hawk shuffled with scaly feet.

'You are a widow.'

'Yes.'

'Then you should not fear this.' His hand gestured toward the bed.

I swallowed. 'I am a virgin. My marriage was never consummated.' I had begun to tremble, now that the moment had come upon me. I glanced up to see that Edward was frowning at me. That was not the answer he had wanted. He had wanted a mistress with some knowledge and experience. All Philippa's planning was for nought. 'I can go, Sire, if you don't want me here.'

'I'll tell you when I don't.' A flash of eye, a brush of temper that surprised me, and then it ebbed as fast as it had flared between us. His voice was very gentle. 'Forgive me. This has to be a very private transaction between us.'

'And you don't trust me to keep my own counsel?'

'That's not what I meant.' His eyes were on mine, fierce and searching again, and I could not look away.

'I know what you meant. I know you don't want to hurt Her Majesty.'

'You think it won't hurt her to know?' Surging to his feet, he was suddenly as far from me as he could get, at the other side of the room. I watched him cautiously. 'Sins of the flesh,' he murmured. 'They will return to haunt us.'

'I am no gossip, Sire,' I replied.

'How old are you?' he asked harshly.

'Seventeen years, my lord, perhaps eighteen.'

'So many years between us, so much experience that I have and you do not. Do you know, Alice? I've never been unfaithful to her. Not in all the thirty years of marriage. No matter the rumours that I have taken lovers—from the day I wed her I have not broken my oath. But now...'

But now she has told you to take a lover!

How to keep all the secrets. Like a weaver, melding all the colours into one seemly whole. Was I capable of such discretion? Such skill? Countess Joan's words returned to my mind. *It is important for a woman to have the duplicity to make good use of her talents.* And there she was with her cruel smile. Until I banished her. There was no place for Fair Joan's cynicism in this manoeuvring between Edward and myself. I waited, the nerves in my belly fluttering like a cage of finches.

'When I touch her she has to sink her teeth into her lips, not to groan with the agony.' Edward turned away from me to brace his hands against the edge of the coffer, head bent, shoulders rigid as he made his confession. 'I love my wife. But I desire you, Alice. Is that very bad?'

'Wykeham would say so, my lord.' I was still chafing at the priest's reproof.

'What would *you* say?'

The only thing I could. 'That you are my King and can demand my obedience, my lord.'

His mouth twisted. 'A simplistic answer to smooth over any complication.' Silence fell. Heavy. Full of decision and indecision. And then: 'If you are to share my bed, you must call me by my name.'

'Edward.' I tried it, as I had written it of late. I smiled. And the King must have heard the smile in my voice and he looked back at me over his shoulder.

'What is it?'

'It sounds strange.'

'Do you know how few people call me by my name, Alice?'

'No, Sire.'

'I could count them on the fingers of one hand. All the friends of my youth—dead within the last two years. Northampton—the bravest of my generals. Sir John Beauchamp who carried my standard at Crécy. Lancaster— the most trusted of all my friends. The years are cruel, Alice. You're too young to see it yet. They rob us of our health and our friends and our hopes, and give nothing back.' His sight was turned inward, his expression melancholy. Another log fell into ash, dislodging others, and as if the sound prompted him to what he was and what he must be, Edward slowly raised his head. His spine straightened visibly, and the lines of his face firmed as his lips compressed. 'I am not allowed to grow old. I am King.'

I stood, my own anxieties obliterated by compassion, not that I would ever have dared reveal it. Here was a proud warrior, who had lived and fought for a lifetime, yet there was no comfort for him. Neither would he ask it—he would bear the burden of kingship to the grave, whatever the depth of loneliness it demanded from him. I walked slowly toward him, presenting him with my own cup since his own was forgotten on the coffer.

'You will not grow old. You will live for ever. And I will call you Edward, if that is what you wish.'

I touched his hand as he took the cup from me, marvelling that I could so easily transgress the honour due to the King, but all my fears seemed to have fallen away. I let my fingers rest lightly on his as his eyes captured mine.

'It's the softness of your mouth that comes to me in my dreams. When you smile, your face is illuminated as if a candle is lit behind your eyes,' he said. 'It lights you from within.'

'You flatter me.'

'Then we will flatter each other.'

Edward kissed me. His lips were firm and warm against mine. An intimate kiss but with no heat of passion. He was not aroused. Perhaps it was the desire of courtly love he wanted to give me rather than the fulfilment of the flesh.

'God will damn me for this but...'

He let his hands drop from my shoulders, for there was harsh conscience again. I thought that in his youth there would have been no hesitation in Edward taking what he wanted, but he was not at ease with either his conscience or with me. His authority, within the bedchamber or without, was supreme, but his memories had roused the spectre of death and decay.

So what was my role? I wanted nothing more than to give him some level of contentment. To make him smile again. But how to distract him from these morbid thoughts that gave him no pleasure? What skill did I have to achieve that? The arts of bedchamber seduction were unknown to me. What might he want most from me that I was capable of giving? What could I do? I could argue and hold an opinion...

My eyes were caught by the documents strewn across the table. Affairs of business and policy. I walked to stand before them.

'Tell me what you are doing here, Edward.'

'Interested in royal policy, are you?' Intrigued, he watched me go.

'Yes.' I looked back at him, a deliberate challenge, which he was free to accept or reject. 'I am capable of far more than deciding the colour of the gown I wear or how my hair should be dressed.'

'Are you, now?' Accepting the challenge, Edward directed me to sit on a stool, reaching to select one of the documents, handing it to me. 'Family affairs,' he said, resting his weight against the table.

'You are fortunate. I have no family,' I said.

'I have sons. Magnificent sons. And they bring me power.' And there was the King again rather than the man, his hand wound tight in the reins to keep ultimate control of the kingdom. 'What do you see on that document?'

He tapped the one I held. The Latin was close-written in the crabbed script of a clerk, but I could read enough. 'Ireland,' I said.

'Good. This is Lionel. He's in Ireland. A difficult province. Once I'd have gone myself but I've sent Lionel as King's Lieutenant. He'll have to tread a path between all the damned interests. God knows, it's a morass of bad blood.'

He took the document from me and gave me another. I felt like a novice again, under instruction, or a clerk under Janyn's scrutiny, but my fascination with the documents was keen. 'And this?' he asked.

This one was more difficult but the names were clear. 'This is Aquitaine.'

'Edward, my heir.' The pride in his voice was unmistakeable. 'He'll rule Aquitaine well as long as he curbs his tendency to stamp on the interests of those he rules. Gascony's restive—he must learn to be patient at the same time as he learns to be King. He is a good commander, a man after my own heart. Now this…'

He was enjoying himself. A man confident and assured as he spread out before me the heirs to his power who would carry the Plantagenet blood and name into history. I took the new document.

'This is John. John of Gaunt. The Duchy of Lancaster is now his. And Edmund? I was planning on the Flanders heiress for him…' he tapped the document with a heavy red seal that had cracked on its journeys '…but the French want her and they have the ear of the new Pope. I'll have to look elsewhere for him. And then there's Thomas…'

'Who's only seven and hunting mad like his father.'

'Yes.' The success of my simple ploy glowed in my heart. Edward was at ease. 'Isabella is the other problem.' He took my cup again and drank as he considered the problem. 'She'll marry as she sees fit. If I took a whip to her sides, it would do no good.'

'I think she will not be averse to any husband of your choice.' I had seen the raging dissatisfaction in Isabella.

'She was more than averse once.'

'But now, with the years passing… She'll accept any man you choose for her, as long as he is young and good to look at and powerful.'

'I'll remember that. You see more than I in the domain of the solar. My fear is that she'll make her own choice—and select someone outrageously inappropriate.'

'Then let her do it.'

'I need her to make an alliance for the good of England— not to choose some landless knight with a pretty face and formidable muscles to entice her into bed.'

He stopped abruptly. I looked up from the vellum to his face, unsure what had silenced him. He was looking at me.

'What have you done?' he demanded.

'Nothing, my lord.'

'You are a cunning woman, Alice Perrers!'

And Edward cast the curling documents onto the table and laughed, enough to reverberate from the walls and wake the hound. With smooth flex of muscle and sinew he pushed himself from the table, stooped with a hand below each of my elbows and lifted me from the stool to place me firmly on my feet. He held me there before him.

'Did I bring you here to discuss matters of policy?' His eyes were now a clear blue, all shadows obliterated, full of humour. And desire. 'Not only cunning, I think. You are a clever woman.'

'Do you think so, Edward?' I tilted my chin, deliberately sombre, exquisitely provocative.

'You've made an excellent attempt at distracting me.'

'Yes,' I admitted.

'And very successfully. I can only apologise for my ill humour.'

'There is no need.' And because I was so close, I touched the King's lips with the tips of my fingers. 'I am pleased to give you pleasure.'

It was a blatant invitation—and it was meant to be.

Edward needed no invitation. With grave courtesy he helped me remove my gown—how did a man of war deal so knowledgeably with female ties and laces?—allowing me to keep my shift for modesty's sake. His patience lulled all my virginal fears. Turning back the bed covers, he helped me to sit against the pillows then doused the candles except for one, far enough away to give me the benefit of shrouding shadows. Without any modesty on his own part, he stripped off hose and tunic, and stood beside the bed.

'I'll make this as good as I can, Alice.'

'I am not afraid.' Neither was I. Now that the moment had come I knew that Edward Plantagenet would not hurt me.

Curious, I allowed my gaze to travel over what I could see of his body in the single flickering flame. I expect the soft light flattered him. Half a century he had lived, but his flesh was still firm and smooth on flanks and chest, neither could the scars and abrasions from a lifetime of battle and tourneys detract from his splendid physique, despite there being more silver in his fair hair than he might wish for.

The evidence of his desire for me was formidable.

'Do you like what you see, Mistress Alice?' he asked.

I flushed brightly, realising that I had been staring with open admiration.

'I like it very well,' I replied as calmly as I could. 'I can only pray that you will find me as pleasing to the eye and the senses.'

'For now, my pleasure in your company is obvious to us both.'

So I lost my virginity to Edward Plantagenet, King of England. It was not an unpleasant experience, and my trembling was from neither fear nor pain. I followed his lead and was brave enough to return his caresses with my own. Sometimes I allowed my own needs, when I recognised them, to prompt a kiss or a caress. Sometimes I made him hold his breath.

And how did I feel? Edward made me feel desired. For the first time in my seventeen years he made me feel valued, beautiful, even when I knew I was neither. I clung to him, drowning in his embrace.

'How did our lives cross, Alice?' he asked when passion had ebbed.

Your loving wife had something to do with it.

I shook my head.

'We keep this between us,' he murmured, 'and Wykeham, who's to be trusted.'

'Yes.'

But Wykeham will damn me rather than you!

And so it was begun: this strange *ménage à trois*, with the Queen a silent partner who neither needed nor wanted to know more than she did, and Edward unaware of his wife's complicity. I would keep the secrets of both. And when his hands explored and his body possessed, we tacitly agreed to keep the Queen distant from the room and the bed. We did not speak of her. Enough time tomorrow to allow guilt to creep in. For now the fluid strength of his body, the slide of heated skin against heated skin occupied all my thoughts.

At the end Edward fell asleep, the fingers of one hand interlaced with mine, but I lay awake, considering the responses of my body. What was love? Love, I suspected, was whatever Edward felt towards Philippa. But did I love Edward? Perhaps I fell in love with him a little, if admiration and respect and loyalty amounted to love. My belly clenched with longing when he kissed me, when his hands stroked down my breast to the dip of my waist. I was overwhelmed by his glamour, that this was the King of England who wanted me enough to throw caution to the winds and own me.

Perhaps that was love after all. I smiled to myself in the darkly shadowed room. I might be uncertain of the meaning of love, but that night I learnt full well the force of ambition.

Later—how many hours later I didn't know, for time had no meaning—Wykeham escorted me back to the antechamber in the Queen's rooms. The same journey but even more spiked with his loathing of what had been done. He was beyond censure. He bowed and left me at the door, not even opening it for me, the bow an empty gesture that denied any courtesy.

I had forfeited his approval. I suspected he thought I had forfeited my soul.

A page returned me to my room where the damsels slept on in ignorance.

A new day and early sunshine filtered into the room as if it were any ordinary day. I washed my hands and face from the ewer of cold water, flinching from the chill. A day like any other day, and yet not so. I dressed hurriedly before my two companions were astir, with the ready excuse that the Queen might need me if she was still in pain, to give her the strength to attend Mass in her chapel.

What would I say to her? I knew only that I must see her, to learn what she might find to say to me in the cold light of day. Last night had been a time of tension and drama when we had both allowed emotion to rule. Today might be a time for regret. The Queen might consider my dismissal a just punishment for what I had done, and, in truth, I could not blame her. I must know. I hurried to her rooms, only to be informed by her tirewoman that she had risen even earlier than I—was that a bad sign or good?—and was already at prayer. I slipped into the chapel. No priest was there, but the Queen knelt before the altar, clasping the altar rail to steady herself. I sank to my knees just within the entrance. I would wait. It seemed to me that the fair face of the statue of the Holy Virgin was particularly austere.

'Alice…'

The Queen's private devotions were complete. I stood, moving quickly toward the altar to help her to her feet.

'Well?' Her eyes were bright and aware. The pain was less this morning.

'It is done, Majesty.'

'It was…satisfactory?'

'Yes.'

So few words, so inconsequential in themselves, to encompass so momentous an act.

'He will send for you again?'

'Yes, my lady.'

'Good. We will not speak of this again.'

A strange relief trickled through my blood, that this three-stranded inter-weaving might not be impossible, if I had the skill to keep the secrets of both and remain true to each. Perhaps I could be loyal to both Philippa and Edward, betraying neither, harming neither. But still the claws of treachery fastened in my flesh. I felt the rip of them as the Queen turned her gaze away from her husband's whore.

When the door opened, disturbing the air so that the candles wavered wildly, we both looked round, expecting a priest. And in a heartbeat the serene, ageless atmosphere of the chapel became heated with fury. It was written on her face, in every gesture. She barely waited to approach us before her voice rang out. Isabella.

'God's Wounds! How could you?'

She covered the distance with long strides, kicking aside her skirts. I thought her attack was for me, but Isabella swept past me as if I were detritus beneath her feet and pounced on her mother.

'Why are you here with her? Do you know what she's done? Wykeham will not talk—at least he's loyal and will keep his mouth shut about this family's affairs—but he was seen last night—with her! And do you know where he took her?' She all but spat the words, her beautiful face contorted. 'She has betrayed you. Your little gutter sweepings, rescued from squalor, spent last night in the King's rooms! In his bed, I presume! And here you are, all but holding her hands!'

'Isabella...!' the Queen remonstrated, to no avail.

'You didn't even know, did you? Don't touch her! She is a vile serpent!' And Isabella struck out at me, making contact with her hand against my shoulder with a forceful blow, so surprising that I lost my balance and fell against the altar rail. 'You will dismiss her. Do you hear me? And if you will not, I'll arrange it myself!'

'I hear you, Isabella.' The Queen sighed.

'Look at her!' Isabella turned on me as I dragged myself upright. Prudently I stepped away as the Princess's fingers curled into claws. 'You have dressed her and polished her until she's halfway presentable. And what has she done? Warmed your husband's bed. As for the King... Is no man honourable? After all you have given him—the respect, the children. I despise him! But I despise you more, little Alice-from-the-gutter!'

'Isabella! You will be silent.' If I had thought Philippa's dignity a thing of amazement last night, today she was glorious in facing her furious daughter. 'I know exactly—'

'She has cheated you! She has turned the gold of your generosity into dross! She should be flogged!' Isabella advanced.

'I have not cheated.' I would not retreat again, even at the risk of Isabella's ire, but my fear was lively.

The Queen in timely manner grasped her daughter's sleeve. 'Isabella!'

'You're not going to make excuses for her, are you?'

'No. I am going to make them for myself.'

'I don't understand you.'

'Then curb your passions, and listen. I know exactly what passed between my husband and Alice. Listen to me, my daughter. Forget your sense of ill-usage and injustice. This is the reality.' The Queen waited until Isabella had at least a semblance of calm. 'What do you think? Am I capable of fulfilling my duty to your father?'

'Your duty?' Isabella looked as if she would rather not discuss it. 'I don't see…'

'Yes, you do see it. Every day you see it. I am incapable of turning back the sheets on my bed for your father. That is the brutal truth.'

'That's not—'

'If you were going to say something so foolish as that's not important, you're no daughter of mine. It is always important. Your father is the man he ever was. Do I condemn him to a lifetime of abstinence because I cannot…?' She brushed aside the words she could not speak. 'Do you understand me, Isabella?'

Isabella's fair skin was flushed.

'And if I cannot give him what he needs…'

'You would procure a mistress for your own husband?' Isabella's disbelief was as strong as mine had been. That gentle, loving Philippa should give her blessing to her husband's lover. 'Why not let him take a palace whore? There are enough of them willing to lift their skirts.'

'No. Before God, Isabella! You try my patience. If it has to be, I would rather it be someone I know and trust.'

How I detested this! There was nothing new to learn here in this confrontation between Queen and Princess of the Queen's motives. Had she not bared her soul to me, in all its agony, the previous night? Yet it made my blood chill. In spite of my loyalty to the Queen I was forced to acknowledge that I was being used. Snarled over like a bone between two royal curs. Better for the King to sleep with an unimportant *domicella* than a high-born titled lady who would use her position to sneer at the Queen's failure as she crowed over her success in bedding the King.

Degradation lapped over me, bitter as the leaves of hyssop. I might have sympathy with the Queen's motives, but the role that had been created for me was a wretched one. I was a creature, a pawn, to be moved around the chessboard at the whim of the player. And what a skilled player the Queen was. How long, before her eye had fallen on me, had she been plotting this deep scenario to preserve the Plantagenets from dangerous scandal?

'Could you not find a more acceptable bed mate than this?' Isabella continued to rage, stabbing her finger at me.

Neither, I realised, my blood now humming with my own anger, did I appreciate this exchange of opinion that stormed over me as if I were invisible. I was not the same powerless woman that I had been yesterday.

You are the King's mistress. You are no longer invisible. Neither are you voiceless. You have his ear. He wants you to come to him again. You do not have to tolerate this. You have power of your own.

The words revolved and repeated like the cogs of Edward's precious clock.

'You will pretend you know nothing, Isabella. You will treat Alice with the respect she deserves for her obedience to me. Do you understand me?' The Queen was laying down her directives with the precision of an army commander.

'And you trust her?' Unimpressed, unmoved, Isabella's contempt would have coated my skin in shame if my fury had not built mightily, from a hum to a roar in my belly. 'What else will she get from him? What gifts will she persuade my besotted father to give to her?'

How much more of this could I withstand? As hot as I was, the Queen was glacial.

'What do you mean?' she demanded.

'She'll not do it for nothing. What whore does? Jewels, money—a title even.'

'And if she does? If Edward chooses to reward her with gifts…'

'You're wrong, *Maman*! You're making the gravest mistake of your life.'

'Not so. It's the best decision I have ever made.'

I could remain a silent onlooker no longer. 'Stop!'

My voice sounded weak even to me. I might as well not have spoken.

'It is an obscenity that she should act as one of your simpering maids and slither into your husband's bed at the same time.' Isabella was beyond subtlety. 'I'll not trim it with the words and gestures of romance. It's lust, and you should be ashamed to encourage it.'

Enough! After my night with him, I could not bear that Edward be discussed in this manner. This time I raised my voice, caring nothing for the words I used in the presence of royal blood.

'Be silent!'

They looked at me, as startled as if the carved figure of the Virgin herself had come to life and uttered.

'I'll not be squabbled over, like a piece of meat on a butcher's slab.' There were things that must be said to Isabella. 'Have you no respect for your father the King? You denigrate him, defile him with crude words. Does he not have enough enemies across the sea, without his own beloved daughter slandering him? His will is law in England and you speak of him as if he were a toothless lion, an aging man who can be pushed and manoeuvred at the will of others. Is he so weak that he needs his wife to arrange for a woman to warm his bed? I say he does not. I say his blood

is high and his spirit great.' I took a breath. I think I had
never made so long a speech. 'You do the King and yourself no honour. He is at the beck and call of no man. And
I deny that he took a mistress at the behest of the Queen.'

'Well…!' Isabella sought for words.

I continued, my voice strengthening with conviction.
'You may consider me despicable, my lady, yet you will
hear me. I am the King's mistress.' How strange it sounded
to say it aloud. I lifted my chin and held her gaze. 'He chose
me. He sent for me, and I will perform my duty with honour. I will be discreet as long as His Majesty wishes me to
fulfil that role. I will not draw attention to what I do—that
is in the King's gift. I will ask for nothing, take nothing but
what the King gives me. If he wishes to reward me, then
I'll not refuse. It is his decision. For myself, I will be loyal.
I will not gossip or spread unseemly calumny. And I will
continue to serve the Queen in every way I can. For as long
as she wishes it.'

Slowly Isabella's lips curved, an expression of sour acknowledgement.

'Well, now. The royal whore has found her voice! I must
curtsey to you.' She did so, all mockery.

'You may mock me, my lady, but this is the King's wish—
and the Queen's. From this day I am the King's lover.'

Isabella's eyes flashed. 'And if the Queen, with some ju-
dicious thought over her poor choice for King's whore, ob-
jects to your new Court position? If *I* object?'

I lifted my shoulders in a perfect, elegant shrug. 'I wish
you no ill will, my lady, but I serve the King first and the
Queen second. And I think *your* wishes are irrelevant.'

'We'll see about that!' And Isabella marched from the
chapel.

I was left to the mercy of the Queen. How could I have

been so insolent, so careless of the difficulties of my new status? I waited for Philippa's judgement.

She laughed shakily. 'Well, I was right in my choice. You are intrepid enough—more than enough if you will challenge my daughter. What a magnificent defence you made for the King.'

She did not despise me, or if she did she hid it well. Tears glinted momentarily on her seamed cheeks until she wiped them away. 'Have you courage enough to withstand the hostility of the Court?'

With shocking naivety, I had not considered the answer to that question. 'We will be discreet,' I said, with more confidence than I felt.

'I'm sure you will. But it cannot be kept secret for ever. And Isabella will be your adversary. I'll keep her from doing too much damage, but she is wilful.'

'And Wykeham is no longer my friend.' I sighed.

I thought about it, my anger ebbing as I stood at the foot of the Virgin, who would surely condemn us both for casting this marriage into adultery. What an impossible burden for me to shoulder. The King's caress. The Queen's respect. And the outrage of those who knew. The loss of Wykeham's regard. Did I have the courage? Whether I took little or much from Edward's generous hand, I would be damned as the adulterous enemy. Not the King for his uncontrollable lust. Not Queen Philippa for her connivance. Only I would be anathema.

I studied the serene painted face but the Holy Mother gave me no guidance.

I had promised Isabella that I would take only what the King offered me. And so I would. But the possibilities were suddenly far beyond my imagining. Woven through this complex tapestry I saw the strand of my own future. It could be as strong as steel if I had the will and the boldness to make it so. It glinted gold in the weaving. I thought, if stitched with a clever hand, it could shine as brightly as the sun at midday, or the stars in the Virgin's crown. On the other hand, Edward might fall out of desire for me within the week and take a different whore to his bed.

I gave a little shrug. I must make sure that he did not. I was young and not without resources, it seemed.

I came of age during that night and the day that followed. I was finished with being a young girl, the pet of the damsels. I played no more. And perhaps I regretted it, but indeed it weighed nothing in the balance against that first heady tingle of power. The King wanted me, desired me. That first night spent in talk and lovemaking would be the first of many. What might the King's lover not achieve in life? What doors might not open to her? It was an enticing prospect, like a starving beggar standing before a table prepared with a banquet spread on gold plate for her personal delectation. I waited to see what my reward might be, my heart racing.

I was the King's mistress. Philippa's damsel by day, Edward's lover by night. What a strange two-sided coin it was. And every day I waited for the repercussions. Wykeham might be furious and stonily silent but my anonymity must be compromised, even though whoever had initially informed Isabella had been effectively silenced. For weeks it was as if I walked on the thinnest of thin ice, waiting with every step for it to give way beneath me to plunge me into a freezing torrent. I was summoned. I obeyed. Wykeham was always my escort. The Queen's health was always the excuse to take me from my room. But was our subterfuge not obvious? I could see the cracks radiating out from my feet every time I trod the same route in that first month.

And then the whispers began amongst the damsels. A slide of eye as I entered the solar. A comment that died into nothingness behind a flutter of fingers. Nothing more than the faintest breath of scandal, the whispering remained barely audible, like the soft shiver of a breeze over a field of grain, as if it was known but agreed that it would not be spoken of. A strange conspiracy of silence, everyone knowing the truth of it but no one prepared to unwrap the secret and lay my deceit open for all to see. No one challenged me to my face.

And why?

Not out of any respect for me. The silence was for Philippa. Such was the love she inspired that it was agreed that she should not be told the terrible truth that her youngest damsel lay naked in her husband's arms.

How appallingly unjust! But the situation hemmed me in and forced me to uphold the pretence that the Queen was as innocent and ignorant as she was believed to be. I was the guilty one. I had slithered my way into the King's bed like Eve's snake. For in all those weeks I heard not one word of condemnation of Edward. The King was beyond reproach.

But why Alice? they asked. I could read it in the slant of their glances. Why not choose someone better born, more talented—someone beautiful—if lust itched at his loins? I was no longer their pampered pet, no longer clasped to their collective bosom.

'Are you made to suffer for this?' Edward demanded in his forthright way. 'Any man who maligns you will be dismissed.'

How typical of a man. It was in the world of women, the

cruelly gossiping henhouse of the solar, where I was held up for judgement.

'No one speaks ill of me,' I replied.

I lied. What point in telling him that the sharp dagger of ostracism was held to my breast every day? It was not that he was uncaring, simply that no one dared whisper when the King was present.

At least my enemies took their lead from Isabella, whose demeanour towards me was rigidly polite, so icy that her stare could have frozen the Thames in August. So cold that it hurt.

It could not last. It was not in the nature of women to tolerate my sins for long without a bite, a snap, a pinch. How publically I was brought to book. For the manner of its doing, I would never forgive them. The occasion was a royal visit in November of 1363 when I had been Edward's lover for a little more than a month. It was a celebration of true splendour, when the rulers of France, Cyprus and Scotland visited the English Court to be awed by our magnificence. At a tournament at Smithfield, Edward would joust and lead one of the forays in the *mêlée*. At Edward's request, we were to attend with the Queen, clad in royal colours to support the symbolic victory of England over her enemies. We gathered in the audience chamber before making our procession to the ladies' gallery, a mass of silver and blue and sable fur, an eye-catching display of royal power as we damsels clustered around the Queen, who also shone in blue and silver with sapphires on her breast. A flutter of anticipation danced through the ranks.

Until the flutter of anticipation evolved into a rustle of shocked delight as I became the centre of attention. As I knew I must.

The Queen's eye fell on me.

'Alice.'

I could have made my excuses and absented myself. I could have hidden, motivated by cowardice. By humiliation. For was that not the intent?

My enemy had misjudged me. I would not.

'Majesty.' I curtseyed. My skirts, as all could see, were not silver and blue and furred with sable.

'Why...?' The Queen gestured towards my clothing: the garments I had first arrived in. Worn and crude, stained and creased from their long sojourn in my coffer, now they clothed me from head to foot as a lowly servant in coarse russet. I stood out in the midst of this jewelled throng, a sparrow invading a charm of goldfinches.

I had thrown down my gauntlet. Now I considered my reply most carefully. Did I state the truth? The idea appealed to me as my temper roiled beneath the rough overgown of a *conversa*. Every one of the innocent-faced damsels would know it, so why not unroll it, like a valuable bolt of velvet? Or did I exert some subtle dissimulation? But how could I be subtle? How could I lie, when fury beat in my head like a blacksmith's hammer?

All I could see in my mind was the beautiful gown laid out for me on my bed, the silk and damask slashed and torn beyond repair, the fur edging ravaged. The veil was rent in half, my embroidered girdle cut in two. I had worked hard on it for so many weeks, yet in the space of an hour someone had wielded a pair of shears with no skill and much vengeance. All my hard-worked stitching—which had taken more patience than I had ever dreamed possible—entirely undone. Someone had delighted in taking out their hatred of me on Philippa's gift: the soft leather shoes with damask rosettes had entirely vanished. I could have wept when I'd seen the destruction, but those who shared my room would have enjoyed my grief far too much. For a moment I had stood and looked, swallowing the tears, moved not so much by this evidence of my isolation but by the disfigurement of so beautiful a thing. I heard a choked giggle, which hardened my resolve. I carefully folded the ruined garment and veil and with fierce deliberation changed into the cheap fustian fit for a domestic drudge. If I could not wear the best, I would not compete with second best. I made no attempt to hide what I had once been and what had been done to me.

Truth or dissembling? I looked around at the waiting faces, hearing the words in my mind.

One of your damsels disfigured my gown out of spite, Majesty.

Well, that would get me nowhere. I had no proof, only the evidence. I would merely look foolish.

'She cannot attend like that,' Isabella observed, when I had still not explained.

'No,' the Queen agreed. 'She cannot.'

'I suppose there is a reason for the disobedience.' I could hear the smile in Isabella's voice. Not that I thought she was the guilty one. Such a vendetta was beneath her and she knew the Queen's wishes in this.

I raised my eyes to Philippa's face. 'I am not wilfully disobedient, Majesty.'

Her face was serene, her eyes clear. 'A misfortune perhaps.'

She had thrown me a lifeline. 'Yes, my lady. It was my own carelessness.'

'And so great a carelessness that the gown is beyond wearing?'

'Yes, Majesty. The blame is mine.'

I looked at no one but the Queen. Praying that she would understand and allow me to retire without punishment.

'Carelessness is not one of your sins, Alice,' she observed.

'Forgive me, my lady.' I lowered my gaze to the silver and blue rosettes on the toes of her shoes.

'Alice…' I looked up, to see the Queen nod briskly. 'I understand. Come with me. And you too, Isabella. We have time, I think.'

I heard an exhalation around me. Disappointment perhaps. But what a sense of exhilaration I felt. I had shown that their hostility meant nothing to me. I would make no excuses, I would not retaliate, I would keep my own counsel. They would see that I had no fear of them. For the first time I learned the true power of self-control.

A half-hour was all that was needed to put in place a transformation. The Queen was soon disrobed of her blue and silver and furred gown. My own disreputable garments were stripped from me—I never saw them again—and Philippa's robes became mine. Far too large but some robust lacing kept them from falling from my shoulders.

Not a word was spoken other than instructions to breathe or lift or step out.

'Good!' The Queen, regal even in her shift, watched as her silver-edged veil and girdle were added to my ensemble. 'Tell the King we will be ready in five minutes, Isabella.' And when the Queen and I found ourselves alone together, she asked: 'Will you tell me, Alice?'

'There is nothing to tell, my lady.'

She did not press me but turned again to the matter in hand.

'Fetch the crimson and gold with the gold over-robe. And the gold veil and the ruby collar.'

We returned to the audience chamber where the atmosphere was thick with the waiting. And there the Queen stood in our midst, glowing like a priceless ruby in the silver and blue setting of her damsels, whom she addressed with hard-eyed severity.

'We will honour the King today. It is my will. Alice is a loyal subject to both myself and His Majesty.' She looked around the carefully bland faces. 'I am displeased at the discourtesy to myself and those who serve me. I will not tolerate it.'

Silence.

'Do you understand me?'

'Yes, Majesty.' There was a hurried bending of the knee on all sides.

What an oblique little statement, saying little but acknowledging everything, and as clear as day to anyone with wit.

'Mistress Perrers will sit at my side at the tournament,' the Queen continued with a flat stare. 'Now, let us put in a belated appearance. It is always good for a woman to be a little late when a handsome man awaits her. Give me your arm, Mistress Perrers.'

The tournament proved to be a superb exhibition of manly warfare, a triumphal celebration of my position at Edward's court. And what a contest he fought. If the visiting monarchs had any thoughts of the waning powers of England's king as he entered his fiftieth year, Edward dispelled them with his mastery of the art of combat.

I should have rejoiced, not least at my own victory. But jealousy is a terrible sin and a vicious companion: an animal that eats and claws and gives no quarter. Thus it attacked me throughout that glorious afternoon. I might be Edward's lover but it was to Philippa that he looked, to Philippa that he gave the honours and the chivalric adoration. Not once did he single me out in my royal blue and silver, neither with look nor gesture. Edward accepted Philippa's scarf as his guerdon and wore it pinned to the sash over his body armour. He kissed Philippa's fingers and vowed to fight in her name. At the end, when he received the victor's prize and Philippa's loving salute, Edward spoke to her alone.

And I? I was woman enough to resent it. Why could he not speak to me? I was ashamed, bitterly remorseful of my envy but unable to quell it. I watched the tournament with a smile painted on my face, empty words on my lips and anger in my heart that the King would take my body in private but not acknowledge me in public. I knew my thoughts were all awry, unfair to both Philippa and Edward, and to the role I had undertaken with my eyes open to the consequences, but still I raged inwardly.

I was simply one of the damsels to fetch and carry.

Until I was in Edward's bed that night.

'That was a good day's work.' He stretched and sighed, pinning me effortlessly to the bed, his body slick and sated.

'Which part of it?' I responded primly, similarly replete, the monster of discontent temporarily laid to rest. I had not known that I could be prim, but I was discovering a multitude of skills to beguile a potent man. Edward had pleasured me with skill equal to that shown in the lists and with far more subtlety.

'Mistress Alice, you have a mischievous tongue. There's life in the old warhorse yet.' He turned his face into the curve of my breast, kissing the damp hollow where my heart still shivered with delight. 'I can still fell a knight half my age with a lance and a good horse beneath me.'

'And still reduce a woman to abject surrender…' I trailed a hand down his shoulder, pressing my palm against his ribs, feeling the answering solid beat.

'I thought I was the one to surrender.'

'Perhaps you did. You deserved to be defeated by a woman after all your male pride today. Wykeham will surely lecture you on how sinful it is.'

He rolled to hold my face between his hands so that I could not avoid his gaze, even if I had wished to. 'My victory was for you too, Alice. Never doubt that.'

'No, it was not.' The green-eyed grub in the heart of the apple was not quite dead. 'You didn't think to ask for my guerdon, as I recall.'

My tone was light but not altogether teasing, and he took me seriously, as he often did when I challenged him.

'The thought was in my heart, Alice. This duplicity does not sit well with me.'

I stifled a sigh and kissed him, allowing him the victory. Were we not both guilty of hypocrisy? 'The Queen was the obvious choice as your lady, and you fought magnificently for her,' I assured him. 'You gave her great pleasure.' It was like executing a complicated dance step to which I was not accustomed but, by God, my skills were improving. 'The Queen dressed in red and gold to please you. To be the centre of your vision and wish you victory.'

'Rich colours always suited her.' He smiled reflectively— and then his eyes focused and sparkled. 'Now, you were perfect in silver and blue. And even more perfect without any clothing at all…'

Edward's energies were prodigious.

As I was preparing to leave him, braving Wykeham's silent enmity, Edward cast a jewelled chain around my neck with thoughtless generosity. He had worn it at the feast that had followed the tournament. I lifted the links in my hand as it lay on my breast, marvelling at the value of it, and stared at it.

'What's wrong?' Edward asked gruffly.

'You don't know?'

'No. I think it becomes you.'

'I cannot accept this, Edward.'

'Why not?'

'I thought you wished to be discreet.' I took it off and placed it over his head so that it gleamed with far more power against the muscles of his own chest. 'There's nothing discreet about this. The golden links would curb a horse and the sapphires are the size of pigeon's eggs!' He was not pleased, as I could see by the flare of his nostrils. I must have a care with his pride, but I must also safeguard my still precarious position. A wise woman would not stir up more trouble than she need. 'Give me this instead,' I said and reached to where the Queen's scarf lay. And with it the brooch that had pinned the scarf to his sash.

'It is a small thing, Alice,' he remonstrated, brows flattening ominously into a line. 'Of no value.'

'It is of great value,' I purred persuasively, holding it on my palm. 'You wore it in the thick of battle. I would like it for my own. And I can wear it without ostentation. See sense, Edward. How could I wear a chain like that without every finger at Court pointed at me?'

Edward grunted his acquiescence. 'Very well, madam. I'll be convinced. But one day I'll give you what I choose.'

'And one day I'll let you.' And I knew that, at some distant point in the future, I would.

Edward pinned the simple jewel, a gold circle set with pinpoints of emeralds, to the linen of my shift, where it gleamed with a strange ostentation against the plain fabric. 'This is not easy for you, is it?' It was not the first time he had asked the question. Neither was my reply any different.

'No. How would it be easy?'

'Am I selfish in demanding that you play this role?'

'Yes. But you are King. Are you not allowed to be self-ish?'

He laughed, his humour restored if a little wry.

I kept the brooch. Amongst the jewels that Philippa had given me it went unobserved. One day, as Edward had inti-mated, I would not be so discreet. One day I would not have need to be, but the obvious reason for this broke my heart. As long as the Queen lived, discretion must rule.

'Are you going to remain silent?' I demanded of Wykeham as he escorted me once more along the route I knew only too well. 'You can't refuse to speak to me for ever. When did you become so prudish?'

'When I perjured my soul in keeping the King's dis-graceful secret,' he snarled in unpriestly manner. 'I'm leav-ing Havering to undertake some building at Windsor,' he added through his teeth.

'I wager you'll find that more rewarding than associat-ing with me.'

'God's wounds, I shall!'

'But I'll still be here when you return.' I could not resist the spark of naughty levity.

'I'll pray for a miracle that you are not!'

Wykeham went to Windsor to build a new tower. I missed him. I missed his severity and his honesty, but I no longer needed him as escort for I was given a room of my own with freedom to make my own way to the royal accommoda-tions. So my position was laid bare before the whole Court, yet the conspiracy of silence for Philippa's sake continued.

And when it did not?

'Whore!' hissed an ill-advised damsel when her moral indignation got the better of her good sense.

The result was a succinct audience with the Queen. The damsel's possessions were packed and she left Court within the day. I had enemies, but I had friends too who were far more powerful. I trod the path of my new role with growing poise and confidence in every step. How would I not? Philippa's royal gown—all blue and silver and costly fur— was re-cut and re-stitched so that it fitted me perfectly. I gloried in its possession, and I wore it with a deliberate arrogance in every graceful step I took. I was no longer an insignificant newcomer to court, to be swept aside or noticed when it pleased my companions. I was no longer to be burdened with all the menial tasks, even if they were for the Queen. I was a woman to be reckoned with.

'You do not know your place,' Isabella remarked coldly.

No, I did not, and never would, I acknowledged in my heart with smug satisfaction. I stared at her, a challenge, and Isabella in her wisdom let it go. As the King's mistress and Philippa's favourite I was invulnerable. I had won this little battle: no damsel would ever dare show me discourtesy again. They might despise me, they might wish me disgraced and banished from Court, but they could not touch me. And I gloried in that as much as I did in my royal gown.

Chapter Seven

Philippa was ill—a return to the old complaint that never entirely left her. I rubbed the new salve into the taut skin of her hands as gently as I could.

'You are sad, my lady,' I observed. Not even the lute music lifted her spirits.

'I feel the weight of every year of my life today.'

She missed Edward. She missed his company and the unquestioning love in his face when he looked at her. With him she was once again a young girl—but without him she sank into gloom and the hours dragged their feet. As if latching onto my thoughts, she winced and pulled her hand away, suddenly petulant.

'Forgive me, my lady.'

She shook her head. 'I need to consider the arrangements.'

'Arrangements, my lady?' She allowed me to scoop up more of the salve, leaves and petals of violets pounded into mutton fat, evil smelling but good to relieve hot swellings.

'For my death.'

My fingers hesitated before continuing their task. I

had not realised the depth of her melancholy. 'There is no need…' I tried to soothe her.

'But there is. I need to prepare an effigy—for my tomb.'

'You have many years, my lady.'

'I do not. You know I don't.' I looked up to find her dark eyes fixed on me, willing me to tell the truth. 'You, of all people…'

And so I told her what I saw in her face, because I owed it to her.

'I know, my lady. I'll not lie,' I whispered back.

A slight smile touched her mouth. 'I want my effigy to look like me, not some slim, flighty court beauty—something I haven't been for too many years.'

'Then we shall arrange it,' I said. 'Tell me what you want me to do to help you.'

Philippa released her hand from mine and placed it under my chin, lifting and turning my face to the oblique light from the window. She ran her thumb over the line of my jaw.

I remained perfectly still, the silk of my bodice barely stirring.

Her hands dropped away as if she had been burned and, thus released, I met her gaze as fearlessly as I could. 'There's a translucence about you, Alice. And a fullness in your face that I don't recall.'

Still I said nothing. The Queen sighed, her eyes clouded with a mix of emotion.

'I've carried twelve children, Alice. With some I've suffered. With some I've rejoiced. I know the signs. I am right, am I not?'

'Yes, my lady.' I would not look away, however sharp my fear.

'I suppose he does not know?'

'No, my lady. He does not.'

I did not know how to tell him. It had been the one thought in my head since that morning, almost two months ago now, when my predicament forced me to my knees with an oath of despair, when I vomited into the noxious depths of the garderobe, then staggered to slide down the wall when my knees trembled and gave way. The King, potent in all things, had got a child on me within three months of Edward's eye and Philippa's mind alighting on me.

I now saw my predicament reflected in Philippa's eyes. Edward valued his image as the King who upheld all that was good and moral in England; a mirror for his people. Would he want a bastard foisted upon him by a hapless girl whom he had honoured with his attentions? Before God, he would not.

And Philippa? If I were the King's legal wife, I knew how I would react to his upstart mistress swelling before my eyes with the evidence of his bastard, forcing her mountainous belly on the attention of the Court. If I were Philippa I would have the whore whipped from my sight. Conscious of how vulnerable I was, I saw my future hanging in the balance as I sat back on my heels and waited for the blow to fall.

Philippa considered me. When she spoke her voice was as hard as the pestle with which I had ground the tender violet petals. 'Go and pack your belongings. I think it's time you left Court.'

'Yes, Majesty.'

Did she mean for ever? Yet how could I blame her? How could she live with this terrible evidence of her husband's infidelity burgeoning before her eyes? I swallowed against the rock of dismay that lodged itself in my throat.

'I'll arrange it.'

'As you wish, my lady.'

Disregarding the pain, she pushed herself to her feet, all

her emotions tightly veiled, her face a stone mask. 'I wondered if you might refuse to go.'

And I bowed my head. 'How can I? I am your damsel, my lady, and if you dismiss me, then I must.'

Philippa's lips twisted. 'I thought you would insist on begging Edward's tolerance. To remain here and give birth under the shocked gaze of the whole Court. When were you going to tell me?'

'When I had to, my lady.'

'Did you think I would disapprove?'

'Yes.' It was little more than a sigh.

Suddenly stooping to seize my hand, her nails bit deep into my flesh. 'Of course I do. I hate it. I despise what you have done. Do you think I wish to see you like this, knowing what you do with my husband? Sometimes I despise you too, Alice. Holy Virgin—I wish I had never set eyes on you.'

Her bosom swelled as she took a deep breath and forced a vestige of a smile to her lips. 'And I despise even more that I cannot blame you, as it was all through my instigation.' Releasing my hands, she turned her face away. 'Get out. I don't want to look at you.'

So I was dismissed from the Queen's presence.

'Will you tell the King that I have gone, my lady?' I asked at the door.

'I will tell him everything he needs to know.'

I walked out of the Queen's chamber, my hand throbbing where her nails had scored me deep enough to draw blood.

Next morning as dawn touched the sky, I left Havering. There was no one in the courtyard to bid me farewell or see me settled into the litter provided for me. Much like my arrival, my departure was anonymous, unrecorded. But then I had had Wykeham with me. Now Wykeham was at Windsor, and Edward at Eltham, neither cognisant of the Queen's decision. The Queen would be in the chapel. There was no one. Isabella, if she had known, would have spat on my feet.

This was it. Dismissed with a royal bastard child and nothing of my own other than the clothes in the saddlebags. The greater the distance I travelled, the more bleak my future became. All was so uncertain—not least what Edward would say when he discovered my absence and the reason for it.

My thoughts drifted. Where were they taking me? Nothing had been said, and I had been too distraught at the speed and finality of it to ask. The Abbey? The thought hit me, like a pail of freezing water drenching me from head to foot.

Not that! I won't go.

But where would I go instead? There was no *where*.

I had always accepted that my good fortune was finite, but on this journey I was forced to accept the implications of it. How terrifyingly reliant I had become on this Plantagenet family with its pride and ruthlessness and complicated plotting. With the presence of this child under my heart, I was nothing to them but an embarrassment. They would decide my future, and I had no choice but to allow it.

The hours passed, and with them grew a knot of fear and anger that I should have so little control over what would become of me and the child that suddenly became very precious. Greseley, I thought. I must write to him at the Tabard, demand that he release some moneys to pay for a permanent sanctuary for me. But as the second day of my journey drew to a close, the autumn sun golden, the shadows extending across the road, dappling the horses, my mind grasped what should have been obvious. I had travelled too far for my destination to be the Abbey. When I had the wit to take notice of the movement of the sun, I found we were travelling west.

A shout from my escort and the hoofbeats of the horses slowed. Curious, I pulled back the curtains despite the evening chill, and caught my first glimpse of the place that was to be my home.

A manor house. A little stone house glowing in the final rays of the sun, the gates to the courtyard and stable block pushed back to allow my little entourage to enter. And there was my new household waiting for me on the threshold—a steward, a housekeeper, to one side two serving maids who bobbed curtseys, and an ostler emerging from the stables. That night the soft welcome of the manor of Ardington, one of Edward's own properties, as I was to learn, closed around me like the folds of a velvet cloak.

But I was not content. Despite the comforts of my rural retreat, I had no serenity, neither of body nor soul. As my belly grew, my spirits declined in counterpoint. I was provided with a home and all my needs, even coin for my purse so that I would not be without resources, but how long would that last? What would happen to me when the child was born?

In a strange way it was like an imprisonment. Although I had my freedom, I was not of a mind to use it. Nothing disturbed my calm, day-to-day existence. I did not travel or visit neighbours. There were books to occupy my mind, and out of boredom I sewed—how frustrated I must have been. I played my part in the running of the household, relieved that Mistress Lacey, the briskly efficient housekeeper, was tolerant of my sudden appearances in her kitchen and dairy. The world of the royal Court seemed to be as far away from me as the fabled land of Cathay. After less than a week in this haven, I accepted that I was not made for the unchanging tranquillity of rural life.

I did write—of course. To Greseley, urgency making me curt and demanding.

Master Greseley—I have need of immediate funds. What can you send me?

I received an equally stark missive in reply.

I will send you a return at Michaelmas after harvest. Do not look for a vast sum. Trade is poor and your manor not yet thriving. My advice, Mistress Perrers, is to be prudent in your demands.

How infuriatingly cautious he was.

So over all hung the terrible cloud of what I would do when the Queen's charity came to an end. When the King's lust died, or was lavished on another. Presumably my successor already trod the corridors to Edward's arms. What value would my child and I be to him then?

For in all that time I received not one word from the King. No letter, no gift. Not even a visit from the priestly Wykeham to pray over my sinful head. Nothing. I thought I would find it hard to forgive Edward that.

I gave birth to my son with little difficulty, my young body resilient and tolerant to the pain. One moment I was sitting in the kitchen with Mistress Lacey, helping her to strip the sloes from their prickly stems for want of anything better to do, and the next my waters broke. Helped to my chamber by Mistress Lacey and visited by the local midwife who declared me to be too much in a hurry, within the day I held my child in my arms.

What a stalwart child he was, with lungs like the blacksmith's bellows until I pressed his mouth against my breast, for I nursed him myself in those early days. I watched him feed with wonder. His hair was fair but I could see no likeness of Edward. His cheeks were round like crab apples, his nose showing nothing of an eagle's beak. Perhaps he would grow into the King's fine features. I prayed that the child, in all his innocence, would be more comely than I.

'You will become a knight and a famous soldier,' I informed him, but he fell asleep, replete, his head heavy on my arm.

I loved him. He was mine. He was dependent on me, and I loved him. But he was also the King's son. I knew what I must do, whatever the outcome.

Finding a long-disused pen, I wrote a letter. My pen hovered over the parchment. To Edward or Philippa? I would write to Philippa, one mother to another, even though it was supplicant to Queen.

> *Majesty,*
> *I am well and my child born. A son. I have called him*
> *John.*
> *Your servant,*
> *Alice.*

That was all I had to say, and I must sit and wait. In my blackest hours I imagined the Queen consigning my letter to the flames.

It was Edward who rescued me, and not before time. Edward, astride the familiar bay stallion beneath the stable-yard arch, the sun gilding his face, at his back a body of gleaming horseflesh and soldiery with the flash of royal pennons and the glint of steel at hand and waist. How many months had it been since I had seen him? Six, I thought. And in that time it seemed, to my critical eye, that he had grown older, a cobweb of fine lines etched beside mouth and eyes, a new austerity in his lean cheeks so that the eagle prow was keener.

Then he smiled when his eye lit on me where I stood in Mistress Lacey's garden, and I decided I was mistaken. Dismounting with fluid grace, Edward strode forward, covering the grass, as energetic as he ever was.

I did not curtsey. I did not smile.

'Alice! My dear girl. You look…' His words dried and gave a shout of laughter, so that a startled blackbird flew up from the branches above me. Despite my standing as stiff as a pikestaff with the child in my arms, his hands were on my shoulders, his lips on my cheeks and mouth. He did not see my anger.

'How do I look?' I demanded, when his kisses stopped. I knew how I looked. I kept no state here. Clad in my oldest gown, my skirts tucked up, my sleeves rolled to my elbow, even my hair was uncovered.

'Disgraceful!' he replied promptly. 'Like a penniless country wench.'

'I *am* a country wench.'

'And this is your son.' Releasing his grip on me, he lifted the child from my arms.

'And yours too. I have called him John,' I said.

'A good name. I couldn't think of better. A splendid name for so small and helpless a creature. He's no bigger than one of my alaunts' pups.' He held him high, so that John's fussing became gurgles of astonished joy. 'He has the Plantagenet nose, I see.'

'I can't see it.'

'Then you must look more closely!' Edward lowered the infant, placing him gently in his basket at my feet. He tilted his chin. 'And what's biting you, Mistress Alice? You're as bad tempered as a squirrel in a trap.'

'Nothing's biting me.' I would not allow his pleasure at seeing his son win me over.

The King looked at me, considering his next move. He brushed a tendril of hair from my forehead and a few crumbs of earth from my sleeve. And he grinned.

'Don't smile at me.'

'Why not?' But he became sober. 'I know what burr's got under your saddle, mistress. You thought I should have come to see you before now. And that's the truth of it,' he added when I opened my mouth to deny such childish petulance.

So I agreed. 'Yes. How many months is it, Edward?'

'Too many. But listen. Look at me.' He shook my sleeve to get my attention. 'You have to accept that you are not always my first priority. I knew you were safe. I knew you were well cared for. I knew that you and your son were in health and lacked for nothing.'

'Why did you not come?'

He pulled me to a bank of grass, where we sat. 'Chiefly because the King of France is dead.' Edward leaned forward, his forearms braced against his thighs, staring at the grass between his feet.

I knew something of this from my Court days: King John of France, defeated in battle and a prisoner in England until his ransom was paid by his penurious kingdom. He had been a man of honour who had waited out his days with good humour.

'He fell ill in March,' Edward explained. 'A month later he was dead. I returned his body to France. His son—King Charles the Fifth now—is reluctant to keep the truce of Bretigny between us. So that means war, God help us. I'm negotiating an alliance with King Pedro of Castile—I think we'll need him. No war yet but the storm clouds are looming and I don't…' His words faded. And it came to me that I had never seen him so lacking in assurance. His brow furrowed. Then he turned his head and looked up at me. 'I am King, Alice. I can't put you before my duties. I must keep England safe. But I am here now, because I needed to see you and could put it off no longer.'

My cold anger melted. Here was no apology but an explanation that I could understand. An explanation from a man who was King, who in truth did not need to explain. And yet he had. I placed my hand on his arm.

'Will you stay?' I asked.

'I cannot.'

'Why not?'

'I have summoned Parliament. It is imperative that the Prince in Aquitaine receives enough finance to pursue his foreign policy. Imperative…' And I saw the line of worry dig deep again between Edward's brows. 'I went out of my way to come here.'

'And I suppose that I, being less important than England, must forgive you!'

I could feel him smile as he sat up and pressed his mouth against my hair. I had gone too far in my selfish displeasure, and I forgave him in my delight at seeing him again.

'Have you time for a cup of ale?' My question was gentle and I touched his cheek.

'I have, and for a kiss from a woman who no longer stares at me as if I were a leper. And let me see my son again.'

Barely an hour we spent together, seated in the garden amidst the herbs and bees. Then he was mounted, the royal escort drawn up in good array, but with one matter still uncertain for me.

'Do I return to Court, Sire? Does the Queen wish me to return as a *domicella*?'

'Can you doubt it?' His regard was quizzical. I did not think that he understood my concerns.

'Yes,' I stated.

'She does, Alice. She has missed you.'

Or was this Edward imposing his will on a reluctant Queen? 'When?' I asked. 'When will you send for me?'

Edward's eyes flashed, temper suddenly simmering close to the surface. 'When I don't have the commons baying at my heels about the rise in prices. It's like trying to legislate against the incoming tide. We're trying to determine what men of rank and no rank might or might not wear— fur or embroidery—or whether the commons should...' Impatience lay heavily on him, and frustration, as he bit off the words.

'What about John?' I asked with false sweetness. 'What does your new law say that a bastard—even a royal one— is entitled to wear?' I knew my humour had an unpleasant edge, but what woman would not dislike being set aside for a discussion over sumptuary laws?

And the temper died, as I had intended. 'By God, Alice! I miss you. I forget to laugh when you are not with me.'

And I reached up to touch the lines beside his eyes, regretting their presence. 'I miss making you laugh.'

'Never doubt that I want you back at Court.'

Then he was gone, leaving me with much to think about that was unsettling. Not so much my own circumstances— still far from certain in my eyes—but the events that were putting the King under so great a strain.

I returned to Court, as circumspectly as I had left. Who should be the first to cross my path, to put me in my place, but Isabella who was crossing the courtyard from chapel to hall. She was just as beautiful and as querulous as I recalled. And quite as extravagant: the gown on her back and the jewels at her throat would have ransomed King John himself back to France, if he were still alive. In my absence no one had managed to wed her and carry her off to nuptial bliss. I was sorry.

She changed direction like one of Edward's ships under full sail, and came to block my path as I climbed the steps.

'So you're back with us.'

Her lip curled. I took a few more steps before I curtseyed. I did it well. The steps gave me an advantage of height over her.

'We haven't missed you.' She eyed me. 'Your looks haven't improved—although your figure has, I expect.'

Her smile was thin, her demeanour haughty. The little knot of the Queen's damsels who accompanied her did not try to hide their amusement at my expense or their disdain at my return. But I had grown daring in my absence and in the light of Edward's visit. I felt strong and would not be provoked. I stood my ground, waited. Sometimes there is strength in silence.

'Nothing to say, Mistress Perrers?' Isabella cooed. 'That's unlike you! And where is the bastard? Does he look like my father? Or one of the scullions, perhaps?'

I was provoked, after all.

'Your brother is well cared for, my lady. In His Majesty's manor at Ardington.' I had left John behind. How difficult that had been—but necessary. And Edward had established a nursery for him with his own servants, a nurse and governess. He would want for nothing. I had kissed him and promised never to abandon him. Now I used my height advantage against the Princess, chin raised. 'He is a true Plantagenet. His Majesty is much taken with him.'

Isabella's nostrils flared. The damsels held their collective breath.

'Airs and graces, Mistress Perrers. How ambitious you are. What do you hope for? A title? A rich marriage on the back of my father's misplaced generosity?'

I replied without inflection. Oh, I was far surer of myself now. 'I hope for nothing but respect and recognition for my services, my lady.'

Anger lay bright on her, the jewels glinting at her sharp inhalation. Isabella opened her mouth to reply with a stream of invective, but we were disturbed, a group of courtiers entering the courtyard from the direction of the stable block. Loud and satisfied after a vigorous hunt, the gentlemen bowed. And I heard Isabella's little intake of breath. Saw a stiffening in her spine as her attention was arrested, her expression softening. She smiled.

Duly interested, I observed the group to see who had been honoured with the Princess's admiration. It would have to be a man of character to put a curb rein on Isabella. Had she not refused every suitor offered to her, a string of the most high-born sons of Europe? I could see no response to her in this group of gentlemen, still revelling in the excitement of the kill. The courtiers moved off, the damsels following.

'Jesu! He's good to look at.' She forgot who I was. Her eyes followed the departing figures.

'Who?'

'Him!'

At the door one of the knights looked back over his shoulder, but then with no more acknowledgement than a nod of his undoubtedly handsome head, he followed the rest. He seemed to me very young.

'I don't know him.'

'How should you?' Isabella's scowl was ferocious. She had remembered again. 'You'd better go and remind the Queen of your existence. She has a new damsel since your departure. You may find you're not as indispensible as you think yourself to be. Take care, Mistress Perrers.'

'I am always careful, my lady.'

But her blow had struck home. My fears loomed large again. At the royal whim, my son and I could be rendered destitute. I would never forget sitting in the parlour of the King's little manor at Ardington, wondering where I would be the next day, the next week. I was nothing, had nothing without the goodwill of my lover and my lover's wife.

Isabella flounced off, while I caught up with the damsels to discover who had taken the Princess's fancy. Enguerrand de Coucy: one of the knights who had come to England in the retinue of the ill-fated King John of France during his captivity. He was still here, unsure of his welcome if he returned to the land of his birth. Was he a suitable mate for Edward's daughter? I doubted it. But if she wed him, and de Coucy succeeded in returning to France, taking his new wife with him…

I prayed fervently that Isabella achieved her heart's desire.

The Queen sat in her solar, her embroidery unstitched on her knee, as I sank to my knees before her, unable to look at her. A silence played out, ominous, full of presentiment.

'Alice.'

'Yes, my lady.' Nothing to read in that. Her embroidery slid to the floor. My fingers curled slowly into fists as I waited.

'You have returned.'

'Yes, my lady.' My knees quivered with the strain of kneeling, but I tensed my muscles to show no weakness.

'Where is the child?' Her voice was harsh, and I remembered how she had ordered me from her presence.

'At Ardington, my lady.'

Then Philippa's hands were stretched to cup my cheeks. 'Look at me! Oh, I have longed to see you, Alice!'

My eyes flew to her face, where tears tracked their silvered path.

'My lady...' It shocked me to see such overt emotion.

'Forgive me,' she whispered. 'I was cruel. I know it— and it was not your fault but I couldn't...' Her explanation dried. 'You do understand, don't you? How impossibly hard it is for me to take you back—and yet I have missed you. It hurts my heart terribly...' The tears fell more heavily.

'Yes, my lady.'

For of course I understood and could afford to be magnanimous. Here was the truth of it: I could not be touched. Isabella's shafts were harmless, for she had no power to undermine me. Even Philippa could not be rid of me now if Edward demanded my return. Within my breast I felt a surge of triumph, which I regretted as the Queen's tears continued to fall. She did not deserve such anguish, yet I would deny that I was the instigator of it. We had all entered into this with open eyes, had we not?

I kissed the Queen's swollen fingers, rescued the stitchery and helped her to dry the tears, all as a good *domicella* should. She had aged in my absence, but still she could manage a watery smile that stoked my guilt to a burning flame. Philippa—kindly, suffering Philippa—kissed my cheek, asked after my son, gave me an embroidered robe for the babe, and presented me with a bolt of red silk for a new gown.

And so I slid back into my place in Philippa's household as easily and smoothly as a trout into a cooking pot of boiling water. I found it hard not to gloat over my restored pre-eminence, but I was never a fool and saw clearly enough the obverse of the coin through the glittering value of it. I was untouchable as long as Edward wanted me. The courtiers and damsels received me back with a careful show of respect as long as I did not look closely into the eyes that followed my progress. It would not do to expose myself to the hatred I might see there—or was it envy? It was unspoken and would always be so, as long as Edward lived—but there was the quicksand beneath my now well-shod feet. There was a finality to my position that could be measured in months, in years. And what of my loyalty to Philippa? My affection for her? It made for bittersweet remorse when she wept over Edward's adultery with me. Had she not made me what I was?

I pushed aside my doubts, for there was no room for them when, in private, Edward enfolded me in his arms and kissed me with Plantagenet fervour.

'It has been a long time, Alice.'

'But now I have returned to you.'

'And you won't leave.'

'Not unless you send me away.'

'I'll not do that.' His elegant hands unwound my hair, his thumbs tracing along my cheekbones as he smiled into my eyes. 'I've been too long without you.'

Too long. I had missed him more than I had thought possible. It was like balm to my soul to be kissed and caressed and loved in Edward's bed. I was returned to where I belonged.

And Isabella? Isabella left us. Isabella, headstrong and in love, flirted, flounced and cajoled de Coucy and defied her father in equal measure. De Coucy looked unconvinced by his good fortune in becoming the apple of Isabella's eye. To wed an English Princess was one thing, to take on Isabella and her formidable father was quite another.

'He's too young, too unimportant.' Edward refused her first request.

'Why can't *you* do something useful!' Isabella muttered privately in my direction. 'You have the use of my father's body, surely you have his ear as well! Persuade him, for God's sake!'

It pleased me to refuse with profound grace, merely to ruffle her royal feathers. 'I fear that I am unable to do that, my lady.'

For the King, with or without my interference, would make his own decisions. And he did. Recognising a lost cause, Edward clamped a tight hold on his true feelings about the match and gave de Coucy the title of Duke of Bedford, made him a knight of the Garter to tie him to English interests, and silently wished the Frenchman well. They were wed in the felicitous month of July at Windsor Castle, with all the pomp and splendour that Isabella could persuade her father to pay for. And by November they had taken themselves off to France.

'I hope you are no longer here when I next visit.' Marriage had not sweetened Isabella's tongue.

'I wouldn't wager Edward's magnificent wedding gift on it.' I could hide my fears with great finesse, or even coarse wagering, when I had to.

Isabella managed the ghost of a smile. 'Neither would I. A lifetime's annuity and a King's ransom in jewels are not to be risked on a certainty! I might even miss your sharp tongue, Alice Perrers!'

Well, well. Was this some manner of a compliment?

'I'll pray you don't breed any more bastards,' the Princess added.

No. Her final sally was not friendly, but I might even miss her, I decided as the year slid towards its end. The Court lacked vibrancy on her departure.

The year of 1366: it would not be forgotten in a hurry. A bad winter, appallingly bad, to bring suffering and worry and grief to the Court as well as to the commons, and it proved to be a turning point in my relationship with Edward. A hard frost kept us shivering from September to April, curtailing most of Edward's attempts to set up a hunt, hurling him into an uncharacteristically sombre mood. Philippa's joints ached beyond tolerance, so much so that she was kept to her bed. The approach of her death kept her occupied more and more as the days passed. Isabella might have brought some light into her shadowed existence, but Isabella was embracing motherhood in France. Edward was little help to her, wrapped in his own melancholy.

Through those difficult months I tried my best to woo Edward from his moody silences. Would he read? No. Would he have me read to him? No. Play chess or the foolishness of nine men's morris? Would he take out the hawks on foot along the river bank, even if too dangerous for the horses on the impacted ground? Would he don skates and take exercise on the Thames like the rest of the frustrated and icebound Court?

'Come and play.' I smiled, hoping to engage him in some light-hearted companionship as the sun consented to put in an appearance. 'You can leave these documents and give me some of your time.'

'Go away, Alice,' he growled. 'I have too much on my trencher to be reading and skating!'

So I went. I learned to skate and laughed with joy. I was still young and enjoyed the speed and freedom, even when I fell.

I lured Edward to his bed on the coldest days but he was not to be roused. He might kiss me but his manhood refused to be enticed—his mind was far distant from me. I wrapped him in my arms and read to him from tales of King Arthur—until he closed the book and refused to hear any more about heroes with magic swords. He took himself off to badger Wykeham for news of his latest building schemes. Even that was half-hearted.

I could not blame him and bore no grudges. Had I not learned my lesson, that I did not always come first with a man of such grave responsibilities? For the King had reason enough for the blackness that wrapped his soul like a shroud. My heart ached for him, for the Prince, his glorious son and heir, lord of Aquitaine, had persuaded Edward to finance a campaign to reinstate Pedro of Castile, who had been deposed by his subjects. A risky project in the depths of winter, as Edward was warned by Wykeham, but, like the King of old, he grasped at the chance to be conqueror once more, forced through a war budget with Parliament, raised an army and handed authority over this invading force to another of his sons, John of Gaunt. He, together with the Prince invading from Aquitaine, would bring a solution to Castile's inheritance problems and glory to England.

'What do you think, Alice?' Edward asked as I sat at his feet before the fire in his chamber—although I think he did not care what I thought. He sipped gloomily from a cup of ale and I sought for something to cheer him.

'I think you are the most powerful King in Christendom.'

'Will England be victorious?'

'Of course.'

'Will I still be seen as the man who holds the power of Europe in his fist?'

He raised his hand and clenched it, the tendons proud against the flesh. Age pressed particularly heavily on him that night. In the shadows the pale gold of his hair was entirely eclipsed with dull grey.

'Undoubtedly you will.'

He smiled. 'You are good for me, Alice.'

I took the rigid fist, smoothed out the fingers between my own and kissed them, aware of my ignorance and deficiencies as King's counsellor. What did I know of the state of England's authority over the sea? Very little, but we were all to learn the truth over the coming weeks. The King should have listened to Wykeham.

Our invading forces, beset by storms and gales and shortage of food, were reduced to a fifth of their original size, with no booty or prisoners to compensate. Sitting in his chamber or pacing the halls of Havering, Edward could do nothing to determine events except to rely on his sons to uphold the English cause. Inactivity gnawed at him day and night. Why did he not go himself, to lead as he once had done? Because he too saw the waning of his powers. The future was with his sons and it hurt him to see the end of his own vitality. However hard I tried through that winter, I could not heal the wounds for him.

As for English affairs in Ireland, they seemed like to sink to their death into the famous bog. Edward's son Lionel scrabbled at an impossible settlement, reducing Edward to vicious oaths against his son's ineptitude.

Philippa despaired and wept.

And I? How did I fare? Did we, Edward and I, emerge from the morass of black despair? Holy Virgin! It was balanced on a knife edge, and I could have lost everything. For we faced a crisis that was in the end, I admit, of my own deliberate making.

Frustrated with the cold rooms of Havering, Edward departed to Eltham at the turn of the year and at Philippa's insistence the whole Court moved to be with Edward.

'You'll see,' she fretted as her possessions were packed around her, setting her teeth against the prospect of journey in a litter, however luxurious the cushions. 'Eltham has more *space*. He feels hemmed in here. And we must hear good news from Gascony soon. We can't leave him to brood. It does him no good.'

But, despite the new planned gardens and Edward's own pride in the new-planted vineyard, he brooded in the spacious accommodations at Eltham as effectively as he had at Havering. He roared through the halls and audience chambers, patient with no one except Philippa, insisting on taking out the hounds, hard ground or no, snarling at the grooms when they were slow, their icy fingers clumsy on the frozen leather. He snarled at me too.

'Come with me,' he snapped. 'I want you with me!'

He kept me waiting, shivering in the cold outside the stables, while he listened to a report of a courier just ridden in. Only the week before he had given me a mantle of sables, wrapping my naked body in his gift in a moment of brittle good humour. I wore it now but I might have been wearing the lightest of silk for all the good it did in the bitter wind.

'Let's go!' he ordered, temper on as short a leash as the hounds. 'What are you waiting for?'

'Her Majesty is not well, my lord. I should be with her.' Not quite an excuse. The journey to Eltham had stirred her joints to a new level of agony. Sleeping was a distant memory without a draught of poppy.

'We'll be back before noon.'

'Jesu! It's too cold for this,' I murmured.

'Then don't come. I'll not force you.' He swung up into the saddle. The courier's news had not pleased him.

For a moment I considered leaving him to his ill humour. Then perversely I joined the hunt. I regretted it, of course, returning with damp hems and frozen feet and mud-splattered skirts. My blood felt sluggish in my veins. Neither had it been a success. We put up nothing for the hounds, everything of sense having gone to ground. We were frozen to the bone and Edward in no better mood.

Neither was I. He had spoken not one word to me—other than to keep up, for God's sake—when we galloped after a scent that proved to be as ephemeral as the King's good temper. Back at the palace, our steaming horses led away to the stables, I trailed after him as Edward stripped off gloves and hood and heavy cloak, thrusting them into my arms as he strode into the Great Hall. Without even a glance in my direction, he raised his hand, a royal summons, without courtesy.

Rebellion spiked my blood, coupled with a rush of despair that I was losing Edward's interest, his regard. As I watched him march away from me my belly lurched and nausea struck so hard that I had to tense my muscles against it. Was this all I was to him, a servant to fetch and carry and obey unspoken orders? If so, my place at court was undermined. If he no longer wanted me, could I accept my demotion to damsel? I closed my eyes shut hard to block out the vision of the Court enjoying my abasement.

No! It could not be. The sense of my rejection, of another woman taking my place in Edward's bed, filled my mind like a blinding flash of light, and my whole body froze as I saw my future mapped out before me; away from Court, without recognition, without influence. I could not tolerate it, losing all that I had achieved since I had first stepped over the threshold of Havering-atte-Bower.

The nausea was swept aside in a blaze of determination. I would not allow it. I would fight for my place.

I halted, my arms full of muddy cloak. It was only when Edward had crossed the antechamber to the staircase leading up to the royal apartments that he realised my footsteps were not following him. He halted, spun round. Even at that distance I could see that his jaw was rigid.

'Alice!'

I moved not one inch.

'What's wrong with you, girl?'

I considered what I should say, what would be wise—and promptly consigned wisdom to the fires of hell and remained where I was.

'I'm cold. Don't just stand there.' Edward was already mounting the stairs.

I abandoned prudence too.

'Is that all you can say?' I asked.

Edward froze, his eyes a steely glint. 'I want you with me.'

For a moment we were alone in the vast arching chamber. There was no one there to hear us. I raised my voice. I think I would have raised it if we had had an audience of hundreds.

'No.'

'I want a cup of wine.'

And at the same echoing pitch I responded: 'Which you are perfectly capable of pouring for yourself, Sire. Or you can summon one of your many pages or even a servant to do it for you. But I will not.'

Edward stared as if he could not believe what I had

just said. Neither could I. I had been his mistress for three years, and never had I addressed him in this peremptory manner. But, then, I had never had the need. I watched Edward's face, the range of emotion, as he absorbed my words. Astonishment. Affronted arrogance. A strange despondency. And a fury that suffused his face with colour. I trembled, and not from the damp skirts clinging to my legs.

Arrogance won. Edward's manner when he replied was as icy as my fingers. 'Mistress Perrers. I want you with me.'

'No, Sire.' My determination now burned like a full-throated fire. 'You kept me waiting until my feet were well nigh frozen to the cobbles. You did not care whether I hunted with you or not. You told me as much—after dragging me from the Queen's side. I made my own decision to hunt, and I will make it again now. I will not go with you. I will wait on the Queen.'

My blood was up and I held my breath. This was no childish temper. This was a deliberate ploy, and a dangerous one to rouse the sleeping Plantagenet lion. I saw anger flash bright as my refusal struck home. It brought the King striding across the chamber until he towered over me. Holy Virgin! In that moment he was the King, not Edward. He grabbed my wrist, even as I still had my arms wrapped around his cloak, and held it tight, unaware of his strength.

'God's blood, Alice!'

'God's blood, Edward!' I mimicked.

The silence was heavy. Thick as blood. Threatening as a honed sword edge.

'You will obey me.'

'Because you are the King?'

'Why else?'

My shivering increased but I held his gaze. 'When did anyone ever deny you anything, Sire?'

'Never. Neither will you.' His fingers tightened still further but I did not wince. 'Do you question my authority?'

'Your *authority*?' I tilted my chin. 'I don't question your *authority*, Sire, only your bloody arrogance.' I bit down on a hiss of breath. 'Do you intend to command my obedience through pain, Sire?'

'Pain?'

'Your royal fingers are digging into my flesh!'

He eased his grip but did not release me.

When I was seventeen and newly come to Court, I would have obeyed the King without question, wary of the repercussions. I did not feel of a mind to do so now. It was a gamble, and filled with jeopardy. He might dismiss me out of hand, order Philippa to dismiss me. But now I was the mother of his son. Now I was a woman full grown, and I did not think he would. I thought I had more power than that, and I thought I had earned the King's respect.

Well, we would see. I would gamble on that power and respect to wean Edward from his black mood.

'You would defy me, woman?' he roared. No respect here. I might just be wrong.

'Yes, when you are boorish and unreasonable, Sire. I've been away from the Queen's side all day. I am her damsel as well as your...' I allowed a little pause. 'As well as your whore.'

Even as rank astonishment ripped across Edward's features, I opened my arms to deposit his garments in a heap on the floor, at my feet and his. Then I let the sables slip from my shoulders to join them. And I stepped around him and climbed the stair, leaving him standing alone with the heap of costly fur and velvet cloth on the tiles muddied from our feet. A page entered at the far door. What Edward might have said if we had remained alone I had no idea. At the top of the staircase I looked back to see him, as unmoving as an oak, hands fisted on hips, looking after me, the garments still at his feet. I waited until I was sure his attention was wholly mine. Then I made a magnificent curtsey. Again I pitched my voice so that he would surely hear.

'There are other palace whores who will be more than willing to keep you company, no matter how sour your humour, Sire. You can give her my sables. I make you free of them.'

I did not wait to see if he would respond. Or if he picked up the garments.

I admit to terrible apprehension as I closed the door of my chamber behind me. I might just have destroyed everything. The terrible melancholy might still hold Edward imprisoned in its shackles, and my position as royal whore might have come to an abrupt end.

I did not wait with an easy mind. The King made his displeasure felt. When he hunted I was not invited. When he visited the Queen, if I was present, he made a point of shunning me, gesturing without words for me to vacate the chamber. There was no question of my sharing his bed. I missed my sable mantle. The damsels gossiped, engrossed in our obvious estrangement. The Queen was anxious but such was our relationship that we both kept our own counsel. Until the tension, colder indoors than out, became more than she could tolerate.

'Have you quarrelled with the King, Alice?'

'No, my lady.' It was not exactly a quarrel.

'Have you displeased him?'

'Yes, my lady.' Definitely.

'He's very restless.'

'Yes, my lady.'

'Should you apologise, do you think?' Her broad brow creased in concern.

'No, my lady.'

So the Queen abandoned any attempt at reconciliation and I waited with increasing anxiety. I did not sulk, for what purpose would there be in that? Edward was not a man to be swayed by an exhibition of female moping, and the damsels would merely enjoy my discomfiture. I preserved an outward appearance of cheerful composure; beneath, my fears leapt and danced at my foolhardiness. Edward was the King and owed me nothing. I had risked all and must pray that I had not staked my future ill-advisedly.

It took a se'nnight.

I was combing my hair in preparation to sleep alone when a soft knock sounded against the door. Wykeham, I thought. Carrying a message from the King, to attend his pleasure. I opened the door, the refusal leaping to my lips.

'I will not…' The words dried.

Edward. He had come himself. And over his arm the glossy pelts of my mantle.

'My lord!'

I curtseyed low on the threshold, hiding my face. The King to come to my room? Was this to be the dismissal I had feared, the sables a final gift to mark my ignominious departure? If I looked at him, what would I see? I raised my eyes to his—better to know immediately, but Edward, master of negotiation, was giving nothing away. If it was dismissal it would be done in cold blood, not in the heat of passion at my lack of respect.

'Well, will you let me come in?' His voice was rough. 'I don't think the King should be expected more than once in his lifetime to conduct an intimate argument in a public space for all his subjects to see and hear.'

I stood back, pushing the door wide, but still for all his impatience he did not step across the threshold. Instead he held out the mantle.

'This is yours, Mistress Perrers.'

I took it from him, tossing it over a coffer beside me as if I did not care.

'I was wrong, mistress. I treated you with unforgiveable discourtesy.'

I remained mute.

'I'm here to ask your forgiveness.' It was still more of an order than a plea.

'It is easy for the King to be uncivil and demand to be forgiven,' I said.

'I don't demand.'

'No?' I folded my arms.

'Mistress Perrers…' Now he stepped in, and thrust the door closed at his back. 'You will doubtless accuse me of overbearing pride but I don't want an audience for this.' And he sank elegantly to one knee. 'I ask your compassion for my lack of chivalry. No true knight would have been as boorish as I was. Will you forgive me?'

He looked magnificent, like a knight from one of the illustrated books, kneeling in a blaze of blue and red and gold at the feet of his lady. Dressed deliberately, regally, to impress me, here was the King of England kneeling at my feet. What's more, he possessed himself of my hand and kissed it.

'No subject has ever challenged me before.'

'I know.'

'Well? Will you keep your King in suspense?' His expression was not that of a lover. The lines of irritation sharpened. 'I have missed you more than I should. You're only a slip of a girl! How could I miss you so much? And all you could do was scowl at me from the ranks of my wife's damned women. Or behave as if I did not exist.'

'Until you dismissed me from the room.'

'I should not have done that.'

'No. And I am not a slip of a girl. I am the mother of your son.'

'I know. Alice...' The formality was waning.

'Neither am I merely your whore. I give you more than the pleasures of the flesh. I thought you cared more for me than that, Sire.'

'I do. God's Blood, Alice! Have mercy. I was in the wrong.'

'We both agree on that.'

He released my hand and, still kneeling, spread his arms wide. 'I have learnt this for you, as any foolish troubadour would to woo his lady. How's that for love...?'

And he pressed his hands over his heart like the love-lorn troubadour and spoke the verse. Ridiculous, foolish, but there was no mockery in his voice or his face. It came from his heart, and with it a sadness, a poignancy for things past. Like youth that was gone for ever.

Fortune used to smile on me:
I didn't have to try:
Good looks and charming manners
Were mine in full supply:
She crowned my head with laurels,
And set me up on high...
But now my youth has faded;
I've seen the petals fall...

He stopped abruptly. 'To hell with verses! My manners have been less than charming. I have no excuse for either, but I beg your understanding.'

I refused to be beguiled. 'A Plantagenet, begging?'

The poignancy was gone. Back was the pride, the authority, even though he still knelt. 'Don't leave me in suspense, Mistress Perrers.'

'I would not dare. I have made my decision, Sire.' What mischief prompted me to keep him in suspense for one more moment? I touched his shoulder, with all the grace of the lady in receipt of her knight's love, to urge him to his feet.

'Well?'

'I forgive you. It is impossible to resist so fine a wooing.'

'Thank God!'

He drew me into his arms, carefully, as if I were some precious object made of glass. Or as if I might still reject him. His lips were cool against mine until I melted against him, and then his embrace became a brand of fire. I had missed him too.

'It's in my mind to give you a gift...perhaps a jewel. You have given me a son, a gift beyond price. I should show my gratitude.' His chin rested on the crown of my head, my hair heavy on his shoulder.

'No...not a jewel.'

'What, then?'

The thought had come immediately into my head, or perhaps it was always there. I knew what I wanted. 'Give me land and a house, Sire.' My insecurities never left me, and Greseley had trained me well.

'You want land?' I heard the surprise in his voice.

'Yes. It is in your gift to give it.'

'You would be a woman of property. Then it's yours. For Mistress Alice who shines a light into the dark corners of my soul.'

It took my breath away. A royal manor for my own, all I could have wished for. 'Thank you, Sire.'

'On one condition…'

I was suddenly wary. It never did to underestimate the Plantagenet.

'That you call me Edward again. I've missed that.'

The rock beneath my heart, which had been there since the day I had dropped my sables at his feet, melted away. 'Thank you, Edward.'

There was love and gratitude in the gift, and in my receiving it. I offered my lips, my hands, my body. All my loyalty. My absence had stirred Edward's passions and he had no thought of celibacy. He made love to me on my less than sumptuous bed that could barely contain his long limbs, and wrapped me again in my sable mantle. I was no longer just his whore. We both knew it. My challenge had awoken the King to the truth of our relationship. There was a permanence.

'I will never dismiss you,' he murmured against my throat in the dying of passion. 'You are my love. Until death separates us.'

'And I will never willingly leave you,' I replied. I meant every word of it. My admiration for him had reached new heights.

He gave me the little manor of Ardington, and as I placed the document into my coffer I acknowledged how much it meant to me, far more than the one I had stolen as my right from Janyn Perrers. Land was power, land was wealth, and Ardington, a jewel of a manor, was now mine. The glow of ownership spread through every inch of my body, as if I had drunk a cup of honeyed mead, until I could feel its heat in my very fingertips.

Lips pursed, I contemplated my new property as I sat on the coffer lid, stroking the glossy wood. Ardington was without doubt a prosperous manor, but not very large. If

Edward was willing to give me one property, then perhaps it would not be the last to fall into my hands. And if Edward was not moved to give me one, why should I not purchase my own? It did not surprise me that I was not satisfied, that I should desire more. I would not leave the comfort of my future to chance.

I carried a second child for Edward—a happy event. Another son, Nicholas. I was free to travel now as I wished to the manor where John grew and played and shouted in his games of knightly conquest. I had no fears that I would not be free to return to Court as it pleased me. My position might still be unacknowledged but it possessed a respectability of its own.

'And what will become of you?' I asked the mewling infant who resembled Edward as strongly as did his brother, John. 'What will be your path to wealth and power?' I thought of Wykeham. An excellent example for any boy. 'When you are older, I will introduce you to a sometime friend of mine.'

'What do I give you, in recognition of this new gift?' Edward asked, holding his son in his arms when he visited us. 'Don't tell me…'

Neither did I have to. He gave me the wardship of the lands of Robert de Tilliol and the gift of the marriage of his heir. It was extensive, four manors and a castle far to the north of England, with the promise of gold for my coffers.

Out of the ordinary, as a gift from the King to a Queen's damsel. It drew attention, but I could withstand the sidelong glances. The conspiracy of silence held fast, for Philippa's sake. I simply informed Greseley that his management on my behalf would take up more of his valuable time.

'I trust you will pay me well for my time, Mistress Perrers,' he wrote back in habitual complaint.

'I will pay you when I see the results,' I replied, then added, *'I will be astonished if you too do not benefit from these investments.'*

To receive back very promptly: *'As do you, Mistress Perrers. Your acquisitions are bringing you—and me— an excellent return.'*

I smiled at his final response. What an excellent man of business Greseley was.

Chapter Eight

A sense of unease touched my spine, like the light scratch of a lover's fingernail on delicate skin. I shivered, every sense alert. It faded as quickly as it had come, and I concentrated once more on the explosion of ill-temper unfolding before me.

This was a high-powered, formal reception, deliberately staged: King and Queen seated in high-backed chairs on the dais in the largest of the audience chambers at Westminster. Before them swaggered a young man, just entering his third decade, boldly clad with all the *éclat* of indulged youth. Despite his shining arrogance he bowed deeply, his entourage following suit. And what an impressive escort it was, weapons as opulent as the jewels and embellished tunics. Philippa beamed, but the King was not in a mood to admire.

'Why are you here?' he demanded.

'I can do no more in that God-forsaken, bog-ridden province.' The young man was not rebuffed. Undeniably handsome, there was a hardness, a carefully shuttered expression and a shocking lack of reverence. 'I wash my hands of Ireland and all to do with the bloody Irish.'

'Did you think it would be an easy task? What in God's name have you been doing?' Edward strode down from the dais to strike the young courtier on the shoulder, a punch of a fist, not entirely a sign of affection. 'Are you trying to destroy all my good work, leaving as soon as you meet opposition? Before God, Lionel!'

So this was Lionel. Edward's second son to survive the rigours of childhood. Handsome, stylish, ambitious and King's Lieutenant of Ireland for the past handful of years, he was as smooth and slick as a coating of goose grease on the chest of a snivelling child. Still, his unwarranted return had brought a flutter of excitement to stir the dark days of the Court. At least Lionel, newly made Earl of Clarence in Edward's birthday generosity, had brought a smile back to the Queen's face. For that I could look on him with more favour than I was at first inclined.

'That's unfair, Sire. I met opposition from the first day I set foot there.'

'I've a good mind to send you back as soon as you can saddle a fresh horse...'

'No, Edward...' Philippa could not stand. It was a bad day for her. 'He is our son.'

'And a thorn in my flesh! No son of mine would have abandoned his charge. We'll have the whole place up in arms before we can sneeze.'

'I see no cause for the peasants to object...' Lionel's voice had acquired an unpleasant whine.

'Of course they will object!' Edward continued to stand eye to eye. 'Your job was to keep the peace, not stir the hornet's nest!'

'Oh, Lionel...' The Queen stretched out her hands.

The young man promptly evaded his father and fell to his knees before the Queen, where he bowed his head in unctuous regret. 'Mother. Forgive me…'

'My dearest Lionel.'

'I can explain…'

'I'm sure there were reasons…'

'But will my father listen?' He angled a sly glance from his mother's face toward the King.

Ah…!

The chill, that same strange sensation of awareness, brushed along my spine again. And again I shivered, an unpleasant prickle of cold on nape and arm. Someone in this room was taking note of me, watching me. Someone had more than a passing interest in me. I looked around, over the men of Lionel's entourage, but nothing came to snatch at my gaze. I could see no face turned towards me. All were intent on the stand-off between King and errant son. And why should anyone single me out? I was simply one of the damsels, anonymous, faceless, to serve and support the Queen.

Yet the feeling remained. Someone had an eye for me.

'Your father will listen,' Philippa urged, soothed. 'But not now. Later. When we have celebrated your homecoming. It's five years since I saw you last.' Her face was luminous with maternal delight.

Edward expressed as little delight as he had admiration, but exhaled on a grunt. 'I suppose the recriminations can wait. Your mother's glad to see you. You need some lessons in managing a difficult province—not everything can be solved with a show of force and sharp-toothed legislation.' He closed his teeth on what was about to become a lecture in high politics. 'But we'll feast your return first.'

He gave the signal for the audience to end. As I began

to help the Queen to her feet, I felt that same scrutiny, as if it were stripping away my skin to peer into my soul. But only Wykeham was interested in my soul and he was still constructing battlements at Windsor. Quickly I looked up, around, determined to catch the culprit who dared to stare at me—and there he was. One of Lionel's coterie, his gaze pinned on me in a vulgar stare.

I refused to return the contact. I would not be intimidated. I allowed my gaze to rove innocently over the ranks as if I sought someone I knew. And all the time I was aware that his gleaming appraisal did not waver.

So be it. Without pretence, I returned his regard, stare for stare.

He was a bold man, for sure. He neither looked away nor smiled in apology. He was older than the Prince but by no more than ten years, to my assessment. A harsh face, not unattractive—if it were not for the saturnine lines drawn from nose to mouth. No, he was not a handsome man. Clean-shaven, I noted, not the usual fashion of the day, and his dark hair closer cropped than the prevailing mode. His eyes were unremarkable in colour, dark rather than light, but direct and with no embarrassment at being detected staring at one of the Queen's damsels. His jaw was disfigured by a faint scar that showed white against skin ruddy from recent campaigning. His clothes were of fine quality but functional, as was his sword, a good steel blade without decoration. As for the jewels of a courtier, alone of all the company he wore none, but I did not think that he lacked the means, rather the inclination. His mouth was set in an uncompromising line. I imagined he gave away no secrets—unless he wished to.

A soldier rather than a courtier, I decided. And, no, I did not know him.

I lifted my brows and he made a curt little inclination of

his head. It pleased me to give no acknowledgement what-soever, but turn my back on him to take the Queen's mis-sal into safekeeping as she made her slow progress to her rooms, Lionel beside her. I followed, feeling that stare con-tinuing to stab between my shoulder blades until we had left the room.

I did not like Lionel overmuch. I liked this man in Lionel's company who had had the impudence to single me out even less. He had too many dark corners for my liking.

In regal style, the King ordered a celebration. Edward revelled in celebrations. It was his delight to glory in splen-dour in which he could play the central role. Was there ever a King to match him, one who could prance and flap with supreme confidence in the gilded costume of a gigantic bird, purely for the entertainment of his children? But not on this occasion. This was a feast with a scant nod in the direction of music and dancing but little else: barely enough of a spectacle to drain the contempt for Lionel's failures in Ireland from Edward's face. Edward handed a purse of coin to Andrew Claroncel, his favourite minstrel, to end the singing barely before it had begun. All in all it promised to be a long evening. I took my seat below the high table with a sharp glance at the man who had been placed beside me on my right.

And my companion for the feast? The insolent man from the audience chamber. And I would have wagered my sables that it was no coincidence that he had the stool next to me. How had he achieved it? A bribe passed smoothly into the palm of Edward's steward? His eyes that raked my face— dark grey, I noted now at far too close quarters—were as audacious as I had first thought.

'Mistress Perrers.'

He stood until I had taken my seat, and it pleased me to make him wait, shaking out my skirts and disposing them elegantly. And wait he did, forcing me to admit that his manners were excellent. With a bland courtesy and a neat bow he finally sat, his actions brisk and controlled but with surprising elegance. So he had not spent all his life in the saddle; he had absorbed some of the skills of the courtier even in Ireland.

'You know my name, sir.' I met his open appraisal with studied disinterest. 'How is that?'

'You are not unknown at Court, mistress.' His voice was smoother than I had expected, and his reply interestingly enigmatic. I thought he masked the full truth. 'You are even spoken of in Ireland,' he added.

So he hoped I would ask what was said of me. I would not. I picked up my cup and drank from it.

'What I *don't* know,' he pursued, imperturbable, 'is what is your family?'

And I remembered, the past suddenly stark and bleak in my mind. The gossip of my infancy. The abandoned child. The bastard of a whore and a common peasant. The purse of gold coin that might or might not have ever existed. And I shrugged. None of it mattered now. But I resented his stirring of the memories.

'I have no family,' I remarked.

And I turned my back, leaning to exchange views with an elderly knight who sat on my left. It was astonishing, the range of topics I could find to discuss with this aging soldier, who looked askance at me and showed more interest in his food. I sighed, weary of his monosyllabic responses. And was unwise enough to glance in my silent companion's direction. He was watching me with rare humour.

'Well?' I should not have responded, but I did.

'Have you finished at last?' he asked, showing his teeth in a smile that made me instantly wary. 'I would not have believed your conversation could be so fatally dull, lady. Sir Ralph must have fallen asleep with the excitement of it. Even I could find it difficult to be enthusiastic about the length of time it takes the Court to transport itself from Havering to the Tower of London!'

'At least I had the good manners to talk to my neighbour, sir,' I retaliated. 'You have failed lamentably.' He had not exchanged one word with the damsel on his other side.

How did I know? Well, I had listened, hadn't I?

'I thought you might wish to know my name,' he remarked inconsequentially.

'Not particularly. But since we are trapped here together for the length of this meal, you may as well tell me.' I could not resist after all. Oh, I knew who he was well enough—I had used my time effectively between audience and feast—but it would not hurt to dent his male pride. 'Since you know *my* name, sir, it would be only common courtesy to tell me *yours*. Particularly since you arranged to sit beside me...'

With a glint of appreciation in his eye, he waited until a page had refilled both our cups with a smooth Bordeaux. He sipped slowly before placing it at his elbow. He would make me wait too. I might have smiled, but did not, suspecting that this man would be quick to detect weaknesses in friend and enemy alike, and be even quicker to make use of them. So far I had no idea which category I fell into.

'I am William de Windsor, madam.'

I gave a little impertinent lift of my shoulder, a gesture I had watched Isabella employ with finesse.

He was unimpressed. 'I have worked in Ireland, for the Earl of Clarence.'

Which told me no more than I already knew. He was

looking at me, still smiling, and to my discomfort I found that my blood flowed warmly into my face.

'Why were you staring at me?' I asked.

'I find you interesting.'

'Interesting? You make me sound like a new battle plan.'

'I think we are very alike, madam.'

'Are we? I don't see it, William de Windsor. You are far prettier than I.'

Which took him aback. He gave a bark of a laugh. 'And you are more forthright than I had anticipated. An unusual trait in a woman. In my experience, women usually dissemble.'

'I do not.' I imagined his experience with women was as wide as the Thames at Tilbury. 'Tell me why we are alike.'

'Oh, I don't think I will. Not yet.' He raised his cup in a little toast.

And I turned back to make another dull stab at conversation with Sir Ralph as if Windsor's reply did not engage my interest. But it did. He knew it did. He waited until my knight buried himself in his platter of roast venison and picked up the conversation as if there had been no hiatus.

'I've changed my mind, Mistress Perrers. You are a woman worthy of my confidence so I'll tell you the manner of our similarity. We are both ambitious.'

I stared at him.

'We are both self-interested.'

Again I kept my counsel, watching him over the rim of my cup.

'We both come from nothing.'

I would not respond. What was this man implying?

'Have you nothing to say to my observations, Mistress Perrers?'

'Do we both come from nothing, sir?'

'In the order of things, yes, we do. My father was a minor knight who made no name for himself in his long life. Windsor of Greyrigg, a poor backwater in Westmoreland with nothing to recommend it but sheep and rain. I abandoned Greyrigg as fast as I could and became a soldier, as any ambitious lad would. Fame, fortune, wealth—that's what I wanted and that's what I got. I fought at Poitiers and made a name for myself. In recent years I have attached my star to Lionel. He may not be perfect, but I consider him to be the most able of the royal brood.' I found myself laughing at so flagrant a criticism, regardless of who might be listening, as Windsor's eyes shifted to where Lionel sat next to the Queen, entertaining her with wit and sparkle. Then back to me.

'We have both made our way in the world. You as a damsel to the Queen—' his remarkable lack of expression told me that he knew exactly the nature of my relationship with the King '—and I as one of Lionel's counsellors.'

'And this is of interest to me, Sir William, because...?'

He frowned. 'I'm not sure, if truth be told. But for some reason I feel our stars might rise together.'

Now, that intrigued me, but I raised my brows in mild interest.

'My skills are in fighting and hard-headed administration,' he pursued without self-deprecation. 'What are yours? How bright will your star shine?'

I flushed. The implication was obvious, his stare as sharp pointed as Master Humphrey's boning knife, but I refused to be needled into indiscretion. 'I think my star shines very brightly without your intervention, sir.'

'Not as bright or as fast as mine, mistress. Military service allows an able and ambitious man to build up a goodly fortune.'

'Through embezzlement, corruption, ransom money and loot?' I had done more than a little investigating of my own.

He laughed, a cheerful note above the noise of the roisterers, causing a few eyes to turn in our direction. 'You have been gossiping, Mistress Perrers.'

'I have, Sir William.'

'And you knew my name from the first.'

'Of course.'

'Well, I can't blame you for it. It's a wise man who knows who he deals with.'

'And undoubtedly a wise woman.' I leaned a little to murmur in his ear. 'But I will not deal with you.'

He took the time to carve through a collop of beef, offering me some choice cuts from the platter. I shook my head.

'What do you want, Mistress Perrers?'

'I don't take your meaning, sir.'

'Well, I'm not speaking of the choice between the venison or the beef—the beef's excellent, by the by, you should try some. If you are a woman of good sense—and I think you are—you should consider where you will be in ten years. It's not a life position that you hold, is it? I'd say you could add up the years left to you at Court on the fingers of your two exceptionally capable hands. Life is finite, is it not?'

And because I understood him perfectly, and it was not the length of my life he was discussing, I followed his eye to where the King sat, leaning back in his chair, listening to Lionel make his excuses. Edward looked well and at ease, but the creep of age was relentless. As for Philippa, her life hung by a fraying thread. William de Windsor was right, damn him. I had no security of tenure here.

'He'll not last for ever, Mistress Perrers. What's for you then?'

My breath caught at this outrage, fear ousted by anger

that this man should read my thoughts. 'What is it to you?' I snapped. 'You're remarkably well informed in Ireland.' A knot of resentment made my tone hostile.

And he was oblivious to it. 'It pays to be so if you wish to make your way in life.'

'Some would say you've done quite well enough for a man of little consequence.'

'Oh, no. They would be wrong. My foot is barely on the ladder. I'll climb higher yet.'

Such arrogance! I was right in my first assessment. I did not like William de Windsor. I studied Edward, remembering his reaction to Lionel's mishandling of Ireland, recalling the disdain that had flattened his fine features as he had cast an eye over Lionel's minions. It gave me pleasure to turn the blade in Windsor's gut.

'I think you're wrong, sir. The King does not like you.'

'He may not like me—but he needs me.'

I choked on a sip of wine. Would nothing put him down? 'To do what?'

'To handle Ireland. It's not a task for a squeamish man. The King trusts my decisions. He may not like them but still he'll send me back to Ireland with even more power than I had under Lionel.'

'You are so sure of yourself!' I mocked.

'Am I not,' he replied, cheerfully unrepentant. 'And uncommonly perceptive. Take heed of my advice, Mistress Alice! Look to your future!'

And after that unwarranted familiarity, for the rest of the meal he gave his attention to the damsel on his other side, presenting me with a view of his perfect silk-covered shoulders, leaving me to the mercy of Sir Ralph, who gobbled the meat and bread as if the meal was his last, and I yawned with boredom. Until the trestles were cleared and

William de Windsor waited for me as we stood to leave the chamber.

'Take some more wise advice, Mistress Perrers?'

'I doubt it.' I was ruffled, intrigued beyond good sense, and was in no mood to be wooed by this wolf that did not even bother to adopt sheep's clothing.

'Who is your enemy? And don't say you have none.'

'You, probably.'

'I'm no enemy of yours, Mistress Perrers! Think of some others who would do you ill.'

'And if I do?'

'Be aware. Be cleverer than your enemy. That's the best advice I can offer. And if you ever need help to keep that enemy at bay, I am your servant. Don't let your unaccountable animosity towards me sway you.' He bowed and kissed my hand, even as I felt an urge to snatch it from him. 'And, no, you are not pretty. But before God, you are the most striking woman of my acquaintance. How old are you?'

Holy Virgin! 'I am twenty-two years. And how old are you, sir?'

'Thirty-seven,' he replied promptly.

'And are you wed, sir?' I asked sweetly, on impulse, while his fingers enclosed mine, warm and firm.

'Why?' He cocked a brow.

'I wondered if you had a son to inherit this great wealth you see yourself earning.'

'No. I have not. I am not wed.'

'Good. Or I would have to pity the poor lady you took to wife.'

His grin was sharp and uncomfortably attractive.

I remembered nothing of what I ate at that meal. The minstrels may as well not have opened their mouths for all the notice I took.

* * *

My exchange with William de Windsor at Lionel's feast was, it appeared, damnably on display, and I wished it undone. Not because I had said or done anything amiss. On the contrary, I had guarded my tongue in the presence of this knight I considered to be more than dangerous. But I found that my reactions to him were unstable. I had no wish to talk about him.

'What did that rogue Windsor have to say to you?' Eagle-eyed as ever for who said what to whom, Edward lost no time in interrogation, his growled demand taking precedence over any lover-like endearments when I sat in the middle of his bed. Perhaps there was more than a dash of jealousy in his unsubtle question. The Plantagenet had an eye to his own.

'Nothing,' I replied, hands folded neatly in my lap. 'Nothing that was not to puff up his own self-aggrandisement. The man speaks of no one but himself.' Not quite true, but close enough.

'Hmm.' Edward's brow furrowed in familiar disquiet. He began to loose my hair from its neat braids, although I thought his mind was not on the pleasures of the flesh. Windsor had even infiltrated the royal bedchamber. Edward tugged persuasively against my hair. 'What do you make of him?'

'I don't like him.'

'Neither do I. Would he be honest in government, d'you think?'

'I doubt it.'

Edward grunted a laugh. 'Well, that's plain enough. Would he be loyal to me?'

'Yes, if it brought him money and power.' Which was as honest as I could be.

'You seem to have read the man in some depth in so short a time.' The frown was back, now turned on me.

'It wasn't difficult.' I smiled ingenuously. 'A more boastful man I have yet to meet. He thinks you will make use of him—send him back to Ireland.' The frown deepened, so I turned my head to plant a kiss on his hands where they were wound into my hair. 'Will you use him?'

'I'm not sure. I think he's got a chancy kick in his gallop.'

So did I, and perhaps not for the same reasons.

Wykeham, returned to Court on the occasion of the feast, was less than polite. Our steps fell into line after Mass next morning. He had not officiated but had stood towards the back of the small body of courtiers. I had noticed him when I had glanced over my shoulders to see if Windsor was present. My lips had curled in high-minded satisfaction as I had noted that he was not. But Wykeham was there. And had waited for me by design.

'I see Windsor has singled you out,' he stated without preamble.

'It is good to see you again too, Wykeham!' I remarked. 'Perhaps you are even pleased to see me?' Wykeham had achieved remarkable elevation: Bishop of Winchester and Lord High Chancellor of England—high indeed for a man whose main interest was the supreme angle of a buttress to prevent a castle wall from collapsing on hapless soldiery. For his impertinence it pleased me to needle him a little. 'Or are you too important now to take note of such as me?'

'It's always an experience, mistress, to converse with you.' Wykeham refused to acknowledge my pert jibe. 'Now, why do you think Windsor is sniffing round your heels?'

'Is he?' I sighed. 'I have no idea.'

'I'll tell you why. To get the ear of the King.'

'Then he won't succeed. I'm no friend of Windsor's. Do you consider me gullible, to be flattered and taken in by every upstart ambitious office-seeker?'

I stared at him, hoping for an apology. There was no apology from the King's new Chancellor.

'I consider that you lack experience when dealing with a man of his mettle,' Wykeham announced, pausing between every word, the echoing thud of his steps providing counterpoint. 'He's proud, ruthless, avaricious, ambitious, opportunistic and quite without principle.'

'You omitted talented.' I smiled at his glower. 'And who isn't guilty of any one of those attributes at this Court, my lord?'

Wykeham scowled.

'Even you, sir. Pride and ambition seem to me to be fair game for a priest newly appointed Lord Chancellor.'

With a curtsey and a swish of my skirts, I left him standing at the door to the Queen's chambers.

Philippa pursed her lips. 'I'd not trust him. I wonder why Lionel finds him such good company.'

'I have no idea, my lady,' I replied.

'You did not find him entertaining at the feast?'

I took a steadying breath. Had our conversation gone unnoticed in *any* quarter?

'No. I can't say that I did, my lady.'

Good company? Entertaining? He had been positively sinister, the manner in which he had poked at my anxieties, undermining my carefully constructed self-possession. Within twenty-four hours of our meeting, it was as clear as the bell on Edward's clock. No one liked or trusted William de Windsor.

The question I was driven to ask myself: Did I? For

William de Windsor had an unpleasant habit of stepping into my thoughts and trampling any attempt I made to dismiss him.

I was present, in attendance on the Queen, when Edward summoned Lionel, flanked by Windsor, to a council of war, to hammer out the thorny matter of Irish administration. Philippa rarely concerned herself with matters of business or politics these days, but her concern for Lionel, and her fear for her husband's temper, brought her to the council table. I was not displeased. How could I have found a reason for being there, to watch Windsor in action, if the Queen had not made it easy for me? I wanted to hear Windsor's excuses for his own involvement in the Irish problems. I wanted to see him squirm.

The King did not use his words with care or reticence.

'God's Bones, Clarence! I thought a son of mine would have more backbone.'

'Do you know what it's like?' Lionel challenged, with what I considered to be an unfortunate degree of heat. 'The native Irish are untameable. The English born in Ireland are only loyal to the English throne when it suits them. The only lot you can rely on are the English born in England, and they, to a man, are nought but a rascally band of brigands.'

'So you hold the balance between them. Do you leave the province in turmoil and make a run for it, leaving them to wallow in their own blood?'

'I feared for my life.' Lionel's pretty face was unattractively surly.

'I expect you to communicate with them, not ban them from your august presence! I expect you to get them to trust you! And don't make excuses for him,' he snapped at Philippa, who had placed a hand on Edward's arm, as if it were possible to stem the tirade. 'Your son is a coward. You're lily-livered, Lionel.' As his ire grew, Edward became colder, the skin taut and white around his lips, his eyes pale with ice. 'In my day...'

I slid my gaze to William de Windsor. His attention appeared to be focused on the carved wainscoting behind the King's right shoulder. How would leaves and tendrils deserve such concentration? Then his eyes moved to mine... but I could not read them. Anger or caprice or even a cool distancing—impossible to say, but an unexpected self-consciousness came to me. I looked away, down at my clasped hands.

'As for the army.' The King brought his fist down hard onto the wood, causing the metal cups to ring and jump. 'I hear there's rape and pillage committed by my forces in my name. I hear they're forced to loot to maintain themselves. What happened to the revenues I directed towards Ireland? What happened to the taxes? Whose pockets did they disappear into...?' Without warning, Edward swung round in his chair to change his target. 'I hear no good of *you*, Windsor.'

And what would William de Windsor have to say about that? I was holding my breath. Did I want him to emerge victorious from this bout, or be buried under the justice of Edward's recriminations? I did not know.

Windsor was entirely undismayed, his harsh features an essay in composure. His voice held neither slick apology nor Lionel's aggression. I should not have been surprised.

'I admit the problems in the province,' he replied. 'I carry out orders, Sire, to the best of my ability. I was paid what was due to me. My lord of Clarence is King's Lieutenant, his is the authority. I am merely a loyal servant of the Crown.'

It was a formidable statement of innocence.

'You're quick to slough off any blame, Windsor,' Lionel retorted fast enough.

'I suppose you take no action on your own authority.' Edward waved his son to silence.

'No, Sire,' Windsor responded, undisturbed, outwardly at least, by either the King's contempt or Lionel's fury. Against my better judgement, he won my acclaim.

'You think Ireland's a lost cause?'

Windsor thought for a long moment, as if it was a new idea, studying his hands that were placed flat, palms down, on the council table before him. If he said yes, he would displease the King; if no, then Lionel's excuses would be undermined by one of his own officers. Which way would he jump? Windsor raised his eyes and cast his dice.

'No, Sire. I do not.'

He did not even look towards Lionel. He had known what he would say from the outset. He had his future entirely planned out, with or without Lionel. Had he not admitted to being ambitious, thoroughly self-interested? He might have omitted unscrupulous, but I recognised it.

'Ireland is dangerous, unpredictable,' Windsor stated. 'It's on the edge of rebellion. But I think it can be remedied. It just needs careful handling.'

'And you could do it.' The King made no effort to hide his distaste.

'Yes.'

'At a cost, I suppose.'

'As you say, Sire,' Windsor concurred. 'With enough power and wealth behind me, I'll whip Ireland into shape.'

'I'll consider...'

Edward fell into abstraction. His fingers began to tap on the table's edge. His deliberation stretched out in an endless, uncomfortable silence and his fingers stilled. His gaze, turned toward the window with its coloured glazing, seemed to lose its focus. Those around the table began to stir in their seats. Still the King made no pronouncement. I became aware of the slide of unnerved glances from one man to another around the table as Edward sat motionless, lost in some inner thought.

'Edward!' Philippa demanded his attention. A hand on his arm. And then apparently apropos of nothing: 'Edward! We must find Lionel a new wife.'

The King blinked, as if drawing back from the edge of some dark precipice.

'A wife! Yes, yes. So we must. I have it in mind.' He was uncommonly brusque, although I knew that Lionel's remarriage after the death of his young wife three years ago now was a matter of policy. A new royal wife would mean the prospects of a new alliance. 'But first this other matter...' Edward frowned, hesitated.

'Who will you send, Sire?' asked Wykeham, who had been an observer throughout of the clash of royal tempers and the unsettling royal indecision at the end. 'Who will go to Ireland?'

'I'll sleep on it.' Edward stood, so did everyone else, apart from the Queen. 'I'll give it some thought, Windsor. Come to me tomorrow, Lionel, and your mother and I will consider the merits of a new bride...'

The council was over with little to say for itself but a lot of bad blood and no outcome. In his youth, I thought that Edward would not have allowed it to be so. Over Philippa's shoulder, as I helped her to her feet, William de Windsor's eyes, with a victorious gleam, met mine. Glancing up, the Queen noticed.

She said nothing but grasped my hand as tightly as she was able.

* * *

After Mass the next morning I found Windsor leaning with studied negligence against the wall outside the Queen's apartments.

'Mistress Perrers. At last.'

His bow was a study in elegance. Or was it no more than a charade? Undecided, I made little attempt at courtesy with the merest bend of the knee. The Queen would have condemned me for my ill manners.

'Sir William. I did not see you at Mass.'

'That, Mistress Perrers, was because I was not there. Where are you going?'

I inhaled sharply. 'Why?'

'I thought I might escort you.'

'To what purpose?'

'Such grace! I had thought better of you, a Queen's damsel—and other things.' Oh, he was a worthy adversary! 'Allow me to accompany you, and you will discover my purpose.'

'If you wish.' I strode ahead of him on my errand for the Queen, but not for long. His energetic stride brought him abreast of me soon enough, closer than I liked. I made a show of tweaking the fall of my sleeve. 'Perhaps if you attended Mass, sir, prayer and supplication would aid your future.'

'Do you think? I doubt it.'

'Confession, then? It is said to be good for the soul.'

'I've found it overrated. Now, *you* could do much more for my future, Mistress Alice.'

'I?' I honoured him with a glance. 'What could I possibly do?'

'Persuade the King to send me back to Ireland, of course.'

Truly perplexed, I stopped and turned to look at him, taking in the uncompromising set of his mouth, the reckless gleam in his eye. 'I don't understand why you would wish to return to the scene of your previous debacle.'

'Debacle? No such thing. Have faith, Mistress Perrers—and tell the King I'm his man. The advantages of having a man of my knowledge there, on the ground, would be invaluable. Will you do it?'

I discovered a mood to be uncooperative. Just to see what he would do.

'No.'

'Why not?'

I knew more about this than I was saying. Should I tell him? Or let him find out for himself? No, I would drop the poison into his ear: it would please me to disturb the smooth exterior. 'There would be no purpose in my taking up your petition with the King, Sir William.' He was on guard in an instant. My smile was serene. 'The King will appoint the Earl of Desmond as the new Governor.'

'What?' Oh, he was shaken, his flirtatious manner cast aside. 'What?'

'Desmond. The King will make him the new King's Lieutenant,' I reiterated.

'Will he, by God?'

'A man of birth and high principle.' I added yet another layer.

'And a man with the intelligence of a gnat. So I've rid myself of Lionel to be saddled with Desmond!' All the warning I saw in the expressive face was a furious clamping of lips, before Windsor strode off, leaving me standing.

I laughed at the success of my ruffling. 'I see you did not seek me out for the pleasure of my company, Sir William,' I called after him.

At which he promptly marched back, brow black, but the formidable control was once more in place.

'Forgive me—although I think my behaviour might have been unforgiveable,' he snapped.

'It was.'

Windsor seized my hand and kissed my fingers, but his thoughts were elsewhere. 'At least Desmond—unless he's changed dramatically in recent months—will stir himself to do as little as possible and leave the ordering of affairs to me. It could be worse. I could be saddled with some interfering old goat who couldn't recognise an insurrection if it fell on his foot…'

He was striding off again before I could think of anything more to say.

Windsor was at Mass next morning. He returned my regard with an atrocious parody of religious solemnity, just as his concentration on the raising of the host was unsurpassed. I was impressed with his apparent unquestioning reverence in God's presence.

Until the end. His grin was quite satanic.

And I was impressed for quite other reasons.

Edward surprised me. Without any advice from me, he ordered Windsor back to Ireland to aid the newly appointed Governor, the Earl of Desmond. Thus a little subtle balancing, I surmised, keeping all parties satisfied and putting an able man at Desmond's right hand. A politic move, without doubt. So Windsor was to go. I did not know whether to be relieved or disappointed that so troublesome an influence should be removed from my life. The decision had more than surprised me.

'I thought you didn't like him,' I remarked to Edward when he told me he was planning to send the thrice damned but clever bastard back to Ireland where he might, with luck, receive his just deserts, skewered to the heart by the sword of an Irish rebel.

'I don't. But he understands Ireland.'

'And you don't fear he'll use your confidence in him to feather his own nest?'

'Of course he will. But he's not without talent.'

'Will you send him soon?' I enquired.

'The sooner the better. It's a conflagration in Dublin, waiting to happen.'

So William de Windsor's visit to the Court would be a short one. Good riddance! I decided. But I would make it in my way to see him before he departed. And why would I do that? Had I no sense?

I had no idea. And sense was definitely in short supply.

I did not know where to find him. Pleading a sore tooth to account for my absence from the solar, I tried all the possibilities, and some I knew to be impossible. Chapel—unlikely; stables, audience chambers, a group of hard-drinking knights in one of the antechambers—now that I would have expected. No sign. Had he gone already? Had he left at the crack of dawn under royal orders to get back to the source of his ambitions as soon as possible?

My heart, inexplicably, plummeted.

You fool, I remonstrated. He is nothing to you but a thorn beneath the skin. He could not even find the time to bid you farewell. He likes you as little as you like him.

And yet I had found an unaccountable delight in our cut and thrust that gave no quarter.

I returned to the stables, to be told that he had not gone. His rangy roan was still there, and his pack animals. So where? Some whore's chamber, perchance. I did not think so. Where might he spend his last day at Court?

And I knew.

Within minutes I was standing, my ear pressed to the door, outside the room. And beyond the door I could hear the rumble of voices. Difficult as it was to distinguish them, I elected to wait to find out, still wondering why it meant so much to me. Before I had settled on an answer that did not increase my sense of self-delusion, the door opened and there was my quarry stepping into the corridor. From an interview with Edward's treasurer. Of course he would be discussing finance…

'Mistress Perrers, as I live and breathe!' He bowed.

'Sir William.' I curtseyed.

'I leave tomorrow.'

'I know.'

'And you have come to find me to say farewell. How kind of you!'

'Wasn't it.'

'You could make my final night here memorable. Unless you have other engagements.'

I stiffened, every sense alert, as when a hare saw the hounds and gathered its whole body to run for its life. My mind repeated the monstrous invitation—how dared he presume? How dared he misread my intentions towards him? My first instinct was to follow the example of the ill-fated hare with the dogs at its heels. But Windsor's hand was beneath my elbow and he was leading me towards an unoccupied sunny window embrasure. My skin beneath his hand felt tender and I knew that hot colour was rising in my cheeks. A sign of anger, I assured myself, of disdain for this man who would either mock or denigrate me. No, I would not allow him to dictate my actions, just as I would never accept his unspeakable offer. I pulled away from him and, shocked as I was at the instant physical response that tightened like a fist in my belly when he merely changed his grip on my wrist, my reply was icy.

'Do you think I would slide into your bed, Sir William? Betray my King?'

'I don't know. Would you?'

'We are not all unprincipled.'

'Oh, I think most of us can be, to one degree or another.' An uncomfortable echo of what I had said to Wykeham. His stare was brazen. 'Is he a good lover? Does he satisfy you?'

'You are impudent, sir. And I'll not betray the King.'

No, I would not betray Edward with one such as William de Windsor, but he was a damnably attractive man for all his impudence. And he surprised me by a sudden change in direction that I was to discover typical of him, a clever stratagem to unsettle the listener.

'No. I don't suppose you will. Will you do one thing for me, Mistress Perrers?'

'Since you obviously don't desire me in your bed, what would that be?'

'Keep me acquainted with Court opinion and any change in royal policy in Ireland.'

So! His interest was political, not personal. Piqued at his rapid rejection of my charms, I asked, 'What's it worth?'

'Do I have to pay you?'

I assayed a simper.

And William de Windsor kissed me. Not a kiss of passion, not of affection, but a firm pressure of lips at the corner of my mouth as if a promise of what might be.

And in instant response, without thought, I struck him with the flat of my hand against his cheek.

Windsor gave a shout of laughter. 'Sweet Alice! Such lack of control!'

'Such lack of respect!' I was shocked equally by both

his action and mine, and fought to claw back the control. My heart was beating faster, my blood was hot, nothing to do with the heat of the sun through the glass. 'I see you've learnt your manners amongst the sluts of Dublin.'

'I match my manners to my company, mistress.'

His gaze disrobed me down to my skin. I reached out to strike him again, fast as a snake, but he caught my wrist, and dragged it to his mouth, kissing the soft skin where my blood beat like a military drum.

'Tempestuous Alice! But seriously.' He released me as fast as he had taken possession. 'Keep me informed. And get what you can for yourself. Without the King or Queen to cushion the blows, your enemies will swoop and swallow you up. Unless your goal is to return to the gutter, fill your coffers now.'

'I'm not so mercenary.'

'We're not discussing something so trivial as mercenary, woman! It's self-preservation. If you don't look to yourself whilst the power is to hand, no one else will. And if you're thinking, "Does this make me too hard, too avaricious?" then consider this. Who will give you a moment's thought the day that Edward goes to his grave?'

I shook my head, horrified by the picture he had thrust so forcefully into my mind.

'Answer me, Alice.'

For a moment I saw compassion in his face. I hated to see it, but I replied with the truth. 'No one.'

With Philippa and Edward dead, the Prince would wear the crown, and Fair Joan would be his consort. There would be no place for me in Joan's Court.

'Did you think to be damsel to Joan the Whore?' Windsor asked.

His crude words, startling me with their mirror image of

my own thoughts, drove home my predicament. It was the last thing I could envisage. As long as she was in Aquitaine I need not fear her, but returned to England she would be no friend to me. I recalled her scorn. Her disdain of all things low born. Her contempt for me.

'Even provision for your sons will not be secure. Have you thought of *that*?'

My hot blood ran cold and sluggish, but I tried to ward it off.

'I am not in any danger. Neither am I without resources.'

'Two tuns of Gascon wine for service to the Queen? Edward is hardly generous!' His laughter was hard and humourless.

'I have property...' I insisted.

'Enough to allow you to live as you do now?' Windsor fired back.

'I have manors and town property...' I clung on desperately to what I had hoped would keep penury at bay.

'So your manors and town properties will keep the wolf from your door, will they, in the hard times? You've had a taste of life cushioned by royal wealth. Will you be willing to accept less? It's a long winter when you have nothing. I should know. But if you will not be open to my advice...'

'I never said that.'

'No. You didn't. But give it some thought.'

I studied the harsh lines of his face. The marks of his experience, not all pleasant.

'Why do you do this?' I asked. 'Why do you bother yourself with my future? I am nothing to you.'

With one hand he raised my chin, tilting my face to the light, and I allowed it since I had asked the question. But what would I make of the answer?

'In all honesty, I don't know,' he said softly, as if searching in his mind for a reason that did not wish to be discovered. 'You're cross and perverse and not my sort of woman at all. But for some reason I would not wish to see you bereft. Now, why should that be?'

I chose not to answer that question. Were we both dissembling? My own emotions were inexplicably in turmoil. Almost in a panic I turned to go, but his hand sliding down my arm to my wrist stopped me. I looked back over my shoulder.

'Well?'

'We'll not meet again.'

For which I am eternally grateful, sprang to my lips. And I saw him brace himself, the smallest stiffening, against what I would say. His fingers around my arm tensed, his eyes darkened as if my reply mattered. So—perversely, as he had accused—I said nothing. And the rigidity of his shoulders relaxed.

'Have you nothing to say?'

'Goodbye, Sir William.'

'Well, at least it's apt.' His mouth had a wry twist. 'And you will write?'

'I'll consider it.'

His hand slid further until he closed it around my hand.

'This is too public…' I remonstrated.

'I care not. And neither do you. I admire you, Mistress Alice. I admire your strength and your loyalty to the King. I admire your singlemindedness and your refusal to be influenced by any man's advice—until you know what is right for you.' I must have looked my amazement. Was that how he saw me? 'I admire your confidence.' He pressed his lips to the palm of my hand. Windsor looked through his lashes. 'Do you admire me at all, Mistress Perrers?'

'No.'

He laughed. 'Which does not change to any degree what I feel for you. I admire your honesty, even though I do not always believe what you say.'

With a little tug on my hand he drew me closer and planted another kiss, this time full on my mouth, with lips that were firm and cool and entirely seductive. It lasted for no time, but it had a warmth that stroked across my skin.

'Farewell, Alice.'

A bow, a wave of his feathered hat and he was on his way to Ireland.

Thank God!

I could not banish the man from my thoughts.

What did I feel for Windsor? I had as little understanding of that as he had for his feelings for me. I knew my feelings for Edward with the intimacy of long association. Admiration. Respect. Compassion. An affection born of deep gratitude. Even—when I was in a mind to admit it—the eroticism of forbidden fruit.

But this man who had pushed his way into my consciousness? A far harsher emotion stabbed at me when I recalled the pressure of Windsor's mouth against mine, against my palm. I did not wish to put a name to this emotion but he made my flesh shiver and I was honest enough to admit that it was not in distaste.

I wished he had not gone back to Ireland.

Do you admire me at all, Mistress Perrers?

Go away!

You could make my final night here memorable.

I was delighted that he had gone. I would never betray Edward. My present and my future rested in Edward's generous hands and Philippa's need for comfort, not in the hard grip of a bold, mannerless man—little better than a lout—who had few friends and fewer morals. William de Windsor was not for me. I scratched at the spot on my palm as if I could erase the memory. There! It was gone. I need think no more about him.

But I did. He left with me a memento of his deplorable regard and his unwarranted warnings of those who had no cause to love me. In the early morning after his departure, I opened my door to a palace servant—one of the many grooms, to judge by his overpowering aroma of horse and straw. He bowed, and handed over a leather leash attached to a very youthful wolfhound. And left before I could question him.

'Oh.'

It—she—sat obediently and looked at me. I looked back. No letter or introduction came with this creature that eyed me like a juicy bone. First a palfrey, now a hound. Suddenly I, who had no affinity with animals, had acquired a surfeit of them.

'I should tell you,' I informed the creature. 'I have no love of dogs, however noble their breeding.'

Unblinkingly, she continued to regard me.

'Why do I know that Windsor sent you to me? And what do I do with you?'

She panted enthusiastically, tongue lolling.

'Send you back to the stables? No place for you in a *lady*'s rooms.'

The wolfhound sighed.

'As you say! Since I am no lady, I suppose you will stay. Does Windsor think I need a guard dog? But to protect me from whom, I wonder?'

So he did think I might be in danger. I would consider that later.

'What do I call you?' I asked as I walked cautiously round

the animal. She sank to her belly and closed her eyes in a patch of warm sun. 'Windsor, perhaps?'

A touch of whimsy. They both shared a knowing expression and more than a hint of ruthless will, even when the creature was half-asleep. As soon as I stepped away, she lifted her head, following my movements with heavy-browed eyes.

'I suppose I had better keep you. And I cannot in all conscience call you Windsor. It had better be Braveheart instead.'

When I sat, Braveheart rested her great head on her paws and slept, and I set my mind to pick apart Windsor's warnings—a far more valuable occupation, I chided, than recalling his kisses. I could not afford to brush aside Windsor's warnings as inconsequential.

Time to contact the Tabard at Southwark again.

Greseley had continued to be busy in his and my interests, even to the extent of a little private money lending. I did not bother overtly with the details of this, leaving my clerk to his own devious devices, only discovering my involvement when the documents of the pertinent court case were sent to me in absentia. One Richard de Kent, a London fishmonger, had been sued by Greseley for return of two hundred marks that I, through Greseley, had lent him. Far more important, my agent had used income from the Gracechurch property to buy for me a life interest in the manor of Radstone in Northamptonshire. And of course I had Ardington…

But I had the ambition to buy more. How incredibly seductive was the ownership of a handful of acres here, a manor house with gardens and outbuildings there, a row of town houses in London or the lease of a castle in the north. The possibilities shone as bright as the North Star, and since the means were available, how could I resist? I might have been born with nothing, but I swore as I knelt beside Edward for early Mass that I would not die empty-handed. Was the serene face of the Blessed Virgin frowning at me? I did not think she was. No, I realised as I clasped my hands in prayer and her gentle smile encompassed my wayward thoughts. I would never be satisfied until my manors numbered the years of my life.

With a sum of money borrowed from the royal treasury— with Edward's permission—I wrote my orders to Greseley. The manor of Meonstoke was acquired for me. My future suddenly seemed far less insecure.

And what do you have to say about that, Sir William?

I thought he would find something suitably disparaging. If our paths were ever unfortunate enough to cross again.

Chapter Nine

The royal castle of Windsor with its massive walls and towers: a magical place. Mirrored rooms glittered with reflected light, or, under Wykeham's flamboyant hand, allowed roses to riot from floor to ceiling in blue and green and vermilion. Too garish for my taste but much admired, and with enough gold leaf to cover Edward's warship, the *Christopher*, from prow to stern. The summer lay softly on this sumptuous statement of royal greatness, but the Queen of England lay immobile on her bed. Even the smallest movement of head or hand racked her with pain. I could do nothing for her. The willow bark now had little effect against such corruption of the body. It had not soothed her for many months and the frequency of the draughts was a nagging concern to me. But Philippa begged for the cup of bitter wine and sank gratefully into sleep when she could tolerate her waking hours no more. I sat with her as she moved between delirium and a keen awareness that demanded the truth. The damsels were not slow to leave me the duties of the sickroom.

I was not sorry. Did I not owe everything to this generous woman who had so much love in her heart, who had
a spirit as strong as a mighty oak, as soft as the feathers
on a dove's breast? Who had seen enough in me to lift me
from obscurity to my strange life in the royal household? I
owed her *everything*. No, I was not sorry to sit with her as
her life ebbed.

'Is Isabella here?' she asked.

'No, my lady. She is in France with her husband.'

'Of course.' Philippa's lips tried ineffectually to smile.
'I'm astonished she hasn't washed her hands of him.' A
breath of a laugh. Then: 'Where is Lionel…? Ah, no… I
remember now…' Tears sprang to her eyes, for her beloved
Lionel was dead. In the wine-fuelled aftermath of a glorious marriage in Italy to the Visconti heiress, Lionel had
succumbed to some nameless fever. Philippa sighed. 'I am
so weary, Alice…'

I bathed her face and lips, my mind gripped with fear.

'Read to me from my missal. The prayer to the Virgin…'

So I did, and it gave her comfort.

'I am dying, Alice?' The assent stuck in my throat. 'Will
it be long now?'

'No, Majesty. It will not be long.'

'Bless you. You have always been honest. Is the King
still in England?'

'Yes, my lady. He is in London—at the Tower.'

'I need him.' Her breath barely stirred the air. 'Send for
him. Tell him…tell him not to delay.'

'I will, Your Majesty. Immediately.'

'Will Edward blame me?' she wept. 'For diverting him
from his duties in France?'

'No, my lady.' I wiped away the tears, a task that she was
unable to do for herself. How could I not weep with her?

'The King will never blame you. He loves you more than life. The King would never forgive you if you did not tell him how you suffered.'

I thought about Edward's sense of duty. It was what I admired in him. When the French had marched into Ponthieu and threatened the security of Gascony, Edward had abandoned his policy of peaceful coexistence and begun to plan for a new war, reclaiming his relinquished title of King of France. Some might whisper that he was too old to plan such a sustained invasion—not like the old days—but what choice did a man of such pride have? The Prince, still laid low from some nameless virulent fever that had stricken him of late, remained too weak to lead an army, so therefore Edward must resume the mantle of command. He was King. All that he had achieved in his lifetime must not be thrown away. So, in that very month, he had sent John of Gaunt to Calais. Edward and an army would follow. Even now he was at the Tower, organising the invasion.

But now he would not go. He would come to Philippa's side, whatever the cost. England's power in France would weigh lightly in the balance if the Queen were in need. I prayed he would be in time. The shade of death squatted in the shadows in the corner of the room, obscene in its presence, growing stronger as the days passed.

Edward arrived by royal barge that beat its way against the tide along the Thames and I went down to the landing stage with others of the household to greet him. Perhaps to warn him. I had not seen him for six weeks and the change in him was unmistakeable.

Oh, I doubt it was noticeable to a subject who simply saw the outer glory of the King of England. Still fair and upright, still handsome with regal presence, he had a smile and a word for those who had rowed him from the Tower. His tunic flattered his broad shoulders, the golden lions stitched against the red were truly resplendent, and the sun gilded the grey in his hair as the barge was manoeuvred into the river landing.

But I was aware of the change, from the moment he stood up from his seat at the stern. Once he would have stood for the whole journey, dignified but approachable, the leader of his people, to see and be seen. Now he sat. Furthermore—I saw it even if no one else did—that he took his page's arm as he stepped from barge to land, not heavily but enough to give him stability. Stretching as if his limbs were stiff, his first strides were uneven. The lines around eyes and mouth were more deeply engraved than when I had kissed him farewell. Oh, Edward! How grief and the passage of years can leave their mark. How the burden of duty can wear away the body's resilience. My first thought was to go to him, to kiss away the sorrow that darkened his eyes, but I kept my distance. This was no time for greetings from the King's lover. I had no place in this homecoming and I knew nothing I could do would assuage Edward's suffering. For a moment I wished I had not come, but stayed at the Queen's side where I had an acknowledged role. And I felt the cold foreboding for the coming days.

No Queen. No place. No position. No reason for Alice Perrers to remain at Court, unless the King…

I pushed away the bleak thought as fast as it assaulted me. Nothing new here, merely the imminent inevitability of it. Now, in this moment, all that mattered was Edward's reunion with his stricken wife.

Lord Latimer, the steward, bowed. I curtseyed. Edward acknowledged the waiting group of courtiers. I actually took a step backwards. But the King's eyes sought me out.

'Mistress Perrers.'

'Your Majesty.'

'Speak to me of my wife.' His voice was low and harsh with unshed tears. 'She is dying?'

'Yes, Sire.'

'Does she know?'

'She is aware. She regretted asking you to come.'

'I could not leave her. How could I? She is everything to me.'

'Yes, Sire.'

I swallowed hard. The heart-rending affirmation could not have made my situation clearer. I stepped back again as the King turned to stride up the steps towards the castle, vigour restored with the urgency to get to Philippa's side before it was too late. But he halted with his foot on the bottom step and looked back.

'Come with me. She will need you.'

And although I shrank from it, I obeyed.

So I was witness to their reunion. It hit me harder than I could have imagined, illuminating as it did the lack in my own life. The love shone between them, undiminished by the prospect of death. Briefly the image of William de Windsor stole into my mind, whether I wished it or not— typical of the man himself. There was something between us, but nothing like this. I could not imagine love like this, beyond the physical, beyond the passage of time. Philippa raised her hand from the bed linen and placed it into the hand of the King, her lord and her love. Edward fell to his knees at her side.

'Dear Edward. You came.' The words were slurred but I heard the pleasure in them.

'Did you ever doubt that I would?'

'No—Alice said you would come.' She glanced momentarily to where I stood beside the door but I had no importance for her. All her focus was on the man at her side. 'What a marriage we have had. All these years.'

'I would wed you again. Tomorrow. This very minute.' Edward smoothed the thinning matted hair back from her brow.

'And you have as much charm as ever.' The gasp might have been a laugh.

'You are all I ever wanted.'

It struck harder than ever. I stepped back against the tapestry—I could feel the stitching and the underlying stone solid against my back—to give them space. *You should not be here!* My conscience was implacable.

'When we are separated…' I heard the Queen whisper.

'No!'

'When we are separated,' she repeated, 'will you grant me three requests, my dear lord?'

Edward inhaled. 'Lady. Whatever you ask, it will be done.'

'Then—settle my debts. I can't bear that they be left unpaid.'

'You always were extravagant.'

The gentleness in Edward's reply caused my tears to overflow.

'I know. Will you do it? And then fulfil the gifts and bequests I've made.'

'I will.'

'And at the last—Edward, my love, will you lie beside me in Westminster Abbey, when your time on earth is finished?'

'Yes. I will.'

Edward bent his brow to her hand. They remained like that, the room still about them, and I left them to their solitude, closing the door quietly. They did not notice. They did not need me.

I walked unseeing through the antechambers, making my way to climb to the deserted wall-walk. My thoughts were appallingly self-absorbed but I could not redirect them. I wept for the two I had just left, but where would I lie when I was dead? Who would lie beside me, at his or my request? I was as alone and friendless as I had always been except for this fast-fading woman and her broken husband. Who could I call friend in the royal household? No one. Who would even have a thought for me? William de Windsor might— but his was a self-interest as strong as mine. Wykeham would condemn me.

So I wept out of grief for Philippa and Edward and my-self. And out of terror of a future I could no longer see.

The end came on the fifteenth day of August, when Wykeham gave the Queen the last sacrament. We were with her, Edward and young Thomas of Woodstock and all her damsels who wept bitter tears, as did the household from falconer to meanest scullion. Philippa had touched the life of everyone. I prayed for her comfort and her soul, touching for the final time her foot beneath the sumptuous bedcover with its embroidered sprawl of Plantagenet lions. Near the end, she raised her hand to beckon me, and whispered, her words barely stirring the air between us.

'Promise me!' she begged.

'I promise.'

Did she know what she had asked of me? Did she under-stand how heavy the burden would become? I think she did not, yet I would do it. I would continue to repay the debt I owed her if it was at all in my power.

The King held the Queen's hand as she drew her final breaths, kissed her forehead.

'Edward. My love. What a family we made together...'

Edward bowed his head and wept unashamedly. I might own his affection, his respect, the demands of his body. Philippa owned his heart and always would, even to her grave. Edward had lost his lode star. His rock. His clear place in the firmament.

So passed the Queen from this life. It was as if the great castle had been hollowed out. Windsor became a dark place. Edward walked the rooms and corridors like a ghost, all his vigour and Plantagenet spirit eclipsed by an impossible loss. He did what he must, what was necessary, but it was as if a husk of a man issued orders. And he did it alone. I, his mistress, had no role in these preparations for his wife's final resting place. His dear Philippa's embalmed body would be transported to the Tower by royal barge along the Thames, and from there in procession through the streets before reaching Westminster, so that all might witness and mourn her passing. She would be buried in the chapel of Edward the Confessor, as she had wished, in the tomb long prepared for her, with an effigy that showed her as she was, a plain woman with an abundance of love in her heart.

In a voice devoid of emotion Edward acknowledged all the Queen's gifts: the Exchequer would pay me—and the other damsels—the sum of ten marks twice yearly at Easter and Michaelmas for services to the Queen. We were given a length of black cloth for mourning garments. I was not singled out in any way.

So it was finished.

What now?

You are the King's lover. That will not change.

But Edward did not want me in his bed. He never sent for me, not once in all those endless days when I could see his suffering. My heart reached out to him but it was as if he was shrouded in an impenetrable mist from which he was unable or unwilling to break free. He did not want me, did not need me, and so I must wait to see my fate.

The damsels had a final task to complete, and I simply took my place amongst them. At the King's command we packed away all the Queen's possessions. The hangings and covers of her magnificent bed were cut and stitched into vestments for the clergy of York Minster in memory of that exultant day when Edward and Philippa were wed there. It kept our hands busy if not our minds, and I could not join in the mindless twitterings of the young women who would go home to their families unless another Court position opened up for them.

And then it was Christmas, a festivity that we did not celebrate. The dancing chambers remained silent, dust eddies patterning the floors. In concern for the King, Gaunt returned from Calais to spend the doleful season with his father, shut away at the hunting lodge at Kings Langley, but Edward did not hunt. Chancellor Wykeham, who travelled frequently on royal business between Windsor and Kings Langley, wore a troubled expression. I remained at Windsor, with the earthly remains of the Queen. I did not see Edward again until I accompanied Philippa's embalmed body to the Tower in the first days of the new year. When Edward stood beside Philippa's coffin as it was placed in the tomb, there seemed to be as little life in his still, silent figure as there was in the body they finally laid to rest. His face was grey and worn, head bowed, fingers flexing convulsively on the hilt of his sword. Age had placed its hand on Edward with cruel precision.

As the solemn words came to an end I watched Wykeham at the King's side make the sign of the cross. His gaze moved slowly from Edward's ashen face to mine, then dropped when he saw me watching him, as if it had been a mere chance meeting of eyes.

I did not think it was.

The solemnities were to last at Edward's orders for six days. I thought, in despair, that for Edward they would never end. He returned to the Tower and shut himself away from everyone in his rooms.

What was I to Edward in these dark days? That was simple enough to describe. I was nothing. I did not exist. I saw him only once and that a chance passing in an antechamber.

Edward walked through with Wykeham, the same easy stride, but there the similarity ended. There was no appreciation of his surroundings, no ready word for those who came within his recognition. I think he recognised no one.

I curtseyed.

Without even a glance, Edward continued to stride ahead with some grim intent.

'Mistress Perrers is here, Sire,' Wykeham murmured to the King, surprising me. He actually touched the King's arm to claim his attention.

Edward stopped. 'Mistress Perrers.'

His eyes slid over my face but they did not linger, did not hold my gaze. His bow had been perfunctory, such as he might make to the lowliest of his servants who performed some menial task for him.

'Sire!' I smiled, struggling to mask my concern, willing him to respond. 'I trust you are well.'

There was no answering smile. Was this the man whose ready laughter had echoed from the roof in the Great Hall at Havering? Sombre black had replaced the crimson and gold of his tunic. Giving no reply, he proceeded toward the door, presenting me with a good solid view of his back. The lover who had stripped the gown from my body and wrapped me in furs was far removed from this man who would leave me without a second thought. All I could do was watch him, in astonishment and despair. Wykeham shrugged helplessly and followed. I was left standing alone.

It seemed that Philippa was not the only one to be interred in Edward the Confessor's chapel: the King's heart was there too. It was as if a hand had been slapped down to still the vibrating strings of a lute.

'Where's the King? It is imperative that I see him.'

'The King is in his private chamber. He will not see you.'

If I heard such an exchange once in those weeks after Philippa was laid to rest, I heard it a dozen times and the answer, delivered in the bleakest of tones by William Latimer, steward to the royal household, was always the same, whether the petitioner was noble or commoner.

'His Majesty will see no one.'

A light had been extinguished in Edward's heart. Abandoning London, he shut himself away in his rooms at Havering where Philippa had loved to stay, letting matters of government slide. The problems in France, where the Prince was increasingly under attack and still not restored to health, might not have existed for all the interest he took. The country shivered under ice and snow as the rooms of the palace echoed in a weird desolation. The Court whispered, uncertain, in a grip of gloom. A country without its head, without its King. Without leadership.

And what of me, my days as a damsel at an end? Philippa's ladies had dispersed to their families or to other noble households where their skills were in demand as confidante or companion. Not I. The pattern of my life hung on the decision of this King who had shut himself away, and I feared the worst. I had never felt so alone, not even when standing in the street, a new widow. At least Greseley had come to find me there. No one saw my need at Havering. Sleep forsook me and I lay awake, planning a future that suddenly had no structure. I would never be homeless, I had enough squirreled away to guard against such an eventuality, but I could no longer envisage my future. Did I really wish to bury myself in some country manor, alone except for a handful of servants, after tasting the sweet delights of court life? I shuddered at the prospect.

You will be lonely without Edward, a voice whispered in my head with terrifying accuracy. I had no friends. Without Edward, I would be truly cast adrift.

I wrote to William de Windsor, as I had promised, informing him of the lack of policy towards Ireland and the reason for it, and perhaps to tell someone of my own insecurity.

> *The King gives no direction to government. I doubt he thinks of Ireland at all. You are your own man, free to administer affairs as you wish. I think you may expect no more information from me. I fear my days at Court are numbered.*

And then on a whim—perhaps an ill-considered one:

> *I miss your forthright conversation, Sir William. Sometimes I wish you were recalled again to London*

to answer for your sins. I think I might give you a
hearing. At the risk of sounding weak and destroy-
ing your expressed admiration of me, I have no one
to talk to here.

Such was my isolation. I sent the letter but had no knowledge of its arrival.

We were a Court in waiting, for Edward to emerge from
his mourning and take up his sword once more. Did not
King Arthur sleep, to return to England in her hour of need?
Surely Edward would do the same.

He did not.

I tried to reach him, only to find a guard on his door. I
was not even announced. I wrote to Edward, persuading
Latimer to ensure my plea was delivered.

Don't shut me out, my lord. Let me talk to you. Let
me give you solace. We both suffer from the loss of
your dear wife. We can mourn together.
Remember what we have been to each other.
Allow me to return to your side.

My pen hovered over the page as I considered whether to
tell him of the child that grew in my belly. I did not. Latimer
took the note but there was no reply.

'Did he read it?' I asked.

'I don't think he did.' Latimer's face was stark with fur-
rows of concern. 'It is impossible to reach him. He won't
see anyone.'

What now? Short of running the guard through with his
own sword and battering down the door, I could achieve
nothing. It broke my heart to leave Edward floundering in
this trough of despondency. Who would talk to him? Who

would read or play chess with him? Who would entice him out of the black pit that he had fallen into?

'Get him to see me!' I ordered, even though I had no authority of my own to order anything. I almost laughed at the expression on Latimer's face. He was unsure whether I was an abomination in the sight of God and man or a heavenly courier sent to release the King from his travails. I closed my hand on his forearm, gripping hard. 'Tell the King I carry his child, if you have to. And if you can't, get Wykeham to do it. But do whatever it takes to get me into the King's presence!'

Latimer eyed me.

'Do it, Latimer.'

Do it! For all our sakes!

Well, my vehemence had some effect. We walked, Wykeham and I, Braveheart pattering after us, through the antechambers into the old section of the palace that was rarely used. At last the Chancellor had come to my room to summon me. Except that this was not the way to the royal apartments.

'Where are we going?' I asked.

He did not reply, striding so rapidly, robes billowing, that I could barely keep up. His expression was stormy, his features tight with displeasure.

'Is it Edward?' I asked. 'Has he asked for me?'

'No.'

Hope died. 'Then where…?'

'Just shut up and wait, woman…'

He marched on in surly mood, with me beside him, my mood was as sombre as his, but in truth I was intrigued. The path to our destination was empty and silent, the walls stripped of their tapestries, the floors unswept. I noticed with interest that others had walked this way before us, and recently, boot prints and scuffmarks plain in the dust. The tracks stopped at a door that Wykeham pushed open, and I was directed with a brusque nod into a chamber I did not know, my wolfhound shut out to whine and scratch in the antechamber. Much like many others, it was a small room built into the curve of a wall, bright with bars of sunshine angling through the narrow window slits. A fireplace was built into the wall but there was no fire and the space was as cold as an unused chamber could be. A standing table occupied most of the room with stools set around, but they were unoccupied. The men stood in a little group by one of the windows. The room seemed crowded with a heavy presence. It looked, I thought, like a war council.

Why was I here? I glanced across to Wykeham for explanation, and did not get it.

'Mistress Perrers. Allow me to introduce you.'

His tone was clipped, hard with distaste—but with me or the body of men, or with the whole situation I could not tell. Neither did I need the introductions. Had I not lived cheek by jowl with them in the various palaces since the day I had come into Philippa's employ?

I curtseyed, my mind working furiously as Wykeham made the introductions. First was William Latimer, Edward's steward. Then John Neville, lord of Raby. A surprise: Richard Lyons—not a courtier but a man of finance, a merchant and master of the royal mint. The others—Nicholas Carew, Richard le Scrope, Robert Thorp. All, I realised in that first greeting, united by one common factor. Ambition. Their eyes were avid with it, young men who hoped to further their careers in service to the crown. I did not know if they were men of talent but I thought that perhaps they were. As Wykeham closed the door behind me, I saw them more as a feral pack of wolves, ready to pounce on any opportunity to step up the ladder to high office and destroy any fool who dared to stand in their way. But how did I fit into their schemes...?

And then there was one more. A royal son, no less. John of Gaunt.

They bowed.

'Please, sit,' Wykeham invited.

I did. So did the conspirators—for surely that is what they were—except for Gaunt, who stood against the wall, arms folded.

'Why am I here?' I asked. No point in adopting innocence or good manners. This meeting was not for public consumption, and I doubted that most of these fine gentlemen, except for Wykeham and perhaps Latimer, would give me the time of day in normal circumstances.

They exchanged glances. Who, I wondered, would be the spokesman?

It was Latimer. 'Can we trust you?'

Well, that was forthright enough. I replied in kind. 'Unless you are plotting rebellion, or the King's death, then I expect you can.' I looked round at the faces. Shuttered. Wary. 'Perhaps you are? Is this a plot?'

'Not quite.' The twist of Latimer's lips in acknowledgement was bleak. 'The King has...' he hitched a shoulder under the rich damask bearing Edward's heraldic device as he searched for a word '...withdrawn.'

'Withdrawn? A milk-sop judgement, by God!' I responded. 'He has incarcerated himself in his rooms and refuses to come out!'

Latimer cleared his throat. 'We must bring him back.'

I looked round the faces. 'And you cannot?'

I knew they couldn't. I caught the eye of Gaunt. Gaunt

had paid a visit to his father less than a week ago, leaving again within an hour with a furious face and spurs used viciously against his horse's flanks. Now I thought he might respond, but he deliberately turned his head to look out of the window, leaving it to Latimer to commit them to whatever devious policy had brought them—and me—here.

'The King sinks further into melancholy. His physicians despair,' Latimer said, and looked at Wykeham, who nodded. 'We want you to speak to him.'

'He will not see me. I have tried.' They must know of my failure.

'We can arrange that you do.'

'And what do you want me to say to him?' I played the innocent after all, enjoying Latimer's discomfiture.

'We want you to…to give him solace…to encourage him to…'

'Say it, Latimer!' Wykeham growled.

Latimer huffed out a breath. 'We want you to give him physical comfort.'

'In effect, you want me to play the whore.'

'Yes.' Suddenly Gaunt was there, stepping up to the table, dominating it. A vitally handsome man with his father's height and fine features but none of his ease of manner, a man notorious for enjoying the value of women in his own life. He waved Latimer aside and spoke bluntly. 'The King is not incapable. He still has the ability to fuck a woman and reap the pleasure of it. It might bring him back to his senses.'

It shocked me to hear it stated so coarsely, and I was not inclined to be compliant, when every one of them would have condemned me for daring to take that role.

'Then if that's what's needed, pay a palace whore,' I replied.

'Unsatisfactory.' Gaunt brushed the idea away, like an

annoying fly, with an open-handed swipe. 'I hope for a more subtle solution.'

'And you think I can be subtle.'

'I think you have a whole range of talents. Discretion being one of them. And you were well-liked by the Queen. You could be the answer to our prayers.'

I laughed, surprising them. What a turnabout from these man who viewed me as some form of pond life, dwelling in the filth of unspeakable sin. I had taken Philippa's place in Edward's bed; did they now want me to play the role of the loving, maternal Philippa too?

'He needs a confidante as much as he needs a whore,' Gaunt confirmed it.

'A concubine, then.'

He bowed. 'Exactly.'

'A wife but not a wife.'

'In so many words…'

'Openly acknowledged by the Court?'

'If we must.'

I looked round them. Not one of them approved. Not one of them wanted this.

'Why me, my lord?' I would make them admit it. I would make them say what had been unsaid through all the years since I had lifted my shift in Edward's bed.

'Because he has enjoyed your body often enough in the past,' Gaunt snapped.

Of course they knew. All the Court had known, even if it was not spoken, except in murmurings over wine cups or whispers between lovers, in their efforts to protect Philippa. Even when she had been the instigator of the scandal. I laughed again at the hypocrisy of it all, to their discomfort.

'So I return to Edward as his lover,' I remarked conversationally. 'What then?'

'Make him return to government. Make him pick up the reins of authority. We can't continue as we are now with the King shut away and the Prince taken to his bed in Gascony.' Gaunt's fist thumped the board.

'I don't know that I can.' Gaunt would get no bloodless victory over me.

Wykeham sighed. 'You can. You're a clever woman, Alice.'

I tilted my head and looked at him, noting his use of my name.

'And you're our last hope.' Latimer flushed at what he had admitted.

I stood as if I might refuse. As if I might leave. How exhilarating was power, knowing that I held them all in the palm of my hand. I took a step...

'Needs must when the Devil's in control!' Gaunt snapped. 'Enough! Here's the truth of it, Mistress Perrers. We are in mortal danger. The days of England's greatness appear to be draining away and I smell rebellion in the air. We need my father at the helm, mistress. He's not young but he's still capable of wearing the crown and ruling if only we can...' He lifted his hands in near despair. 'If only we can catch his interest and bring him back to life.'

We. We were in collusion. We were a circle of plotting. I surveyed the faces once more, all taut with expectation, all driven, all concerned for the future, their own and England's, but their repugnance for this negotiation smeared the air like the miasma of pestilence. Quick anger shook me, and I turned my stare on Gaunt. By God! I would make him beg.

He turned away to drive his fist into the stone lintel at the window. It was Wykeham, generous Wykeham, who spoke the words.

'Will you do it?' Wykeham asked. 'Will you rescue our King?'

Again, a beat of hesitation. I luxuriated in making these men of power and breeding wait on my decision.

'Yes. I will.'

And I saw the relief sweep through them, muscles relaxing, smiles appearing. The business was done—or so they thought. But it was not—not to any degree. 'And what, my lords, did it take for you to trample over your damned morality and ask me, the King's whore, for help?'

To do him justice, it was Gaunt who replied. 'It will be worth *any* price if we can restore the King to his powers.' Walking round the table, he raised my fingers to his cold mouth. 'We are grateful.'

'How can I refuse so gracious an admission?' I murmured.

There was a concerted sigh. And in that exhalation I realised what had been done here. The power of these courtiers—excepting Gaunt—their wealth and place in government rested in truth on the King's pleasure, but now their ambitions were dependent on me. We all had everything to lose if the King was allowed to fade into obscurity. We were indeed in collusion. But I would not let them off the hook quite yet.

'What's in this for me?' I asked, frankly.

'What do you want, lady?' Latimer asked, amusing me with the form of address. Much had changed in the last hour. I took a little time, as if the ideas were new to me.

'Nothing much, my lords.' And smiled sharply at their palpable relief. 'A servant for my comfort. A bedchamber and a parlour with an outlook over the gardens. Clothing and jewels fitting to my new position. An income so that I am not penniless. Am I not worthy of all of that?' And then—what I desired most of all to expunge my memories of past humiliations. 'I want recognition, my lords. I want acknowledgement that I am the King's Concubine. I refuse to live longer under the shadow of embittered silence and rancorous rumour. There is no one to hurt now, by stripping the covers from my relationship with the King.'

Their gratitude was risible, thinking that I had made an easy bargain. What fools they were, as were most men. Did they not know that I would have gone to Edward freely? My compliance did not need to be bought. But a woman must seize her opportunities, as Windsor would have said…

'Furthermore,' I added, 'if I am to be involved in the running of the royal household, I need access to the royal Treasury for funds…'

There was an exchange of glances, an uncomfortable lift of shoulders, but what choice had they?

'It can be arranged.' And Gaunt led me to the door, his hand light on mine. I knew little of him other than that Edward had a high regard for him, knew nothing of his ambitions. He was not the heir to the throne. What did he hope for from this agreement? He did not have the look of a man satisfied with life. A premonition touched my nape, that one day I would find out.

At the door I smiled and curtseyed again in a parody of deep respect.

'I will do it, my lords. I will be Edward's concubine, openly in the full knowledge of the Court. I will, if it is in my power, restore your King to life.'

So much settled in a dusty room in the old palace. I allowed my eye to travel over the familiar faces, enjoying their unease, their underlying distaste for this offering of apparently limitless power on a gold platter. Did they truly realise what had happened there in that cold chamber? I did, and for a moment I was stunned at the scope of what they had done. The potential dominance they had tipped into my lap. I would be the King's Concubine, free to stand at the King's side, to share his bed, acknowledged by all. Obeyed by all. I felt the weight of power on my shoulders as the thrill of it raced through my blood so that I could barely contain my tumbled emotions.

But was it settled? Now I must turn my mind and all my persuasive powers to the one obstacle to the success of our venture. It was in my mind that it might not be an easy task.

'Will he respond to me?' I asked Braveheart, retrieving her from her unhappy vigil outside the plotters' door.

She sneezed as she stood and stretched. She had as little an idea as I.

Not wishing to let grass grow under my feet, for I could not afford to be squeamish about such matters, I wrote immediately to Greseley.

'I anticipate having funds at my disposal, sir. Buy or lease whatever you can for my future comfort.'

Greseley acted with exemplary speed. Within the month I was the leaseholder of the Orby lands with the control of the wardship and marriage of the young heir. Ten manors all told. I clapped my hands and pressed my lips to the document of ownership in a fervent salute. I was becoming a woman of means.

I had been Edward's lover for six years, but in all that time I had never been the one to take the initiative. Edward had always sent for me. Yes, I had challenged him on the day of the hunt, but never again. I knew how difficult a proud man could be, how his pride must be allowed to dominate. Edward demanded and I obeyed. A Plantagenet never asked for favours. I had never removed my garments without his invitation or without his participation. He was the King: I was his minion, and I would not have had it any other way. A strong woman needed a wilful man to match her. If not, respect flies out of the window.

Now I stood outside Edward's apartments, my limbs trembling, and not with the cold air that shivered the tapestries. My belly lurched at what I must do. Tactics, I decided. It must be like planning a battle campaign. Knowing when to attack and when to retreat. What, I wondered, would William de Windsor advise this time?

Attack the weakest element in the fortifications and give no quarter until the battle is won. In fact, never give quarter, or the opponent gains ground.

That was no help to me. I must simply use my instincts as a woman and pray that Edward would respond. *Holy Virgin, let him not turn me away!* I stepped over the threshold, closing the door softly behind me, relieved that my path had been smoothed for me.

First an antechamber, empty and uncannily still. Then an audience chamber in a similar state of abandonment. Finally the Halidon Hill Chamber, a private room, where a man could take his ease with books and music. I knew the room well with its magnificent tapestry of Edward's first great military victory, when, still a young man, he had demonstrated to the Scots who was master. On a low stool was a chess game, set up but unplayed. A fire burned low, gleaming on the polished wood of a settle and a cupboard. A great chair was set beside the hearth, next to it a coffer set with a flagon and cup, a neglected dish of sweet pasties. Someone had left a candle bracket that was in danger of burning out.

And there was Edward. Every inch the King, bejewelled and clothed in costly fabrics, the mighty Plantagenet,

Edward the third of that name who had made England a great power for all of forty years, stood as if carved from stone. He did not even turn his head.

I waited, neither speaking nor moving.

'Leave the food and go,' he ordered.

He stared out over the gardens and enclosing walls to the distant meadows and encroaching forest. Or perhaps he stared at nothing at all. He stood straight, legs braced, shoulders firm. Nothing amiss with his health, I decided, and my heart lifted a little, but the room, apart from the neglected chess game, was curiously impersonal. No books. No documents on the table. No habitual hawk on its roosting pole. Only the magnificent battle scene on the walls, its colours stark, even brutal in their vibrancy as the golden sun glinted on blade and armour sewn in silver thread. It seemed to me that the stitched battlefield dwarfed the King with its splendour. He could not have chosen more apt surroundings in which to sink into oblivion.

Edward did not turn to see if his order had been obeyed. I did not think he cared.

I would have to make the first move after all.

'A cup of wine, Sire?'

My request dropped into the heavy silence. His body tensed. Slowly, very slowly, he turned round, one hand resting against the stone ledge against which I now saw that he leaned. Perhaps he was more fragile than I had first thought.

Then, as the light fell fully on him, I saw what had previously been hidden.

Oh Edward! What have you done to yourself? And as it hit home: *Did you love her so very much?*

What weight could my scribbled notes possibly have against this evidence of abject loss? Edward's face had thinned, the lines between nose and mouth deeply gouged, cheeks hollowed. His throat and neck showed a deterioration of flesh that he could not afford. Worse—far worse—was the dimness of his eye, the blue faded almost to grey, and the pale transparency of his skin. His mouth had not smiled, I thought, for weeks. The hand on the window frame was almost translucent. It looked incapable of wielding a sword.

First compassion. It flooded through me, almost reducing me to tears. But then fury as bright as the King's gold-crowned helm in the tapestry. What was he doing to himself? How could the victor at Crécy wallow in miserable self-pity? But I forced my unwarranted anger to drain away. Ungoverned emotion would achieve nothing: the air around me was stuffed full of it, like goose feathers in a cushion. Smothering. All-enveloping. Edward had allowed it to gain the upper hand. Emotion would not serve to accomplish my quest, but female cunning might. It might just save this man from himself and restore him to his uneasy realm. Perhaps in the end Fair Joan's conclusions on a woman's need for guile and duplicity were not incomprehensible.

So be it. I trod into his direct line of sight. 'My lord.'

'Alice.' His eyes were unfocused, his voice, without its impressive power, grated from disuse.

I walked slowly forward, halting within an arm's length, interested in Edward's reaction. He seemed uncertain. And so he would be. I had dressed most conservatively, quiet and discreet, as would befit a nun. As a wife, in fact. I had laughed as I had donned the sombre dark-hued gown and cotehardie more fitting to a housewife than a royal mistress. And so I played out my allotted role: I neither curtseyed nor lowered my eyes in dutiful respect. I certainly did not kiss him in greeting, as I might have done in the past.

'Yes, Sire,' I stated in a cool manner, hands folded demurely at my waist. 'As you see. It is Alice.'

He frowned. 'Who let you in?'

'Wykeham.'

'I don't want to talk to you.'

'As I am aware. But you don't have to, Sire. I'll talk to you.'

There was quick surprise in his eyes. Perhaps irritation. 'I didn't send for you.'

'No. I gave up waiting.'

Edward's surprise was overlaid by disquiet. Not quite disapproval, but not far off. Good! That was what I wanted. Would he order me to go?

'I would rather you weren't here. I would be alone.' Not quite an order to leave, although I doubted he would see the subtlety…

My reply was as flat as Wykeham's new paving in the great Court at Kings Langley. 'Time for reflection is good, my lord. And I have reflected much.' I put a hint of bite into the words. 'Over the two months I have reflected—since you last spoke with me.'

'Two months?'

'It is more than two months since you buried Philippa and shut yourself up here.'

The vertical line dug between his brows. 'I had not realised…'

'Then you should. It's far too long for a King to isolate himself from his subjects.'

I waited to see if the Plantagenet temper would surface, and was disappointed when it didn't. My success was not a certain thing, even though I had thought long over this as I had unpacked my clothes in the new rooms that had been immediately set aside for me—Latimer was nothing if not an efficient steward. If Edward rejected me now, how should I force him to take note of me? Sexual allure? Not that. He was too solitary, too worn down. Later perhaps, but seduction was not yet the path forward. Stern admonitions—not that either. Plantagenets did not react well to stern admonitions from their subjects, even their lovers. Compassion? No—he would see that as pity.

I was here to draw Edward back from the brink of whatever hell he had made for himself, with cold logic. Had I a view to my place at Court? My own financial security? Of course I had. But my future and Edward's healing need not be entirely separate. I had no guilt as I poured two cups of spiced wine—no longer warm but still palatable—and held one out. He took it automatically.

'I am considering leaving Havering tomorrow. Drink with me to my safe journey.' I did not smile. I was brisk.

'Leaving…?'

'There's nothing to keep me here now.'

'Where…?'

'Ardington. I have a mind to see if it suits me to live there permanently.'

Edward did not reply. So I would stir the pot a little more. I sat, even when he did not—such a breach of royal etiquette!—sipped the wine, inspected one of the cherry tarts on the plate and bit into it. 'This is delicious. Come, Edward.' Making deliberate use of his name. 'I can't eat all these myself.'

He sat, but not close, regarding me as if I had transformed into a hunting cat that had just unsheathed it claws. 'Why are you going?'

'I am no longer a royal damsel. I am not needed.'

I let the silence play out, finishing the tart, licking my fingers, but in a businesslike manner. And then: 'Have you thought about me at all through the past weeks, Edward? I think not. What have you been doing?'

'I have been thinking…' His voice trailed off.

'I expect you've been thinking of all you've achieved,' I observed. 'All that you've done since the day you cast off your mother's authority and seized the ruling of England in your own hands. I imagine that took a lot of courage for a young man barely reaching maturity.'

'I have thought of that.'

'Philippa helped you, didn't she?'

For the first time Edward smiled, but it was a strained affair. 'She was my strength.'

'Tell me about it.'

'I don't think I could have done it without her. My mother was a ruthless woman and I was considered to be of an age to need a regent…'

It was as if a wall had been breached, allowing the pent-up waters to escape. First a trickle, then fast becoming a flood. The old tale of the beautiful but vicious Queen Isabella, who would have ruled England with her notorious lover, Roger Mortimer, at her side, keeping the young Edward as close as a prisoner. Until Edward had arranged a coup to bring Mortimer down, to strip his mother of her regency. He had been all of eighteen years old, but the memories of that night in Nottingham when he had taken power were as vivid as if they had happened yesterday.

I nodded. 'And Philippa helped you to stand firm, take back your birthright.'

Edward's face was alight with it. 'She was magnificent.'

'She must have been very proud of you.'

And the light vanished. The rush of words dried up in a summer drought. Edward frowned, staring down into the cup, and I saw the muscles in his jaw clench at some unpalatable truth. I knew what it was. I would say it.

'Philippa would not be proud of you now, Edward.'
'No.'

'She would be horrified. She would berate you! Philippa would order you to look forward, not back.'

At last his eyes lifted from whatever images he saw in his wine and slid to mine, and I saw true recognition there, and a flash of resistance. Good. Excellent.

'Have you come to berate me too?' he asked. 'It is not your place.'

'No, how should I? I am the lowest of your subjects and no longer have a claim on you or the Queen. I have come to say goodbye.'

'I suppose you wish to be reunited with your sons.'

'Yes. *Our* sons. Sons are very important. They are the only family I have. So will you drink to my safe journey?'

He sipped the wine absently, his mind still far distant.

'My son. My heir, the Prince. He is so ill...' His words were spoken with difficulty as if he had to search for each one. 'When I was his age I rode at the head of my army. What a sight we were. But my son cannot ride. He is carried into battle in a litter. All I have achieved, destroyed.'

Panic fluttered, rapid wings beneath my heart. I was losing him again between the victorious past and the desperate present. I stood up, placed the cup on the coffer. I had to throw the dice with callous disregard, and risk the outcome.

'It seems I must leave without your good wishes after all.' I walked to the door. My hand reached for the latch, and still there was no response. I would have to admit my failure. To Wykeham and Gaunt and the rest. I would have to leave my King, even though my heart urged me to stay.

'Don't go.'

It was quietly spoken, but very firm. I exhaled slowly,

but still I addressed my question to the smooth grain of
the wood under my hand. 'Give me one good reason why
I should not.'

'I want you to stay.'

I held my breath.

'I need you, Alice.'

I held still, eyes closed tight. I heard the brush of his tunic
as he stood, the click of metal on wood as he placed the cup
beside mine, his soft footsteps. I felt his body fill the space
behind me, but he did not touch me.

'I was wrong, Alice. Don't go.'

Against all my inner compassion, I kept my back to him.

'God's Blood! Look at me!' Edward demanded. 'I would
rather not be addressing the back of that excessively unattractive hood you've chosen to wear.'

There it was. The command was back. But I must not
succumb too quickly. I was not a fortress driven into surrender by a light threat and a call to parley, and I admit to
a ripple of old jealousies, however unworthy they might be.

'Two months—and you haven't once asked to see me.
You feel lost without Philippa—I understand that—but you
must know how unwanted *I* have felt,' I said. 'I see no future for myself here if you don't need me.' His hands were
on my shoulders, turning me round so that I must face him.
He was really looking at me, seeing me. At last!

And Edward tilted his chin. 'Is that why you've clothed
yourself as a drab? Some penurious widow about to enclose
herself into a convent and fill her life with prayers and good
works? Perhaps I should send you off with some new gowns.
How will you catch a man's eye otherwise?'

And there was the humour I had missed, a glint of it as
the sun struck obliquely across his features.

'The only eye I wish to catch is yours,' I remarked with the slightest lift of my chin to match his. I would not smile yet.

Edward bent his head and kissed me, my brow, then my lips, at first as if it was a difficult thing for him to do, this contact with a woman, revisiting an old memory, uncertain of what he would discover on the half-forgotten journey. But then his mouth warmed against mine as his hands slid from my shoulders and closed around mine.

'Why is it that you make me feel renewed?' he asked.

I could feel the growing strength of his intellect as he sought my face for the answer. And as if he had found it, he raised my hands, still cupped in his, and pressed his lips to each palm, to the tip of each of my fingers, reacquainting himself with me after a long absence. Yet still we had a way to travel.

'How I have missed you, Alice. Why did I not realise it?'

'Because you closed yourself off to all but grief.'

'Will you change your mind and stay here?'

'You too might change your mind. Tomorrow you might banish me.'

Temper flashed in Edward's face. 'I order you to stay! Your King orders you. I need you to remain here.'

The temper. The possession. The authority. There they all were, returned in good measure. I hid my smile but stood on my toes to kiss Edward's cheek. He was already stripping the maligned hood from me so that my hair, unbraided beneath it, fell over my shoulders. He clenched his hand in it, into a fist.

'What lovely hair you have. Why do I feel that I have been outmanoeuvred? You have never worn anything half as ugly as this.' He dropped the hood to the floor.

'I have not needed to,' I replied. 'I had to do something to catch your attention.'

And Edward laughed softly. At last he laughed. I led him over to the settle against the wall and pulled him down beside me. I would not let him go quite yet. I didn't trust his mood sufficiently. Reaching for the platter on the tray, I offered it.

'Eat one of these. You must be hungry.'

'I suppose I must be. And if you eat them all, you'll lose your figure.'

The final attack, the lethal thrust against which I prayed he would be helpless.

'I will anyway, my lord, with or without the sweetmeats.' His stare was instant and knowing, on my face, my waistline. 'I am carrying your child. Are you pleased?'

The King abandoned the sweet delicacy and turned his face into my hair. 'I didn't know. You have to stay with me. I'll not have a child of mine raised without my knowledge. Stay, Alice. In God's name, stay.'

I kept my incipient victory close as I unravelled yet another skein of my plotting. Edward must return to his people too. 'Only if you'll take me hunting tomorrow. Please do,' I invited, leaning against his shoulder. 'I have no one to ride with who does not damn me as a daughter of Satan. Wykeham has taken to praying over me. Besides, my mare needs exercise. She's eating her head off in the stables.'

'You have been lonely.' How clever he was at reading between my words. 'I've neglected you, haven't I?'

He was mine. Colour stained his cheeks, the years dropped away. Inwardly I rejoiced as I saw that the Plantagenet had returned. 'Yes, you have,' I said solemnly. 'And now you must make recompense.'

He stood and pulled me to my feet. 'As I will. What is it my lady wishes?'

'Call a hunt, Edward. Let your Court see you. Let them know that the King is come again. Promise me.' Still the slightest hesitation. 'Promise me! Soon it will be too late— I will be too large to climb onto a horse!'

'I promise. Stay, Alice. I have missed you.'

So I did. His kiss was long and deep with relief and an awakening of passion. 'Come to bed, Alice. It's been a long time.'

And so we returned to the vigour and heat of past days in the royal bed, where we could pretend that all was well. Edward took me with mutual satisfaction, confirming Gaunt's crude assessment of his male powers, and that I could make the King forget the encroachment of age.

'You are a pearl, my beloved Alice.'

'And you are King of England. England needs you.'

'I shall rule.' The self-regard was restored. 'With you at my side.'

Triumph surged through my blood as I gave my body to him once more. *I will look after him, Philippa,* I vowed. *I will care for him, nurture him and love him.* And I kissed his mouth for my own pleasure, even as I acknowledged within my heart: Edward was not the man he used to be, the man who had first commanded me to his bed. But for now I had pushed back the shadows.

The hunt met in the courtyard, the denizens of the Court clad in velvet and furs. Horses stamped in the cold and side-stepped at the delay. The huntsmen swore as the hounds swarmed under everyone's feet. There was a sense of anticipation in the air that had been missing for a long time.

We waited. Would the King come?

We shuffled and puffed clouds of mist into the icy air. Squires brought round cups of spiced ale. We began to shiver at the delay.

Dark and saturnine in the middle was Gaunt astride a glossy bay that resented the lack of action more than most. Beside him in the hands of a groom was the rangy grey that Edward loved. Deliberately Gaunt's eye found me in the crowd. No need for him to voice his concern, his blame at what he obviously saw as my failure. I returned his stare with stony expression. I had done all I could.

Time passed.

Expressionless, Gaunt motioned to the groom to lead the grey stallion away. He drew on his gauntlets. 'We'll go.'

He raised his hand to draw the attention of the crowd, for the huntsman to blow the horn for moving off. I sighed and admitted defeat, turning my mare's head toward the stables. I had no belly for it.

'You'll wait for me, Gaunt.'

He always was the master of surprise, of display and self-aggrandisement. The King strode down the steps and across the courtyard, taking the reins from the groom and swinging into the saddle with all the agility expected of him. By chance—or was it royal command?—a shaft of sunlight broke through to gild his leather and fur, sparking glints off the ruby that pinned the peacock feather to his cap and the jewelled chain on his breast. He smiled around at the expectant crowd.

'An excellent morning. My thanks for waiting for your King—and my apologies. You need wait no longer.' Self-deprecating with the same formidable charm that had won him more friends than enemies in his long reign. There were murmured greetings from all sides.

The huntsmen began to move from the courtyard, Edward

riding beside his falconer, taking a hawk onto his wrist, as if he had never been absent, except perhaps for the first moments of stiffness in his posture as he settled into the saddle. The air of melancholy had vanished with his donning of the handsome wolfskin cloak against the cold. As I hung back to take my habitual place at the rear with the women, I felt a warmth spread through my belly where the child lay. And heard what I had prayed I might hear as Edward turned his head to address his son.

'After the hunt, come and see me. We must make plans—for our armies in France. It's more than time.'

'Yes, Sire.'

Gaunt in his swaggering arrogance, as much part of him as his raptor's face, he gave me no recognition, but I could see the depth of his gratification as the brisk wind whipped colour into his cheeks. Father and son exchanged a hand clasp, reunited and set to enjoy the occasion. I tucked my skirts securely beneath my legs and nudged my mare forward to follow the rest. I too would enjoy the hunt. When the huntsman lifted his horn to blow the gone away call, I gathered up my reins.

The huntsman did not blow, his action arrested by Edward's hand on his arm.

'Mistress Perrers…'

All eyes fastened on the King, who had called the halt. And then shifted to discover me in the crowd. My hands closed sharply on the reins, causing my animal to jib. Never had the King addressed me so openly in public.

'Sire.' I sounded breathless, even to my own ears.

'Ride with me.'

I hesitated, but only for a moment before I pushed my horse through the brightly clad *mêlée* to Edward's side.

'Sire…'

'You said you wanted to hunt. So you shall.' He grasped my bridle to pull my mare closer, took my hand in his, then leaned and kissed my temple. 'You were right. It's good to hunt and I have been remiss.' His voice fell to an intimate whisper. 'You will not be lonely today.'

Around me there was a general intake of breath. To single me out in so obvious a fashion! The Court was astounded. Hot blood rush to my face so that my cheeks flamed with it. To be kissed so wantonly in public—but was this not what I wanted? This acknowledgement in the face of lords and commons alike?

'Will you ride with me?' he prompted, forcing me to make a statement of our relationship. No one was to be allowed to fail to understand its meaning.

'I will, Sire.'

As I fell in beside him, my hand still in his, the courtiers streaming out into the water meadow, the huntsman blowing the gone away at last, I could do nothing but smile as brightly as the fitful sun that chose that moment to bathe us in gold. Edward had given me recognition in public. I was the acknowledged royal favourite.

I suppose my enemies multiplied that day. Did I care? I did not, for the flame of my ambition burned fiercely. It was a momentous day. The hounds ran to ground a particularly fine and royally tined buck. Edward's features sharpened and glowed with the exercise as his body relaxed into the familiar demands of the saddle. His laughter rang out and the Court breathed a concerted sigh of renewed confidence. Even Gaunt looked content, despite my having replaced him at the King's side.

I rode beside Edward for the whole of the hunt. When the hounds picked up the scent and the riders spurred into a gallop, he restrained his mount to ride beside me, conscious of my state of health. He could not have made his choice plainer if he had ordered Chester Herald to announce the news with a blast of his trumpet.

Alice Perrers was the King's Concubine.

I had to ponder this reversal in my fortunes, and did so in my room where I stripped off my hunting finery and ordered my maid to fill the copper-bound tub with hot water. I sank into it with a sigh. I had not hunted for some weeks; my muscles complained, but not beyond what was tolerable. In the herb-scented water I inspected my belly, which was rounded with the growing child. It would not be possible for me to hide it, and neither did I need to. For the first time I could display my increasing girth brazenly.

For my name, in one form or another, had been on every pair of lips that day. Edward's very public showing of what all the Court knew, but pretended not to, had seen to that. No longer secret, no longer hidden, no longer a source of shame for the Queen, my position was exposed naked for all to see and speak of. It was Edward's gift to me, to give me his recognition before the whole of the Court, with a generosity I could never have imagined. Made public and acknowledged by all, I was secure under the King's protection.

I repeated the epithets I had heard as the hunt had pursued the hapless deer.

Alice the Whore: not one I would choose.

La Perrers: better—but it had been said with a sneer.

Royal mistress, royal paramour: a ring of authority here perhaps.

But this one I liked much better. King's Concubine. Official. Untouchable. Powerful. My sharing of the King's rooms and the King's bed was an undeniable fact; lacking legal sanction, but the King's stated preference gave me status. No one, *no one*, would dare slight me, the King's chosen companion. Even Gaunt had managed to mark my presence with a deep obeisance as the hunt had dismounted. I had never dreamed of such a gift, made in the face of the great and good, of which I was neither.

'Thank you, Edward,' I whispered, my hands protective over my belly.

I let my head fall back on the rim of the tub and closed my eyes, enjoying my achievement.

Chapter Ten

Edward went into immediate conference with Gaunt. I knew nothing of the discussions, always the preserve of men, but I saw the results. The King was once more at the head of affairs, the reins firmly in his fist: Gaunt was ordered to Gascony with an army to give the beleaguered Prince some aggressive support against French incursions. Even more impressive, Edward ordered a second attack from Calais under a tough old campaigner, Sir Robert Knolles. If I had needed any evidence of Edward's recovery, it was this planning of a two-pronged attack from north and south, which he had used in his early campaigns to good effect. At the same time a whirlwind of envoys was dispatched to the Low Countries, to Germany and Genoa to enlist allies against the King of France.

Edward's nights were spent with me, where anxieties still gnawed at him.

'I should be leading the attack,' he fretted. 'Am I not strong enough?'

'Of course you are.'

But the depredations of Philippa's death had dug deep. His strength was much restored but however much I might like to argue against it, Edward's mind had lost its incisive edge. Playing chess, reading a book of favourite poetry, enjoying the music of a well-played lute and sweet singing, his concentration could vanish, his awareness of his surroundings drifting away like high clouds under the strength of a summer sun. Even his confidence waned. And as it faded, my fears for him grew. He would never lead his troops with the same superb flamboyance, if at all. And yet I gave thanks: the isolation was over and Edward was reunited with his Court. A victory at Gaunt's hands in France would in some measure restore Edward's confidence in his ability to make well-balanced decisions. I poured two cups of fine Bordeaux, a wine symbolic of Edward's possessions.

'To England's victory!' I raised my cup, and drank.

'To England! And to you, my love.' Edward kissed me with all the passion of a mighty King.

I celebrated too soon, of course. The news that trickled in over the coming months was not good. In the north King Charles of France had learnt from past mistakes and refused to be drawn into battle against a major force. Knolles, increasingly vilified, lost impetus and authority, his troops becoming separated and easy meat for the French vultures. In the south we fared better. Limoges was sacked and burnt, which put a stop to the French cause in that vicinity, but all we heard were tales of the Prince being forced to return to Bordeaux, abandoning the attack, defeated not by the French but by his own pain-racked body.

All Edward's convictions drained away.

'Gaunt is there,' I soothed. 'He will take control. There is no need to worry.'

But increasingly he looked inward and was reluctant to

talk to me. Neither did I realise the problem until I saw him waiting on the battlements for news that did not come, with young Thomas clamped to his side by a heavy hand on his shoulder, even though Thomas shuffled and twitched, clearly wishing to be in the stables or practising his sword-play—anywhere but with his burden of a father.

'Then go!' Edward snapped, releasing the boy, and Thomas went with alacrity.

When I took the boy's place, tucking my hand within his arm, Edward smiled, but there was a loss in his face. I was not who he wanted, and although the remedy was clear to me, it was not a pleasant one. I thought I would not enjoy the outcome, but I was woman enough and confident enough in my new role to do it. For the sake of the King's health, I would risk the consequences.

I wrote a formal invitation on good-quality vellum, complete with wax and Edward's seal, and prepared to dispatch it with a courier in full regalia. Wholly illegal, for the King's Concubine to employ the royal seal—but why not? It could not help but have the desired effect. With a duplicity for which I made no excuse, I kept it from Edward. What point in raising his hopes if by some chance it never came to pass? Neither did I sign my name—it crossed my mind that I might just live to regret this missive. Indeed, I stood before the fire in my chamber, holding it between my finger-tips as I considered consigning the document to the flames.

Could I not provide all the affection that Edward needed?

But news arrived. Devastating news that drove Edward to his knees in the chapel, his face ravaged with distress. The Prince's tiny son and heir, Edward of Angouleme, heir to England's crown, had died in Bordeaux. The Prince was too ill and distraught to carry on the campaign. He would return to England, leaving the campaigning in the increasingly ineffective hands of Gaunt.

Edward wept.

In the same hour I sent the letter. All was to play for. I could not afford to change my mind.

I wrote again to Windsor, with rigid formality.

> *I am restored to Edward's pleasure. And to his confidences. He has no interest in Ireland. The Gascony situation takes all his attention, which at best is wayward. You are still your own man in Ireland and I think there will be no interference from London.*

And I received a reply by return of the courier in Windsor's trenchant style—he wrote as he spoke.

I received your two letters within days of each other, such is the difficulty of communication. I am relieved that you are restored.

For me or for him? I grimaced cynically.

Keep my name in Edward's mind. This is a hard road and I need all the help I can get.

The final paragraph surprised me.

> *I would give you one more piece of advice. You have experienced what it will be like for you without royal patronage. I did warn you when we last met. You rejected my advice. Now you know it for the truth. Your position as royal mistress can be undermined in the blink of an eye. Make the most of your opportunities. It will be a long winter for you when the King is dead. I doubt the Prince and his ambitious wife will make a place for you at Court.*

And then I was more than surprised.

I think of our meetings more frequently than I might wish. Yours was not a comfortable companionship but I find that you dwell in my thoughts. It might not surprise you to know that you are, on occasion, impossible to dislodge. You have claws of steel. So accepting that, I admit that your wit and charm give me consolation in my isolation in this place. I do not see myself returning to London within the foreseeable future with some regret. I think we would have dealt well together if events had fallen out differently.

Keep well, Alice. Keep safe. Your supreme position will make your enemies more lively than you might imagine. Take care that you do not put any weapons into their hands.
Accept this advice from one who knows.

I laughed softly, and then stared as I unwrapped the package that accompanied Windsor's advice, its content obvious even before I unrolled the soft leather. A slim-bladed knife that could be secreted in a sleeve or bodice. A lethal means of protection from the assassin. How ridiculous of him! Who would possibly wish me physical harm?

I found that I too regretted Windsor's absence from Court. I doubted he would be faithful to that final less than chaste kiss. But, then, as King's Concubine, neither was I.

He had my protection in mind. A foolish dog and a slim blade.

Should I have been afraid? I was not. My mistake perhaps.

* * *

The reply to my royal invitation took longer to arrive than Windsor's letter, but was far more impressive when it did. It came in person, arriving at Windsor with palanquins, outriders and an impressive military escort with its pennons fluttering bravely. Eye-catching and ostentatious, there could only be one owner of such an entourage. Yes, I conceded. I might just regret this. But it was the only answer to the problem that I could see.

Family!

Edward needed family around him. He wanted—as he had all his life—his children and the memories they brought him. He might be heroic on the battlefield, he might be a superb administrator, his physical presence might be matchless, but at home he needed the anchor of family. The absence of humour and affection played on his temper, his spirits. Philippa and the offspring she had borne for him had been so vitally important to him after his own childhood of loneliness and isolation under the selfish hand of his mother. Creating his own family had been vital to him, giving him all the stability and love he had never had.

But what now, now that his family had dwindled? Two sons in France, both heavily committed to war. Lionel dead in Italy. His daughters, except for one, dead. Young Thomas too young and self-interested with the occupations of youth to give his father real companionship. Edward needed family around him.

Why can't you *give him what he needs?* I demanded crossly, but honesty made me admit: I could give him much, but not the sense of belonging that Edward needed. And the remedy? Isabella, his much-loved daughter. Wilful, capricious, impossibly haughty and no friend to me she might be, but she was the remedy.

Now below me, emerging from the swagged and cushioned palanquin, was the unmistakable figure of Isabella, without her much-desired husband but with two little girls with the same fair hair and dawning beauty as their mother. I watched her arrival from the little chamber above the main door. Hardly had she set foot on the ground then she began to issue orders as if she had never been away.

I tapped my fingers against the window ledge as Isabella laid claim to Havering. Should I waylay her? Or let her settle in and meet Edward on her own terms? I mentally debated the choices. If I went down now, there would only be a clash of words and personalities, with no one to cushion the resentment that would erupt, like a flame applied to dry tinder. Ah! But if I let her see Edward, make her own rules, order her own accommodations, I would immediately put myself at a disadvantage. Isabella would take control before we sat down together for supper.

Well, now! I stilled my fingers, considering the appropriateness of my garments for the occasion that I foresaw. Since when had I retreated from a little unpleasantness? Was I not chatelaine of this palace? Who supervised the money and the housekeeping? God help me to harness my words and my temper—I needed her as my ally. So, having the niceties of Court ceremonial at my fingertips, I was standing on the dais in the Great Hall, clad in Court finery, Latimer and a servant at my side, when she eventually swept in.

'Are my rooms ready?' she asked of no one in particular, imperious as ever, magnificent as ever, superbly gowned despite her long journey in an over-robe of silver and dulcet green that I instantly coveted. If I had not deliberately selected my newest gown, very much to Edward's taste, rapidly replacing the dull robe of leaf-green that I had been wearing when I had set eyes on Isabella's splendour, I would have paled into insignificance. Isabella retained her old habit of cutting one's confidence off at the knees. But I was now prepared to herald my new wealth and status in a startling figure-hugging robe of violet silk patterned in vermilion and blue. It was impossible to pale into insignificance in such a gown coupled with a cotehardie of gold damask. I was mistress here, and I signalled to the servant to lead Isabella's entourage and her two daughters to the accommodations I had had made ready for them.

Isabella remained. Her eye avoided me with careful nonchalance but considerable displeasure, and fell on Latimer instead.

'Latimer! It's good to be back. Some wine, if you please.'

'Of course, my lady.' Latimer bowed to the Princess—and then to me, before exiting to obey the command. Isabella caught the action, as she must, and her brows rose into perfect arches, her gaze finally becoming fixed on me, as I knew it would when she deemed it suitable. She had seen me the moment she had stepped across the threshold. How could she be blind to violet and vermilion?

'Mistress Perrers!'

'My lady.' I curtseyed.

'I didn't expect you to be here still. And what role is it that you occupy now that you are no longer a damsel?' Her disdain might have cut me to the quick if I was of a mind to let it. 'Can I guess? Palace whore?'

I stayed unmoving on the dais. 'Things have changed, my lady.'

'They must have, if you are giving orders to Latimer.' A sudden frown. 'Does my father know? I presume he does.'

'Of course.'

'So you have stepped into my mother's shoes.'

'One might say.'

She was uncomfortable, and I enjoyed it. Would she ask me outright? A servant entered with a tray of wine, and offered it, kneeling before me. I motioned him to offer it to the Princess instead. What pleasure it gave me.

Her lovely face had acquired the consistency of granite. 'You are controlling the household, it seems.'

I inclined my head. 'Someone must. It pleases the King that I do it.'

Isabella deliberately ignored the wine. 'I'll soon change that.'

'Certainly, my lady. If you intend to take on the burden yourself...'

I knew that the Princess had no intention of taking on such a role. So did she.

'Where is the King?' she demanded.

'In the stables, I believe.' Isabella turned on her heel. 'Wait!' I had to speak now. 'There's something you should know.'

She halted. 'And that is?'

'The King has not been robust.'

'So?'

'Have a care in your choice of words to him.'

'I don't need you to tell me.'

I stepped down and faced her, our eyes much on a level.

'But you do. You have not seen him in the weeks— months—since Her Majesty's death. I have.'

She considered this, momentary indecision clear in her pursed lips, then spun around to accost Latimer, who had stepped quietly into the Great Hall again.

'I understand the King has been ill, Latimer.'

'Yes, my lady. But now much improved.'

So she did not trust me to give her the truth even about her father. I had some bridges to mend if I would make use of this Plantagenet Princess. And seeing the ingrained hostility in the set of her spine, in her rigid shoulders, I thought I might have wagered wrongly in that damned invitation.

'Have you taken advantage of his kindness?' she demanded, jealousy thick in her voice. 'I see you've been more than busy.' Now that I was close, her eyes narrowed on my expanding waist. 'Another bastard? Who'd have thought you'd have the wit to rise so high. But beware, Mistress Perrers, you'll rise no more.'

I swallowed a smart retort. Isabella was an intelligent woman and I must appeal to that. I walked beside her, keeping step even when she quickened as if she would shake me off. Isabella had no idea how single-minded the Queen's erstwhile damsel could be.

'He can't be too ill,' she announced. 'He invited me here to participate in a celebration.'

'I know.'

'He said he was arranging a tournament.'

'Yes.'

'Would a man who was ailing commit himself to a tournament?'

'No.'

'When is it to be held?'

'It isn't.' That stopped her. Once again we faced each other like two cats posturing on a roof-ridge. 'There is no such arrangement,' I stated.

'Who wrote the letter?'

'I did.'

I heard the intake of breath, saw her nostrils narrow, and awaited the outburst, but it did not come. Rather a speculative stare. 'To what purpose? You would invite me here?'

'You sound surprised.'

'If you wanted to rule the roost, you would not bring

me back to England. We both know my inclination is also to rule.'

'That I know.'

'So why?'

'The King's spirits are low. The Prince's state of health is uncertain and his little son is dead. The King's in no mood for tournaments. Unless you persuade him, of course.'

'I'll speak with him.' She eyed me thoughtfully.

I smiled thinly. 'I wish you well, my lady.' And I did. Edward needed the distraction. 'And I should tell you. The King does not know I sent for you.'

I watched her go, the energy in her step that was undoubtedly a flounce. She would not like what Latimer had to show her. I sighed and looked down at Braveheart, who pressed against my leg. God help me! Had I invited the vixen into the chicken run?

Isabella was in a conflagration of temper when I walked through the gardens to join the royal father and daughter and test the air between them.

'I have been turned out of my rooms!'

'Turned out?' Edward chuckled at the drama of it. 'I expect you've been provided with something larger and far more fitting—you've brought the children, I presume.'

'The rooms were mine—you had them built for me!'

'So I did. But they were empty. Why not make use of them? You rarely visit, and Alice finds them very comfortable.'

Did I not say? Edward had moved me into the sumptuous royal apartments. When I had listed what I had wanted, I could not have envisaged what I got: the suite of palatial rooms constructed for a Princess. And how I relished them.

A taut silence fell on us like a hoar frost, sharp and cold, broken only by the strident cry of a magpie in the stand of trees. Isabella took a breath. I wondered what she would say, if she could manage to be diplomatic. The line of her jaw had the tension of a bow string. She stopped on the path with a swish of embroidered skirts, and turned four-square to Edward.

'You would put your mistress in my rooms?'

Careful, I breathed. *Careful, Isabella. He may be aging but his pride is as strong as it ever was.* In confirmation, Edward's hand close tightly into a fist.

'I think you should ask pardon for that,' he remarked mildly enough.

'Do we pretend she is not? That she was not, in all those years when my mother was alive?'

The ermine mantle of royalty slipped invisibly but impressively back onto Edward's shoulders. Even his shoulders braced as if to take the weight of it.

'I'll tolerate much, Isabella. But not that. You will not judge me or your mother. I have given Alice the authority to administer my household.'

'I don't like it.'

'You don't have to. You are a guest, Isabella. If you do not like it, there is no compunction on you to remain.' Isabella's lips parted, then clamped together. 'There, you are not without sense, my daughter.' Edward smiled but the warning was still there. He knew exactly what he had achieved for me. 'Now that the formalities are over, how long will you stay? We must see what we can do to entertain you.'

Isabella's glance slid to mine. I left them planning. They were two of a kind when it came to outward display and spending money. So Isabella would stay for some weeks, but I was secure in Edward's favour. Daughter and mistress could work very well together when they had to, to ward off the dread melancholy.

Isabella had other ideas, of course. She whispered in my ear as we entered the Great Hall together for supper. 'Don't expect to win my regard. You won't succeed. You're an up-start, Mistress Perrers.'

True. I was, and always would be, but I worked hard for my position. I decided to flex my claws a little.

'I don't need your regard, my lady.' I remained solemn as her brow furrowed ominously. 'His Majesty needs me in his life far more than he needs you.'

'He'll listen to me.'

'No, he will not. Ah…' Edward was there to lead me to the chair at his right hand. 'Perhaps your daughter should take the pre-eminent position,' I suggested smoothly. 'For tonight at least. As an honoured guest.'

I showed my teeth in a smile that was not altogether false. How could it be when I had emerged triumphant from this little clash of wills? Realising that she had met her match, Isabella returned it but with a flash of her eye as she sat. It was an excellent evening, with food and wine and music and entertainment. The King's spirits revived under his daugh-ter's ready wit and I felt the soul-enriching heat of victory fill my belly, even when Isabella paced beside me as we left the chamber, the tint on her lips stretched into a bitter smile.

'Have a care, Queen Alice.'

I laughed softly. How exhilarating it had been to watch Isabella, seated in pre-eminent position at Edward's side— but only at my instigation. Because I *allowed* her to be there. 'I always do, my lady,' I replied. 'I always do. As I have a care for the King.'

She was furious, she would remain my enemy, but I knew she saw the truth in what I had said. I ruled the royal roost, and I would abjure that power for no one, not even a royal princess. Edward could have Isabella for a little time, with my blessing, but it was me he needed. I was the centre of his ever-decreasing world. My blood hummed as I retired to my chamber, allowing my serving woman to divest me of jewels and gown, stretching out my hands so that she might take my rings. Queen Alice? I liked it. The title would never be mine, but—and I clenched my hands into fists—I would enjoy the power as if I were truly Edward's queen.

I left the field to Isabella through necessity, for I could barely see my toes over the swell of my belly. When the child kicked incessantly and I began to find life at Court wearying, I announced my intentions. Edward kissed my lips and my hands and packed me into one of his royal barges as if I were a precious piece of glass.

I had just acquired the house and manor of Pallenswick through Greseley's clever negotiation and my borrowed gold coin, courtesy of the royal Treasury. And Pallenswick was a gleaming gem of a property on the banks of the Thames. My access to Edward and the Court was as easy as donning a pair of silk slippers.

'I'll come if I can,' Edward assured me.

'I'll do just as well without you.' I knew he would be engaged in the progress of the war, and would be barred from the birthing chamber, King or no. Isabella would keep his spirits in good order.

'I'll have masses said for your safe delivery. Send me word.'

'I will.'

'I'll be content if you bear me a daughter.'

'As long as she's less combative than Isabella!'

'Difficult not to be.' Edward's laughter startled the ducks

that quacked in the shallows. Then, as I settled myself against the pillows: 'Don't go!'

The tightening of his hands around mine was a consolation but I knew I must. In some matters I valued my independence. I wished to be under my own roof when I gave birth. And so I left Court. There was no secrecy now. My departure was marked with banners and pennons and a royal escort, such that all the world was aware that the King's Concubine would bear him another child. Isabella found other affairs to occupy her so that she would not have to pretend a degree of concern. Good practice, all in all.

My wolfhound travelled with me, nervous of the water. A more misnamed animal I had never met. I carried Windsor's dagger in my sleeve.

A basket of new-laid eggs rested on the table in the kitchen at Pallenswick, where I was engaged in helping my housekeeper to clear out boxes of wizened fruit from the previous autumn. And tucked between the eggs was a letter. An unconventional delivery, forsooth. Intrigued, an eye on Joan, my new daughter, who slept in her crib beside the hearth, I retrieved it and unfolded the single page. A brief note, no superscription, no signature, no seal. So someone wished to remain anonymous but had gone to a deal of trouble.

It is necessary for you to return to Westminster. Personal circumstances must not be allowed to stand in your way. It is for your good and that of the King.

A clerk's hand. But from whom? I tapped the note lightly against the brown egg on the top of the pile. Not Edward. Not his style, and why the need for secrecy? Wykeham? He would not stoop to unsigned missives. He would not need to, surely as Edward's chancellor. Edward's physician? If

Edward was ill, a courier would have arrived with a horn blasting out its warning. None the wiser, I dropped the letter into the fire with a wry smile. Who would actually want me to return? I might be the acknowledged concubine, but most would happily clap me in a dungeon as far away from the King and Court as possible.

For the length of time it took me to walk from kitchen to parlour, the sleeping infant in my arms, I considered taking no heed of it. But, then—it was a warning. It was for the good of the King. I could not afford to ignore it—or could I? I did not appreciate an anonymous request that smacked of an order. I would think about it overnight.

I wished the anonymous writer a close association with the fires of hell.

I was, of course, up betimes, ordering my belongings packed and barge made ready. I kissed my new daughter—fair and blue-eyed like her father—named Joan after Edward's beloved dead daughter who had been taken by the plague. I had balked at the name, it being uncomfortably reminiscent of the woman who had disparaged my low birth and consigned me to a life of drudgery, but on this occasion Edward's wishes took precedence. So I bade my daughter and sons farewell, admonished nurse and tutor with a multitude of unnecessary instructions, and set off for London within the hour. The writer of the note would make himself known soon enough.

I arrived to find that in my absence Edward had summoned a Parliament. It did not disturb me in any manner. With a new campaigning season approaching, a Parliamentary session to give approval for taxation to raise the moneys to pay the English forces was an obvious step. It gave the palace at Westminster where Edward was in residence an air of turmoil. There was an unusual scurry and bustle, the stabling overcrowded and the accommodation for lords and bishops at a premium. The commons had to make what shrift they could. It would not affect me. Closing my door against the commotion without, I sighed with the pleasure of arrival. But not for long. I expect I scowled.

'You took your time!' John of Gaunt announced.

'What are you doing here?' I was not gracious. Why was I rarely gracious around John of Gaunt? And to find him here in occupation of my rooms, without my invitation. I think I always feared him. Gaunt was as ever impervious, sitting on the window ledge, his foot braced against the stone coping.

'I'm waiting for you, Mistress Perrers.'

He'd had little to do with me since our initial plotting. Oh, his public recognition of me was superb, he might be forced to accept my importance to Edward, but still I thought he despised me. So what was he doing here? Unless... Suspicion began to flutter over my skin.

'I came as soon as I could,' I said.

'I expected you yesterday.'

I was right. Plotting again. 'So you sent the letter, my lord.'

'That's not important. It brought you back. It should have been sooner.'

I resented his tone, the peremptory demand. His overt criticism. My response was biting. 'You didn't have the courage to sign it, did you, my lord?'

'Nothing to do with courage. More to do with discretion.'

'So that no one knows you sent for the King's paramour? How unfortunate for you that you are driven to consort with such as me, having to admit that you actually have a need of me. Once was enough. But to have to ask again! How can you tolerate it, my lord?' How savage my taunts, but he had caught me on the raw.

Gaunt was on his feet, striding towards the door. I had pushed his pride too far.

'Wait!'

He halted abruptly, his expression stony. 'I don't have a need of you. I was mistaken.'

'Obviously you do.' I removed my mantle and hood, giving myself time to struggle against the inclination to let him go and slam the door at his back. It must be serious for Gaunt to come to me, therefore it was for me to make the first gesture to this man whose conceit was vast. 'Let us begin again, my lord.' I stretched out my hand in a gesture of conciliation. 'Tell me what the problem is and I will answer you.'

Serious indeed! Gaunt needed no second invitation. 'He refuses to do it. And he must. You are the only one he'll listen to. Regrettable, but a fact. You've got to persuade him.'

Typical of the man to dive into the middle of the problem without explanation.

'I presume you mean the King. And I might persuade him if you are more specific. Come and sit with me, my lord, and tell me what's stirred this particular pot. Is it Parliament?'

He sat, and told me all in short, bitter sentences.

Parliament had begun the session in an unfriendly mood. Their list of complaints would carpet the floor from Westminster to the Tower. All the money granted by the previous session—what had happened to it? Vanished without trace and with no achievement for it! England's proud name had been ground into the mud of Europe. Gascony was more or less lost. Where was the English navy? Were there not rumours of French invasion plans? And now the King was daring to ask them for more coin. Well, they wouldn't! It was throwing good money after bad.

I listened, honestly perplexed.

'I do not see how I can help in this matter,' I observed at the end.

'They are looking for scapegoats,' Gaunt snarled, as if I were witless not to see it. 'They are unwilling to attack the King directly, but they are intent on drawing the blood of his ministers, accusing them of poor judgement. And unfortunately Parliament has discovered a weapon. What do all Edward's ministers have in common?'

I saw the direction of this. 'They are all men of the church.'

'Exactly! Priests, to a man. What do they know about warfare? Nothing! Parliament wants them removed before they'll consider taxation.'

It was now very clear, my role in Gaunt's plans. 'And Edward will not do it.'

'No. He is driven by loyalty. I can't move him. And if he won't comply…'

We would have a crisis at home to match the one in Europe.

'If I persuade Edward to dismiss his clerics, who will replace them?' I asked.

Gaunt smiled bleakly. 'Here's my suggestion…'

I listened to his planning. It was masterly. I could not find fault with it.

'Will you do it?' he urged at last.

I stared at him. 'Will your new ministers not be unpopular?'

'Why should they? They're not clerics.'

'But they'll be seen as your men.'

'They're men of talent!'

So they were. But for a moment I simply sat and considered the whole, making Gaunt wait, because I was in a mood to do so. I could see no fault with it—and it would rescue the King's relationship with Parliament. It had much to recommend it.

'I will do it, my lord.'

'I'm obliged!'

The agreement was accepted by the curtest of nods, and Gaunt strode from my rooms, leaving my previous good humour disturbed. Gaunt and I might be allies in this but it would never be an easy alliance. It crossed my mind that it might be like getting into bed with a viper.

Together Gaunt and I found Edward engaged in some heated conversation with Latimer. He greeted me with a smile, saluting my cheeks, but the welcome was notable by its brevity, even a touch of irritation.

'You should have told me you intended to return, Alice. I can give you only a few minutes because…'

The burdens were hemming him in again. I saw the strain of holding his far-flung possessions together dragging at the muscles of his face. He looked beleaguered.

'We're here to talk about your ministers, Sire,' Gaunt intervened gently.

'You know my feelings about that…'

There was an irresolution about Edward that worried me. I touched his arm, drawing his eyes to my face.

'I have talked with your son, my lord. My advice is to do as he says.'

'My ministers have served me well.'

'But Parliament will not give them the benefit of the doubt. You need money from Parliament whether you like it or not, Edward. How can you fight without their support? You must dismiss your clerics. Now is not the time to be indecisive.'

I think I said no more and no less than Gaunt must have said, but Edward listened to me.

'You think I should bow to Parliament's will?' His mouth acquired a bitter downturn.

'Yes, Edward. I do. I think it would be good politics.'

So he did it.

And the men who came forward in the place of the unfortunate clerics? The little coterie of men who had met with me in the circular room. All friends and associates of Gaunt—young, able, ambitious men. Men who would serve Edward well and be loyal to Gaunt. Within the week the reorganisation was complete. Carew became Lord Keeper of the Privy Seal. Scrope took on the burden of Treasurer. Thorp the new Chancellor. William Latimer was Royal Chamberlain with Neville of Raby replacing him as steward to the royal household. A Court clique to close around Edward and cushion him against the world that he found increasingly difficult to recognise.

I watched them bow before the King. Gaunt had it right. They were his men, bound to him, and since it was my influence that brought them to the forefront, they would be loyal to me too. Not one of them would dare oppose me, giving me for the first time in my life friends at Court who would not neglect my interests.

It was my first overt step into government circles.

'You must not worry, my lord.' I raised one of Edward's hands to my lips. 'They will serve you well.' The days when his palms were calloused from rein and sword were long gone. The strain in him, his lack of vision for the future, was pitiable. He was like an aging stag, still leader of the herd but the weight of years beginning to grey his muzzle, to dim the fire in his eye. Soon the hounds would be baying to drink his blood. Perhaps they already were.

'It is good that you are back,' he said. 'Have you brought the infant?'

'No. She is with her nurse. But I will. You will see her.'

I accompanied him to the mews to inspect a new pair of merlins just taken into training, relieved to see him enjoy the moment as he handled the birds. Edward must not worry. But I would. I would do all I could to keep the dangers at bay.

And Gaunt? I expect he was satisfied with the outcome. He made no genuflection in my direction but I felt the shackles that bound us together drawing tighter: we were undoubtedly in league, although whether I had sold my soul to Gaunt, or he had sold his to me, was a matter for debate. This was a marriage of convenience, and could be annulled if either saw fit. We were too wary of each other to be easy bedfellows but, for better or worse, in this political manipulation we were hand in glove.

The result of our conspiracy was immediate and inspiring. Edward addressed Parliament with all his old fire and won their approval, and the money was forthcoming. England could go to war again, whilst I smugly castigated the far distant William de Windsor. Look to your enemies, he had warned me. He had been wrong. I had friends at Court now. Perhaps I should write to tell him. I consigned his dagger to a coffer.

'And I don't need you!' I informed an entirely unimpressed Braveheart, who had curled up on the hem of my gown.

And if I needed confirmation of the rise of my bright star in the heavens of Court politics, that was immediate too. Gifts were exchanged between the royal Plantagenets, as was habitual at Easter. And what was it that my lord of Gaunt gave to me? The sense of his obligation must have struck him like a blow to the gut. He proffered an object wrapped in silk.

I took it, unwrapped it.

Holy Virgin! It was an exceptional thing, a hanap such as I had never seen. A bejewelled drinking vessel, fashioned in silver and gleaming beryls, fit for a King.

Oh, I read Gaunt well. He had a need to keep my allegiance. My voice in his father's ear was worth every ounce of silver, every one of the jewels set in the hanap: a gift to buy my favours, if ever there was one. And why was it so very necessary for this Plantagenet Prince to have a royal mistress on his side? Because, as every man in the land knew, the state of the succession rested on rocky foundations. With the rumours flying out of Gascony of the Prince's health, no one would wager against the Prince dying before his father, and then the crown would pass to the Prince's son Richard—a child of four years. A state did not thrive with its ruler not yet out of his minority.

Did Gaunt see the crown of England falling into his own lap? Children's lives were cheap. Richard's elder brother was already dead in Gascony. Richard might not live.

But Gaunt was not as close to the succession as he might like to be, for would not Lionel's issue stand before him? Lionel, who had died so tragically in Italy, had produced a daughter by his first marriage. This child, Philippa, wed to Edmund Mortimer, the young Earl of March, was now mother to a daughter. If that young couple proved sufficiently fertile to produce a large family, a Mortimer son would take precedence over any offspring of Gaunt.

Not something to Gaunt's liking, I judged. There was no love lost between him and the Earl of March.

My thoughts wove back and forth as I inspected the splendid cup. It was all too far in the future for speculation, but without doubt Gaunt had all to play for. For who would be a better King within the next decade? The child Richard? A Mortimer son as yet unborn? Or Gaunt in his full strength?

And just supposing the situation was solved and Richard lived? Still all would not be lost for Gaunt. A Governor would be needed for the young Richard. Who would be the obvious choice to educate and protect and direct the young King? Gaunt, of course. Gaunt would be in control. And he might still see the Crown as a not impossible prospect for his own son, young Henry Bolingbroke. To have an ally of the King's Concubine who had the ear of the ailing King was not to be sneezed at, Gaunt seeing me as a useful arrow in his bow in ensuring the succession fell into the best hands, for nothing would persuade me that he did not have some scheme in mind. He was not a man to take second place, even to his brother, the dying heir, however deep his affection for him.

Of course, it was treason on Gaunt's part.

I smiled, in no manner seduced by the quality of the gift, understanding the motives of the giver perfectly, and yet how could I not appreciate it? If I needed any outward sign of my pre-eminence in the royal household, this was it, a gift from an arrogant Prince who would have no reason to notice me, much less seek my allegiance. How magnificent that the all-powerful John of Gaunt should honour lowly, base-born Alice Perrers. I found the urge to laugh almost irresistible.

'Thank you, my lord.' I curtseyed, duly solemn, but when I rose to my full height, I made sure that my eyes met his. I would accept the gift but my loyalty would remain true to Edward.

'It is my pleasure, Mistress Perrers.'

Gaunt too smiled, sly as a fox.

I was not without regrets in all this realigning of alliances and royal ministers. Wykeham, the man who trod the line between friend and enemy. Wykeham was the one victim in all this political manoeuvring that Edward truly regretted. I doubt a more honest Chancellor ever existed, but Wykeham was swept away in the anti-clerical hysteria. It was impossible to save him.

Edward's departure from his minister was formal. Mine was not. He was packing his possessions, his beloved books and plans for even more building that would never now see the light of day at the hand of a generous King. Standing at the open door, I watched him fold and place everything with meticulous neatness. William de Wykeham, Chancellor no longer. The closest thing to a friend, even if an unnervingly judgmental one, that I'd had.

I did not call Windsor a friend. I was not sure what Windsor was to me.

He did not even turn his head. 'If you've come to gloat, don't bother.'

'I have not come to gloat.' Wykeham continued to wrap a bundle of pens in a roll of cloth. 'I have come to say farewell.'

'You've said it. Now you can go.'

He was hurt, and with every justification. I had stood at Edward's side and listened to the empty phrases of necessity and regret and well-wishing. It had been necessary, and Edward felt the hurt just as keenly as Wykeham, but the man deserved more. I walked round the room, to force him to face me. He foiled me by picking up and rummaging in a saddlebag.

'Winchester will see more of you,' I remarked, holding out a missal to him.

He snatched it from me. 'I will apply my talents where they are appreciated.'

'I'm sorry.'

Now he looked at me. And I saw the pain of betrayal in his doleful eyes. 'I never thought *you* would be the instrument of my dismissal. I thought you valued loyalty and friendship.' He sneered. 'You have so many friends, do you not? You can afford to be casual with them.' I felt the blood stain my cheeks. 'How wrong a man can be when he doesn't want to see the truth!'

'I don't think I was the instrument,' I observed, keeping clear of sentiment. 'Parliament wanted you gone. All of you.'

'For crimes none of us committed. For lack of ability— and with what proof? We've more experience than the whole job lot of Parliament put together!' He shrugged, placing two more books into the bag. 'I didn't hear you trying to persuade Edward to be loyal to old friends!'

'No, I did not.'

'Neither did Gaunt.' Wykeham glanced up under frowning brows as if to seek proof of what he suspected, and read the answer in my face. 'Take care, Alice. You're swimming with big fish in a small pool here. Gaunt is a powerful man and might wish to become even more powerful. And when he does—when he doesn't need you any longer—he will be quick enough to rid himself of you.'

'He doesn't threaten me,' I replied. I thought about our last exchange when I had returned to Court after Joan's birth. 'I think he would protect his father, by whatever means. And to do that, he needs me.'

'*I* think he would feather his own nest.'

'Who doesn't?'

'One day you will not be indispensible.' A travelling ink-stand followed the two books. 'Stay away from him. He's not known for being scrupulous.' When he looked up again his expression was smoothly bland, as if it was simply a piece of advice to a friend. But it was not. I knew it was not. It was a warning.

'I can't afford to antagonise Gaunt,' I stated harshly.

'What? When you are the King's sight and hearing? His right hand?' Wykeham was mocking me now.

'For how long? You know my circumstances better than most. I need all the friends I can get, as you so aptly stated!'

'Then you should turn your mind to making some, rather than antagonising the whole Court!'

'How can I, when what I am to the King lies at the root of all the hatred? To my mind, I am stuck between a rock and a hard place. If I lose Edward, I lose everything. The Court will crow with delight. If I stay with Edward, I have a legion of enemies because they resent my power. What do I do, most sage counsellor?' He was not the only one who could stoop to mockery.

He thought about that. 'I don't know.'

'Well, that's honest enough,' I growled moodily. 'You could pray over me, I suppose.' I wished I hadn't come.

'I will.'

'Don't. I could not bear your pity.'

'You need someone's.'

I flung away to the window, leaving him to his books, fighting against a ridiculous urge to weep.

'You could try the Prince when he returns,' Wykeham said eventually, when he had allowed me time to recover. A man of cunning politics, Wykeham, in spite of being a man of God. I shook my head. There was no path for me

to follow there. Joan would be no friend of mine. 'He's expected home any day now.'

'That's as may be.' Adroitly I changed the direction of
our exchange. 'But what of you? At least you'll not be without comfort in your political exile. A dozen castles, palaces
and houses to your name at the last count...'

His smile was wry. 'But all belonging to my office. None
of them mine. I too am vulnerable.' The warmth was gone.
And I was sorry.

'I'll see that you are rewarded,' I found myself saying.

'Now, why would you do that?' How calm his voice, how
trenchant his words. 'Do I look as if I need your charity?'

'No, and I've no idea why I offered it. Since you are so
unfriendly, I should consign you to the devil.'

'I'll not go. I'm aiming for a place with the angels.'

'Then my advice is don't associate with me.'

His smile, a merest breath, was a little sad. 'You do yourself down, Alice.'

'I merely follow the fashion.'

'I've seen you with Edward. You are good to him, and
for him.'

'But only for my own ends.' The scathing quality of my
reply mirrored his and shook me by its virulence.

'I'll not argue the case since you're determined to douse
yourself in self-pity today. You clearly don't need me to
point out your sins.' He looked around the bleak, empty
room. 'Well, that's it.'

I was sorry I had tried to provoke him. 'When do you go?'

'Now.' He bowed, quite formally. 'God keep you, Mistress
Perrers.'

'He's more likely to keep you, my lord bishop.' And when
he laughed, I leaned and kissed his cheek. 'Do you know?'
I whispered, in a moment of gentle malice. 'I sometimes

have thought that we could have been more than friends, if you were not a priest and I a whore.'

Wykeham's solemn face creased. 'Sometimes,' he whispered back, 'I have thought so too. If you ever need me...'

He stopped at the door, and then went out, closing it quietly behind him so that I stood alone in the deserted room. Finding a forgotten quill on the floor, I picked it up and slid it into my sleeve. Bishop Wykeham was a friend worth having, and he was right to castigate my slide into self-pity. I had made my bed and for the most part enjoyed lying on it. It would be an unforgivable weakness if I were to whine about the repercussions.

I must be strong. For Edward, if not for myself and my children.

I watched Wykeham ride out, astonished at the sense of loss that was almost as painful as the guilt was. He should not have had to forfeit his offices and his estates, and my guilt increased when Edward gifted one of Wykeham's estates to me. The pretty, desirable, extremely valuable manor of Wendover in Buckinghamshire with its fertile fields and timber, its easy routes to London. I was nudged into making reparation. Greseley had acquired for me the manor of Compton Murdak, and so I granted its use and income to Wykeham. I grimaced as I signed the document. Who said I had a heart of stone? But the grant was for a limited term only and Compton Murdak would return to me. I was not too soft-hearted. It behoved me to have an eye to my own wealth after all.

So Wykeham left, and I turned my mind to a meeting I really did not wish to have but could not avoid.

I was late. When I arrived, father and son were in the midst of clasping hands in what was undoubtedly a joyful reunion. The Prince had returned to England—a moment for national and personal rejoicing, if it had not been so shattering for any onlooker.

I knew of the Prince being stricken, knew that he had needed to be carried into battle as if a man of twice his age, that his strength had waned so rapidly that he resembled in no manner the knight who had led his troops at Poitiers. We had all mourned the death of his first-born son. But nothing could have prepared me for *this*. Whatever the disease that afflicted him, he was wasting away, his face a gaunt death's head. Even from a distance I could see that Edward was as aghast as I.

'Thank God…!' Edward wrapped an arm around his son's shoulders.

'It's good to be home.' The Prince stiffened as if he could not bear to be touched.

'I have longed for this day.'

Edward ushered his son to a seat. Isabella spoke softly, with something like despair freezing her features into what might pass as a smile. And there at Edward's side, her hand on his arm as she smiled up into his face, was the Princess Joan.

The Fair Maid of Kent.

I had last seen Joan brushing the dust of Barking Abbey from her skirts.

Now I took stock. The years had not been kind to her, her face full and round like a new-made cheese, flesh encroaching on her slight frame so that her once fastidious features were now flaccid, coarsened, and the remnants of her earlier prettiness wholly overlaid by excess. Over all, gouged in the soft flesh next to mouth and eye, were lines of grief and worry.

Edward was busy with the Prince. Isabella and Joan stood

a little apart, two forceful women. As I walked towards them, Joan looked round, her expression such as she would direct at a servant tardy in bringing wine.

'Here is Alice,' Isabella announced with a face and voice as bland as a dish of whey.

'Alice?' Joan's lips pursed.

'Alice Perrers. The King's whore.' Isabella stated it without inflection.

'We had heard. So it's true.' Joan stilled as she saw me, really saw me, for the first time.

I curtseyed, my expression, my bright smile, one of ingenuous welcome. 'My lady. Welcome back to England.'

Joan's brows snapped together. Memory returned, as it must. 'The Abbey!'

'Yes, my lady. The Abbey.'

'You know each other?' Isabella was jolted out of her blandness, like a cat spying an approaching mouse.

'Yes,' I replied smoothly. 'The Princess was kind enough to give me a monkey.'

'How unfortunate that it did not poison your blood with its bite,' snapped Joan.

'I have proved to be exceptionally resilient, lady,' I assured her with impeccable serenity. 'You will be gratified to know that I found your advice most pertinent.'

'Fascinating.' Isabella purred. 'A reunion—how charming…'

And Joan's gift for razor-edged comment returned with polished venom. 'She was nought but a clumsy, nameless servant. Lent to me to fetch and carry.' She turned on me with fire in her eye. 'God's Blood! By what ill chance did you become…?' She gestured to my clothes, my person.

'The King's lover? No ill chance, lady. I am mistress of my own destiny now.'

'Fortunes change, dear Joan,' Isabella interposed with sparkling devilment. 'As you yourself should know. Alice is a remarkably powerful woman.'

'It's not fitting,' she spat. 'And now I've returned…'

'I doubt you'll change the King's mind.'

'The King will listen to me!'

I waited, sure of my ground. I would not antagonise—that would not be politic—but neither would I give way before such impertinence at the hands of this woman who expected to slide into the pre-eminent role as the next Queen of England. The pre-eminent role was mine.

Edward became aware of my presence.

'Alice!' His touch of greeting on my hand was unmistakeably intimate.

'My lord. The Princess has been telling me how much she anticipates renewing my acquaintance. It is my greatest wish,' I said, placing my hand softly over Edward's. 'We will do all in our power to make Joan's return a happy one. I have ordered the apartments at Westminster to be made ready.'

'Excellent!' said Edward.

'A family reunion, no less!' Isabella smiled.

Joan scowled at my use of her given name. Then quickly hid it behind a tight curve of her mouth and an unmistakable barbed response. 'I cannot express my gratitude.'

So the battle lines were drawn. Joan regarded me as less than a beetle to be squashed beneath the sole of her foot. She might justifiably expect to order affairs in England to her liking, with the approval of a father-in-law who remembered her fondly as a child brought up in the royal nursery. And now, in the space of a half-hour, she had learned that she had a rival. I was the one to order affairs at Court. But a warning tripped its way down my spine. At some point in the future, which I would not contemplate, Joan would be the one to hold all the power.

'We should celebrate my son's return,' Edward announced, oblivious to the antipathy amongst the women in his household.

'I will be gratified to arrange it, my lord,' Joan responded, seizing the chance to make her mark.

'No, no. We won't ask that of you. I think we can give you time to recover from your long journey, my dear.' Edward looked across the Princess to me. 'What do you think, Alice? A tourney?'

It was not done deliberately. Edward had little guile in him these days, but the effect was like a bolt of lightning. Joan inhaled sharply, hands clenched in her damask skirts.

'I should take up my responsibilities immediately,' she stated. 'As your daughter by marriage, I should be hostess at a Court function.'

'But Alice has the knowledge and the experience,' Edward demurred. 'She's the one to ask. What do you say?'

'A Court banquet,' I replied. 'To organise a tourney would take too long.'

'Then a banquet it shall be.' Edward was turning away, back to his son, content.

'I would organise a tourney!' Joan's demand sliced through the air.

'As you will. Talk to Alice about it!'

With true male insouciance, Edward cast aside the matter to return to the discussion of military tactics with the Prince, leaving me to fight a war in his wake, but, unlike my days in the Abbey, I had the skills to avoid and manoeuvre. And attack. And, surprisingly, an ally.

'It is my right, and you will not usurp it,' Joan declaimed. 'Now that I am returned—'

'Of course,' I interrupted pleasantly. 'I will tell the King you insisted. A tourney? You'll need to speak to the Steward, the Chamberlain, the Master of Ceremonies. The Master of Horse, of course. Chester Herald if you intend to invite foreign knights—which I'm sure the King will insist on... I'll send them to you. I'll send Latimer to discuss the ordering of food. The annual cleaning of the palace which is now pending. And where will you live? Do you intend to stay at Westminster? The accommodations are not very spacious.'

The planes of her face tightened. 'The Prince has not yet decided.'

'Then do you wish to interview them in my rooms?'

'No.'

I spread my hands. 'What do you wish?'

'Let it go, Joan.' Isabella chuckled. 'Hold a banquet. It's much less hard work in the circumstances. And let Alice do it.'

'I thought *you* would understand.'

'I understand that Alice is a past master at arranging these affairs.'

'Which I intend to change.'

'And I also understand that you are *jealous*, dear sister.'

'Jealous?' Joan's voice climbed. 'She has no right!'

'Sometimes, Joan, it is necessary to accept the inevitable.'

'That this woman rules the King?'

'Yes. And you should have the wisdom to give her the credit for what she does well.'

'I will not listen to you!' Joan stalked away to her husband's side.

'Then you are a fool,' Isabella murmured after her, *sotto voce*.

'Whilst I,' I added, astounded at this turn of events, 'am entirely perplexed!'

* * *

'What I don't understand,' I murmured to Isabella, when the Prince and his wife had departed for a temporary stay in the royal apartments at Westminster, and I was left to consider the burden I had just been handed, 'is why you would throw in your lot with me rather than with the Princess? Why not plump for a tourney and let her get on with it? Would it not please you to put my nose out of joint?'

'She's nought but a block of lard!' Isabella announced.

'So?'

'I dislike her.'

'You dislike me.'

'True—but if truth be told, perhaps not as much as I dislike her. I always have.'

'Joan will one day be Queen,' I warned. 'I have no long-term prospects.'

'I know who holds the power now, and it's not Joan.'

Which was like balm to my soul. But: 'I still don't understand why you would stand at my back when Joan tried to stab it.'

Isabella frowned at me, clearly considering whether to take me into her confidence. 'We'll need a cup of wine. Or two...' Her eyes gleamed.

We sat in the solar, two conspiratorial women.

'Not a good marriage,' Isabella pronounced, and proceeded to inform me of all the facts that Fair Joan, newly widowed, had failed to impart to me about her marital affairs in those far distant days at the Abbey.

A clandestine marriage no less, Joan, at the precocious age of twelve, with Thomas Holland, who promptly abandoned his child bride to go crusading. Meanwhile, in his absence, Joan was forced by her family into a second marriage with William Montague, son of the Earl of Salisbury.

Unfortunately Holland returned. For a good number of years he held the position of steward in William and Joan's household.

'Can you imagine,' Isabella gloated in unseemly mirth, 'what a convivial household that must have been. What an amazing *ménage à trois*. Whose bed do you think she shared?'

Until Holland had petitioned the Pope for the return of his wife, and had got her back after an annulment of the Montague union, living with her for good or ill until he died in the year Joan came to the Abbey, a new widow, to cleanse her soul through prayer and seclusion. I doubted Joan had taken any benefit from it. She had certainly not mourned Holland to any degree that I recalled, taking more interest in her jewels and her lute than in confession.

'But Montague was still alive,' Isabella was continuing. 'A living husband, even a dubiously annulled husband, did not make Joan good material for a royal bride. It smacks of bigamy to me. Many might consider so unorthodox a situation to be an impediment to the legitimacy of any child my brother got on Joan. Is their child Richard a bastard?' Isabella wrinkled her nose. 'Hardly good news for the succession! The Virgin of Kent she was not! But my brother closed his ears and the marriage went ahead. Joan had him in her thrall.' Her lip curled. 'She's an ambitious woman.'

I could not blame her for that. 'Like me?' I asked wryly.

'Exactly. That's why she hates you.'

But Joan had every right to be ambitious. On Edward's death she would see her ambition fulfilled and I would find myself effectively banished. My fingers clenched into the silk of my gown, my nails scoring the fine material as Isabella inadvertently brought the terrible presentiment of

Joan's crowning into sharp focus. Joan would celebrate, and with great glee she would toss me into the gutter.

'Did you see her?' Isabella continued, oblivious to my thoughts, not mincing her words. 'Joan the Fat! She still preens and smirks as if she were beautiful. And that makes it all the more incomprehensible to her—that you should have such power with the King—when you are *not* beautiful.' Her stare was uncompromisingly critical. 'Famously ugly, in fact.'

'My thanks for the compliment.' But I think I had become resigned to it. It no longer hurt.

'It's true.'

'The King does not think so,' I observed.

'The King is blind.'

And I thanked God for it. What a rewarding exchange of information this had been. Princess Joan would be my enemy. But Isabella... Here was a strange twist in our troubled relationship, yet it would be an unwise woman to put too much weight on any new intimacy. I raised my brows, determined to prod and pry.

'Do I understand that you will be my friend, my lady?'

The reply was as sharp as I expected. 'I wouldn't go as far as that.'

'I have never had a friend,' I added, to see her response.

'I'm not surprised. Your ambitions are beyond what most people can stomach.' She perused me, her eyes bright with anticipation. 'But I'll say this. It will be interesting to watch the battle royal between the pair of you. I'm not sure that I wish to wager on the outcome. It wouldn't surprise me if the banquet never happens.'

In that moment I found myself wishing for the one thing I had never had. A friend, a woman to whom I could speak my mind with confidence and trust. A confidante. What would it be like to say what was in my heart, to bare my soul, and know that it would be treated with respect? How would it be to have a woman to turn to for understanding, even for judgement? I had never known it.

A little breath of sadness surprised me. Was this melancholy? I twitched it off with a swirl of my skirts. Since my star had risen high in Edward's firmament, I was not given to melancholy humours. Briskly, I took my thoughts in hand. How was it possible to miss what one had never had? Far better to keep my ambitions—and my fears—close to my heart than to drop them into the ear of some mythical female confidante. To give any information to wily Isabella would be dangerous.

I arranged a banquet to mark the return of the Prince and Princess and I was suitably extravagant. The only whining voice raised in protest—our eminent Princess—was drowned out by the din of the feasting courtiers.

'What did you wager on this banquet ever coming to fruition?' I asked Isabella.

'Not a silver penny!' she replied archly. 'I thought the planning would shatter on the rock of Joan's disgust.'

I smiled in pure joy. 'You were wrong.'

'So I was.'

Joan was not finished with me. She had not even started. With a smooth exchange of seats as the feasting ended and the wine flowed, as the minstrels dived into their unmusical renderings, encouraging the Court to leap and caper with riotous levity—she leaned close, eyes hard as jade.

'When I am Queen of England, I will destroy you for what you have done.'

I returned the gaze, a little contemptuous. 'And what have I done?'

'You have entranced him! You have taken the King's mind and twisted it! You have usurped a role that is not yours to take. Nor ever will be. You have schemed and manipulated until he sees nothing but your desires. You trick him at every step and turn.'

I was startled by her unsubtle accusations, but not perturbed. I would use her own words against her.

'As I recall, my lady, you advised me that a clever woman should always be capable of dissimulation. You mocked me when I did not comprehend.' I smiled as her face became suffused with colour. 'I have no need for guile or trickery. I show the King the respect he deserves. Which is more than you do, my lady. Do you think him so weak of mind that he cannot withstand the wiles of a woman?'

For a moment she stared, open-mouthed. 'How dare you!' She had not expected me to retaliate.

'I have brought nothing but pleasure and contentment to an aging man.'

'Is that all? I see more, Mistress Perrers. You dip your fingers into the royal Treasury. Who paid for those garments you wear? You walk these corridors as if you were Queen. I've seen you—you wheedle and connive until you squeeze all you can of land and estates and wardships from the King. When I am Queen I'll strip you of all you've filched and send you packing back to that dire convent with only the clothes you stand up in. And not even those, I swear.' Her eye travelled over my new velvet sideless surcoat in royal crimson, the jewelled cauls that encased my hair. 'Then who will remember Alice Perrers? And if I discover you have at any time stepped even an inch outside the law, I'll make sure there is a cell to confine you for the rest of your earthly existence. A pillory would not be too good for such as you!'

I looked across to where the Prince sat beside his father,

allowing her invective to pass for the most part unheeded. Her accusations were not new to me. They could be heard in every quarter of the palace, with or without evidence to prove them. I had learned to live with them.

'Look!' I interrupted her with a nod of my chin. And she did, the words drying on her lips.

'Do you truly look? And acknowledge what your eyes show you? When will you become Queen of England?'

Two men. One old, one in what should be his prime. One fading, slowly as the years took their toll, the other racing to his death. Unless there was a miracle, there was not one man in the country who would wager a purse of gold on the Prince outliving his father. Edward might be fifty-nine, the Prince a mere forty-one years in comparison, but I knew who would die first.

So did Joan.

And I saw the emotion that took a grip of her features so that any remnant of good looks was transmuted into ugliness. So she loved him. Despite everything, I felt a tightening around my heart and an unexpected lurch of compassion.

'It must be hard for you,' I said.

But my compassion was wasted. Joan's eyes might be bleak with despair but she thrust aside my observation with the flat of her hand slapped down on the table. 'My lord will recover with rest and good nursing. And your days will be at an end. The Prince will live. You'll see. And my son after him. I will be Queen of England. Your present good fortune will be laid waste before your eyes.' Her hands curled into fists on the table before her.

'I wish you and the Prince well, my lady.'

I shrugged off Joan's answering stare that could have pierced a shield at fifty yards. Her plans for the Prince would never come to fruition and Joan was wretchedly, hopelessly building a bulwark against the truth. I moved to stand beside Edward, enjoying the brightness of his face as he conversed with his son.

Edward's restored vigour with the return of the Prince had its own consequences. I fell for a child at Easter. A girl, Jane, to join her sister in their little household at Pallenswick. Not a pretty child, for she inherited my heavy brows and my dark colouring, but I lavished love on her because of it, and Edward presented her with a silver bowl that I stored away with the other three. Edward had no imagination for birth gifts, but his acknowledgement of this dark-browed daughter was magnificent.

Edward's return to good heart proved not to be transient. Despite the Prince's weakness, his inability to visit Court with any frequency, Edward began to turn his ear to what was happening outside the walls of Westminster where we were settled for the term.

'Consider Parliament's grievances,' I advised Edward.

And so he did, meeting with his council at Winchester as in the old days. Graciously conciliatory, listening to the endless petitions, promising redress but doing nothing to undermine his own prerogative, regal authority sat well on him with his ermine robes. Returning to me from the success of his meetings, his enthusiasm filled the rooms of Westminster with a blast of energy.

'I will rebuild our defences,' he said. 'And then we will go to war again. I will restore Gascony to English hands. Gaunt will help me…'

'You will do all that is necessary,' I assured him.

His smile was almost a youthful grin. 'I feel the years falling from my shoulders.'

We went hunting, the best sign of Edward's renewed spirits.

Gaunt acknowledged his father's initiative with a bow in my direction. 'My thanks.'

'It is my pleasure, my lord.'

I needed no more. Edward was himself again.

Beware fickle fate! Never turn your back on her. If you do she will sink her teeth into your unprotected heel. If there is to be any maxim applied to the conceit of my life, that will be the touchstone. My spirits, one minute soaring as high as Wykeham's new towers at Windsor, in the next collapsed as if the foundations had been fouled by a detail of zealous sappers. Edward sat in stunned silence, his knuckles white as his hands gripped and kneaded the arms of his great chair. I stood at his side, even going so far as to touch his shoulder to remind him of my presence. I don't think he felt it. His mind, his inner vision, was across the sea with this ultimate, irreconcilable loss. All my hopes, all Edward's optimism destroyed in one piece of news from a royal courier. The King aged before my eyes.

'This day will be engraved on my heart,' he murmured in broken accents.

I would have saved Edward from knowledge of the devastation, but how could I? He was the King and so must bear the ultimate responsibility. Unaware of the latent strength in his hands, seeing nothing but the bloody massacre that had been recounted, he gripped my fingers as if to draw the life-blood from them, and there was nothing I could say to him to soften the agony.

The English fleet had been lost. All of it. Completely and utterly destroyed when pounced on by a Castilian fleet in opportunistic alliance with France, in the seas off La

Rochelle. Our ships were swept by fire. Terrified horses stampeded, breaking apart the wooden vessels that contained them. The English commanders were captured.

A terrible scene of wanton death and carnage.

Edward gazed unseeingly at the wall before him, seeing nothing but the destruction of his life's work in this, his first major military defeat in his long reign. He said not one word, even sitting through the night staring into the flames of the fire he insisted on having lit in his room despite the heat of the summer. I sat with him. I feared for his reason through those long hours. Next morning, as light filtered into the room, he stood.

'Edward…you haven't slept. Let me—'

His words startled me.

'I'll have my revenge,' he said, low and even. 'I'll lead the greatest army England has ever seen into France. I'll fight to take back all I have lost. I'll not return home until it is done.'

But it was a charade, laid bare by the transparency of his skin pulled tight over spare cheekbones, the trembling in his hands.

Should I have tried to dissuade him? Should Gaunt? We did not. There was about Edward a hardness that I recognised and knew I could not fight against. He might be aging but he was a lion still and needed to prove to himself and to England that he was a King worthy of his crown and his people's loyalty. I let him be.

The preparations were magnificent, the army vast as, flanked by Gaunt and even the Prince, who was roused by the crisis of the moment, the whole force embarked on the Thames with appropriate fuss and splendour. Pride filled my heart, for a short time sweeping away my doubts as I watched from the shore. Edward stood at the forefront in gilded armour and helm, his heraldic lions resplendent above him as the war banners whipped in the wind: a sight to stir the senses. I had already made my farewell. Now I must leave him to God's grace and pray for his success.

'I'll die on French soil before I allow them to take what is my inheritance!' he had sworn as he had boarded his flag-ship, *Grace de Dieu*.

It frightened me, to tempt fate in so bold a manner.

By the Virgin, my fears were well founded.

Three weeks later, the vessels had not stirred from port, contrary winds battering Sandwich and the brave plan into pieces. In Gascony, our beleaguered town of La Rochelle fell to the French. In utter despair, Edward called off the campaign. It was a sad, hopeless old man who returned to London to my waiting arms, and I could offer him no solace.

The humiliation broke Edward. His world fell apart around him. Philippa's death had wounded him sorely but the failure in war broke him beyond repair. And the follow-ing months, with Edward sitting helpless in London? Every English-held fortress came under attack, every English de-fence was obliterated. By the end of it, Edward's Gascon territory was even smaller than that bequeathed to him by his father.

All his life's work destroyed.

If England was humbled, Edward was trampled under-foot. He had lost everything, a thing that his mind found it difficult to comprehend. He tired quickly, losing the thread of conversations in the middle of a thought. Sometimes he fell into a silence from which he could not be roused. Sometimes he did not recognise me.

Chapter Eleven

Sir William de Windsor! Back in England! Back within my orbit!

He might have thought it a matter of pure chance that I was crossing the vast space of the Great Hall at Westminster when he arrived, but I could have put him right if I had chosen to do so. I knew exactly when he dismounted from his travel-weary mount, when he dispatched his horses, baggage and escort to the stabling, exactly the moment when his foot struck the first of the steps into the great entrance porch.

I stood in the shadows cast by a pillar to catch a glimpse of him, the first for nigh on four years. I had been expecting him, for before the debacle of the English fleet off La Rochelle, when Edward had turned his mind to England's precarious hold on Gascony, he had also picked up the rumours emanating from Ireland.

It was not good news. It never was, and here was the usual trail of accusations of inefficiency, bribery, corruption and back-stabbing in the highest circles. Which put Windsor directly in the firing line, for no one doubted that the power was in Windsor's hands rather than in the hapless Desmond's. He had no warning from me. Had I not promised to apprise him of royal policy towards Ireland? The last time I had written had been to tell him that there *was* no policy. By the time I knew of Edward's renewed interest, events had overtaken me. In an unusual burst of anger, and a flash of the old independence, Edward had ordered Sir William to get himself to London on the next available ship and deliver an explanation in person.

When he would come, *if* he would come, was a matter for conjecture. It was easy enough to claim the message lost *en route*, but I thought he would obey the summons. Windsor was not a man to hide from notoriety. And so I had been watching for his arrival, unsettled by the range of emotions that were stirred up in me. Some trepidation. Some anticipation. A good deal of mistrust. And more than a pinch of pleasure.

And here he was. My first impression—more than an impression, more a certainty—was that Windsor was not in a good mood. I would not have expected otherwise given the tone of the royal demand. Crossing the threshold, he looked as if he had been thrust into the hall by a blast from a raging storm. His clothes were wet and mud-spattered, a hint of stiffness in his muscles told of long days of travel. Driven, furiously engaged with the direction of his thoughts, as if the storm had entered his brain, he marched forward. I thought he would stride straight past me. Did he even see me?

I waited until he drew level, even two steps beyond, picking apart my own wayward reaction to this man as my heart beat a little more quickly, my mind bounding ahead to the prospect of his caustic observations. Unexpectedly my lips warmed. That final kiss had been compelling.

If I did not speak now, he would be gone…

'Sir William…'

He lurched to a halt, wheeled round, eyes fierce as if expecting an enemy to leap from concealment. Then a sharp, impatient exhalation of breath.

'Mistress Perrers.'

A scratchy bow, irritable beyond words. To which I responded with an equally brief curtsey. Braveheart, older but no wiser, pushed hard against my legs to give her courage.

'Is that all you have to say?' I asked sweetly.

His eyes narrowed. 'What do you want me to say? I'm back. And not best pleased.'

An understatement, seeing his expression clearly for the first time. His face was hard, engraved with a faint cobweb of lines by eye and mouth that were new since I had last seen him. His tight-lipped mouth and flared nostrils spoke of temper. His whole body was a study in contained fury, with all the allure of a shard of flint. But my heart shifted at the proximity of his lean frame and sardonic features. When he snatched his hat from his head in a gesture of furious impatience his hair clung, sleek as moleskin from rain and sweat, against his skull. His eyes, dark and hostile on mine as he waited for me to speak, were no darker than his mood, which was dangerous and volatile. And still I felt that uncomfortable thrill of attraction. New to me but frighteningly appealing.

I set myself to speak of immediate affairs. Indeed there would be no point in doing otherwise since the man was too caught up in the moment to think beyond his grievances.

'I hope you've come prepared to answer for your actions in Ireland, Sir William.'

'I might have hoped you'd have warned me, mistress,' he snapped back.

'And I would have.' I tilted my chin a little. I did not

appreciate his criticism. 'It was too late. The King's summons would have reached you before any warning of mine. Besides, would it have made any difference?'

He shifted his shoulders irritably. 'So he's angry.'

'He's not pleased.'

'I thought the King was fading,' he growled. 'I had hoped the Prince might have spoken for me.'

'The Prince is ill.'

'I had heard.' Windsor sighed, his thoughts momentarily diverted. 'And God knows I'm sorry for it. Once we were close enough, fighting side by side, campaigning together—twenty years ago now.' His frown deepened as he stared down at his fist clenched on his ill-used cap. 'We were both young and loved the soldiering life. He was the best commander I ever knew. And now...'

'Now those days are gone; the Prince is dying.'

'Is he, now? It raises a question over the succession.'

'It does. A question where more than one has an interest.'

'The child is too young...five years?'

I sighed silently. Politics and policy. Court intrigue. This was not what I wanted to talk of, when my heart was beating and my blood racing: that same strange reaction to this man whose principles were questionable, whose motives were driven by personal ambition and whose actions did not bear close scrutiny. I realised that a silence had fallen between us, and that for the first time Windsor was concentrating on me.

'You look well,' he announced brusquely.

'I am.'

'I see my wolfhound fulfils her role.'

'Not to any degree.' I dug my fingers into the rough hair at Braveheart's neck, causing her to whine in delight. 'She needs my company to make her feel brave, and even then a mouse would frighten her. Your choice was not a good one, Sir William.'

'And the blade?'

'I have had no occasion to use it, unless it be to cut my meat.'

'For which it was not intended.' For the first time his eye glittered with more than ill humour. 'Tell me that you keep it in your bodice.'

'I'll tell you no such thing.'

I waited for a provocative reply, but he surprised me.

'I hear you've made a reputation for avarice. Your hold on power has grown apace since I saw you last. I commend you.'

It hurt a little. I did not expect that from him. 'And I hear that you are much disliked by those whom you rule.' I would give as good as I got.

'I also hear that you are making a name for yourself acquiring rights over property by fraud.'

Acquiring property? He would know, of course. It was no secret—but fraud? Oh, he was in a vicious mood. I raised my chin.

'Fraud? That's unproven! My agent, Greseley, is a man of high principle!' My response was sharp for I would defend my business dealings until my last breath. 'If you refer to the fact that I acquired the manor of Compton Murdak with some difficulty, then that is so. Are you so interested? Then let me tell you. I sued John Straunge for poaching in my new rabbit warren—did you hear of that too? He was as guilty as hell and deserved the fine. His wife foolishly wore a rabbit-skin hood.' I smiled at the memory. 'I sat with the judges in the case and pointed it out to them. They were not pleased at my interference, but they ruled in my favour. How could they not? If that is fraud, then I am guilty.' I grew solemn. 'I hear that *you* are guilty of exploitation and bribery.'

It was like setting a match to dry timber.

'God's Blood! Of course I am. Which Governor of Ireland has never been guilty of bribery?' His jaw visibly clenched. 'When will he see me?'

His admission shocked me. 'I don't know.'

'Then I'd better find someone who does.'

'There is no one.' I had not done with him yet. 'Who knows but the King himself?'

His stare became ferocious. 'The longer Ireland is without a head, the sooner it will descend into revolt and bloodshed. All my work undone in the time it takes for Edward to decide that he has no one, other than me, to take on the task.'

And without another word or even a gesture of respect, he spun on his heel, damp cloak billowing and shedding pieces of twig and leaf, and marched off. I watched him go. I was sorry, even in this foul mood. I trusted him as little as I trusted Gaunt, but there was a visceral connection between us. I might have wished there was not, but so it was. I waited until he reached the staircase at the end of the Hall. I raised my voice.

'Windsor.'

He turned but did not reply. Even from a distance I could tell that his humour had not softened. There he stood in the shadow, the light from a flickering torch picking out the edge of his cloak, the glint of the metal at his side. A man of shadows, a man of unplumbed depths. It would be a brave woman who claimed to know him.

'I can find out for you,' I suggested.

'Then do so.'

Once, four years ago, he had marched back to finish a conversation, apologising for his rude manner. Now he stood and waited as if I might approach him. I did not. A neat stalemate of our joint making.

'I do not answer to your beck and call, Sir William.' My reply echoed in the vast space.

Windsor bowed low, the gesture dripping with malice.

'Sweet Alice, sweeter than ever. Will you be there when Edward tears my morals to shreds and damns my actions to hell and back?'

'I wouldn't miss it for the world.'

'And will you speak out for me?'

'I will not. But neither will I condemn you until I've heard the evidence.'

'So you are not my enemy?'

'Did I ever say I was?'

A hard crack of a laugh was his only reply. At least I had made him laugh. He ran up the stairs, every action speaking of annoyance but perhaps a lessening of the anger. Until at the head of the stair he halted and looked down to where I still stood below.

'Were you deliberately waiting for me?'

'Certainly not!'

The bow, the flourish of his cap suggested that he did not believe me for a moment. I watched him disappear through the archway.

What now? I was not satisfied, not content to leave matters as they were. Never had I felt this need to be close to a man of the Court. Yes—through necessity, through courting their regard, through a need to win their support in a bid to protect Edward. But this? Windsor's friendship—his regard—would bring me no good. And yet still I wanted it.

I considered as the distant sound of his boot heels died away. I did trust him more than I trusted Gaunt. And then I pushed it aside, unable to make sense of my troubled thoughts. Time would tell. I would certainly be there when Edward dissected his morals and his character. And, no, I would not condemn him until I had heard his excuses.

Windsor's presence continued to nibble at my consciousness. Nibble? Snap rather. Like a kitchen cat pouncing on a well-fed and unwary rat.

Edward ordered Windsor to present himself one hour before noon on the following day with no prompting from me. The King was lucid, furious. It was, I thought, very much a repetition of his interview with Lionel without the close redeeming relationship of father to son. In the end Edward had forgiven Lionel. Here there was no softness, only accusation following on accusation. Edward was angry and seethingly forthright: there was no impediment to his memory or his powers of speech that day.

Windsor proved to be equally uninhibited beneath the gloss of respect.

As I had intended, I sat beside Edward, fascinated at the play of will between the two men, impressed by Edward's grasp of events, anxious that Windsor would not overstep the mark. Why was I anxious? Why should I care? I did not know. But I did.

Edward's litany of crimes against his Governor of Ireland rolled on and on.

'Bloody mismanagement…inglorious culpability…disgraceful self-interest… Appalling fiscal double-dealing.'

Windsor withstood it all with dour expression, feet planted, arms at his sides. I did not think his features had relaxed for one minute since his arrival the previous day.

Was he guilty? Despite his callous acceptance of my initial accusation, I had no idea. He argued his case with superb ease, not once hesitating. Yes, he had taxed heavily.

Yes, he had used the law to support English power. Yes, he had empowered the Anglo-Irish at the expense of the native Irish—to do otherwise would have been political suicide. Was not the revenue needed to finance English troops to force the Irish rebels to keep their heads down? If that amounted to extortion and discreditable taxation, then he would accept it. In Ireland it was called achieving peace. And he would defy anyone to instigate peace in that God-forsaken tribal, war-torn province by any other means than threats and bribery.

'And the royal grant made for such purposes?' Edward was not impressed.

'A grant I thank you for, Sire.' At least Windsor tried to be conciliatory. 'But that was spent long ago. I am now on my own and have to take what measures I can.'

'I don't like your methods and I don't like the rumble of dissatisfaction I hear.'

'When is there not dissatisfaction, Sire?'

'You are very voluble in defence of your innocence.'

How would he answer that? I waited, my heart thudding against my ribs.

His eyes never flinched from Edward's face. 'I would never claim innocence, Sire. A good politician can't afford to be naive. Pragmatism is a far more valuable commodity, as you yourself will be aware. And who knows what's happening while my back is turned?'

'They don't want you back,' Edward accused.

Windsor shook his head, in no manner discomfited. 'Of course they don't. They want someone without experience, to mould and turn to their own will. I am not popular but I hold to English policy as best I can with the tools I have. A weaker man would have the Irish lords singing his praises and licking the toes of his boots, all the time while they are sliding Irish gold into their own pockets.'

'They want me to send the young Earl of March,' Edward announced. 'At least I know his honesty.'

'I rest my case, Sire. Doubtless an able youth. But with neither experience nor years to his advantage.' Windsor left the thought hanging, his opinion clear.

'He is husband to my granddaughter!'

Edward was tiring. He might wish to champion the cause of young Edmund Mortimer, Earl of March, wed to his granddaughter Philippa, but I could see the tension beginning to build in him, wave upon wave, as weakness crept over mind and body. Time to end this before his inevitable humiliation, I decided. Time to end it for Windsor too. I leaned across with a hand to Edward's sleeve.

'How old is the young Earl, my lord?' I murmured.

'I think…' A frightening vagueness clouded his eyes.

'I doubt he has more than twenty one years under his belt.' I knew he hadn't.

'But he is my granddaughter's husband…' Edward clung to the single fact of which he was certain in the terrible mist that engulfed his mind, his voice growing harsh, querulous.

'And one day he will serve you well with utmost loyalty,' I agreed. 'But it is a difficult province, for so young a man.'

Edward looked at me. 'Do you think?'

'There may be much in what Sir William says…'

'No!' he huffed, but with agonising uncertainty.

I had planted the seed. I looked at Windsor, willing him to a mood of diplomacy, and for the first time in the audience he returned my gaze. Then he bowed to Edward.

'Do I return to Ireland, Sire? To continue your work to hold the province? Until the Earl of March is fit to assume the role?'

It was impeccably done.

'I'll consider your guilt first. Until then you'll stay here under my eye.'

It was not an out-and-out refusal but I doubted Windsor accepted it in that light. He bowed again and stalked out. I may as well not have been there.

'Come,' I said to Edward, helping him from his chair. 'You will rest. Then we will talk of it, and you will come to a wise decision—as you always do.'

'Yes.' He leaned heavily on my arm, almost beyond speech. 'We will talk of it...'

So Windsor, against his wishes, was restored to the complex round of Court life where all was seen and gossiped about and it was increasingly difficult to keep Edward's piteous decline from public gaze. For the first week I saw nothing of him. Edward languished and Windsor kept his head down. No decision was made about the future of Ireland. How did Windsor spend his time? When last at Court he had sought me out. Now he did not. When Edward was strong enough to dine in public with a good semblance of normality, Windsor was not present. After some discreet questioning I discovered that he visited with the Prince at Kennington.

I wished him well of that visit. I thought there would be little satisfaction for him.

And then he was back, prowling the length and breadth of one of Edward's antechambers, a black scowl on his face, a number of scrolls tucked under his arm. At least the scowl lifted when he saw me emerge from the private apartments. He loped across as I closed the door at my back. He even managed to smile, though there was no lightness in him. It gave me an urge to shock him out of his self-engrossment—

except that I could think of no way of doing it. Neither did I have the energy. Edward had been morose and demanding. If there had been other courtiers waiting in the antechamber, I might even have avoided his harsh, brooding figure. As it was…

'The King has not decided?' he demanded without greeting.

'No.'

'Will he never make a decision?'

I sighed, a weary hopelessness settling on me. 'In his own good time. But you know that. You must be patient, Sir William. Are you waiting for me?'

'Certainly not.' A wolfish grin as he deliberately repeated my previous denial.

I laughed, some of the weariness dispelled. 'What are you doing to pass the time?' We were close enough that I tapped my fingers against the documents.

'Buying property.'

'In Ireland?' I was surprised.

'In England. In Essex, primarily.' I was even more surprised, since his family estates were far to the north.

'Why?'

'Against hard times. Like you. When we can no longer depend on royal patronage.'

He looked at me, as if weighing up a thought that had entered his head. Or perhaps it had been there for some time.

'What is it?' I was suspicious.

'I have a proposition, Mistress Perrers.'

A little tingle in my blood. A faint warmth that dispelled the smothering lethargy, product of sleepless nights.

'A proposition?' I turned to go, feigning disinterest. 'Now, what would that be? You've had little enough to say to me in the past se'nnight.'

'I've been busy.'

'And so? Now that you are no longer busy?'

Again, for a long moment, he studied me. Then gave a decisive nod. 'Let us find a little corner where the hundreds of courtier ears in this place will not flap. It's like a beehive, a constant buzz of rumour and scandal.'

He escorted me—not that I was unwilling for had he not stirred my curiosity?—into a chamber used by the scribes and men of law, angling me between desks and stools into a corner where we could sit. There were no courtiers here. The young scribes continued to dip and scratch and scribble without interest in us. Idly I picked up a document from a box on the floor and pretended to be engrossed in it. A bill of sale of two dozen coneys. Presumably we'd eaten them in the last rabbit pottage.

Windsor came straight to the point. 'I think we could make a killing.'

We? I said nothing, fanning myself with the coney document.

He grinned. 'You give nothing away, do you? A killing of a financial nature.'

I tapped my foot against the base of the box.

'Would you care to throw in your lot with me on the purchase of some excellent little manors?'

A proposition indeed. My interest was snared like one of the unfortunate rabbits. That he would desire someone in partnership with him—and that he would look to me. I smoothed out the roll of parchment in my hands as if the coneys were of vast importance, playing for time.

'And why would I do that?'

'Against the hard times,' he repeated. 'They'll be harder for you than for me.' And he began to juggle with two lumps of red sealing wax swept up from a nearby desk, adding a third and then a fourth with amazing dexterity.

'Perhaps.' My eye might be caught by the clever manipulation of the wax, but my mind was working furiously. Would they be harder for me? I expect he was right. It was always harder for a woman alone. I slid my eye from the wax to the sharp stare turned on me. 'Why invite *me* to share in your project?'

'You have an interest in purchasing land.' The wax, unheeded, fell to the floor with a soft clatter. 'You have contacts. I expect you have access to funds. Need I say more?'

It was an impressive tally, of which I was justifiably proud. 'What do *you* have?' I demanded.

'Business acumen.' He was not short of arrogance.

'Do I not have that also?'

'Amazingly, yes, but…'

'Don't say it! Amazingly for a woman!'

'Then I won't.' His mouth twitched. 'What do you think?'

I waved the forgotten document to and fro, giving it some thought.

'Don't you trust me?'

'No.'

He laughed. 'So what's your answer? Is that no, too?'

'My answer is…' And because I did not know my own mind: 'Why do I need you? I have acquired land perfectly adequately without you.'

'Sometimes you need a man to push the negotiation forward.'

'I have any number of men who are ready to work with me, for our joint benefit.'

'Do you?' He looked surprised.

So I allowed myself to crow a little. 'Did you not know? In the last handful of years I have purchased any number of manors through the offices of a little cabal of most trusted men. I use them as feoffees who—Master William Greseley in particular—undertake negotiations in my name. It is a perfect arrangement, for a *femme sole.*'

'Where did you learn that?'

'A long time ago. A different life.' I remembered standing outside Janyn Perrers's room, my bride gift clutched in my hand. I smiled a little. How far I had come. Then I dragged my mind back to the mercurial man who sat before me, leaning forward, having rescued the wax from the floor and tossing it irritatingly from hand to hand. 'If I do not help myself, who will?'

'Clever!' Windsor's eyes narrowed as he considered what I had achieved. 'I admit your success. Tell me, then, a mere curious man, how many manors have you actually snatched up?' I shook my head. I would not say, which he acknowledged readily enough. 'I'll find out one day! I still say you need an astute man, who has a more personal view of your future.'

'And you are he.'

He bowed, seated as he was.

'Ah, but I think my little cabal of moneyed men have a very personal commitment to my success. If I fall under attack, so will they, so they will defend me to the death. I find them hard-working and unswervingly loyal. And so my answer is, Sir William—no. You might need me, but I do not need you.'

'Then our conversation is at an end, Mistress Perrers.'

Abruptly, he tossed the wax into my lap and left me to the company of the incurious clerks. I had surprised him with my refusal. And he did not like it.

For the whole of the next week he kept his damnable distance from me. During that time I considered Windsor's offer. I had many hours. The King was full of lassitude, his mind sluggish. When awake Edward felt an urge to confess his sins and so spent many hours on his knees in the chapel. Sometimes he stood alone on the castle walls, looking abstractedly out towards France. Since I was not in demand, my thoughts turned inward to the unexpected proposal.

There was much to recommend it in spite of my cavalier rejection. Was it not always easier for a man than for a woman to indulge in binding agreements with those with land to sell or lease? Yes, I used Greseley but would it not be more advantageous to have an equal partner, a man with some status and authority, whose interest was as strong as mine? A woman was considered an easy target. I might have the King's ear but not everyone was willing to accept my jurisdiction.

Yes, I had won my case over that unattractive rabbit-skin hood, but my mind swerved to a more recent clash with the local population near my manor of Finningley, a valuable little property in Nottinghamshire. My manor no longer! For what had the local mob done? Only attacked and stolen my cattle. And not only that: my crops were destroyed; my men and servants imprisoned until they swore to renege on their oath of fealty to me. Which they did, the words tripping over their tongues in their desire to obey the vindictive rogues with hard words and harder fists who had set on them.

Now, if I were in partnership with Windsor... Would it be to my advantage? I imagined Windsor more than capable in negotiation. But would I wish to work with one such as William de Windsor? *Do you trust me?* he had asked. *No*, I had replied. And yet I thought it would be exhilarating to work in tandem with such a man. I imagined him taking a select group of armed men to sway the decision of the local population, and ensure that Finningley remained my property.

On the other hand...

He would make me take the initiative! If I kept my distance he would find someone else to work in partnership in his ventures.

So must I agree to work hand in glove with him? A bold woman might be persuaded to accept a glove from Windsor. A smile touched my mouth. I would do it. But I would take him by surprise, on my own terms. I would put him at a disadvantage, and enjoy every minute of it.

I wrote two fast notes, much with the same purpose. One to Master Greseley, one to Windsor. The response from both was prompt. I set myself, with some careful arrangements, to luxuriate in the outcome.

I was always fond of the drama of a mummers' play.

The whole occasion had a delicious *frisson* about it. I chose late afternoon, for obvious reasons, when the light in the audience chamber would have dimmed, and I had no torches lit. I took my place on Edward's throne, clad in dark skirts and veil, Greseley at my side. Only when I was ready did I raise my hand for the attendant at the door to admit Windsor who was waiting in the antechamber. I heard his words.

'You will be seen now, my lord.'

And I recalled my little note. Not malicious, playful only. I hoped Windsor would appreciate it.

His Majesty has made a decision relating to the governorship of Ireland. You will be informed in the Panelled Chamber at four hours after noon.

He was very prompt. He strode in. Halted. Bowed, keeping a keen eye to protocol.

'You may approach,' the attendant advised, before closing the door behind him.

So we were alone, the three of us, as Windsor advanced. He had dressed with impeccable neatness in dark hose and close-fitting cotehardie in black and green damask, cinched with a jewelled girdle on his hips. Very fashionable—even to a parti-coloured shoulder cape and gold-edged baldric, although he had abjured the extravagant long-toed shoes for good-quality leather boots. He was out to make a solid impression; he would not lose this position through inattention to detail. He was, I recognised anew, a man who could play whatever role he set himself.

The thought shivered momentarily along my spine, but I sat perfectly still.

When did he realise it was not the King who occupied the royal throne?

When he was halfway down the length of the room. I saw the moment, the second look, the recognition. To his credit, there was barely a hitch in his step. He continued until he stood just below the dais and bowed again with the same depth of respect, the feathers of his cap sweeping the floor. Straightening to his full height, he looked up at me. His eyes were sombre in the shadowed light, but they gleamed when I motioned to Greseley to light the bracket behind me. And there we were, a dramatic little scene in a pool of golden illumination.

'Sir William. How good of you to come.'

'Isn't it? I could not resist the invitation.'

'And so promptly.'

'I dare do no other. Queen Alice, is it?'

I would not smile! 'I think that is treason, my lord.'

'I'm sure it is. As is impersonating royalty.'

'Impersonation? I wear no crown.'

'Forgive me! Is that not the throne that you are occupying?'

'Where would you have me sit, sir? On the floor?'

'Many would…'

'I make no claims to royal authority, Sir William.'

'Impressive, mistress.'

My whole body felt alive, my breath quick and shallow. This was exhilarating. And beneath the sharp cut and thrust, did we not understand each other very well? I stilled my tongue, I made him ask. And he did.

'You have news for me?'

'Yes.'

'Well?'

'I will do it.'

'Do what?' And I saw the fingers of his right hand stretch slowly against this thigh. So it did matter to him, as I had thought.

'I will become your associate in buying land. This is my agent, Master Greseley.' Greseley bowed. 'He deals with many of my ventures and handles the finances.'

Windsor's brows snapped together. 'Why have you changed you mind?'

'Sometimes it is necessary to work through a second party. I have decided that I will work with you.'

He made no reply while his regard was fixed on my face.

'It is also,' I suggested, smoothly, 'a woman's privilege to change her mind.' I rose to my feet, considered remaining above him, then stepped down from the dais so that we were all on equal footing. 'I trust your offer is still open? If not, then Master Greseley and I will continue to purchase land in the same efficient manner that we have always done. But if you are still of a mind, Sir William…'

'I am.' Was his reply not quite as smooth as his wont?

'What do you think, Master Greseley?'

'I see advantages, mistress,' he replied in his undemonstrative way, as if nothing could surprise him.

'So it is done,' Windsor observed.

'So it is,' I agreed.

We clasped hands, the three of us.

'Are we business associates, then, Sir William?'

'So it seems. I rarely enjoy being wrong-footed by anyone, much less by a woman. But on this occasion I believe it will be a lucrative venture.'

Not only did he clasp my hand but he kissed it. His smile held the sharpness of a man acknowledging that he had been outsmarted.

My carefully staged little drama had taken him by surprise. To the advantage of both of us, of course. But my planning was nothing to what Windsor achieved to stun me, to all but shake me out of my wits. What's more, it took no staging on his part, merely a diabolical cunning and an outrageous confidence.

I suppose he thought I deserved it. Perhaps I did.

Meanwhile, as my new associate planned his private campaign of revenge against me, we celebrated our first joint step into property with a cup of wine. It was a fine Bordeaux, to toast the acquisition of the land, rents and services of the equally fine manor of Northbrokes in Middlesex. Greseley was lugubrious but satisfied. I was full of delight at our smooth purchase. Windsor was not. Although he worked hard to keep his frustrations smothered beneath a brittle jubilation as we lifted our cups in mutual appreciation, his mood was sombre.

'Can you not get the King to make a decision on Ireland?' he asked when Greseley had left us.

'Edward is not capable of deciding what he will eat to break his fast. You must be patient.'

'It is not in my nature.'

As I knew. I would miss him when he was gone.

I made an error. Or perhaps it was not an error, because it was an outcome I desired, but it turned out to be a dangerous choice on my part. Where had my sense of clear judgement gone? Buried under my successful enterprise with William de Windsor, I expect, thrust aside by my delight in Edward's felicitous return to health. We were at Woodstock, where Wykeham had gloried in the freedom to rebuild the old manor into a stately palace. The hunting was good and Edward, rallying as he often did in new surroundings, was renewed in body and spirit. Or perhaps I was driven by my lamentable ambition to own a King's ransom in fine jewels. That I cannot deny.

Or was it, in some basic manner born of my treatment at Joan of Kent's hands, to prove that I was now a woman worthy of such gems? Well, perhaps it was, and I think I was not entirely to blame. A package had been delivered to her during her stay at the Abbey.

'Open it,' she had ordered.

I had unrolled the leather to find a set of jewelled buttons clustered in the palms of my hands: a fire in each heart. Sapphires set in gold.

'Don't touch them,' she spat, snatching them from me, impossibly wayward. 'Do you know what they cost me? More than two hundred pounds. They're not for such as you.'

But now they were for such as I. My jewels—Philippa's jewels—were far superior to any that Fair Joan owned. I would wear them and relish Joan's envy.

Why was I incapable of seeing the consequences of my request to Edward? I had stepped carefully all my life and yet here I leapt into a morass that was ultimately to drag me down. And what was it that caused the conflagration? Philippa's jewels. Some inherited, some gifts, some brought with her to England all those years ago. All magnificent.

'They're yours.' Edward placed them on the bed in the room he had had constructed with such love for Philippa, and which I now occupied. With the jewels was a letter in his own hand.

...we give and concede to our beloved Alice Perrers, late damsel of the chamber of our most dear consort Philippa now dead, that to her heirs and executors all the jewels, goods and chattels that the said Queen left in the hands of Euphemia, wife to Sir Walter de Hasleworth, and the said Euphemia is to deliver them to the said Alice on the receipt of this command...

Philippa's jewels. What woman would not want them? They took my breath as I lifted a string of rubies, a collar set with sapphires, a heavy emerald ring, and allowed them to fall back to join their glittering brethren in the metal-bound coffer. Edward had given them to me.

But on whose initiative?

On mine, for my sins. I had asked for them. Since Philippa's death they had never seen the light of day, but had languished in safekeeping with one of the senior ladies of Philippa's household. And so I had asked for them, and Edward, in his magnificent generosity, had arranged it. Legally and officially they were now mine. And with this simple acquisition of Philippa's jewelery, I helped to dig my own grave. Thoughtlessness on my part. Greed? I did not think so. They ought to be worn—and who better than the King's Concubine?

I wore the sapphire collar when the Court met for supper.

It was, of course, immediately recognisable and the whispers had begun to circulate, between the minced meatballs in jelly and Edward's favourite dish of salmon in rich cream sauce, damning me for my impertinence. Did I not see the eyes slide disbelievingly over the wealth that gleamed on my bosom? And the murmurs multiplied when next morning I pinned a ruby brooch to my mantle. Disgraceful avarice, they said. The jewels were not mine to take. The King must be besotted or bewitched, one as bad as the other, to give his wife's jewels to his whore. If they were to be worn, was it not more fitting for them to be seen around the neck of Isabella or even Princess Joan? Certainly not adorning the neck of Alice Perrers. Had Edward lost his wits entirely?

I could answer my critics. Not that I ever did—why would I? Any reasoning of mine would be rejected out of hand. But of what use was it for such glorious jewels to be shut in a box in a dusty cellar in the home of Lady Euphemia? Far better to be worn and enjoyed, and how I enjoyed the weight and warmth of them on my skin. How I relished the glitter of the stones, the dull gleam of the gold. I would challenge any one of those sharp-tongued courtly vipers not to covet the glory of Philippa's jewels as I did, and I smiled as I flaunted them with ostentatious pride. It was not as if I was wearing the royal regalia, was it? If Philippa had wished them to be worn by Isabella or Joan, she would have willed them. She did not. Did she will them to me? She did not do that either but I did not think she would object to seeing them on my person. And I think, truth to tell, she might have seen the humour in it.

Did I have an eye to the coming years? Of course I did.

As Edward's life-force failed, my preparations for an uncertain future quickened. Greseley might decry gemstones
against the lasting value of land, but both were of equal
value to me, and what woman could resist a collar of sapphires and pearls? Besides, I could not afford to be complacent. And Edward knew it too, although we did not speak
of it beyond his solemn assertion: 'At least they'll put cloth
on your back, Alice, and bread in your mouth when I'm not
here to provide them.'

Oh, yes. I could make every excuse, but I never did. All
I knew was that Edward loved to see me wearing them,
and to me that, and my own pleasure, was reason enough
to flaunt them before the censorious Court.

'They become you as well as they became Philippa.' The
smile that almost refused to come to Edward's mouth these
days, so weak were his muscles, was very gentle.

'I am not Philippa, my lord.' Equally gentle. Some days
I was not sure that he even distinguished between us. But
on that day he did.

'I know that very well. You are Alice and you are my
beloved.'

In response to my wearing a particularly fine emerald
ring that Philippa had much loved, and a gold-linked belt
set with equally fine stones, Princess Joan's descent on
Woodstock was immediate and vicious. Someone had ensured that the gossip reached her. 'They're Philippa's!' She
launched into invective before the door to my parlour was
closed. 'By what right do you dare to even touch them?
Much less wear them!'

On that occasion I was wearing rubies. Well, she would
notice those that adorned my hood, as large as cherrystones,
wouldn't she? They were difficult to overlook. At least we

were private when Joan grabbed my wrist for her inspection. 'I don't believe it!' She twisted my arm so that the light glittered on the ring and the blood-red clasp around my wrist. 'Did you steal them?'

I raised my brows. I would not answer such an accusation.

'Did you?' Joan was always obtuse. 'I know you did. It's the only way you would get your thieving hands on them. They're the Queen's. They're not yours to wear.'

'Oh? I think they are.' My gaze never wavered beneath hers, and at last gave her pause.

'He gave them to you?'

'Of course he did.'

'What did you have to do to get them from him? No—don't tell me, I might vomit.'

Without doubt I should have been more circumspect in my reply. 'Am I not worthy of them?' I asked, in retrospect not circumspect at all.

'By God, you are not.'

'By God, I am.'

She dropped her hold, retreating in obvious disgust, lips drawn back from her neat teeth. But I followed her. I was no minion to be put in my place. And I was weary of baseless accusations.

'If we are talking of worth and payment, then consider this, my lady. How many nights have I sat beside the King when he is sleepless? How many nights have I talked or read to keep the nightmares at bay? How many days have I devoted to the melancholy that drags him down?' I pushed on to make her think beyond her prejudices, to make her acknowledge me and what I had achieved. 'You know what it is like when a strong man suffers. He is demanding, and yet inconsolable in his weakness. It is not easy for a woman to stand as buffer against the horrors that attack him. You know this from your own experience.'

For a moment I saw her hesitate. She understood what I meant. But not for long.

'The Prince is my husband! It is my right and my duty to stand with him! You have no right!'

Any prudence I might have had melted under Joan's scorn. 'And the King is my lover,' I rejoined. 'He gave me Philippa's jewels and I will value them. I will wear them and enjoy them.'

'You wear them like a slut—shamelessly—a Court harlot who has demanded jewels for her body.'

But I did not think I was. These were not gifts given in a spirit of payment for services rendered; the jewels had been given out of love. Yet I was without redress. My reputation was made and I must live with it, but sometimes it was very hard to accept the consequences. Joan's savage attack wounded me after all, and that was why I said the unforgiveable.

'I had no need to demand, my lady. The King obviously considers gold and gems suitable payment for my superior skills in the bedchamber.'

'Whore!' She stormed from the room.

I was to pay a high price for my heedlessness, higher than I could have dreamed possible, even though I made an attempt at conciliation, for Edward's sake. I was not entirely heartless. Unfortunately my good intentions made matters worse.

Edward decided to visit the Prince at Kennington, where I accompanied him with serious intent, for Edward, I decided, deserved some peace in his household. War between his mistress and his daughter-in-law—no better than two screeching, scratching cats—should be avoided. Within minutes, King and Prince were deep in discussion of the state of the present truce with France, and I, my feet on a path towards what I suspected would be a lost cause, was shown by the steward into Joan's solar.

Joan sat at her embroidery, by her side on the floor her young son, turning the illuminated pages of a book. A charming boy with fair hair and round cheeks, Richard leapt to his feet and bowed with quaint grace.

I curtseyed. 'My lord. My lady.' I would be courteous.

Joan remained seated with flat denial in her eyes. 'Mistress Perrers.' Her voice was as flat as her stare.

'His Majesty has come to speak with the Prince.' I was very formal. How to broach this. Head on as if in the tilting yard was the only way. 'How is the Prince?'

I had not needed to ask—had I not seen it for myself? His loss of weight was pitiful. Eyes feverish, skin grey, hair dull and lank, the basin positioned beside his daybed was ominous in itself. And Joan's features closed, tight with distress. Unable to hide her fears, she shook her head. For once her guard was down, with even the moisture of tears in her eye. This was my one possibility, for Edward's sake, of draining the poison from her hatred of me.

Grief strong in the set of her mouth, the hard lines engraved deep from nose to chin in her soft flesh, Joan forgot she spoke to me. One tear rolled down her cheek. Then another. 'I don't know what to do for him.' It was a cry from the heart.

'I can help.'

'You! What can you do?' Furiously she wiped away the tears.

I could have retreated. I should have, if I had known where this would lead, yet faced with such grief, knowing the terror of helplessness for myself when Edward looked at me as if I did not exist, I could not. In my arms I had a little coffer, a delight of sandalwood with ivory corners and metal hinges, and an intricate little lock and key. It was a costly gift in its own right but its contents were of far greater value to the Prince. I had brought the only offering I could think of that might be acceptable. For sure the Princess would take nothing else from me. I placed it on the chest that held a tangle of her embroidery silks.

'What is that?'

'A gift.'

'I have coffers enough. Of greater value than that.' She barely looked at it, setting a number of stitches, stabbing clumsily at the panel for a purse or an altar cloth.

I thought it unlikely, given its value—for it was a gift to me from Edward—but I let it go.

'It is the contents,' I explained gently. The nuns would have been proud of my humility. 'A number of nostrums and potions. They will give the Prince ease…'

'And do these nostrums and potions work?' She stopped stitching.

'They soothed the King in his grief after Philippa died. They helped Philippa too.'

Joan cast aside her sewing and I saw her fingers twitch over the little domed lid. Surely such a gift was impossible to resist. She lifted it, to reveal the carefully folded packets of herbs, the glass phials of intense colour.

'They are distilled from common plants,' I explained. 'I learned the skills at the Abbey. Here are the leaves of lady's smock to restore a lost appetite and soothe digestion. A tincture of primrose to aid rest and a quiet mind. White willow bark when the pain is too great to bear. I have written the amounts.' I indicated the sheet of parchment tucked under the lid. 'Either you or the Prince's body servants can mix them with wine as indicated. I'm certain the Prince would enjoy the effects.'

Joan looked at the coffer, the neat arrangement of packets and bottles. Her teeth bit hard into her lower lip.

'I can speak well for their effectiveness,' I encouraged as she made no move. 'There is also the pulp of dog rose hips—to staunch bleeding and the loss of bodily fluids.'

We had all heard of the Prince's appalling symptoms, the constant flow of blood and semen that could not be halted.

Joan moved. It was as if I had thrust a bunch of stinging nettles into her unprotected hand as, with a jerk of her arm, she swept the box from coffer to floor. It fell with a crack, damaging the hinges, so that glass from the phials shattered and the liquid ran. A dusting of herbs covered the whole, swirling into intricate patterns. Richard squeaked in horror, then was quick to investigate, poking his fingers into the debris until Joan took a handful of his tunic to pull him away to stand beside her.

'Don't touch that! It's the work of the devil!'

'Indeed it is not,' I remonstrated.

'Satan's brew! And you are his servant!'

Her words were a shock, running cold through my blood as we looked at the mess between us, Joan still seated, I rigid with what she had implied. Until Joan raised her eyes to mine, holding them as she clicked her fingers for one of her women to approach from the far end of the room.

'Get rid of this. Burn it. And the box. I don't want to find any trace of this on my floor.' And when the woman gawped at the detritus: 'Do it *now*!' she hissed, like the kiss of a steel blade against its adversary.

As the woman busied herself the Princess stood, gripped my wrist and leaned close, her mouth against my ear. 'Did you think I would be such a fool?'

I was still stunned by her outrageous response to a gift that could have brought nothing but good. 'I thought you might accept what I could do to give your husband ease,' I remarked, watching the play of fury—and was that fear?—across her face.

'Ease! Distilled from common plants,' she spat. Her voice fell to a whisper that shivered in the corners of the room. 'I hear you employ witchcraft to achieve your ends, Mistress Perrers. I think you have *maleficium* in mind. Not *compassion*!' Spittle sprang to her lips on the word.

But there was only one word that I heard out of the whole rant.

'Witchcraft?' I repeated, voice equally low. It was not a word to shout to the rooftops. I had heard much said of me but not that. A little breath of fear beat in my mind, but I managed a sneer coated in laughter. 'And what do *they* say? Whoever *they* are. That I eat the flesh of children? That I keep a familiar and feed it from the blood of my own body?'

'They say you call up the Devil's powers. That you have skills and knowledge that no God-fearing woman should have.' I watched as Joan's fingers on her left hand circled into the sign against the Evil Eye. 'How in God's name could you explain Edward's fascination with so ugly and ill-bred a woman as Alice Perrers?' Her jaw snapped shut on my name.

It was a slide of a knife between my ribs, but I ensured that my reply gave away nothing of her wounding, or of the fear that spread to fill the spaces around my heart. The cold along the length of my spine deepened, as intense as ice in January.

'It is inexplicable, I grant you,' I remarked, refusing to defend my birth or my looks. 'But my lord's love for me is no product of witchcraft. Neither was this gift.' I slid my shoe over the sifting of dried heart's-ease flowers that still marked the floor. 'But if my husband suffered as yours does, my lady, I would use the powers of the Devil himself to give his body relief. I would leave no stone unturned between here and the depths of hell, if it would allow my husband a restful night and an end to pain.'

'Get out.'

'My lady.' I curtseyed.

'Get out. Or I will lay evidence before the authorities that you plied me with witches' condiments.'

'Your evidence is worthless.' For Edward's sake, I would not allow my temper to rule.

'Get out of my sight.'

I did. I did not try again. Joan was too eaten up with hatred. I told Edward nothing of my interview. He did not need to know.

Witchcraft. Maleficium.

The vicious accusation continued to buzz in my brain, like a persistent bee in the depths of a foxglove flower. There was no evidence that Joan could use against me, of that I was certain since there had never been any bewitchment, but it was too dangerous an accusation to be taken lightly.

Evidence could be fabricated, could it not?

Chapter Twelve

I had caught Windsor off guard in the audience chamber. If I had jolted him out of his habitual *sangfroid*, he all but stunned me. He swept the rushes from beneath my feet.

It did not start off well. We had moved on in our royal perambulations from Woodstock to Sheen, where a weighty delegation had arrived from France to begin negotiations for a permanent truce. I intervened. On instructions from me, Latimer sent the delegation away. I watched them go, aware of their furious dissatisfaction at the slight to their importance. They made no attempt to hide it.

'Dangerous, Mistress Perrers!'

The voice was at my elbow.

'And what does that mean?' I scowled indiscriminately at the departing delegation of angry, high-born Frenchmen and at Windsor.

'It won't be popular.'

'What won't?'

'Dictating who will and who will not see the King.'

'Do you think I don't know that?'

How could I not know? This was not the first time Latimer and I had intervened between King and petitioner. Did I need Windsor to tell me how much resentment there was? As for resentment…I glared at the man at my side. I resented his presence. I resented his opinion. In that moment I resented everything about William de Windsor.

'You're playing with fire.'

'I know that too.'

'It will put a weapon into the hands of those who would be rid of you.'

'Tell me something I don't know.'

'So why do it?'

He could think ill of me if he wished. There he stood, regarding me with an element of deep suspicion that did nothing to improve my mood. I did not need this, not at this precise moment, but if Windsor would condemn me without a hearing, then so be it!

'I won't talk to you now! I don't have to answer for my actions to you!'

And then suddenly, overwhelmingly, I wished he would wrap his arms around me and allow me to lean against him. What I would not give for a moment of ease, to realise that I was not alone? I would like him to stroke my arm as if I were a soft-furred cat, fold my fingers close within his, and tell me that all would be well.

Of course all would not be well. Immediately I took a step back, away from him, shivering at my appalling show of weakness, determined that Windsor should never read the turmoil in my mind. I would not make excuses. I would not explain. I realised that he was staring at me intently and so I hurried to follow Latimer and the angry delegation, to make my escape. I did not think I could keep my reactions under a firm hand for much longer, when hot tears gathered in my throat.

Windsor stopped me by the simple method of stepping in front of me. 'Come with me,' he ordered curtly.

'No.'

Regardless, he took my wrist and pulled me out of the now-deserted audience chamber.

'And let go of me. Do you want all the palace riff-raff talking about us?' He released me, but I followed him, knowing that if I did not comply he would repeat the performance. 'Where are we going?'

Since I got no reply, I marched sullenly at his side, still disturbed by the recent confrontation, the disbelieving stare of the French when Latimer had offered to begin the negotiations himself, and even more unsettled by Windsor's judgement of my motives. When I found myself hustled into a corridor leading to an outer door, I balked. Halted.

'No.'

'Why is a woman always difficult when a man has her best interests at heart?' he asked, returning to intimidate me with his height and breadth in the narrow passage.

'You have only your own interests at heart. I've never met anyone as self-interested as you,' I fired back, all my thoughts awry.

'By God, woman!' He pinned me against the wall, regardless of who might be traversing the corridor—fortunately no one—and he kissed me. It was not a kiss of mild affection, or of compassion. I wasn't sure what it was. When he lifted his head, I had no breath left to speak.

'Silence! At last!'

'Are you out of your mind? Release me!' Lord, how that kiss had stirred my blood. My heart bounded against my ribs like a ferret in a hunter's cage.

He kissed me again, all heat and power—appallingly seductive—and my will to resist was stripped away. When he released my mouth I simply stood, every sense compromised.

'Excellent! Now, be a biddable girl for once in your life.'

He had kissed me, as far as I could tell, with thorough enjoyment but his face was stern, his thoughts preoccupied. And because I wanted to, I walked beside him, conscious of his nearness, the brush of his tunic against my arm at a turn in the stair. And then we were out in the open, climbing to the wall walk, under clouds that were low and brooding, much like my humour. There we came to stand, looking east, and I waited, limbs still shaking, wondering if he would kiss me again, hoping that he might, despising him for trapping me in this unexpected passion. Despising myself. I had no intention of cuckolding Edward, in private or under public gaze. The palace guards were far too obvious, far too watchful, and I retained some sense of honour even as my heart galloped like a panicked horse.

'Tell me what's troubling you,' he invited when the silence between us grew heavy.

'Nothing. Since you think the worst of me.'

'It's the King, I presume.'

'How should it be?'

'Alice…! You can't deny it any longer. He's beyond sense. At this moment you need a friend, and I'm the nearest you'll get. So tell me the truth.'

My determination to keep silent, to protect Edward at all costs, drained away. Yes, I needed a friend to help me shoulder the increasingly difficult burden. Wykeham was in Winchester. I would not put myself in Gaunt's hands. So that left Windsor. But was Windsor that friend? There he stood, dark and saturnine, the epitome of louche self-serving. And yet there was in his face, completely unexpected, kindness. Why not…?

'Yes. It's Edward.'

'You're guarding him.'

'Yes. What would you have me do? Put him on show in London, for his subjects to gawp at?' Still I was defensive.

'At least then you could not be accused of manipulating an old man for your own ends. Keeping it secret is dangerous, Alice.'

'You are not helpful.'

'I'm trying to be realistic.'

Still I resisted, but in the end I told him everything. How Edward's bright spirit was once more in eclipse, his actions unpredictable. Who could persuade him that it was not good policy to order *every* bridge in Oxfordshire to be repaired or rebuilt, simply because he wished to go hawking from Woodstock? I could not. The King was not capable of committing England to any future policy. How long could Latimer and I, and the rest of the loyal ministers, pretend that Edward was fit to be King? Edward barely knew the day of the week. His physicians could do nothing to alleviate his loss of awareness.

'And so that's why I try to protect him as much as I can,' I finished. 'Next week—tomorrow even—his senses may return.'

'How admirable you are.'

'No. I'm not. But I care too much to allow him to come under attack from those who might question his right to rule.'

'Some would say that you do it for your own ends.' Propping his shoulders against the wall, he turned to watch me as his accusation sank in. 'To bolster the King's power is to preserve that of Alice Perrers.'

'Which is entirely true, of course.' Sharp irony coated the air between us. 'How could anyone think I had any concern for the King's well-being?' I turned away, furious that once again he voiced familiar calumny against me.

'I didn't say *I* believed it,' he retorted. 'I think I need to distract you a little.'

'By kissing me?' Suddenly I was afraid of my weakness with this man, afraid of the burn of tears beneath my eyelids. I was far too emotional. 'I hope you won't.'

'No. Or not yet at any rate.'

The preoccupation was back. Windsor had other thoughts on his mind. Woman-like, I resented his preoccupation and strolled away, angry with my twisted emotions, despairing at how easily I was manoeuvred into opening my heart to this man, leaving him to lean against the stone coping and sweep an arm over the battlements to take in the view.

'I have a handful of estates in Essex,' he remarked.

Neutral territory. I strolled back. 'I know.'

'I plan to have more.'

'I know that too. Have you brought me all the way up here to tell me something of so little news?'

'No. I want to ask you something. And from the scene I just witnessed, it's becoming imperative.'

He braced himself against the parapet, chin resting on his folded arms, and glowered at the scene below, where one of the palace cats took its morning slink amongst the rabbit holes on the river bank. I waited in silence, until he angled his head to look at me again.

'Alice...'

'William?'

He eyed me speculatively.

'Alice, will you marry me?'

My mind scrabbled for understanding, for any sensible

response, finding none. After all the emotion of the morning, I could not deal with this. I was forced to drag air into my lungs.

'Are you mocking me?'

'Now, there's an intelligent reply. I often propose marriage to a woman in the spirit of mockery. The country is littered with my proposals. Will you marry me?' he repeated.

Did he mean this? I could read nothing in the hard lines of his face.

'Marriage…! But why?'

Immediately he straightened, then, shockingly, went down on one knee. For a moment of blazing memory I recalled Edward in his strength and power wooing me with poetry after my outburst, but there was no similarity here at all. Edward had wooed me from the heart: this was a charade, a travesty of honour and chivalry. Surely it was.

'I love you,' Windsor announced. 'Why else would a man ask a woman to wed him?'

'And you are a liar, Windsor.'

'Ah…but how do you know?' Those bold eyes glinted in a sudden bright stroke of sunlight through the heavy cloud.

'Sense tells me… God's Blood! Stand up—the sentries will see us and the whole world will know you are making mischief within the hour!' When he rose to his full height, the light spread over his harsh features, gilding him in an enticing softness. Pouncing, he clasped my hand and pressed his lips against my fingers.

'It's not such a bad idea, you know. Wife and Concubine—not an easy role to pursue at one and the same time, but I swear you have the talent for it. Will you?'

'No.' I had no breath, no wit to say more. What an appalling morning this had been. Was he indeed ridiculing me? If so, there was an edge of cruelty to it that I would never have expected.

'Listen to me. I'm quite serious.' He leaned back against the parapet once more, looking up to where a pair of crows somersaulted on the thermals. His voice was clipped, his hand still firm around mine, and he was deadly serious. 'I foresee advantages...'

'You would, of course!'

'For you, woman! For you! Just listen. When Edward dies, what happens to you? Alone, unprotected, you'll be a perfect scapegoat for those who have loathed you since the first day you crawled into the King's bed.' How sordid he made it sound. 'From the first day that you stood at the King's side and blocked their way to power. They'll not accept that the King is too ill to hold the reins of government. They'll blame you, and they'll take utmost pleasure in throwing you to the dogs.' His eyes slid from the tumbling crows to me. 'And I wager that none of this is new to you. You've seen the threat of the storm clouds building on your horizon, just as those birds know the power of the thermals to lift them. Look at them! Storm crows. Birds of ill omen.'

Who'd have thought Windsor would be superstitious? 'I have seen the storm clouds,' I replied. 'And I see the crows every morning without fear. I have made provision.'

'I'm sure you have. Squirrelling away wealth for your old age.' How cynical, how practical. No superstition here! Did he think I had been robbing the royal coffers? 'But what if your enemies target your sources of income?'

'I have taken precautions.'

'I know. I know how clever you are.' I thought it was no compliment. 'But that's another reason for you to watch your back. Men don't like it when a woman oversteps the line of what is acceptable for her sex. A man would get away with it. A woman? She will be damned as impertinent, presumptuous at best. Immoral at worst. A woman who fights for herself, who is bold and outspoken and fearless, and is successful at what she sets her hand to, is instantly vilified, whereas a man is praised for his perspicacity. You've made yourself notorious.'

'As have you,' I retaliated.

'That's not relevant,' Windsor fired back. 'Just as your innocence or guilt is irrelevant. They'll be snapping at your heels as soon as the King is laid out in the chapel. Now, if you wed me, I would stand protector for you and your property, through the courts if need be.'

Ah! Of course. 'And what would you get out of marriage?'

'Someone to watch over my interests in England when I'm in Ireland.'

I frowned. 'That's not an answer a woman wants to hear. It's a marriage, not a business deal.' I pulled my hand free, and turned my back on him. 'Are you still so sure you'll be allowed to go back?'

'Yes. As I said—who else is there?'

'Then pay an agent to look after your properties for you. It's cheaper than marriage. With far fewer problems,' I added dryly. 'I'll get Greseley to recommend someone.'

'I want someone who will do it for better motives than a paid clerk. I want you!'

I want you! I shook my head, to jangle my thoughts into order. 'No.'

'Why *not*? Give me one good reason.'

I fell back on the practical because I dared not contemplate my initial reaction. 'I can't. Edward…'

'Edward would not need to know.'

'What? We would keep it secret?' My sensation of shock doubled.

'Why not? Would it be so very difficult? If we did take so momentous a step, it would undoubtedly be better if the Court didn't know of it.'

I followed his line of sight, the crows twisting and falling in unison, a mating dance, and, brusquely, asked the primary question in my mind: 'Why would you consider— why would any man consider—making such a proposal to the King's mistress?' I swallowed against the constriction in my throat and made my question plainer. 'Why would you wish to share your bed with the King's whore?'

'I've thought of that. I've decided it doesn't matter.' When I looked at him in amazement, he returned my gaze with frank assessment. 'What are you to him, Alice? What are you to him *now*?'

It took me unawares, and I sought for a reply that would not betray Edward. I would never speak of what passed between myself and the King.

'What are you to him?' Windsor continued. I must have looked momentarily lost so he made it easy for me. Who would have thought that he would do that? 'Friend?' he asked.

'Yes.'

'Counsellor?'

'Yes. When he asks—and sometimes when he does not.' I smiled sadly. 'Edward likes to talk. Or he did.'

He cocked his head. 'Confidante?'

'Yes. Always.' I set my teeth. I knew what was coming. 'Lover?'

My reply stuck in my gullet.

'Be honest with me, Alice. For God's sake. I'll not spread it through the palace.'

Should I give him the answer he wanted? The one that was the truth? Blessed Jesu! I found my nails digging deep into my palms.

And seeing, he took my hand, smoothing out my fingers, asking gently: 'Are you still lovers?'

'No.' I sighed, with infinite sadness at this ultimate decline in so great a man. 'No longer.'

'As I thought.'

I felt the need to explain, to defend the King when he could not defend himself. I could not bear that he be sneered at for losing that essential masculine power that made him the crowned stag, the vigorous stallion. Edward would hate it, shrink from it. But I did not need to explain. Windsor showed no scorn.

'The sad depredation of old age,' he remarked matter-of-factly. 'It strikes us all down eventually. How long since?'

'Two years or more now,' I admitted.

'And yet you stay with him.'

'Yes.'

'For the power it brings you?' His eyes bored into my soul.

'I can't deny it, can I?' I demanded bitterly.

'I think you are better than that.'

He reminded me of Wykeham. It should have been a comfort to have two men who believed that I had even an inch of a better nature, but it did not. When the whole world railed against me, sometimes it was difficult not to believe the defamation. Perhaps I did not deserve happiness. Not when the length and breadth of my sins were tallied up.

'He needs me,' I stated, consigning self-pity to the Devil. 'I cannot leave him.' To my relief, Windsor made no comment, letting the moment draw out between us. 'He loves me, you see,' I continued. 'Even though he cannot play the man any longer, he loves me. Does he not deserve my loyal service to the end?'

Windsor turned back to the wall, resting his chin on his hands again. 'Think of it like this. If you are not intimate, would it matter if you were wed to me? It would not be a physical betrayal, would it?'

'But the King would see it as a betrayal—and rightly so.'

'I can't agree. How often does he not know you when you walk into his chamber?' He must have felt my resistance. 'Be honest again. You've nothing to lose. I'm no gossip.'

No, he was not. 'Too often...' I sighed

'Here's the thing,' he drove on, the timbre of his voice deepening. 'You are vulnerable. And when the King's dead, you will be on your own.'

'And if I wed you, you will stand for me.'

'I will.'

'And in return I administer your property.'

'Yes.'

'Still a business arrangement, all in all.'

'If you wish to call it that.'

'It's what it seems to me.' Dismay, like a reaction to the cool breeze after a hot day, shivered over my skin.

His glance was a direct challenge. 'Wed me, Alice. Do you have the courage?'

'I don't think I lack for courage.'

'Then accept!'

I let the idea tumble through my mind as the crows dived and rose once again on the air, a pair enjoying the freedom of their kind. I did not think that I had any freedom.

Windsor sighed. 'Alice...'

'No. I won't. I can't.'

He did not press me but abandoned me alone to ponder the joy of the two crows flirting above me. I was left trying to deny the effect of his mouth against mine, to deny what I wished for rather than what I was duty bound to do.

Windsor's proposal made an uncomfortable bedfellow and I did not sleep that night.

Marriage? A business agreement was one thing—but marriage? To a man whom I found inordinately attractive? It had an appeal, until integrity demanded that I reconsider. Edward. Where was my loyalty to the King? Did he not deserve my fealty, my steadfastness?

Edward smiled serenely, uncomprehendingly, as I wished him goodnight, kissing his cheek. I might have been the servant who brought him wine at the end of the day to help him to sleep. I had not shared Edward's bed for physical gratification since he'd returned from the desperate attempt to invade France. How terrible the advance of age, his failure rendering him impotent, his physical desires vanished entirely, his passionate need for my body transfigured into mild affection—when he recognised me. Just as all at Court knew that Edward would never again lead an army into France, I knew that he would get no more children on me. He might need me to share his bed but for comfort only: the years imposed their cruel sway.

But marriage to Windsor?

When the tenure of my royal position ended, I would have the wealth I needed to bolster the rest of my life and ensure security for my daughters. What more did I need?

You need a man to stand protector.

Did I? No. I had married once and had found no joy in it. I would not do so again. I did not even know if I *liked* William de Windsor. His touch might set fires ablaze in my blood, but that was mere lust. No, he was not for me. If I wed it would be to some mild, biddable soul who could be managed by a strong-willed woman: I would be no one's chattel. No, marriage was not for me, and it would be a brave woman who agreed to take on William de Windsor.

Are you not a brave woman?

I buried my face in my pillow. He said he loved me but I did not believe him. His proposal had smacked of a transaction to buy property. I should know, should I not?

Not one soft word had he spoken.

I abandoned sleep, taking up a quill to record in my ledger my most recently purchased manor of Gunnersby, a property on the Thames that would prove far more trustworthy than William de Windsor.

'Good morning, Sir William.' I stood in the little group of shivering courtiers with Edward, who had expressed a wish to fly the falcons. We were on foot, ambling along the river bank at a speed that would suit the King, who seemed not to feel the cold. 'I did not expect to see you so early in the day. Or are you hoping to win royal favour?'

He ignored the bait. 'Have you thought about it?'

'I have.'

'Second thoughts, Mistress Perrers?'

I inclined my head in parody of regal dignity that I knew he would appreciate. 'No, Sir William.'

'Let me know when you do.'

'I will not.'

He grinned. 'I think you will.'

On our return, as the falconer retrieved his birds and carried them off to the royal mews, there he was again at my shoulder.

'Think of the advantages.'

'There are none.'

'I say there are.' His gaze, forthright, lingering, drove a

shaft of heat through my body. I felt it colour my cheeks and quickly turned away.

'You are presumptuous, Sir William.'

'I am indeed. Would you cast my offer into the flames without giving it due consideration? You would do as much for an offer on the feudal rights of a manor.'

So I would, damn him!

'A woman would enjoy some words of courtship, Sir William.' I was atrociously demure, studying the gold embroidery work on my new gloves.

'I am not a man of soft words, Mistress Perrers.' A statement of fact, not an excuse, and I could not resist abandoning the stitchery to search his face. There was no subterfuge in the man. He said what he meant, both fine wine and bitter lees of sediment in the cup. If I drank, I would have to accept both…

'You might try.' Still I hoped for something that might have a leaning toward courtship. 'If you truly want my hand in marriage.'

'I have no poetry in my soul.'

Neither had I—but I would have liked to hear some from him. I think he saw my disappointment for, stretching out his hand, he drew the tip of his finger along the curve of my cheek.

My heart turned over, a little leap of pure delight.

I thought about it again. I thought about Janyn Perrers. I thought about Edward. I worried the subject to death in the early hours. What would it be like to be tied to a man who did not need my care? A man whom I was free to choose or reject? I had no experience of such freedom. What would it be like to *love* a man of my own free will? I had no idea.

It would be far better for you if you loved no one!

As for that…

Discreetly I watched Windsor fit seamlessly into the daily pattern of the Court. His undoubted agility with horse or sword in mock combat, his merciless single-mindedness in hand-to-hand conflict, the tip of his sword resting against his opponent's throat—until he put it aside to grasp the man's hand in mutual congratulation. The arrogant lift of his head. The proud knightly stance.

He may not have been a handsome man but he took my eye.

I felt again that unexpected caress of his fingertip that made my face burn.

And I watched Edward slip further and further away from me, until the morning he demanded in querulous manner as I curtseyed before him: 'Philippa? Where have you been? Have you persuaded Isabella not to wed de Coucy? Tell her I'll not have it…'

It tipped me over the edge.

He saw me coming, immediately stepping away from where he was loitering in an antechamber by a huddle of equally dissolute idlers who were casting dice to pass the time. Inactivity did not suit him. I kept my expression stern.

'Change of heart, dear Alice?'

'Yes.'

His brows climbed infinitesimally, but at least he did not allow victory to descend into smugness. 'Are you sure?'

'Yes.'

'Good—I like a woman who does not mince her words.'

I left the arrangements to Windsor for he had the freedom from the public eye that I did not. Still, it was a simple matter for me to make the excuse of visiting my little girls at Pallenswick. I was free to travel, had been so since the birth of John, and after a brief halt at Pallenswick I would make my way to Gaines near Upminster, a manor bought in partnership, and in Windsor's name. Edward stared vaguely at the wall beyond my shoulder and gave no recognition when I touched his hand in farewell.

I did not try to explain. John Beverley, his body servant, would care for him. My absence would not be a long one.

Windsor travelled separately. Seated alone in my barge, rowed swiftly by the oarsmen who made easy weather of it with the pull of the tide, with every mile my nerves leapt like crickets in the summer heat. There in Upminster I was wed in a simple service in the village church with no fuss and no guests, no bridal ring for me or gifts exchanged between us at the altar. Nothing to mark the occasion but for a solemn taking of vows, Windsor's steward and William Greseley stood as stolid witnesses. Greseley, perhaps recalling a previous marriage, managed what might have passed for a smile.

'I always knew you would have an adventurous life, mistress.'

'And I have you to thank for much of it.' I knew what I owed him.

'I have a manor in mind to purchase, not too far from here…'

I stopped him with a hand to his arm. 'Tomorrow, Greseley. That will keep for tomorrow. For today—I am busy.'

It had been many years since acquisition of property had not been my prime concern. But not today. Today was for my marriage. Today was for the man who stood at my side and was now my husband.

I stood in the porch of a house I did not know, feeling

nothing but shock, blind to the assets of the little wood and plaster manor of which I was now joint owner. I had done it. I had married him. And there he was, throwing back the door, gesturing for me to walk into the entrance hall, smiling at me.

Words would not come. In all that I had done in my life, I had no experience of such a relationship, stepped into at my own behest. It was like hopping from familiar territory into a strange land, all subtle shadows and traps for the unwary. As I entered, my heels echoing disconcertingly on the wide oak floorboards patterned with their whorls and knots, I was afraid.

'Well, Lady de Windsor?'

And I shivered a little. Then laughed at how easily it had all been achieved. Yet perhaps it was not easy at all. How much did I really know about the man who stood regarding me? It was not easy at all to untangle my feelings towards him.

'I suppose I am lady of the manor.'

'You are indeed.' He took my hand to lead me through the nearest doorway, rubbing my fingers between his. 'You're cold. Come in—there should be a fire lit in here. Can't have my wife being cold, can I?'

I hardly registered the small panelled parlour, the pleasurable warmth, the polished furniture. Every sense was fixed on this man who had swept me off my feet. And had I not allowed him to do so? I removed my hood and mantle, placing them on a gleaming settle. 'I suppose you intend to consummate this business arrangement in the proper manner?'

'Of course.'

'A cup of wine and a signature on a document?'

He was already pouring the wine with solemn concentration, the flagon and cups having been made ready for us.

His preparations had been meticulous. I took the one presented to me, raising it to my lips.

'I had a more energetic consummation in mind!'

And I laughed again. How easy he was to talk to, to laugh with. And how much my body desired that consummation. And then a thought wormed its way into my mind, for no apparent reason.

'Have you shared a bed with many women?' I asked bluntly.

'Yes.' He lifted his cup in a silent toast. 'Does it matter?'

'No.'

'I won't ask you the same.'

'No.' I sighed a little. 'But I was a virgin when I went to Edward's bed.' And wished I had not brought the spectre of the King into the room. I grimaced mildly. 'Forgive me…'

'It's not easy, is it, Alice?' He touched my hand with such understanding that my heart lurched.

'No. It is not.'

'We knew it would not be. This day is ours. We'll not let others intrude.'

We consummated our union in time-honoured fashion, between the lavender-scented linen of Windsor's bed—what an efficient housekeeper he had acquired. How thoughtful he had been of my comfort, and for a soldiering man astonishingly so. And how careful he was with me. An unexpected gentleness. Until his energies got the better of him, and he approached the task of disrobing me like initiating a campaign against the Irish: with a wealth of cunning and stealth to destroy all barriers. Not that there were any real obstacles to overcome between us—were we not both experienced? Only my own unusual, unsettling reticence.

'Alice.' I had felt my muscles stiffen as he unfastened the

lacing on my gown, allowing his fingers to trail across my nape. 'You are allowed to enjoy this.'

'I know. It's just that…'

'I know what it just is. You think too much. Let me seduce your mind as well as your body.' His breath was warm, his lips soft, along the line of my shoulder.

'You don't know any poetry,' I managed on an intake of breath as he kissed the sensitive skin below my ear.

'But I do know how to use my lips for other purposes than mouthing meaningless sentiments. Like this…'

He was inordinately successful.

I did not compare him with Edward. I did not. I would not. There were no ghosts there with us, not Edward, certainly not Janyn Perrers. As for the nameless, faceless wraiths of Windsor's ghostly amours, I did not feel even one of them treading on my hem as he led me to the bed. And then Windsor filled my entire mind. A new lover, with new caresses and heart-stopping skills. A resourceful lover it would take time to get to know.

As things were, I did not think I had that time.

On a practical note—a very necessary one—I took care to protect myself with the old wives' nostrum of a carefully placed fold of wool soaked in cedar gum, messy but essential. It would not do for Windsor to get a child on me, and I bred easily. Were we not, even through our marriage, opening Pandora's box, allowing the escape of a multitude of dangers? A child would put weapons into the hands of those who did not love me. Besides, I was in no doubt. Whatever censure might be levelled at my own actions, Edward must be protected. I would not carry another child. I would never foist another man's child on Edward, or brand him as a cuckold.

And Windsor? He understood, and accepted. We both

saw the yawning perils of our position, the strange delicacy with which our marriage must be conducted.

I received no bride gift after my wedding night. I did not care. For the first time in my life I had been given a gift that was far more precious than monetary value. I could not yet put a name to it, but I knew its value.

A strange happiness settled within me, like a bird come home to its nest. Physical delight made me languorous. A meeting of minds satiated me with pleasure. And so we experienced a little idyll lived out at our manor at Gaines, far from enemies and Court intrigues and the pressures of the world. The few days we snatched away were long and warm, perfect for new lovers.

For that short time I was able to set aside my nagging fears for the future. I laid aside my anxiety over Edward in my absence. He was well cared for. My children were safe and lacked for nothing: I had enough wealth in land to protect them. Why should I not allow myself these few days for my own enjoyment? Without guilt I wallowed in sheer self-indulgence as we spoke of the inconsequential things that came to those who shared a bed and experienced a creeping, blossoming contentment in each other's companionship. Certainly nothing of our lives outside the walls of the manor was allowed to intrude. We sat or strolled as the mood took us, rode out in the meadows, ate and drank. Made love. Like the young lovers we were not.

Did I regret my precipitate decision? Not for a moment.

Did Windsor? I think not.

When, as it must, my mind began to escape the confines in which I had set it, to reach out to that other life, there remained a fine solace, to my very soul, wrapping around me like a fur on a winter's morning. When Edward died,

God rest his soul, I would not be alone. I would be with this man whom I—

My careless thoughts slammed up against a barrier like a battering ram against a stone buttress. Uninvited, horribly intruding, fear bit deep. The words refused to form in my mind, although my heart urged them on.

With this man whom I had an *affection* for. That was enough.

Windsor's touch awakened my body to an awareness of him that I had not anticipated. All my earlier reticence swept away by his experienced caresses, I used my skill to make him shiver.

'I told you you would not regret your decision,' he whispered against my throat. 'Why are you always so reluctant to believe what I tell you?'

'Because I know you for a devious man. And you, Will? Do you wish you had never made me that offer?'

'I knew I wanted you from the first moment I saw you. It was merely a matter of timing.'

'Long-term planning.'

'I am a master at it. And I am content.'

I believed him. So was I too content. I would change nothing. But did I wish to commit myself in similar words? *It is dangerous to open yourself, body and soul, to a man you barely know and whom you suspect of less than altruistic motives.* And yet I did speak them.

'I am content.'

And what did I do? I destroyed this new contentment. Wilfully, wantonly.

Because I was afraid.

Every day I was conscious of the moods of my new husband, learning to read them, learning his interests, the workings of his mind. I grew to know his care for me, the tenderness that sometimes undermined all my determination to remain a little aloof, the fire of passion when we came together within the curtains of his bed. And throughout our rural sojourn I was conscious of an energy burning deep within him, to be, to do, to act, to be engaged with the world beyond our bedchamber. It burned quite as strongly as the passion. He never spoke of it. He never said a word of his ambition to be elsewhere. And I loved him more for that…

Love?

My realisation of it tiptoed into the recesses of my mind and stole my breath. Too soon, too reckless. Too hazardous. Why would I seek an inner fervour that robbed me of my freedom? I feared it like the plague. I would flee from it if I could.

In the end, honesty took me in hand and I could no longer deny the murmurings of my heart, but it was only to my own innermost thoughts that I spoke the word, savouring it on my tongue. I had hidden my emotions for so long I was incapable of baring my soul to anyone. I had never done so to Janyn, to whom I had been a means to an end. Or to Edward, who had not been interested in my soul. Before God, I could not expose my vulnerability to William de Windsor, who seemed against all the laws of nature to hold my heart in his hands. For if I did, would not that double, treble, quadruple my weakness? Better that I keep my own counsel. He did not love me. I would not put the power to wound into his hand.

So what did I do to our magical sojourn together? I destroyed it.

Here was my inarguable logic. If I did not destroy it, it would destroy itself, imploding on its inward-turning sweetness. We could not stay together away from the world of the Court where our ambitions must be played out. Windsor could not; and I had a duty elsewhere. At least this destruction was on my terms, with the hope of a renaissance, a reconciliation at some point in time in the future. My love for this man was not on my terms, because I did not want it, but this decision would be. I would claw back control. Simply to preserve what we had, frozen in that sweet ice, would kill it slowly, for neither of us was made for domesticity, for happiness confined within four walls.

And yet in my heart I yearned for it. What I *wanted* and what I knew I must *not* want warred within me. And the victory of common sense near broke my heart.

On our return to Court, separately, discreetly as we must, I went immediately to Edward.

'Alice! Come and play chess with me.'

He recognised me, welcomed me, defeated my wayward manipulation of my knight against his bishop with a few clever moves that I had been too preoccupied to follow, but I think he did not know that I had been absent for more than a few hours. I talked to him and explained what I wanted him to do. And he did it, accepting the rightness of my advice, signing and sealing the document.

My heart wept and my mind rejoiced at my success.

I took it to Windsor's room, little more than a passageway, in one of the distant wings. Indiscreet perhaps, but I chose my time, closing his door at my back, wishing there was another way, as I offered the document at arm's length, stepping no closer. If I did, I might be seduced by the strength of his arms. And if he kissed me… I thrust the document forward between us. 'This is what you want, Will.'

He took it, his eye travelling down, then up, his face illuminated with this victory, and I knew that I had done the right thing.

'Ireland!' he said.

'Yes. Ireland.'

'King's Lieutenant.'

'A valuable office.'

'So you will be rid of me sooner than we thought.'

'Yes.'

He folded the document carefully, his mind suddenly arrested, as I knew it must be. 'Is this your doing?'

'No.' I perjured myself without regret.

His glance was sharp. 'What made him change his mind?'

'Who's to say?'

So great was my sense of impending loss that I actually turned to leave him to enjoy his achievement alone.

'Is this difficult for you?' His question stopped me.

To persuade Edward, or to let you go?

And I knew he suspected my hand in it, despite my denial. Our knowledge of each other had grown apace.

'No.' My voice was steady. 'Edward needs a man of ability, not a young man barely out of adolescence—and as you so frequently say, who is there but you?'

'You knew it would be like this, Alice.'

'Yes.'

Still the space yawned between us, until Windsor was the one to close it, to kiss me with a familiar echo of the passion I had come to find essential to my happiness.

'It's what I want, Alice.' Did he think I did not know it? For a brief moment it grieved me that he should desire that distant office more than he desired me, but with his words the sorrow passed. 'I'll miss you more than I ever thought I could miss a woman.' The wound healed a little and I pressed my forehead against his shoulder. Until he lifted my chin so he could look at my face. 'I'd ask if you'll miss me…but you'll never admit to that, will you?'

'No. How can I?' I frowned helplessly in the toils of the dilemma I had helped create. And he rubbed at the groove between my brows with his fingers.

'What's this? Guilt?'

'A little,' I admitted. 'Perhaps the King's Concubine is not free to miss you. Perhaps she is not free to have her emotions engaged.'

'Does the King engage them?'

'With friendship. Compassion. Respect. All of those. I will not leave him, Will. I am not free to do so until his death.'

At last the document that would take him from me was cast aside, and Windsor's voice was tender. 'Then I would say that the King could have no more loyal subject. And still I say you are free to miss me.'

'Then I will.' I would give him that at least, and I thrust my guilt away.

His lips were soft on my brow. 'Write to me.'

'And risk interception?'

'You don't have to admit your undying love. Not that you would anyway!'

We understood each other. 'I'll write.'

We made use of that one snatched opportunity to be together, in Windsor's sparely furnished room. Unsatisfactory, all in all, both of us with senses stretched against possible discovery, struggling to make the best use of the narrow pallet. Little clothing removed, a hasty coupling, it was a reaffirmation of our commitment to each other rather than an outpouring of passion, and yet I would not have him leave me without experiencing the intimacy once more. How many months would it be before I saw him again?

We exchanged few words. What was there to say?

'Keep safe,' he whispered.

'And you.'

'I'll keep you in my thoughts, Alice.'

'And you in mine, Will.'

He was gone within the week. I could not put my loss into words; it was too great. He had said he would think of me, which was as much as I could hope for. For the first time in my life I knew what it was to have a broken heart.

I upbraided myself for my foolishness. *Your heart cannot be broken unless you love him. And of course you do not!*

And William de Windsor? I received an unexpected communication from my absent husband within the month. After a brief summary of events in Dublin, he added, *I said that I would miss you, Alice, did I not? I do. You belong to me, and it seems that I belong to you. Keep in good health. I need to know that you are safe for my return, whenever that might be.*

It was the closest to poetry that I would ever get from Windsor. It was a precious thing. And, yes, I wept.

Chapter Thirteen

How could I have been so disastrously short-sighted? I was terrifyingly, inexcusably complacent, blinkered, unforgivably so, and with no excuse to offer other than that the normality of affairs lulled me into believing that no change was imminent. Why worry? There was nothing to suggest that the ambience of the long warm days in the summer of 1375 held any sign of danger. Edward was strong enough to host a tournament, and the spectacular Smithfield festivities in which I played the supreme role of Lady of the Sun left a sweet taste on the palate. So did Windsor's assertion that he would miss me.

There was no obvious cause for concern.

Why is it that we never see disaster approaching until it overwhelms us, like failing to foresee a winter storm lashing onto a lee shore, crashing down with terrible destruction and heartbreak? I never saw it coming, but it broke over our heads with disastrous force.

Looking back, I realise that I could not have foreseen what happened. The year-long truce with France was draw-

ing to its close with the prospect of new hostilities, but not
quite yet for a while. Perhaps another truce could be cob-
bled together. Certainly neither side was urging the other
to a further bout of bloodlust.

Edward's health teetered on a knife edge but did not fall.
Some days were good, in others he drowned in melancholy
that I could not lift from him, but death did not approach.
The Prince was far beyond help. He would be ordering his
shroud within the year if I knew the signs. Joan, her eye to
her son's future, was wound as tight as wool on a begin-
ner's distaff. Her temper, ever unpredictable, was danger-
ously short. But the King held onto life, and he had his heir
in young Richard.

Windsor was in Ireland, communication erratic, but I
knew that one day he would return to me. I refused to admit
my longing to see him again.

In the early months of the new year, a Parliament was
summoned. The upkeep of an army was paramount and taxation was essential to raise the revenue: the royal Treasury
needed a substantial input of gold. All in all, it was nothing
out of the way. Even the Prince rallied to be present at the
ceremonial opening beside Gaunt and the King, an impressive trio of royal blood, their robes of scarlet and ermine
hiding the frailty of life beneath.

Joan stayed away from Court. No one mentioned witchcraft.

And so the days passed inexorably into the summer of
1376. Who could have foreseen the outcome of Edward's
calling that thrice-damned Parliament? There was no inti-
mation of danger as magnates, clergy and commons came
together in the Painted Chamber at Westminster with formal greetings and dutiful smiles on all sides. There was
no undue restlessness in the ranks. Why would there be

any barrier to royal demands? Parliament would act as it had always acted, giving its consent to the subsidies. The Commons retired, as they would, to the Abbey Chapter House to elect their leader and consider the proposals to raise coin for the royal coffers. The debate would be brief and productive.

God's Blood! It was neither. And I learned of it soon enough.

Gaunt, driven by pent-up anger, divesting himself of gloves and hat, thrust open the door of Edward's private parlour where I sat. Shouldering Latimer aside, he slammed the door before striding across the room, where he halted in front of me.

'Where is he?'

Gaunt rarely lost control, but stark fear entered the room with him. Sweeping together the papers I was studying into a rough pile to tuck them under the edge of a chest that held my pens and ink, I stood, my heart beating with sudden apprehension.

'The King is resting…' I stepped before Edward's door. Edward was prostrate with exhaustion.

Gaunt took a turn about the room, unable to remain still. 'The Commons! They've elected Peter de la Mare as their Speaker.'

'Ah…!'

'De la Mare, by God!' Gaunt's teeth bared in a snarl of temper. 'That name means something to *you*, of course.'

I allowed my raised brows to make my answer. Every man and woman at Court knew of my recent confrontation with a member of the de la Mare family. It had been a regrettable incident. Wisdom said that I should not have stepped into the argument, but when does wisdom count against a denial of justice towards an innocent man? I had become involved in a dispute that was not mine and, truth to tell, the outcome had given me much pleasure.

'Our new Speaker is no friend to either of us,' Gaunt remarked, twitching a curtain into shape then punching it so that it billowed again into disarray. 'I'm not sure which of us he despises most.'

'I could hazard a guess.'

Considering Edward's privacy relatively safe from invasion, I abandoned my stance and sat so that I could keep Gaunt in view as he continued to prowl. My recent adversary was a cousin of this Peter, now Speaker of the Commons: Thomas de la Mare, Abbot of St Albans, a man with a famous reputation for erudition but none at all for charity or compassion. And not a man open to compromise.

Our clash of wills was to do with the ownership of the insignificant little manor of Oxhay. Fitzjohn, a knight living there, was ejected from his property, the Abbot claiming ownership. So what did Fitzjohn do? Before marching once more into the manor to take hold of it, with worthy cunning he enfeoffed the property to me. And the Abbot, all prepared to summon the local mob to seize the manor in St Alban's name and force Fitzjohn out, decided at the last moment that Alice Perrers was not one to tangle with.

And the consequence? I kept the property with Fitzjohn as my tenant for life; the Abbot called down curses on my soul. Unfortunate all in all, given the choice of the new Speaker, cousin to the Abbot.

'So where does that put us?' I asked, surveying my loosely linked fingers. There was no tension there. Still I did not see the danger. Could Gaunt not use his influence against an upstart leader of the Commons?

'Under threat,' Gaunt ground out through clenched teeth.

I frowned. 'What possible mischief can he and the Abbot make, even if they combine forces?'

'Think about it.' Gaunt swept across the room and gripped the arms of Edward's chair in which I sat, trapping me. His eyes were a bare hand's breadth from mine. I refused to allow myself to blink as I saw myself reflected there. 'Who is Peter de la Mare's noble employer?'

'The Earl of March...'

'So do I have to spell it out?'

Gaunt reared back and stalked to the window to look out, although I swear he did not see the scudding clouds. No, he did not have to spell it out. I had simply not made the connections, but I did now. Peter de la Mare was steward to Edmund Mortimer, Earl of March, husband to Edward's granddaughter Philippa. The man who was not lacking in influence as Marshall of England. Who would be more than happy to see his infant son as the next ruler of England.

'And March is involved...'

'I'm sure he is!'

'Because of the succession...'

'Exactly! The whole lot of them shackled together with my own princely brother into a plot against me.'

Now my fingers tightened together, white knuckled. Had I not always wondered how loyal Gaunt would be to the true succession to the English crown?

Gaunt turned his head to stare fiercely at me over his shoulder. 'It's a conspiracy against me and those who stand as my friends. A neat little plot concocted by the Abbot of St Albans and the Prince. Did you know they had long conversations together when the Prince stopped on his way from Berkhamstead to Canterbury earlier this year?'

No, I had not known.

'The Prince was not too ill to spend time putting weasel

words into the ear of the Abbot. So there it is. March, the de la Mare cousins and the Prince, all tied into a stratagem to keep me and my heirs from the throne.'

Never had Gaunt spelt out his ambitions so clearly. Not to me. Not, I surmised, to anyone, for it was dangerous talk. Treasonous, in fact, for it all came back to the problem of the future succession. If the Prince's son Richard died without issue, the son of March and Philippa would rule England through order of descent, for Philippa had carried a son, a lad of three years old now. Not Gaunt. Not Gaunt's boy Henry Bolingbroke. Would Gaunt be vicious enough, ambitious enough to destroy the claim of his nephew Richard? Or that of the infant son of March? Watching his fist clench hard against the window ledge, I thought he might. But thought was not proof.

Whatever the truth of it, rumour said that the Prince lived in fear that his son might never rule if Gaunt had his way. And the Prince, from his sick bed, was using the allies he had to hand; the de la Mare cousins and now March, who had apparently discovered he had much to gain in opposing Gaunt.

I forced my mind to untie the knots. I couldn't quite see where this was leading. Unless the new de la Mare Speaker of the Commons intended to use the one weapon he had to get what he and his co-conspirators wanted. My mind began to clear. The one weapon that would give him much power.

'Do you think that the Commons will grant finance for the war?' I queried.

'At a price. And I wager de la Mare has it all planned to a miracle of exactness. He knows exactly what he will ask for, by God!'

'What?'

'I scent danger on the wind. They're planning an attack. On me, on my associates in government. Latimer and Neville. Lyons. The whole ministerial crew, because I helped them to office. De la Mare and March will plot and intrigue to rid Edward of any man who has a connection with me. Gaunt will be isolated, that's the plan. Brother warring against brother.' Gaunt's smile was feral as his eyes blazed. 'And they will declare war on you too, Mistress Perrers, unless I'm much mistaken in my reading of de la Mare's crafty mind. Any chance that I might step into my brother's shoes will be buried beneath the crucified reputations of royal ministers and paramour alike.' He folded his arms, leaning back against the stonework. 'I did not think March had such ambitions. I was wrong. Being sire to the heir to the throne obviously appeals to him.'

Sire to the heir? But only if Richard were dead. Or perhaps Richard did not need to die… The complications wound around my brain, like a web spun by a particularly energetic spider. March—and even Gaunt—might challenge the boy's legitimacy because of Joan's scandalous matrimonial history. They would not be the first to do so, but I could not think of that yet. There was a far more urgent danger.

'Can you hinder him? Speaker de la Mare?' I asked.

'What can I do? The Commons are elected and hold the whip hand over finance,' Gaunt responded as if I were too much a woman to see it. 'I'd look a fool if I tried and failed.' When he rubbed his hands over his face, I realised how weary he was. 'You have to tell the King.'

My response was immediate and blunt. 'No.'

'He needs to know.'

'What would be the point? If *you* can do nothing, what do you expect from an old man who no longer thinks in terms of plans and negotiations and political battles, who cannot enforce the authority of royal power? You've seen him when he is as drained as a pierced wine flask. What could he do? He'd probably invite de la Mare to share a cup of ale and discuss the hunting in the forest hereabouts.'

'He is the King. He must face them.'

'He can't. You know he can't.' I was adamant. I watched as the truth settled on Gaunt's handsome features, so like his father's. 'It will only bring the King more distress.'

Gaunt flung his ill-used gloves to the floor. For a moment he studied them as if they would give him an answer to the crisis, then he nodded curtly. 'You're right, of course.'

'What will you do?' I asked as he recovered his gloves and walked towards the door, thoughts obviously far away. My question made him stop as he slapped the gloves against his thigh, searching for a way forward.

'I'll do what I can to draw the poison from the wound. The only good news is that the Prince is too weak to attend the sitting in person. It might give me a freer hand with Speaker de la Mare. If we come out of this without a bloody nose, it will be a miracle. Watch your back, Mistress Perrers.'

'I will. And I will watch Edward's too.'

'I know.' For a moment the harshness in his voice was dispelled. 'I detest having to admit it, but you have always had a care for him.' Then the edge returned. 'Let's hope I can persuade the Prince to have mercy on his father and leave him to enjoy his final days in peace.'

He made to open the door, clapping his hat on his head, drawing on his gloves, and I wondered. No one else would ask him, but I would.

'My lord…'

He stopped his hand on the door.

'Do you want the crown for yourself?'

'You would ask that of me?'

'Why not? There is no one to overhear. And who would believe anything I might say against you?'

'True.' His lips acquired a sardonic tightness. 'Then the answer is no. Have I not sworn to protect the boy? Richard is my brother's son. I have an affection for him. So, no, I do not seek the crown for myself.'

Gaunt did not look at me. I did not believe him. I did not trust him.

But who else was there for me to look to? There would be no other voice raised in my defence.

Gaunt was gone, leaving me to search out the pertinent threads from his warning. So the Prince was behind the Commons attack, intent on keeping his brother from the throne. Every friend and ally of Gaunt would be dealt with. And I saw my own danger, for I had failed to foster any connection between myself and the Prince—but perhaps I was a fool to castigate myself over an impossible reconciliation. Could I have circumvented Joan's loathing? I recalled her vicious fury over the herbs, her destruction of the pretty little coffer. No, the Prince would see me as much a self-serving whore as his wife did.

Could I do anything now to draw the poison, as Gaunt had so aptly put it? I could think of nothing. Edward was not strong enough to face Parliament and demand their obedience as once he might have. He needed the money. And what would the price be for de la Mare's cooperation to keep the imminent threat of France at bay? Fear was suddenly perched on my shoulder, chattering in my ear like Joan's damned long-dead monkey.

'Watch your back, Mistress Perrers!'

I considered writing to Windsor, but abandoned that exercise before it was even begun. What would I say? I could expect no help from that quarter before the axe fell. If it fell. All was so uncertain. I shivered. I would simply have to hope that its sharp edge fell elsewhere.

In those days following Gaunt's warning, sitting tight in Westminster, rarely leaving Edward's side, the name of Peter de la Mare came to haunt my dreams and bewitch them into nightmares. I gleaned every piece of information that I could. Neither Edward nor the Prince attended any further sessions so all fell into the lap of Gaunt, who tried to chain de la Mare's powers by insisting that a mere dozen of the Commons members should present themselves to confer privately with Gaunt in the White Chamber. De la Mare balked at the tone of the summons. How clear was the writing on the wall when he brought with him a force of well over a hundred of the elected members into a full session of Parliament? There they stood at his back, as their Speaker put forward his intent to the lords and bishops in the Painted Chamber.

It called Gaunt's bluff. It put the fear of God into me. This might be a dangerous game de la Mare was playing, and one without precedent as he challenged royal power— but I would not wager against his victory.

Oh, Windsor. I wish you were here at Westminster. To stiffen my spine.

I must stand alone.

Gaunt's description of events of that Parliament, for my personal perusal, was grim and graphic. Thud! Speaker de la Mare's fist crashed down against the polished wood. Thud! And thud again, for every one of his demands. Where had the money gone from the last grant? The campaigns of the previous year had been costly failures. There would be no more money until grievances were remedied. A smooth smile. Smooth as new-churned butter. Now, if the King was willing to make concessions… It might be possible to reconsider…

Oh, de la Mare had been well primed.

There must in future be a Council of Twelve—*approved* men! Approved by whom, by God? Men of rank and high reputation to discuss with the King all matters of business. There must be no more covens—an interesting choice of word that ripped at my rioting emotions—of ambitious, self-seeking money-grubbers to drag the King into ill-conceived policies against the good of the realm.

And those who were now in position of authority with the King? What of them?

Corrupt influences, all of them, de la Mare raged, neither loyal nor profitable to the Kingdom. They must be removed, stripped of their power and wealth, punished.

And when Parliament—when *de la Mare*—was satisfied at their dismissal? Why, then the Commons would consider the question of money for the war against France. Then and only then.

'Do they think they are Kings or Princes of the realm?' Gaunt stormed, impotent. 'Where have they got their pride and arrogance? Do they not know how powerful I am?'

'You have no power when Parliament holds the purse strings,' I replied. The knot of fear in my belly grew tighter with every passing day, as we awaited the final outcome.

And there it was.

Latimer, Lyons and Neville, singled out as friends of Gaunt. And the charge against them? De la Mare and his minions made a good legal job of it, ridiculously so. Not one, not a score, but over sixty charges of corruption and abuse, usury and extortion. Of lining their pockets from trade and royal funds, falsification of records, embezzlement. And so on and so on. I had a copy of them delivered to me, reading them with growing terror. De la Mare was out for blood, nothing less than complete destruction.

I tore the sheet in half as the motive behind it swam as clear as a silver coin dropped into a dish of water. The guilt of these men was not an issue here. The issue was their tight nucleus of control, a strong command over who had access to the King and who had not. Latimer and I might see it as protection for an increasingly debilitated monarch; de la Mare saw it as a blight that must be exorcised by fire and blood. What did it matter that Latimer was the hero of the nation who had excelled on the field of Crécy? What did it matter that he ran Edward's household with superb efficiency? Latimer and his associates were creatures of Gaunt. De la Mare was delirious with power and would have his way. Gaunt was helpless.

Throughout the whole of this vicious attack on his ministers, Edward remained ignorant.

I was trying to keep the whole disaster from disturbing Edward, whose hold on reality weakened by the day. And I would have managed it too, swearing all around him to secrecy, except for a damned busybody of a chamber knight, friend of Latimer and Lyons, who begged Edward's intercession.

I cursed him for it but the damage was done.

After that there was no keeping secrets.

'They'll not do it, Edward,' I attempted to soothe. Dismissal. Imprisonment. Even execution for Latimer and Neville had been mooted.

'How can we tell?' Edward clawed at his robe, tearing at the fur so that it parted beneath his frenzied fingers. If he had been able to stride about the chamber he would have done so. If he had been strong enough to travel to

Westminster he would have been there, facing de la Mare. Instead tears at his own weakness tracked down his face.

'This attack is not against you!' I tried. 'They will not harm you. You are the King. They are loyal to you.'

'Then why do they refuse me money? They will bring me to my knees.' He would not be soothed.

'Gaunt has it in hand.' I tried to persuade him to take a sip of ale but he pushed my hand away.

'It is not right that my ministers be attacked by Parliament.' His mind, besieged by all manner of evils, could not see the full scope of what de la Mare was planning. I enfolded Edward's icy hand, warming it between both of mine. 'I want to see the Prince…' he announced, snatching his hand away.

'He is not well enough to come to you.'

'I need to listen to his advice.' He was determined, struggling to his feet. I sighed. 'I want to go today, Alice.'

'Then you shall.'

I could not stop him so I would make it as easy as I could, arranging everything for Edward's comfort for a journey to Kennington. I did not go with him: I would not be welcome there and it would do no good to add to Edward's distress by creating a cataclysmic explosion of enmity between myself and Joan. I prayed that the Prince would be able to give his father the comfort that I could not.

And so I made my own preparations. No longer could I delude myself that Latimer, Lyons and Neville would escape without penalty. And when they fell…

So far my name had not been voiced in de la Mare's persecutions. I had remained unremarked, but that would not last: I saw retribution approaching. I had myself rowed up the Thames to Pallenswick—a cautious measure, removing myself from Westminster and from any of the royal palaces. Discretion might be good policy. What effect would it have on Edward's failing intellect and body if the one firm centre of his life was removed? For once the prospect of Pallenswick, the most beloved of all my manors, and reconciliation with my daughters, did not fill me with joy. Rather a black cloud of de la Mare's making settled over my head.

Storm clouds. Storm crows.

The words came back to me, Windsor at his most trenchant. The presentiments of doom were gathering.

I shivered with fear as the days passed, heavy with portent. Even though isolated from the Court, could I not see the future danger, teeth bared like a rogue alaunt? I read the signs for myself, sitting tight at Pallenswick, every nerve strained. And how strange it was. Braveheart slept at my feet, unconcerned, lost in a dream of coneys and mice. Windsor's blade lay forgotten in a coffer upstairs. The threat to me came not from an assassin's dagger but from the heavy fist of the law.

The three royal ministers were dealt summary justice, their offices stripped from them, as were their possessions. They were confined to prison, but the demands for execution died a death. Not even de la Mare could make the charge of treason stick. There was no treachery in these men to endanger King or state, unless acquiring a purse full of gold was treason, and if it was, then every man in government employ was guilty. But imprisonment was considered a just punishment. Thus the reward for royal service, the price Latimer and Neville and Lyons paid for their association with John of Gaunt and Alice Perrers!

Would I be next? Gaunt, a royal son, would be safe, but the royal concubine would be a worthy target. I too might end my days in a prison cell.

My mind leapt to Ireland, as it often did in those days.

Did Windsor know of my plight? It gave me some foolish comfort to think of him riding to my rescue. But of course he would not and was too far away to stretch out a hand to me. I shut out the image of his arms protecting me, his strength resisting any attack. It was too painful to imagine when I had no weapon that I might use. I had given Edward all I could. My youth, my body, my children. My unquestioning allegiance. Now I was truly alone.

And then, as they must, the charges against me arrived, ominously red-sealed. I had to sit, my legs suddenly too weak to hold me upright, when I read de la Mare's accusations, a pain hammering at my temples as I absorbed the astonishing scope of it. What had they concocted to make my freedom untenable?

As I read the first, the pain lessened. My breathing steadied. Predictable, nothing outrageous to shock me. I could answer this. I could state my defence. This was not so very terrible after all…

She has seized three thousand pounds a year from the royal purse.

From where had they conjured that sum? Any monies I had taken were gifts from Edward. I had stolen nothing. It was his right to give gifts where he chose, and when I had borrowed to purchase some manor or feudal rights, it had never been without Edward's consent. Except for the purchase of the manors of Hitchin and Plumpton End, that very year, when Edward's mind had slipped into some distant territory. And the borrowings had been paid back, for the most part, anyway… And if I had not repaid them, through some oversight—well, I defied Parliament to find me guilty of fraud or embezzlement in that quarter.

She has seized Queen Philippa's jewels. She wears them.

She has no shame in proclaiming her immorality with the King.

Yes, I wore them. Yes, I had no shame. Had Edward not given them to me? No illegality here. I read on.

She has shut the King away from his people. The only influence over him is hers, so that she might squeeze him dry of wealth and power.

True. I had kept him apart, protected. If it was a crime I must answer for it, but it was not a matter of treason.

And then a charge with more than a snap of teeth. My heartbeat jumped again.

She has made use of the King's Court in her acquisition of land. She has been so bold as to sit beside the judges, influencing their verdicts in manorial disputes to her own ends.

And I had. If I had been a man, intent on urging my interests in the courts, there would have been no accusation made. Was it a crime to do so? Would they punish me because I had stepped beyond the remit of my sex? Windsor's harsh warning came back in a flood. They would seek to punish me for overstepping the boundaries suitable for a woman—but it was not treason.

My heart settled again. It would all come to nothing. By the end of the year there would be some new scandal to stir Parliament's ire. Edward need not be troubled, for the threats against me were empty ones and would die on their feet. Reassured by the power of my logic, I returned to Westminster and from there, my mind more at ease, as the heat of June began to press down on us, I wrote to Windsor.

Latimer and Lyons and Neville languish in prison, for which I am sorry. I have no power to help them. Gaunt is furious. Edward is inconsolable for reasons which will be known to you. De la Mare is frustrated

that he can find no evidence of treason against me. I
think that they might be content to let me go.
    There is no need for your concern about my safety.
    Of late I have wished you here with me.

Edward is inconsolable, I had written. Not in reaction to
my own predicament because I told him nothing of the accusations levelled at me. How could I? The loss of his beloved son was too much for him to bear.

The Prince was dead.

I was with the King in those final days of his son's life,
as were many from London and far beyond who travelled
to see the end of this great warrior, struck down before
his allotted time. They filed before him as he lay between
sense and delirium at Westminster, men and women both,
weeping openly. Joan remained with him, rigid and tear-
less in her grief.

I did not weep for the Prince, but I did for Edward, for
it was Edward's burden that he must watch the Prince die,
his favourite son, his firstborn, his hope for the future and
the protector of England. What hope could Edward have in
Richard, the nine-year-old child who was ushered into the
death-ridden chamber to make his nervous farewell and be
recognised as the future King of England? So the Prince
slid in and out of consciousness, the pain great enough to
disfigure his noble face, and Edward remained throughout to witness his passing. The outpouring of grief was too
much for his spare frame, his face was grey with fatigue.

I helped Edward to turn his stumbling steps back to his
rooms when it was over, where he lay on his bed, unseeing, unmoving, as if the Prince's death had drawn some of
the life from his own body. Sitting beside him well into the
night hours, I knew that I would not tell him of Parliament's

attack on me. I told myself, willing myself to believe, that the Commons had slaked its thirst for blood on Latimer and Lyons. The evidence against me was weak, and they would abandon me as not worth their effort.

Wrong! How desperately wrong I was. De la Mare would summon the evidence from the ashes in the fire grate if he had to. I should have known he would not let me be. Yet if I had, what could I have done?

I soon learned the depths to which de la Mare could sink in his desire for revenge.

We were at Sheen, where I hoped that the superb quality of the hunting would give Edward's mind a more optimistic turn. Wykeham, restored to earthly glory as one of the newly appointed twelve high-minded men to counsel Edward in place of his scurvy ministers, arrived at the same time as a group of merchants representing the City of London had come to petition the King. Complaining bitterly over the parlous state of law and order in the capital, they were determined to be heard, much as I would have preferred to send them away. They had been invited to send a delegation, so here they were, to see the King and beg his intervention. Accepting the rightness of their cause, and perhaps conscious of the hate-filled de la Mare breathing his foetid breath down my neck, I allowed it. Yes, I had escaped the Speaker's campaign against me, but I had no intention of adding further fuel to the fire by keeping Edward shut away from his people. We worked hard to make the best show we could, not in the great audience chamber but in a smaller one where the King was already seated when the petitioners arrived.

They bowed before him. Edward made no gesture of recognition.

Forgive me, Edward! Forgive me! I could have wept again for him. How close tears were in those days when for most of my life I had been dry-eyed. Could de la Mare, in rare pity for his King, not acknowledge the truth of why I had kept Edward from the public eye?

We had swathed him in cloth of gold and tied him as well as we could into his chair so that he at least gave the appearance of normality, but it was as if a statue filled the royal throne, not a living, breathing man. He looked vacantly at the merchants when they complained that the peace of the realm was in jeopardy. And when they went on to detail the lawless behaviour of the mobs and John of Gaunt's troops, and the scandal of an attack against the Bishop of London himself, Edward, uncomprehending of the whole proceedings, gave a reply that was a mumbling of incoherent words that no one could hear let alone understand.

'This is a travesty,' murmured Wykeham in my ear where we stood a little removed from the audience.

'But I must allow it,' I stated.

'Why?'

'Because de la Mare accuses me of standing between the people and the King—and before God, what he says is true. I have done exactly that.' I could hear despair building in my voice. 'You can see why...'

'Yes...' Wykeham looked back to where Edward remained engraved in stone. 'The Commons should not have to see this.'

'Neither should the King have to suffer this humiliation,' I added more curtly than I had intended. 'To put him on show in this manner is...' I recalled having the same argument with Windsor. Suddenly I felt very tired.

'Is cruel,' Wykeham finished my train of thought with a sigh.

One of the knights standing beside Edward leaned to grasp his shoulder and keep him upright.

'End this, Alice…' Wykeham murmured. 'It can't go on.'

The delegation stood uncertainly, a mix of horror and pity on their faces, and I hurried forward.

'The audience is at an end, gentlemen.' And as the merchants bowed themselves out, gestures that Edward did not see, I touched Edward's hand but he did not respond. 'Take the King to his chamber,' I instructed. 'I will come to him.'

'I doubt he will know whether you do or not. I had not known he had faded so quickly,' Wykeham murmured.

'It is the Prince's death.'

'Before God, it's pitiful.'

'It's more than that.' I could not watch as the knights lifted Edward from the throne and led him stumbling away. 'Now, why are you here, Wykeham? I hope it's good news.' I did not need to ask, now that I had time to read his expression.

'No.'

'Then tell me. It can't be worse than what we have just seen.'

'I think it can, mistress. Let us find somewhere where you can be emotional.'

'Emotional?'

'You might feel the need to throw something.'

It sent a bolt of fear through my body.

'I thought you should know, mistress, what it is that de la Mare is saying to stir the Commons against you.'

I was in no mood for guessing games. 'What now? That I have secreted the whole of the crown jewels—including Edward's crown—in a cache to ward off future poverty?'

'It's far worse.' He waited until there was no one within earshot, and whispered, 'De la Mare is citing necromancy.'

I came to an abrupt halt, my hand fastening like a claw around Wykeham's wrist.

Necromancy? *Witchcraft!*

I think I laughed at the absurdity of it—until my throat dried, my thoughts tumbling. This was no time for laughter. There was no possible evidence of necromancy that could be laid at my door...unless... Joan's accusations and the box of remedies! But surely her impassioned words would have no bearing on de la Mare's attack. My notions had been what any good wife could have produced.

'He can't accuse me of that!' I retorted.

'You might listen first, mistress, to what I know.'

I took him into the garden where we could walk or sit without eavesdroppers. Onlookers might wonder at a conversation between King's Concubine and the Bishop of Winchester, but, in the circumstances, they might consider my need for confession to be urgent.

Confession, by God!

'I am no witch!' I could barely wait until we were secluded, apart from the bees enjoying the heady flowers of lavender and thyme.

'That's not what your physician is saying!'

'My physician?' Father Oswald, a gentle, unassuming Benedictine monk, attached to my household for many years now. Unswervingly loyal, I would have thought. 'What has he said?' I racked my mind for anything that could be construed as dealing with the Devil. A few foolish love potions for the damsels—but they were far in the past. As were the salves and draughts to give Philippa ease from pain. No witchcraft there. Neither would Father Oswald have any intelligence of them.

'Your physician's been put under some...pressure to

speak of what he knows.' Wykeham was deadly certain. 'His accusations against you ran like a stream in spate.'

'Torture?'

'So I understand.'

This was dangerous stuff. How many times had a difficult woman been accused of being in league with the Devil, ultimately to face death by drowning or the excruciating pain of fire... I shuddered in the warmth of the parterre.

'I am no witch,' I repeated stalwartly.

'Then let me tell you what's said, mistress.'

Wykeham pulled me further along the pathway until we stood in the very centre, facing each other on either side of the sundial. There we were, whore and priest, standing in a summer landscape, and I felt the jaws of death closing in around me. 'So that you should be clear about it,' Wykeham said dryly, his face severe but not without compassion. 'They'll hound you to death if they can, Alice.' He had a way with words did Wykeham. Probably from preaching so many sermons to the damned.

'Where did the evidence come from?' I asked.

'John de la Mare, brother to the Speaker of the Commons— how fortunate!' Wykeham explained with blistering brevity. 'He visited Pallenswick with a chamber pot of urine. He asked for help to have his malady diagnosed—and in pious charity your physician agreed.'

'Father Oswald always was a gullible fool when it came to judging others!' I observed irritably. 'Had he no suspicions?'

'Apparently not. He was brought to London and questioned. I've no doubt force was used.' Wykeham eyed a lively flight of goldfinches in the adjacent bushes. 'Your admirable physician admitted to a remarkable range of activities on your behalf.'

'The last he did for me was mix a salve to calm my chilblains.'

Wykeham grunted. 'It's far worse than that. By the by, they said you were there, at Pallenswick. And that you grew pale with fear when you saw your man under restraint.'

'By God! I was not!'

'I think God has no role in this. Rather the Devil. This is what your man did for you, if he is to be believed.'

Wykeham ticked them off on his fingers while I absorbed the depth of my supposed guilt, far more weighty than fraud and embezzlement. The accusations smeared the soft air in that pretty spot with the taint of necromancy. All of it false. All of it impossible to prove to be false, but Father Oswald's confessions cast me into the pit.

'Your physician claimed that upon your order he created two images of yourself and His Majesty, binding them together to make an indissoluble bond. Thus Edward's infatuation with you. Their words—not mine. Your physician made two rings with magical properties for you to put onto Edward's finger, one to refresh the King's memory so that you would always be in the forefront of his thoughts. The other to cause forgetfulness of all else but yourself. And he made love potions and spells suffused with herbs picked at the full moon, at your request, to work your magic to bewitch the King into infatuation.' He paused, eyeing me. 'You have been very busy, it seems, Mistress Perrers.'

'Have I not? And do you believe all this?'

Wykeham shrugged. 'He also said he made a spell so that you could charm Gaunt and the Prince to your own ends.'

'Both of them?' My voice was no more than a croak.

'Yes. I think he added both for good measure.'

'It says little for Father Oswald's skill.' Should I laugh or weep at the outrageousness of it all? 'I failed singularly to win the Prince to my favour, and Gaunt's allegiance is an unpredictable thing governed by self-interest.'

A silence fell between us. I had nothing at hand to throw.

'The Speaker is making much of it,' Wykeham said.

'He would, of course.' I tried to predict the next step in this battle, for surely that is what it was. 'What have they done with my poor physician?'

'Sent him back to St Albans, in a sorry state, to face his superiors. They've done with him, mistress. It's you they want.' Wykeham's gaze was cool and direct. I waited for his condemnation, but it did not come.

'You were kind enough to come here to inform me.' It seemed hours since Wykeham had first breathed the word 'witchcraft', since my world had become a thing of terror, but the line of shadow on the sundial had barely moved, and now encroaching clouds blotted out the sun. 'You still haven't said whether you believe the charge or not.'

'The sin of avarice, perhaps. Of pride, certainly...'

'Oh, Wykeham...!' Would he list all my failings?

'But witchcraft? No, not that. I believe you have a deep affection for the King. I don't believe you would ever do him harm.'

'My thanks. You are one of very few.' It gave me some comfort but not much. We began to walk back toward the palace, driven in by the birth of a sharp little breeze that had driven away the bees and promised rain. Here was blatant propaganda of the worst kind to blacken my character. I stopped, regardless of the spatter of heavy drops.

'Will they find me guilty?' And when Wykeham hesitated: 'Don't give me a soft answer. Tell me what you think.'

'I'd no intention of hiding the truth. I think they will. He's like a hound slavering for the kill.' I flinched. 'With

Latimer and Lyons under his belt, de la Mare's confidence shines like a comet. I find it difficult to meet with him without addressing the sin of pride.'

'And the punishment if it's proven? Will it be death?'

He thought for a long moment. 'Unlikely. Penance and fasting probably. You haven't killed anyone. Imprisonment at the worst.'

I barely felt the rain on my face. 'Then I'll plan for the worst. I don't see de la Mare being content with a few missed meals and a Pater Noster.' The thought of imprisonment was bad enough to me. I closed my mind to it. 'What do I do, Wykeham?'

'You could take refuge at Pallenswick.'

Inwardly I recoiled at the implication, that making a defence against the charges would be a waste of his breath and mine. But flight? 'No.' I didn't even consider it. 'I cannot. You've seen the King. He needs me.'

'Then you remain here and do nothing. Just wait. The Speaker might abandon it…'

I completed his sentence when he hesitated again. 'If he finds something worse to pin on me.'

Wykeham's eyes bored into mine. 'Why? What else have you done?'

I shook my head and looked away across to the trees that were now shivering in the wind. There was one secret I prayed would remain hidden from public knowledge for a little time yet. It would bring too much pain to Edward.

And if it didn't?

Back in my room, where I retired to change my muddied skirts, I hurled a handsome glazed jug at the wall, and then regretted it. I felt no better for it, and one of the serving maids had to clear up after my uncontrolled temper.

* * *

Wykeham gone, I returned to Edward's side in his great chamber. The cloth of gold folded away, he was now wrapped in a chamber robe, the scarlet and fur at odds with the wasted figure it contained. Before the fire—he always felt the cold even on the warmest day—he slept in his chair, his head forward on his chest, a cup of ale at his side. John Beverley, his body servant, stood within call if he should wake and lack for aught. I gestured that he should leave and sat on a stool at Edward's feet as I had been wont to do when he had still been in his prime and I a young girl. But my thoughts were not of past memories. As I leaned my head against the chair, Wykeham's warnings echoed strongly in my mind. He might be sanguine about my punishment but I was not convinced. Prison walls seemed to hem me in.

When Edward moved, I looked up, grateful for the distraction. His eyelids lifted slowly and, gradually, his eyes focused on me. Because they were lucid and aware, my heart leapt with joy.

'Edward.'

'Alice.' Even his voice was stronger. He could still surprise me. 'Dear girl. I have missed you.'

'I have been here with you while you slept. You had an audience with some of the worthies from London.'

He sighed a little. 'I don't remember. Bring me a cup of ale.'

I reached to pick up the forgotten cup beside him and placed it in his hand, curling his fingers around it. Sometimes he was still very much the King.

He sipped, handed the cup back to me. 'Will you sing to me?'

How little he remembered! 'I would, but it would not be to your pleasure! I'm told I have a voice like a creaking door-hinge.' I smiled as I recalled one of Isabella's more vulgar remarks, and saw an answering gleam in Edward's eyes. 'But here is a verse I have found and liked, because it speaks of old lovers, as we are...' I sank back against his chair, arranging my skirts, drawing the little book from the purse at my belt. 'It is about the cold of winter, and the warmth of enduring love. You will like it too.' I began to recite, slowly, gently, forming the words clearly so that he might follow.

'The leaves are failing; summer's past;
What once was green is brown and sere;
All nature's warmth has faded fast and gone from here;
The circling sun has reached the last house in its year.'

'You have it right, Alice. Winter has me in its thrall even in the heat of summer.' Edward dragged in a breath as if it were painful for him to speak it. 'I am no use to you as a man. I regret it, but am unable to remedy it.'
'No, but listen, Edward. It is not sad at all.'

'The world is chilled in every part:
But I alone am warm and grow
Still warmer. It delights my heart to feel the glow:
My lord made the burning start—I love him so.'

'Alice... You have a beautiful voice.' The slight slurring of his words that always returned when he grew weary was very evident. 'I think that was one of the first things I noticed about you.'
'I doubt it!' I laughed a little at the memory. 'I think I was shrieking like a fishwife in the chapel at Havering when I was accused of theft! And you were tied up with your clock.'

'I had forgotten…' He sought my hand and his fingers tightened around mine. I could feel his eyes on my face, on my lips as I read the final tender lines.

This fire in my heart is nourished by
My lord's kisses and his gentle touch;
And shining from his radiant eye the light is such
That neither earth nor brilliant sky can show as much.'

'There, you see.' I closed the little book. 'Love remains even in the depths of winter and the fullness of years.'

Silence settled around us. He was asleep again and my heart full of sorrow that he should mourn the loss of virility so keenly and above all else. We might no longer be lovers but we were bound together by our past that stretched over well nigh thirteen years. Even in sleep, his fingers held mine and I knew he was pleased.

For a little time my fears of witchcraft were banished. I would allow nothing to separate us. Not until death released Edward from his present sufferings.

'Is it true?' Wykeham demanded, voice raw and positively vibrating with disbelief. Wykeham come to Sheen again in a towering fury.

'Is *what* true? If it's more empty mouthings of de la Mare that you've come to report, then don't. Just go away!'

I reacted without patience, weary beyond my soul. There was no royal audience to distract us this time. Lost in the past, Edward was dictating orders—full of cloth of gold and torch bearers—to mark the occasions of the deaths of both his mother and Philippa. And this after a week when he had spoken not one word to anyone: not to his servants, not to God. Certainly not to me. I had made myself scarce until the doleful task of remembrance was done.

'Is it true?' Wykeham bellowed.

I stood in the centre of the Great Hall. 'Is what true?'

But when Wykeham shouted back, careless of who overheard, I knew my fate was sealed. When Wykeham had come to warn me about the charge of necromancy hanging over my neck, he had been the concerned and courteous priest. Now he was the dread harbinger of doom, the executioner. There was no escape for me.

'You actually *married* him?'

Holy Mother! 'Who?' I played desperately for time.

'You know who!'

Wykeham watched me. He was waiting for me to deny it. Knowing that I couldn't.

'Yes.' I raised my chin. 'Yes. I did.'

'I don't believe that you would do anything so…so…' he groped for self-control '…so ill advised!'

'Well, Wykeham, how mealy-mouthed.' There was nothing genial about my smile. 'And how did de la Mare mine that little gem?' I asked. 'I thought no one knew.'

'Does it matter?' His voice had dropped to a hiss. *'When?'*

'Just before he returned to Ireland.'

'That was when? Two years ago? You've been wed for two years?' The volume grew again to echo above us. 'In God's name, Alice! What were you thinking?'

I did not want to explain. I did not think I could.

'Does Edward know?' Wykeham threw up his arms as much in despair as anger.

'No.'

'Don't you realise what you've done?' At least Wykeham now had the sense to lower his voice. 'You've made him an adulterer!'

I lifted a shoulder. 'And so were we both when Philippa was alive. Edward did not step back from it then, when he had all the knowledge. What difference?'

Wykeham kicked a foot into the ashes of the open fire, sending up a shower of sparks.

'Why, Alice? Why do it? If it's just a roll between the sheets you wanted, why not just do it without the sanction of Holy Mother Church? As for the man you chose—God's Blood! A more self-interested, unprincipled bastard I have yet to meet...'

I watched the sparks die as they fell into grey dust. Because beneath the hard-edged ambition and ruthless temperament, there was in Windsor a man of rare honesty who actually cared for me. But I would not say this to Wykeham.

'I wed him because he asked me.'

'Alice!'

I abandoned the flippancy. 'Don't lecture me, Wykeham. You, of all people. I must make my future secure. I come from nothing and will return to nothing if I don't make provision. I will not have my children live in penury or on the charity of others, as I did.'

'Surely you have enough property by now to keep shoes on their feet?'

'Perhaps I need a man to stand for me.'

'But to *wed* him.'

'He offered when no one else would. It is not adultery. Not in the letter of the law. The King and I are no longer intimate.' The priest in him flushed to his hairline. 'Don't be prudish, Wykeham. It can't be a surprise to you that the King is incapable.'

'But the King recognised the children you had together. They will never suffer.'

'Yes, he made provision. But will Princess Joan allow

the provision to continue when her son is King?' It was a shallowly buried fear that was quick to resurface. 'I dare not risk it. If marriage to Windsor secures my daughters' dowries and marriage, I'll not regret it.'

'What will Edward say?'

Which brought me up short. As he intended. I replied slowly. 'He will be hurt, of course.'

'You must tell him. Unless he knows already.'

'Pray God he does not.'

As Wykeham left me alone in the Great Hall, all its spaces empty around me, I thought of the one thing I had not said. I had wed Windsor—a name that had not once been voiced between us—because I loved him. How weak did that make me?

Edward knew. How swift could gossip fly? There were always those at Court who would make mischief and Edward's mind was clear enough.

'You betrayed me, Alice. You betrayed my love for you.'

He rubbed his hands together constantly, in incessant repetition, one over the other, his fingers tearing, his nails marking his skin. Guilt-ridden, I fell on my knees, trying to still his fretful clawing, but he would not. Edward turned his face from me as he had never done before.

'I don't want you here.'

I deserved it. All my senses were frozen.

Did the Commons have mercy on me? By God, they did not! In a mood of vengeful exuberance they ordered me to appear before them in the Painted Chamber at Westminster. And I obeyed—what choice had I?—seeing nothing but the lugubrious face of de la Mare gleaming with unholy virtue as I set my mind to hear and accept my punishment for bringing the King of England into adultery. By now I feared the worst, gripping my hands together as I sat on the low stool provided for me. At least they allowed me to sit.

I sat straight-backed, determined to hear my fate with dignity. I would never bow my head before de la Mare. Whatever punishment they meted out, nothing could be worse than Edward's rejection of me.

Nothing?

Ah, no! There was worse, far worse. The door to the magnificent Painted Chamber opened and there was Edward, brought to appear before his own Parliament for my sins and his, and I saw the panicked fear in his eyes as they skittered over the vast assembly. I stood abruptly, I even think I reached out to him in my guilt and misery, but he did not look at me, all his efforts fixed on walking to take his place on the throne. Slowly, one step after another, he dragged himself there, and once there he pushed himself upright and faced his accusers while I prayed that they would direct their vengeance at me, not at Edward, who did not deserve this. I willed him to look at me. Whatever was asked of me, I would not betray him more than I already had done. I would do or say nothing to increase his humiliation. Was it not terrible enough that he must be there?

De la Mare bowed. 'We are honoured, Sire.'

And I sank back to my seat as I waited for the blow to fall, as de la Mare faced Edward.

'Majesty. We are concerned that Mistress Perrers has acted towards you with a degree of insincerity that is beyond belief.'

How smooth he was. How terrifyingly, horrifyingly respectful, before plunging the metaphorical dagger into Edward's unsuspecting heart.

Edward blinked, hands clutching.

'We believe she has put Your Majesty's soul in mortal danger.'

Would he dare to accuse Edward of being complicit in adultery? My nails dug deep into my palms.

'Were you aware, Sire, that Mistress Perrers had entered into matrimony? That she has been married to the knight, William de Windsor, for two years or more?'

Bewildered, Edward shook his head.

'Were you so aware, Sire?'

'No…!' Again I was on my feet. How dared they question him! This was my guilt, not his.

'Be seated, Mistress Perrers.'

'It is not right—'

'It is very right.' De la Mare swung back to the King. 'Did you know, Sire?' I sat again, forcing myself to look at Edward in his extremity, forcing myself to accept that this was all my doing. 'Were you aware, Sire, that the woman who is acknowledged as your mistress is married?' The question was hammered home once more.

And I heard Edward reply. Calm and clear. Unemotional. 'I was not aware.'

'Would you swear to that, Sire?'

The Speaker would dare to ask the King of England to swear an oath? Edward's face was ravaged, but he replied.

'I swear on the name of the Holy Virgin. I did not know.'

'So she tricked you, Sire.'

'I don't know. How could I know…?'

Oh, Edward! How could I have put you in this position?

It was all de la Mare needed. Facing me now, he flung out an arm in a dramatic all-encompassing gesture.

'You are guilty. You have wilfully put the King into the state of adultery. You tricked him with your lies and deceit. The fault is yours.'

I waited for the noxious taint of witchcraft to fill the chamber.

'What is the punishment for your crime? There are those here who demand your execution. The means you have used are unholy, disgusting in the sight of God. We have evidence of...'

I tensed. This would be the moment. *Maleficium!*

'Sirs!'

I looked across the chamber. It was Edward. De la Mare hesitated.

'I beg of you,' Edward said, each word carefully formed as at last he looked at me, his eye weighted with sorrow and confusion. And astonishingly a hard-won determination. My heart was wrung. 'Show her mercy, sirs. I beg your compassion. She does not deserve execution. If you have any loyalty to me, your King, you will show this woman leniency in your judgement. She has done wrong, but she does not deserve death.'

I held Edward's gaze. In that final sentence he had both betrayed and upheld me. All hung in the balance.

'Mistress Perrers deserves a lesser punishment than death,' Edward repeated. 'I beg of you...'

And grief all but overwhelmed me.

'We honour your request, Sire.' De la Mare could not disguise his self-congratulation, so smug that I felt an urge to vomit. 'Stand up, Mistress Perrers.'

I did so, bracing knees that refused to obey me.

'We are decided.'

De la Mare spelt out the terms of my punishment. As it flowed from his lips, detailed, thorough, I knew that it had been decided all along. There had been no need to put Edward through this. Grief was transmuted into an anger that shook me as I absorbed the extent of his revenge. Even Princess Joan could not have thought up any better.

Banishment!

The single word hung in the air with all the heaviness of its meaning. I was banished. Never to see Edward again.

'You will live at a distance from the royal Court. You will not return. If you disobey, if you make any attempt to approach the King, you will lose everything you own and suffer permanent exile overseas.' The Speaker's lips widened into a rictus of a smile over his discoloured teeth. 'If you force your way into the King's presence, all your property, your goods and chattels will be seized and confiscated.' His pleasure disgusted me, but I stood unmoving, unresponsive. I would never give him the satisfaction of seeing how much this penalty wounded me.

Glancing at Edward, I knew that he did not understand. His eyes were closed, his mouth lax. He had no inkling of what they had just done. If I walked across the chamber to him now, I would be left with nothing and banished from England.

With blood drained from my face, my hands as cold as ice, I did what they wanted. My lips pressed to the crucifix presented to me, I swore that I would never return to the King. I would live apart, away from the royal Court. I would never see Edward again.

Thus I abandoned him, or so it felt in my heart.

Where to go? I collected my immediate possessions and went to Wendover, Wykeham's old manor that Edward had gifted to me. My sore heart urged Pallenswick but I knew Parliament would consider it too close to Sheen, or the Tower, or Westminster, wherever Edward might be, with too easy a route along the Thames. So I went to Wendover to lick my wounds, after I had risked seeing Edward for the last time. Surely a final farewell would be allowed.

He did not know me.

'Edward!'

There was no flicker of acknowledgement in his empty gaze.

'I have come to say farewell.'

Nothing. I was not pardoned. His wayward mind could not encompass me or what I had done. I kissed his forehead and curtseyed deeply.

'Forgive me, Edward. I would not have it end like this. I would never have left you.'

At least he was spared the pain of parting. I closed the door of his chamber, swallowing tears. Alice Perrers, King's Concubine no longer, humiliated, repudiated, maliciously destroyed.

Who had not been in the Painted Chamber to witness my downfall?

Gaunt.

Who had made no attempt to see me, to stand for me?

John of Gaunt.

He too had abandoned me. The alliance, tenuous at best, did not bring him to my side when I most had need of him. I was no longer of any value to him. Refused the position of Regent for his nephew Richard by the magnates who feared his power, Gaunt found that I had no influence to help him. Neither would it be good for Gaunt's name to be coupled to any degree with mine.

He turned his back on me.

And my poor, lost Edward? I had Wykeham tell me how he fared. Of the days when he was driven by anger, accusing Windsor far more harshly than he accused me. And then there were the hours when old loyalties returned to Edward, when he looked for me, asked for me, and was told that I could not come. Days when his senses deserted him. I knew of the hours when he sat in uncomprehending gloom with tears on his cheeks. The King was nothing but a lonely, forgotten old man, with no one to stir his spirits to life. Who would reminisce with him? Who would talk to him of the glory days, as I had done?

No one.

Gaunt was too busy plotting revenge against de la Mare and the Earl of March, who now stood with Wykeham as one of Edward's councillors. Isabella was back with her husband in France. There was no one to remember the past.

And I also knew of the increasing number of days when Edward's thoughts turned inward.

'I will bury my son, my glorious Prince, and then I will die.'

I swallowed the tears no longer, but wept for him. I did not write to Windsor. I could not find the words, neither could I bear his pity.

Chapter Fourteen

For the first days at Wendover I grieved. Until hot rage blew through me like a wind before an August storm. It shook me by its virulence as I heaped my hatred on the absent, crowing, self-satisfied Master Speaker.

'May Almighty God damn you to the fires of hell! May your vile body be gnawed on by worms. Your balls roasted in everlasting flames and...' I was not circumspect in my choice of language but it brought no release.

Never had my life stretched so emptily, so helplessly before me, my hands so idle and without power. My knowledge of the outside world in those terrible weeks was reduced to common gossip, brought into the house by my servants and passing pedlars. Poor stuff! The Prince's body lay embalmed in state in Westminster Abbey week after week. There were no moves to bury him, Edward unable to make a decision. Princess Joan and the young heir were at Kennington. Gaunt was biding his time but furious with events. The Good Parliament had ended its days, preening over its successes.

'And I am banished, by God. How dare they!'

With a need to occupy my hands and my mind, I swept through the manor, stirring up steward and servants to clean and scour and scrub every surface, every nook and cranny. There was absolutely no need for me to disturb their daily routines but I could not rest. They would have to suffer me, perhaps for the rest of my life. God's Blood! At thirty-one years I could not contemplate it.

Braveheart slept at my feet oblivious to my mood, uncaring of whether we were at Wendover or Sheen.

I stalked from room to room, my pleasure in my surroundings and my acquisitions dimmed. Even the magnificent bed—a gift from Edward—carved and swagged with deep blue damask hangings, the oak tester and pillars polished to a rich gleam, did not satisfy me. I saw far too much of that fine weaving that closed me in, for my nights were troubled. If I had had a looking glass, I would have abjured it. It would have shown me all too clearly the effect of my lack of appetite and restless thoughts. My collarbone pressed against the cloth of my gown and my girdle must be tightened or it would fall around my ankles. As I pressed my fingers against my sharp cheekbones I grimaced, suspecting that the dark thumbprints of weariness would not enhance my looks.

Lured by the soft warmth of autumn, I took the side door out into the orchard where the apple trees hung heavy with the fruit and doves preened in the dove cote, a lovely scene if I was of a mind to admire it. Before I could take a breath, all unbidden the image leapt into my mind, so that I sank down on the grass, helpless, enclosed in that one moment of the past.

* * *

'Today you are my Lady of the Sun,' Edward says as he hands me into my chariot.

And there I sit, garlanded with flowers, swathed in cloth of gold, a cloak of shimmering gold tissue, opulent in its Venetian style, is spread around me, so disposed to show a lining of scarlet taffeta. My gown too is red, lined with white silk and edged in ermine. Edward's colours. Royal fur fit for a queen, no finer than the myriad of precious stones refracting the light—rubies as red as fire, sapphires dark and mysterious, strange beryls capable of destroying the power of poison. Philippa's jewels. My fingers are fretted with rings.

'Today you are the Queen of the Ceremonies, the Queen of the Lists,' Edward says. He is tall and strong and good to look on.

I am Lady of the Sun.

I blinked as a swooping pigeon smashed the scene, bringing reality back with cruel exactitude. How low I had fallen. I was caged in impotent loneliness, like Edward's long-dead lion. Powerless, isolated, stripped of everything I had made for myself, I could not tolerate this absence from what had been the centre of my world for—for how long now? Ten years? It seemed to me that I had lived my whole lifetime in one royal palace or another, the vivid colours of luxury and royal privilege quite obliterating my early origins and crude memories. I needed to be at Court now, even if it was only for one more time while Edward lived. Not here, not at Wendover, however good life was, however much I might love the solidity of the manor that had been gifted to me by Edward. The Court was my *métier*. The glamour, the pageantry, the outward show. The gossip and intrigue behind every tapestry. The *power*—power so strong that it could be tasted on the tongue, could almost be seen, like a dusting of golden pollen on the bees that haunted the lavender hedges in high summer. That was where I wanted to be.

At night sleep evaded me, a persistent grinding ache between my brows nailing my head to the pillow. When I arose it was little better, leaving me dull and listless. Even the compresses of lavender or pennyroyal gave me no ease, even when I took myself to task. What were my sufferings compared with Edward's? I should be there, with him, to lure him from his ill humours back into the present world where he was still King. Frustration clawing at me, I tore at the grass, scattering handfuls into the air.

At court I was *someone*. Here I was nothing but a country wife with grass seeds lodged in the lacings of her bodice.

Irritated with myself and my morose self-pity, I rose to go back inside and torment someone into doing something, but was stopped by my two girls, Joan leading her younger sister, in their escape from their governess. Joan, five years old, fair and strong-limbed like her father. Jane, two years younger, a shy child, not like me at all despite her dark hair and plain features. They ran laughing through the orchard, shouting to each other in their joy of freedom. And my heart tripped a little at their innocent pleasure. I did not remember running, laughing in my childhood. I recalled very little joy. God help me to keep their lives safe.

Seeing me, they ran to jump and caper, full of chatter and news. With promises that we would ride out in the afternoon, I dispatched them back to their lessons. They would read and write and figure. No daughter of mine would lack for such skills, and neither would my sons. I wanted no ignorant, untutored gentleman with the King's blood in his veins and nothing between his ears. John, as befitted a lad with royal blood in his veins, learned the lessons of a page in the noble Percy household. Nicholas at eleven was taught his letters by the monks at Westminster. I had such pride in them. As for my girls—they would have an advantageous marriage as well as an education. I smiled a little as I stooped to pick up a much-worn doll that Joan had dropped on the grass. Combing my fingers through its disordered hair, I vowed that I would ensure that my daughters were capable, even without husbands.

A movement caught my eye. A robin flew up into the boughs of the apple tree, making me look up.

'Is this you?'

I hadn't heard. Neither the approach of horses nor the soft footfall. Or had even felt the movement of air. Startled for a moment, the fear still lively that Parliament might not quite have finished with me, I took a step back. And then clutched the doll to my breast, because I knew the voice, and the solid figure outlined by the sun through the branches.

The years rolled back and away. To the day I first set eyes on Edward in the great hall at Havering, back lit by the low rays of the afternoon sun with his hounds, the goshawk on his wrist, a corona of light around head and shoulders. Crowned with gold. I had simply stared at such an aura of power.

But this was another time, another life.

Windsor stepped forward, and the moment passed as he was enclosed in dappled shadow. All was suddenly upheaval in my belly, my mouth dry with nerves, my whole body weak with longing. I would run to him, cast myself into his arms, press my mouth against his, feel the solid beat of his heart under the palm of my hand. Three years since I had seen him last. Three long years! I could cover the distance between us within the space of one heavy beat of my heart and…

No, no. I must guard my response. I must be measured and calm. Lightly controlled...

Why? Because it was never wise to give weapons into the hands of others, even the man I loved with a physical desire so strong that it shivered through me like an ague. How terrible it was to fear putting oneself under the dominion of a man whose affection I craved, but if my life had taught me one indisputable fact it was the need to be resilient, self-reliant. I must not show my husband how afraid I was of giving him power over me, power to hurt and wound and destroy.

But he will not hurt and wound and destroy! You know him better than that.

No, I do not know him at all!

But I could not stop my mouth curving in a smile when my eyes lifted to his.

'William de Windsor! By the Virgin!'

'Alice Perrers! As I live and breathe!' The familiar goading tugged at my heart. 'Picking apples?'

'No.' I held up the doll. 'And I thought I was Alice de Windsor, your wife.'

'So did I. But it's so long since our ways met...' He took off his hat, sweeping a splendid bow. 'I didn't recognise you in this rustic garb. It took me some days to find you.'

'I suppose you thought I was a servant.'

'Impossible!' His voice was warm, but he did not approach. A tension in his stance warned me that all was not well. Skin was stretched taut over his cheekbones, the habitual cynicism touched his mouth with what was barely a smile. Momentarily I wondered why, but my own anxieties prevailed. I took another step away, thoroughly irritable with myself and with him, as he observed: 'I hear you're banished from Court by the great and the good.'

'Yes, as you see. The Good Parliament in its wisdom decided to sweep the palaces clean of all unwholesome influences. Latimer, Neville, Lyons…all gone.'

'And you.'

'And me. They left me until last, to savour the moment. They cast me into outer darkness.' All my pent-up frustrations overflowed. 'And if I set foot within a yard of Edward they'll rejoice in taking every last inch of my property and packing me off even further into oblivion. Your wife will be living somewhere in France for the rest of her life so you'll never see her at all!'

'They've got your measure.' Windsor's teeth showed with a wolfish grimace. 'Is that why you're holed up here, not a silk ribbon or a jewel to be seen, rather than banging on the door at Sheen for admittance?'

'Yes.' I looked down, smoothing my hand over the plain russet kirtle beneath the unfashionable open-sided cotehardie, miserably unadorned even if the wool was a good weaving. 'My new role in life. Rural seclusion.'

'Perhaps we'll both grow to enjoy it.'

'I doubt it.'

'So do I. But we are no longer invited to dine at the royal table, and so must make do with the scraps dished out to us.'

It was almost a snarl, enough to give me thought, to snatch my mind from my own ills. How could I not have *seen*? I should have asked him the moment he stepped into my orchard.

'What are you doing here?'

'You haven't heard? Summoned—again! In disgrace—again! Relieved of my position.' The words were clipped, every vestige of edgy banter gone under a layer of black temper.

'Edward's dismissed you…'

'Yes. My services are no longer required. There will be no further re-instatement. I shouldn't be surprised, should I?'

'Oh, Will!' And I held out my hands to him. Of course he was aggrieved. The ultimate courtier and politician, he would hate it as much as I to be thrust into this power-less obscurity. I could remain distant from him no longer. I crossed the grassy, apple-strewn divide in easy strides. 'I'm so sorry, Will. Oh, Will—I am so very glad to see you.'

Even his name on my lips was a soft pleasure. All my intentions to remain aloof scattered in the face of his dismissal, I stepped into his arms and they closed around me.

'That's better,' he said after a moment when he almost resisted the intimacy. 'It almost makes it worth my while returning.'

For a little while we stood silent and unmoving, savouring the shifting patterns of light and shade, my forehead pressed against his shoulder, his cheek resting on my hair, the doll still clutched in my hand. I felt him relax, slowly, gradually, beneath my hands. The robin trilled above but we let the deeper silence enfold us.

'So what's the King doing?' Windsor asked eventually when the robin flew away.

'He's not doing anything. He's old and lonely. I don't think he understands.' I placed my fingers against his mouth when he opened it to deliver, as I supposed, some sharp comment on the King accepting my banishment without redress. 'He deserves your compassion, Will. Did he not plead for me? And Edward needs me—he is helpless. Who will know how to care for him?' And tears began to slide down my cheek into the damask of his tunic.

'I've never seen you weep before. For sure you've never wept over me. I think you had better tell me all about it.' Windsor led me to a grassy bank set back near the perimeter hedge and dried my tears with the edge of my cotehardie. Taking the doll from me, sitting her down between us as a quaint chaperone and taking my hands between his, his eyes narrowed on my face as I sniffed. 'I see you, Alice—before you even think to hide the truth. You're too thin. When did you last sleep through the night? Your eyes are so very tired.' When he ran the edge of his thumb under my eye it took my breath away, and then his mouth was warm against my temple. 'What terrors have you had to face on your own, my brave girl?'

His compassion all but undermined my self-control. 'I am not brave. I've been terrified out of my wits.'

'Why didn't you send for me?'

'What could you have done?'

'Perhaps nothing. Except be here to make sure that you eat and sleep and don't malinger. You've always stood on your own feet, haven't you?'

'There is no one else.'

'I see.' As his brows snapped together, I thought I had hurt him. But what could he have done at so great a distance? 'I'm here now, when you've fought your enemies alone. I admire you for it. So tell me what terrified you.' The earlier sharpness crept back. 'Unless you prefer to keep it all to yourself.'

Yes, I had hurt him. But that was the life we led.

'I will tell you.'

And I did, with strange relief, even though I had determined not to. I told him of Parliament's vendetta. The accusation of necromancy and Joan's probable involvement. My ultimate banishment. Edward's brave defence of me at the last, when his heart was split in two.

I sighed. 'It's been quite a month,' I finished.

'So Edward knows about our marriage. And blames you.'

I nodded and sniffed again. 'Yes. But he blames you more.' I would tell him the truth. What harm would it do? 'Edward damns you for the whole. He blames me for the hurt I caused him, but in his eyes you were the instigator. He thinks you have corrupted me. He even purchased a chest to lock away all the accusations made against you for his future reference. He sits and looks at it and plots his revenge, so I'm told.' I touched his hand. 'I don't think it can ever happen. He no longer has the will to carry it out.'

'Perhaps not, but I am relieved of my position,' Windsor responded, a bright spurt of anger erupting again. 'For fraud. What is fraud? A mark on a line of necessity. I have taxed them heavily. I have made my own fortune. But I have kept the peace and the government is at least efficient. I have kept those arrogant lords on a short rein. And all I get is dismissal.' He shrugged and I saw the fire die in his eyes, to be replaced by resignation. 'It's out of my hands. A man who wields authority must always risk losing it.'

'And a woman who has power, unless born to it, makes enemies.'

'So both our names are to be trampled in the mud.' He dried my tears again with his own dusty sleeve—I think I no longer cared if he left smears on my cheeks—and, dislodging our ineffectual chaperone, kissed me, a demanding assault on my lips, a little rough, as if he had indeed missed me.

Windsor raised his head and looked at me, his dark eyes holding mine, his thoughts beyond my imagining.

'Don't weep, my resourceful wife. We shall come about. Is there anything for a much-travelled man to eat and drink in this pearl of a manor?'

I shook myself into the reality of my orchard at Wendover and the practicality of a long-absent husband returned to me. This was no time for dreams. 'There is,' I said. 'I've been an unthinking hostess.'

'And hot water to remove the filth of travel perhaps?'

'I could arrange that.'

'Even to remove the odd louse? By God, I've stayed in some miserable inns.'

'I can arrange that!'

'And perhaps a bed?'

'I expect so.'

I led him into the house, some semblance of good humour restored between us. We banished our concerns to some distant place beyond our bedchamber door and made of our reunion a private celebration. I had forgotten how resourceful he was. His hands and mouth woke my body to a depth of desire that consumed me. Even the worries that had stalked me vanished. How could they exist when he was intent on possessing my body, and I was equally intent on allowing it?

Next morning Windsor was up at dawn. I awoke more slowly, my mind full of spending the day with him, renewing the tentative bonds that had been first created so long ago. But I saw that his sword was gone from where he had dropped it beside the door, and I could hear the sound of the house astir and busy between kitchen and parlour. I dressed rapidly, knowing what I would find before I entered. Windsor, dressed for riding, was already breaking his fast. On the coffer by the door was a leather wallet, topped by his gloves, sword and serviceable hood.

All my bright anticipation fell to earth with a crash. I should have known, should I not? The pleasures of the bedchamber would not keep Windsor from what must be faced and challenged. For a little while I stood on the threshold, studying the stern lines of his face, the quick movement of his fingers, strong and capable, as he sliced and ate, my mind reliving the recent dark hours when he had ignited a flame. Then I stepped in.

'Are you abandoning me, Will?' I asked, a bright smile despite the chasm that his imminent departure had opened up before me.

'Yes, but not for long. I'll take a look at my estates. In spite of an excellent steward, the mice will have been playing while the cat's away in Ireland, and you, I think, have been preoccupied,' he said round a mouthful of home-cured ham. 'But I'll return by the end of the week.'

I would not have wagered on it but it had to satisfy me. I came to sit across from him, resting my elbows on the board, taking a sip from his mug of ale. 'Will you find out what's happening at Court for me?'

'If it pleases you. What's Gaunt doing? Do we know?' Windsor stood, snatching the small beer back again and finishing it, brushing any trace of crumbs from his tunic.

'I don't know. But he'll not be content. Parliament humiliated him.'

'Hmm! So he'll be looking around for opportunities for revenge.' He smiled thinly as if on a new thought, his hands busy tucking documents into the wallet. 'Life might become interesting. I might even become acceptable again.'

I followed him out, deciding to allow him his enigmatic statement. I doubted he would explain, even if I asked.

'Will you try and get news of Edward? Wykeham is a good correspondent but...'

'I will. He might wish me to Hades, but I'll do it. God keep you, Alice.' He strapped the wallet to the saddle, whilst I stood like a good wife to wish him God speed. Then he turned and surprised me by cupping my face in his hands.

'I'll do what I can. Don't fret. I can't have your sharp wit and intelligence wasting away to a shadow. What would I have to come home to?'

'An amenable wife?'

'God preserve me from such!' A kiss and he was gone, less than twenty-four hours after he had arrived, with not one word of affection. Or love.

I raised my hand in farewell, retreating briskly into the house as if I did not care. Oh, but I did, and when Windsor did not return within the week I mourned his loss beyond all sense, as if it were a death.

Despite his absence, Windsor did not forget my need for news, sending a courier with a scrappily written note. I read it again and again, a lifeline to Windsor, as well as to Edward and the Court, absorbing every word.

Gaunt, magnificently vocal and brimful of revenge, had declared war on the actions of the Good Parliament.

You will be interested to see how busy he has been in your absence from Court.

And I was, revelling in the details, admiring Gaunt's ruthless efficiency. He announced that the Good Parliament had proceeded contrary to Edward's commands, thus rendering all its actions null and void. Edward's new body of twelve councillors, appointed by Parliament to keep such malignant forces as I from his door, was summarily dismissed. Poor Wykeham, once more deprived of royal office. And the Earl of March, for whom I had no sympathy. Gaunt would relish that dismissal, holding the young man wholly accountable for the clever plot with the de la Mares to undermine Gaunt's own power.

Latimer is released from his imprisonment. I know this will please you.

And then Gaunt began hunting in earnest, his own forces taking Peter de la Mare prisoner.

He is held fast in a cell in Gaunt's castle at Nottingham. The word is that there is no prospect of a trial. Try not to be too overjoyed. It is unseemly in Lady de Windsor.

I laughed aloud. I had no tender thought for the man who had forced Edward to plead for me in public. Ah! But I did not enjoy the next paragraph. I think Windsor must have known I would find it hard, because it was written plainly, without comment.

Gaunt has charged Wykeham with fraud as Edward's Chancellor. I am told that the evidence was thin, but Wykeham is deprived of all his temporal appointments and forbidden to come within twenty miles of Edward's person. He has retired to a monastery at Merton...

I regretted it, Wykeham once again suffering for his loyalty to Edward.

And the one name omitted in all of Windsor's comprehensive summary?

Alice Perrers.

What of *me*?

Well into the third week, at the end of a sultry day that weighed us down with damp heat so that even taking a breath was wearying, Windsor returned. I was out of the house, into the courtyard, in the instant I heard the approach of a horse. I hardly allowed him to swing down from the saddle before I was at his shoulder, pulling on his sleeve.

'What's happening?'

'Good evening, my wife!'

'What about me?'

'Ah! No one is mentioning your name, my love!'

'Is that good or bad?'

'Impossible to tell.'

'And Edward?'

He shook his head. 'He's ill. It's thought to be only a matter of time…'

He looked tired, on the edge of a short temper, as if he had ridden long and hard. As if business had not gone entirely as he would have liked. I sighed. 'Forgive me, Will. What of you? I've been selfish…'

'Let us say single-minded.'

Tossing his reins to a groom, we walked into the house, side by side. He drew my hand companionably through his arm.

'You sent me no word of your fate,' I accused as we moved into the rooms dim with evening light.

'What's to write?'

I saw the glint of anger in his eye despite the shadows. I had been selfish. After a lifetime of major and minor selfishnesses, I was learning that there were others who needed my compassion. An unlikely man to need it—and he would never ask it of me—yet Windsor might actually need my comfort. I was beginning to know him better. So I applied myself to the skills that still came unhandily to me, relieving him of his gloves, hood and mantle, dispatching a servant to bring ale, pushing him to sit on a settle beneath an ancient oak to the side of the house that would allow us the blessing of any movement of air, conscious of how weary he was. I sat beside him, leaning to push wayward strands of hair back from his brow where they had stuck with perspiration.

'Very wifely.' He smiled. But even the usual mockery was missing.

'I'm practising. Allow me to try my skills.' I poured the

ale when it was brought to us, and gave it to him, waiting until he had drunk deep. 'You have been to Court.'

'Yes. To Sheen.'

'And?'

'My dismissal is confirmed. I've been handed a paltry pension of one hundred pounds a year for my past services. And should be grateful for it. The King wouldn't see me. He sent a thin-lipped lawyer with the message.'

'Perhaps he couldn't see you,' I ventured, to lessen the slight.

'Perhaps. I doubt the message would have been any different.' He sat and brooded, staring at the scuffed toes of his boots. 'It was strange.' He looked up at me. 'It was as if the heart had gone out of the palace. Everyone waiting for the King to breathe his last.'

I could not reply. We sat in our own little silence.

'What will you do?' I asked eventually.

Windsor hitched a shoulder. 'Decide where to live— Gaines, I expect. Administer my estates.' His smile was wry. 'Much as you will, I expect.'

I knew what I wanted. I had thought about this. I knew what I wanted more than anything. I said it before I could tell myself that it would be better not to.

'Stay with me, Will. Stay here. Don't go back to Gaines.'

His agile brows rose. 'How conventional. Set up home, like husband and wife?'

'Why not?'

'I could think of worse things.'

'I wasn't sure you wanted it,' I said. For, apart from the brief days after our marriage, we had never lived together. Secrecy and Ireland had kept us of necessity apart, and since our union was of a practical nature, perhaps he envisioned us always living apart. But now there was no need for pretence.

'I admit I had not seen us living in connubial bliss,' he said. 'But since we are both here, both outcast…'

'Could you think of any better outcome?'

'I don't know that I could.' He leaned and pressed his lips against mine, a very soft caress as if he was unsure of my response—or even his own. I returned the salute, my lips warm and inviting. Suddenly I wanted him, deep within me, a stroke of heat.

'Take me to bed, Will.'

We looked at each other. And smiled.

'Will…?'

'Go on. Say it.'

'Do you have any affection for me?'

'Is that in doubt?'

'Everything is in doubt.'

'Then I do.'

'That sounds as if you are placating a child.'

The harsh lines softened into amusement. 'Hard questioning, Alice. Worthy of Gaunt himself.'

'You can tell me the truth. I won't weep on your shoulder.'

'I wouldn't mind. I have a very handy shoulder and it's yours for your use.'

'Will…!'

'Do I have an affection for you…? Who did I seek out first when I returned to England?'

'Me. I think.'

'Who did I write to, most inconveniently?'

'Me.'

'There you are, then. I think I even told you I missed you.'

I punched his shoulder with my fist, my heart already lighter. 'Is that all I'm getting?'

'Yes. I'm tired. Come and be wifely in the bedchamber.'

Not love. Affection. But enough—it would have to be enough. And later, when we were entwined, sweat cooling on naked limbs: 'Alice. Do you have an affection for me?'

So he had noticed that I had not reciprocated. Of course he had. I made him wait as I always did.

'Yes, Will. An affection.' Only my heart knew that I could lie as well as any man.

And later. I sat and combed my hair at the open window, my husband still nothing more than a heap in the bed. I heard the eventual upheaval but did not look over. My thoughts were not at ease, despite the pleasure of the last hours.

'What's going on in that marvellous brain of yours?' he asked, soft-voiced.

'Edward.'

'I should have known.'

But there was no judgement in his voice that I had brought the King into our bedchamber. I turned my head.

'Do you think I'll see him again before he dies? I don't want him to die alone, the hard words still standing between us.' It was not easy to recall the last time I had seen him. 'He never pardoned me, you see. I would like to see him once more.'

'Don't set your heart on it. Who's to say you'll ever be given leave to return? It's in the hands of the gods.'

'More like Gaunt's.'

Windsor's silence spoke for itself—and gave me little comfort.

I was difficult to live with. I knew I was and could make neither excuses nor amends. After the years as Edward's lover, confidante and soul mate, and recently his solace, I found the distance insupportable. He had made me all that I was, all that I could ever be, and to be separated from him now at the end was beyond tolerating. If Windsor regretted moving his household to join with mine, he gave no indication of it, although I think that a less confident man would have washed his hands of me, miserable creature that I was, and packed his bags. Instead he gave me space in which to mourn the King, who was not yet dead. At night he held me in his arms when he knew I did not sleep. He did not chide me as I deserved, even when I snapped and snarled at him because he was the only one I could snap and snarl at.

Until it became too much for any man and he challenged me.

'What are you doing?'

I was staring out of the window. 'Nothing.'

'Which is useless. Go and interfere in one of your estates, woman. Just how many do you have?'

'Fifty-six at the last count,' I replied without thought. '*What?*'

'Fifty-six.' He looked stunned. 'And before you ask, only fifteen of them are gifts from Edward. I am quite capable of purchasing for myself.'

'By God!' He paused, as if he could not believe what Greseley and I had done over the years. 'I didn't know I'd wed a woman of such means! No wonder they've got you in their sights! If you were a man, it would qualify you for an earldom.' And he gave a sudden loud roar of laughter. 'And you do realise, my dear one, that all your fifty-six estates now belong to me, as your husband?'

Which got my attention fast enough.

'Only in name!' I snapped. Which was not true, but I was in no mood for legalistic banter.

'Now, why do I think I might find some noxious and fatal substance flavouring my ale if I lay claim to them?'

'Hemlock, I was thinking.'

But he had defused my quick anger. I managed a smile, if a pale travesty, remembering the day when, in my innocence, I had sworn to pursue the acquisition of land until I had as many manors to my name as I had years. I had not known the half of it, how the hunger for more and more would take possession of me so that I might never have to face homeless penury when Edward's protection was no longer mine to call on. Or perhaps it simply became an all-consuming passion, a need to acquire, that I was incapable of denying. If that was so, then I had undoubtedly fashioned the weapons that had brought my downfall—and yet it came to me that Speaker de la Mare would have created his own, with or without my help, to oust me from power.

I did not know…neither did it greatly matter now.

Windsor's voice became gruff with an underlying concern.

'But that's by the by. Sitting there will not help. Take the girls and—'

'Edward has made his will.'

'Oh. Are you sure?'

'It's the talk of the market. He's dying, Will. He must know it.'

I heard him exhale, abandoning any argument he might have made. Rejecting words as a lost cause, he took my hand to lead me into the parlour, which he had taken over for his own business affairs, and sat me down before a pile of accounts.

'Check the figures for me, Alice. If that won't distract you, nothing will.'

'Who are you? Janyn Perrers?'

'Why?'

I smiled, really smiled, for the first time for days. I had never spoken of the details of that marriage. 'It's how I passed the nights of my first marriage.'

'God save you!' He kissed the top of my head. 'But I'll still crack the whip. To work, woman!'

Holy Mother! It was dull work at that.

'And if you could finish them before the end of the day...'

'Am I your clerk?'

'No. You're my wife and you are suffering.'

I felt another light kiss on my hair before he left me to it. And through those drear November days I concentrated on Windsor's finances and my own. I was grateful, even through the fear that this might be all that my future life held for me.

One morning, when the frost was white on the hedges and I was so bored as to be near to ripping the pages from the ledger, Windsor entered the room and took the pen from my hand.

'What now? I refuse to look at one more document of tenure or—'

'There's a man on a horse just ridden into the courtyard.'

'A pedlar?' I yawned. I supposed I would value the distraction.

'More official than that. A royal courier, I'd say.' I was out of my seat. 'Alice! It could be to your danger.'

'How can it? I've obeyed them to the letter in their damned banishment!'

'But still...'

'They'd have sent a force to arrest me.' And I was down the stairs into the hallway before the man had climbed the steps to the porch.

'Mistress Perrers.'

Not another nail in the coffin that the lords had constructed for me! Far less confident than I seemed, I snatched the missive from his hand, tearing it in my urgency. 'Fetch him ale…' I had time for nothing but the contents. For a moment I closed my eyes, then opened them and read…

I skimmed over the word 'banishment', flushed with the heat of panic despite the cold of the dull November day. Then forced myself to read more slowly.

And the fear began to drain away. For there it was. Written by a palace clerk in the name of Gaunt. My banishment was no more. I was free to return to Court, to Edward. So much in so few lines. My head felt light, my senses adrift, and I sank to the settle at my side.

'Will?' I called.

He was standing in the doorway, looking at me, reading my face before I spoke.

'You are free?'

'Yes.' I sighed. 'Oh, yes.' And I pressed the document against my heart.

I had Gaunt to thank for it, for what reason I knew not. Past loyalties? Sympathy for his dying father? To spite Parliament more like. I cared not. He had had the banishment revoked by the Royal Council. I was free to travel, free to return to Court. To see Edward again.

'Well?' Windsor still waited.

I stood, feeling stronger, full of light and power, and walked slowly across to him. I think my words surprised us both.

'You are my husband. I need your consent.'

'That's the first time in your life you have asked for it.'

I flushed. 'I need your approval.'

His gaze was quizzical. 'Would you go if I did not give it?'

I hesitated.

'There has always been honesty between us, Alice.'

'Then, yes, I would go with or without your permission. If I did not see him, it would be on my soul.'

He closed his hands on my shoulders, kissed my forehead and then my lips. Our final embrace was strained with unspoken words and longings.

'Do I come with you?' he asked, his arms banded round me.

'No.'

'I suppose I must find a clerk to finish the accountings.' I heard the smile in his voice.

'He won't be as accurate as I am.' And I laughed softly into the fine wool of his tunic as the endlessly nagging fears of the past weeks loosed their grip.

'Go to Edward.' His compassion for me struck deep. 'And then you will come back to me when you can. When it is over.'

I allowed myself to look at him, rubbing my knuckles over the line of his jaw, running a finger over the hard line of his mouth. I knew him well enough to read the concern for me behind those austere, resolute features. I pressed my lips to his.

'Yes. I will return.'

My belongings packed and loaded onto two horses, a groom and one of Windsor's household mounted to accompany me, I kissed my daughters and rode like the wind to Eltham, to Edward. And the official document detailing my release? What happened to it? I had no recollection. With unusual carelessness I did not keep it.

Afterwards I wished I had.

Chapter Fifteen

Eltham

Leaving my baggage to be unloaded, I stepped in, good memories of this palace with Wykeham's new rooms sweeping back to lift my spirits. But as I walked purposefully, absorbing the atmosphere, I was forced to accept that much had changed. It was, as Windsor had said, as if the heart had gone out of it. It had, as I imagined, the still, dust-laden quality of a stone coffin. The servants I passed looked at me askance. All bowed or curtseyed as they had in the past, no one stopped me, but one, hand half-hidden against his hose, curled his fingers against the power of the Evil Eye. I saw it. My reputation as a witch had sunk deep.

That was not all. It would be no easy task to return to my old position. Legs braced, arms folded as if to repel a troop of invaders, Roger Beauchamp, Edward's new chamberlain, the man to replace Latimer, stood foursquare before the door to Edward's accommodation, drawing himself up as his eye lit on me. I had come so far and so fast, and now this paid minion would keep me from Edward's side. *I* might know that my banishment had been lifted but the speed of my arrival had pre-empted the news. The word had not yet reached Eltham—or perhaps it had and he would still deny me.

Here I would discover how much power remained to me. Not much, I thought.

Beauchamp regarded me like one of the vermin that could never be exterminated from even the public rooms of the palace. 'You should not be here! The law forbids it.' No respect, all denial, Beauchamp's challenge confirmed my fears.

'I wish to see the King,' I replied without heat.

'I say you will not.'

'And will you stop me?'

'I will, madam!'

'My banishment is lifted.'

'And you have proof?'

No, I had not. In my urgency I had not seen a need. Not that Beauchamp would have accepted anything less than a royal declaration, stamped and sealed.

'The decisions of the late Parliament have been declared null and void,' I stated calmly. 'By Gaunt himself.' Surely the name would have some power.

'I have no knowledge of it.' Beauchamp's stance remained implacable.

How I wished for Latimer's return. And how had this monster escaped Gaunt's purging? I gestured to the door at his back.

'Let me pass. The King will see me.'

'The King will not.' Beauchamp drew his sword.

I retreated not one inch. 'If you intend to stop me, you will have to use that, sir.' I pushed the flat of the blade to one side with my hand. 'I wear the Queen's jewels. I have borne the King's children. Will you deny me?'

I hammered with my fist on the door to Edward's chambers.

No reply. However assured of my welcome I might appear, I was far from it. I hammered again, fear building layer upon layer so that I could barely breathe as Beauchamp's fingers clamped peremptorily, unforgivably, around my wrist. I thumped again on the door with my free fist, raising my voice.

'Sire! It is Alice.' I tried to wrench my wrist free but Beauchamp held on, and suddenly all was blackness in my mind. I would be cast out. Gaunt's promise was nothing but a charade...

'Majesty!' I heard my voice, harsh with terror.

The door opened.

'What's all the noise and fuss, Beauchamp? It's enough to wake the dead. Be still, man...'

My wrist was released.

Once I would have gone to Edward, touched him, spoken with him, no matter who stood between us. Now, considering our parting words, I could not. But to see him standing alone, unaided, to hear him speaking without difficulty, his words clear and authoritative, the impact of it clenched around my heart. Edward, still King, still regal even with the stooped shoulders and hollowed cheeks of old age, was standing in the doorway. Not robust but steady enough with one hand clawed around the edge of the door jamb.

I sank into a deep curtsey.

'My lord. I am here.' I waited until the faded blue eyes tracked across my face, and only then did I rise to my full height. 'It's Alice. I have come to you. Let me in, to be with you.'

Would he turn his face away, would he reject me? Would his wayward mind recognise me beyond this first second of reunion? That moment when Edward looked at me seemed to last a lifetime, until the focus sharpened with recognition. And there in that acknowledgement was an astonishment that held unmistakable joy.

'Alice…'

'I am here.'

'I asked for you. I was told that you could not be here with me…' And then he was holding out his hands to me and I placed mine there.

'Now I am here. Let us go in,' I said, confidence surging back, and I stepped inside the room.

Moisture glistened in Edward's eyes but his command was still strong, and so were his memories. As he would have done in the past, he bowed and raised my fingers to his lips, first one hand, then the other.

'I have missed you,' he said simply.

'I couldn't bear that you should be alone.'

'They kept you from me…'

'It was not my choice. But your son has rescued me. I am free to be here with you.'

'Then come. We will talk.'

As he led me through the rooms, it was impressed on me how harrowing the intervening months had been for him. We were forced to walk slowly, Edward's right foot dragging a little with every step, his arm beneath my hand tense with the effort to walk unaided. But he was determined and we reached the great chamber.

'Alice…' Before he could say more I sank to my knees before him. 'What's this?'

'I need to ask your pardon, Sire.'

'A minute ago you called me Edward and demanded admittance. Now you are on your knees. This is not the Alice I recall.' The ghost of a laugh was tragic on the once fine features, the muscles on the right side of his face refusing to obey the demand to smile.

I bowed my head. I could not laugh. 'I hurt you. I betrayed you.'

'So you did. You should have told me about him. I think I would have understood.'

'What man could understand that I had married another in secret?'

'What I don't understand is why Windsor? Why such a man?'

I could think of no reply that would explain the call of blood one to another. 'He will care for me,' I managed.

'Yes. I expect he will.'

'My loyalty to you has not changed, my lord.'

'But you are a young woman and I...'

'My lord... I am so sorry...'

'We must have the courage to face our limitations. My flesh ignores the demands of my heart.' Again that heart-wrenching smile. 'How many old men have said that when their young lover looks elsewhere? I am not the first. I won't be the last.'

His candour overwhelmed me. Neither could I explain that my attraction to Windsor was more than physical satisfaction but also a meeting of minds.

'It was not my choice to leave you, my lord. Will you forgive me?'

'You know I will. Come, stand. It's too exhausting looking down at you.' And he raised me to my feet with a remnant of his proud grace. 'Have you come to stay?'

'I have. If you want me.'

'Do I not want the sun to rise tomorrow? You are mine

and I have a need of you if you can tolerate the weakness of an old man.'

'This is where I wish to be.'

Edward's brow creased, for which I was sorry. 'Those who have no love for you say you have no heart, Alice. That you are as cold as stone and hard as flint. What do *you* say?'

I regarded him gravely as I swallowed against the press of tears. 'What I say has no weight. What do *you* say, my lord?' Enclosing his cold hands between mine, in a deliberately intimate gesture, I placed them, flat-palmed between my breasts where my heart beat. 'What do *you* say?'

'I say that you are never cold to me.' Leaning a little, he pressed a kiss between my eyebrows. 'You are as gentle as a blessing, as warm as the sun in summer.'

We both knew that Windsor would not be spoken of between us again. A tacit agreement that for the length of Edward's life my husband did not exist. Edward turned from me to shuffle towards his bed with its embroidered heraldic hangings. 'I am weary, Alice. I have not slept well since you went away. Or at least I don't think I have... Memory plays tricks on me...'

'Then you must sleep now. I'll stay with you.'

I helped him to lie down on the magnificent bed that we had shared. And I sat beside him, curled against the pillows, his hand in mine as his eyelids began to droop.

'Do you know?' he murmured. 'When they told me that you were not allowed to come to me, that we would be parted for ever, I was destroyed. Not an emotion appropriate for a King, is it?'

'No. But it is the emotion of a man of honour and courtesy. Of a lover.' I folded his hand between mine.

'I thought I would never see you again...'

'But I am here now.'

'And all will be well.'

'All will be well.'

I sat with him until sleep claimed him. I would have liked to have told him that he would grow strong, that he would resume the mantle of Kingship. I would have liked to assure him that his present clear understanding would remain; that he would know my love and care of him for all the remaining days of his life. But I could not. This lucidity, I suspected, was transient. I tucked the memory away for the difficult days.

Did I weep for him?

Not then. He would not have wished it. I would do what I could for him. I would stay until the end. Windsor would understand.

For that I was surely blessed.

Despite my fears, Edward's grip on life proved to be ferocious, his mind set on one final splendid gesture. He was in no fit state to travel, but his resilience was a fine thing.

'I will do it. I will not be gainsaid on this! I will do this one thing! Do you hear me, Alice?' I heard him as I saw the flash of the old imperious Plantagenet regality. But so brief, so painfully brief. His head lolled forward, his chin against his chest, and he dozed. But on his awakening, the thought was still firmly lodged in his unsteady mind.

'I will sit at the table in Wykeham's Round Tower at Windsor, even if I have to be carried into the chamber in a litter.'

This would be the last St George's Day that Edward would ever see, whether he went to Windsor or no. His physicians warned against the exertion. I shrank from the bathos of the scene that would ensue if I consented. I could not bear it for him.

'Arrange it for me, Alice.' His twisted mouth could still issue orders. 'Would you stop me from doing something that will bring *you* such personal joy? I don't think you'll refuse me.'

I flushed at the accusation, but held my ground. 'Your health is of prime importance to me, Edward.'

'I know. But I also know you'll allow me to see this through.' His speech was slurring as his energy waned, but he could still grip my hand.

How could I not? Edward dragged himself through the days with sheer willpower. He wanted to do it—and so he would.

'I will arrange it. But you know what I will ask,' I said.

'Yes.' His sigh acknowledged the burden I had put on him. 'Do I not know you, like I know my own soul? A difficult request, Alice.'

'Simply to be there, to watch? Is it so difficult?'

'Unorthodox…' His tongue struggled a little over the word.

'You have the power to make the unorthodox the most acceptable thing in the world.'

Oh, I wanted to be there, more than I could express. This occasion to mark St George's Day meant as much to me as it did to Edward. I did not expect the flood of vitriol that was to be unleashed against me. Or perhaps I did…

'It is not appropriate, my lord! She will not be admitted!'

Princess Joan. Whose nose for Court intrigue had sharpened with her widowhood. She was haranguing Edward before the week was out.

'But on this occasion…' Edward might regret the onset of a battle with the Princess, but was still prepared to argue my case.

Except that Joan rolled over him like the English cavalry destroyed the French at Poitiers. 'She is not a Lady of the Garter. Only those of royal blood qualify for such high recognition. Only Philippa and Isabella. You, yourself, would have it so, my lord. Would you put a low-born woman on the same footing as your wife?' She wilfully ignored my role as Lady of the Sun when Edward had done just that. 'Even *I* am not allowed...'

'I hear you, Joan.' Edward raised a weary hand. 'Tradition weighs heavy—and since I was the one to create it...' He smiled apologetically at me.

Since you created it, you could claim the right to change it! But seeing the fretfulness in him I closed my mouth on any counter-argument I might make. I allowed Joan her little victory, for did *I* not have one even greater? It would be for me a moment of pure joy.

'You will come with me,' Edward ordered, gripping my hand.

'I will come to Windsor with you,' I agreed.

'But not to the ceremony,' Joan added for good measure.

Well, we would see what we would see.

We arranged it most carefully, travelling by river to arrive on the day before the ceremony so that the inhabitants of Windsor would not see Edward lying on a litter rather than riding on a warhorse to their gates. I would at least guard him against that ignominy. But would he be able to walk into the chamber? Would he be able to lift the great sword of state?

It was in God's hands.

And so the day dawned. Edward broke his fast, a cup of wine driving colour into his cheeks and strengthening his sinews. I withdrew into the background as his servants clothed and prepared him for his celebration and his ordeal. With lambskin and fur to protect him, fine robes covered his wasted body, giving him a semblance of majesty. I stood aside as he lifted his head and walked slowly into the chamber, his hand pressing hard on the shoulder of one of his knights, to take his seat at the vast circular table.

He was thinking of his first inaugural ceremony, more than thirty years ago, when he had been in the full strength of his youth, attended by the flower of Europe's chivalry and Philippa, who had presided over the subsequent festivities. There would be no festivities to preside over this year— Edward could not maintain his strength for more than an hour. At least Joan would not have the excuse to lord it over the proceedings. And I, the whore, the mistress, would be shut out of the sacred ceremonial. The solemn rituals had no role for the King's Concubine and, unlike my splendour as the Lady of the Sun, Edward could not make one for me. All I could do was imagine.

My eye was taken by the approach of young men clad in scarlet robes, and all my desire was centred on the one fair face in their midst.

I would not be absent from this most glorious acceptance of what I had done in my life. I slipped inside the door and stood to the left in the shadow of a great curving tapestry. I would simply be there. A witness.

Twelve youths, the new generation of England's rulers, royal blood flowing through an impressive number of veins. I recognised them all. Edward's two grandsons were the first to kneel to feel the kiss of the sword on one shoulder then the other. Richard of Bordeaux, slight and fair, Edward's heir. Henry Bolingbroke, Gaunt's son. Followed by Thomas of Woodstock. Then the young men: Oxford; Salisbury;

and Stafford. Mowbray, Beaumont and Percy. All the great names of the Kingdom receiving Edward's final gift of a knighthood. I had been right. So weak was his arm that the great sword of state quivered, but his will was as strong as ever. I knew he would see it out to the bitter end, even if he needed to take a sip of wine to fortify himself.

They knelt to receive the honour of knighthood, stood, stepped back. There was only one face I looked for, only one who made my heart bound against the cage of my ribs. And there he was at last. The final youth to kneel before his King—and his father.

John. Our son. *My* son!

Pale, with nerves chasing across his features, John sank to one knee, his hair bright in the light through the high windows. At thirteen years he still had the uncoordinated limbs of youth, but he had been well schooled for this day. I held my breath as Edward raised the great sword for the final time, and our son lifted his head to receive the accolade. Pride warmed my blood. Such public recognition of what had been vilified, my place in Edward's life. I slipped out. I had seen all I needed to see. My son, a knight of the garter. Emotion choked me.

'Take me to Sheen,' Edward ordered when the young men, released from their ordeal, had toasted themselves with relieved laughter. 'I'll die there.'

I was afraid that he would.

'What is it?' I asked, seeing the shadow of grief as we began the journey.

He shook his head.

'I shall nag at you until you tell me!'

'There's one regret I have…'

'Then it can be remedied.'

'No. It cannot. I allowed matters of state to step in front

of friendship. It was a grave misjudgement, and I don't think it can be forgiven.'

He closed his eyes and would say no more. And however much I worried about it, I could not think what it was that disturbed his rest. And if I could not decipher it, how could I put it right?

And then in the night it came to me. I knew what I must do. And quickly.

Edward lay on his bed, his chest barely moving, his skin so thin and pale as to be almost translucent, like a pearl from the Thames oyster beds. Occasionally his breath fluttered between his lips but that was the only sign of the life that remained to him. The day had come. That long, courageous life, lived to the full for the glory of England, was drawing quietly to its close.

The last time I had kept vigil beside the dying it had been Philippa. I smiled a little at her amazing duplicity born out of compassion. Then my smile faded for who could have believed it possible? That Edward's loss of his most dear wife should place his feet firmly on the path to deterioration. Every day for the past eight years he had missed her keenly, until his mind could bear it no more. I was second best, and so I had always been. I had known it and accepted it. Today Edward would lay the burden aside.

And so would I.

At the foot of the bed knelt Edward's confessor, a furious eye cast in my direction. Father Godfrey de Mordon, a man of erudition and superior oratory, a man of narrow morals, as narrow as his unfortunate features, reminiscent of a ferret. I disliked him as much as he disliked me, but I let him pray. I simply sat and watched as Edward's life ebbed, until the priest's voice broke into my thoughts.

'His Majesty needs to repent.'

'Later.'

A pause.

'It would be better if you were not here.'

I turned my gaze on him, ignoring the deliberate absence of respect in his address. 'Yet I will stay.'

'You have no place in this final confession of the King's sins.' The priest's scowl informed me that I was the most virulent of them.

I considered as he made the sign of the cross and launched into yet another *Ave*. Father Godfrey had revered Philippa as a saint while I was the worst of Eve's daughters. I folded my hands, one over the other in my lap. What would this priest say if I announced that I *was* innocent once. Who did he think arranged that the King of England should take a girl with no background, no beauty and no breeding as his mistress?

Edward sighed, his hand clutching convulsively against the bed cover. That was all in the past. This priest would not want to hear my justifications. Here we were at the end of that supremely difficult road. It was in my heart to pray that Edward might keep hold of the thread that bound him to me, but I could not. He wanted to let go. He had had enough of weakness and forgetfulness, of lack of dignity. So I prayed that death would be quick now, and painless, that he would slip away into soft oblivion.

And when it was over?

Why, then my position at Court would be at an end, my time as King's Concubine numbered in hours and minutes, no longer years. When Philippa had died and my role as damsel had ended, Edward had been there to rescue me. Now there was no one.

So what would I do?

I would go to William de Windsor, of course, but with the King's death the wolves might be howling at my door again, and Gaunt might not be able to hold them at bay. The thought of Windsor settled me. He would strengthen me, he would hold me in his arms and keep the nightmares away by the force and heat of his body against mine.

In the shadows beyond the bed, John Beverley tidied and arranged with his usual quiet competence, having done all he could to make the King comfortable.

'Go now,' I murmured. 'You can do no more.'

We were alone, the priest and I, with Edward sleeping the precursor of death. I closed my eyes, suddenly very weary.

The priest's voice scraped along my nerves as he stood. 'Mistress Perrers! His Majesty must confess before God…'

'Of course.' It would be necessary, but my eye gleamed. It was in my mind to reduce this pompous cleric who despised the ground I trod on. 'Now that you've got up off your knees, make yourself useful and light more candles. It's too dark in here.'

Edward would die with light and power surrounding him, not in some darkened room without trappings or recognition. He was no peasant.

'It's not fitting…'

'Do it. Why should he not die in the light? He lived his whole life in it.'

Reluctant to the last, Father Godfrey obeyed until the chamber shone as if for a royal feast, as I touched Edward's hand, unsure even now that he would wake. But his lids lifted slowly.

Edward turned his head toward me. 'I'm thirsty.'

His voice was laboured and low, his breathing heavy. I poured a cup of wine and held it to his lips so that he could sip, then banked the pillows behind him, lifting him so that he might be aware of his surroundings. And his eye fell on the crown that rested, by my orders, within his vision on the bed beside him.

'Did you do that?' he asked with a movement of his lips that was all that remained of his once captivating smile. 'Thank you.' Stretching out his hand, he touched the jewelled gold. 'I hope I have kept faith with the power that God gave me...' My heart swelled with admiration for him, and with imminent loss. Edward sighed again. 'It is mine no longer. The boy will wear it, God help and strengthen him. How can a ten-year-old child...?'

The priest stepped up to the bed. 'There are more important things for you to face now, Sire.' He held up the crucifix around his neck. 'Your immortal soul...'

'Not yet. My soul can wait.'

'Sire—I urge you to make your last confession.'

'I said not yet. Talk to me, Alice.'

So I would. Without sentiment or pity. We would pretend that there was all the time in the world and I would entertain the King as I had always done. Edward would die as he wished. I sat on the edge of the bed, turning my back on the priest, so that it was as if we were alone as in the days of our past together.

'What do we talk about?' I asked.

'The glory days. When I was the mightiest King in Europe.'

'How can I? I didn't know you when you were the champion of Crécy.'

'Ah...! I forgot. You were a child...'

'Not even born.'

'No... It was Philippa who was with me then.'

'So she was. And loved you for every moment of your marriage.'

'Sire…!' The priest hovered at my side.

'Let him be!' I snapped.

'Talk to me about the last day we hunted the deer at Eltham,' Edward said.

'Your hounds brought down a tined buck. You had a good horse and rode as well as any man.' It had been one of his good days. My throat clenched hard.

'I did, didn't I? Despite the years…'

'No one could match you.'

'It was a good day.' Edward closed his eyes as if he could see imprinted there the memory of his greatness.

'It is sacrilege that you speak to him of hunting,' Father Godfrey growled at me. 'That you encourage him.' He turned to Edward. 'Sire…!'

The tired eyes opened. 'I'm not dead yet, Godfrey.'

'You must make your peace with God!'

'For what?' Suddenly those eyes were unnervingly keen. 'For all the dead on the battlefields of France? Will He forgive me for those I sent to their deaths, do you think?'

'He will if you repent.' The priest held his crucifix higher.

'How can he repent of the deeds that made him the great King he is?' I challenged the priest.

'Leave it, Alice!' Edward as ever was more tolerant than I. 'Do you remember the day we flew the falcons from the battlements at Windsor? Now, there was a sight…' Edward breathed laboriously through a long silence. And then: 'Alice?'

'I'm still here.'

'I'm…sorry it's ended.'

Father Godfrey swooped like some form of venomous insect. 'He's slipping away. Get him to repent. He mustn't die unshriven.'

'He'll do as he wishes.' I stroked Edward's hand, careful

of the fragility of his skin. 'He always has. He has enough
favour notched up with the Almighty to get him into heaven
whether he dies unshriven or not.'

'Get him to make confession.'

It was too much. I stood, making the priest step back.
'Get out!'

Father Godfrey held his ground but his eyes could not
hold mine. 'I will not.'

I strode to the door and opened it. 'Bring Wykeham as
soon as he arrives,' I ordered the squire who kept watch
outside, and saw Edward's face light with joy. Edward's
one regret, his alienation from Wykeham. I had been right
to send for him. If anyone was to shrive Edward it would
be Wykeham.

Father Godfrey stalked out. 'When the King is dead, who
will save you then, mistress?' he snarled.

Wykeham arrived and Edward rallied, with a delicious
levity that failed to rile the imperturbable Wykeham.

'Wykeham? Is that you? You were almost too late! Let's
get it over with. I ask your pardon for a dismissal you did
not deserve. And I repent of all my sins. Will that do it?'

'For myself, I'm deeply grateful.' There was the shine of
unshed tears in Wykeham's eyes. 'As for the Almighty, I
think he might need rather more than that, Sire.'

'Intercede for me, damn it.' A spark of the old fire.
Edward's lips attempted a smile. I stood, content with the
much-desired reconciliation. 'Why did I make you bishop
if you won't speak for me at the feet of God?' Bold words,
but his voice was failing.

'I doubt God will accept intercession by a third party for
fornication.' Wykeham's harshness surprised me but then,
he was a priest after all. 'And adultery,' he added. 'You must
confess your sin if you hope for forgiveness.'

'Then I'm condemned to the fires of hell. I'll not betray Alice in repentance. Neither will we argue witchcraft. I was not bewitched. The decisions and actions were all mine, and I'll answer for them.' Edward's hand closed around mine as his breath caught. 'Sooner rather than later. I can see Death waiting beside the door. Edward looked up at me but his sight was blurred now. 'Do you suppose Philippa will be waiting for me?'

'I expect she will.'

'Yes. It will be good to see her.' It hurt me, a blow delivered without intent but one I should have expected. But still it hurt. 'Hold me, Alice.'

I knelt on the bed, and stretched to put my arms around him, horrified at how thin and insubstantial he had become. I had anticipated this moment for so long, but now it stared me in the face with all its horror. He was leaving me. I would lose him and the life I had built around him. My mind was so frozen with the inevitability that words would not come. It was Edward who spoke.

'You never were a witch, were you?'

'No. I never was. You knew what you wanted without my intervention.'

'So I did.' He drew in a breath. 'Take them…' A ghost of a laugh shivered under my palms. 'Take them, as I said you must. I can't do it…but you can. They're yours…your final insurance against dreaded penury…' He took another difficult breath. 'You were the light of my final years. The joy of my old age.' His breath caught again on a harsh intake. 'Do you ever have any regrets, Alice?'

'No. I regret nothing.'

'Neither do I. I love you…' His voice died away. Until the final whisper: 'Jesu, have pity.'

Then his breath was gone.

So England's great King died in my arms, his head on my breast, light blazing around him as if he were already in heaven. And I had perjured my soul, denying any regrets.

'God have mercy.' Wykeham, still on his knees, made the sign of the cross.

'Farewell, Edward.' I would not weep yet. 'Philippa will stand beside you when you approach God's throne.'

I stood to perform my final tasks for him, removing the pillows so that he could lie flat. I combed my fingers through his hair, arranged his linen so that it fell gracefully against his neck as he would have wished, before placing his hands palms-down at his sides.

And then...because he had remembered...I began to take the rings from his fingers. A cabochon ruby. A sapphire flanked with diamonds, heavyset with pearls. A trio of beryls. A magnificent amethyst, set alone. I took them, one by one, watching my hands complete the task, all emotion suspended by sheer force of will. The gems glittered as I dropped them into my palm.

With a sharp oath of distress Wykeham sprang to his feet, prayers forgotten. 'In God's name! What are you doing?'

And I turned to look at him. The bright light illuminated the expression on his face, every deeply marked line making it clear exactly what he thought of my actions, overlaid with a loathing of me so savage as to pierce me to the heart. For a moment it shocked me into immobility. Did Wykeham, the best man of God I knew, believe me capable of robbing the dead? Of stripping Edward's corpse of everything of value out of pure avarice? Would Wykeham of all men consider me guilty of such a final infamy? *Do you have any regrets?* Edward had asked, and I had denied it. But sometimes the reputation I had made for myself was a heavy burden. Why should I alone be the one to deserve the world's scorn?

Emotions raced through me to match Wykeham's, and I think far more deadly. Twining with my anguish, bright anger melded to create a vicious brew. So Wykeham believed the worst of me, did he? If he would damn me just as readily as Father Godfrey for my sins, then let him. In my torment a desire to hurt and to be hurt was born within me, a vehemence that would not be restrained. Fury was there. But also self-loathing. And an urge to destroy.

So be it!

I would destroy Wykeham's so-called friendship. I would destroy any good standing I had with him. I would live up to the worst of my reputation. For who would care? The only man who had cared was dead.

Windsor cares!

I slapped the thought away.

Oh, I had an enormous talent for dissimulation. For self-mockery. I held up the rings on my palm so that they glimmered with a myriad of reflected candle flames. Wykeham had already tried and condemned me. I would give him the evidence.

'Don't I deserve this for giving my youth to an old man?' I demanded. Never had I sounded so cold, so unfeeling.

'You are robbing the dead.' Wykeham was aghast, as if he could not believe what he saw. I drew a ring set with opals from Edward's thumb, feeling the force of Wykeham's stare as I did so. 'It is an abomination!'

'Hard words, Wykeham!' I placed the ring with the others on my palm.

'Once I thought you worthy of my friendship. I would not believe what they said of you...'

Friendship? By God. I had just seen the limits of friendship, to be condemned without trial.

'Foolish Wykeham. You should have listened to the common gossip.' I raised my chin, praying that the tears that had formed a knot in my throat would not betray me. 'What do they say about me? What do the courtiers and the Commons say?'

'You know what they say.'

'But *say* it. Humour me. Let me hear it spoken aloud.' How I wished to lash out, to cut and wound. And be wounded. I would hear anew the dregs of my reputation. In my grief and anger I had no control.

His lips were a thin line in disgust. 'They say you're an unprincipled slut...'

'Well, that's true.'

'...and without shame.'

'Is that all?' I think I tossed my head. 'I'm sure it's worse than that.'

His eyes blazed as bright as the candle flames. 'You're a grasping, self-seeking whore.'

'That's closer to the truth, forsooth!'

'Will nothing shock you?' His rage was suddenly as great as mine, his tongue unbridled. 'They say you fucked the King to drain him of his power. You're nothing but an adulterous bitch who betrayed Queen Philippa and—'

I struck him. The hand that did not clasp the rings struck flat against his cheek. The man who had always stood my friend, who knew the truth behind all the Court scandals.

'My lord bishop!' I upbraided him. 'So shocking! And for you to repeat such vulgar language!' And I began to laugh.

Cheek aflame, he retaliated. 'You don't like the truth.'

'I didn't think you'd actually say it to my face. I really didn't... But there's your answer: always believe the gossip of the stews and the whorehouses. Always believe what's said of a woman who makes use of the talents God gave her.' I poured all the scorn I could into my voice.

For a moment he was speechless. Then gestured to the rings in my hand.

'Are you *proud* of what you've done?'

'Why not? I'd be living in the gutter in London if I'd been less than an unprincipled slut. Or dead. Or a nun—which is probably worse.'

'God have mercy on you.' He flung out his hand, stabbing with his finger. 'You've missed one! He's still wearing the emerald. Don't let that one escape. It's worth more than all the rest put together. It will keep you in silk and fur until the day of your unworthy death.'

The emerald. I made no move to take it.

'Why stop now? Have you suddenly developed finer feelings? You squeezed him dry of everything you could get out of him. You took what should have been Philippa's. His company, his loyalty, his devotion into old age…' I flinched at the hard words, but recognised them for what they were. Wykeham's own grief, lashing out at me, as I had allowed him to. 'Take it!' he hissed. And drew it from Edward's finger, holding it out to me.

'I can't.'

'Oh, I'm sure you can!'

'It's the royal seal.' I took a step away.

'Since when would such niceties stop you?'

'The coronation ring belongs to Richard. It's not for me.'

It was a mistake. I knew it as soon as I had opened my mouth. My deliberate construction destroyed in those few careless words. Wykeham simply looked at me, the emotion draining to leave his face white and drawn except for the print of my hand. His hand with the emerald ring dropped to his side.

'Oh, Alice!'

All the fury leached from the room, leaving it still and

cold despite the constant shimmer from the burning flames. At last, as grief descended on me in a winter's deluge, I felt tears threaten, however hard I tried to staunch them.

'Alice…'

'I don't want your pity, Wykeham.' I turned my face away, all my defiance drained away. 'Goodbye, Edward. I hope I made you happy when you thought there was no happiness left in life.' For a final time I knelt and kissed his hand. 'I loved him, you know. In spite of everything. He was always kind. I think he loved me a little. I was not Philippa—but I think he loved me…'

'Where will you go?'

'To Pallenswick.'

'To Sir William?'

'Yes.'

'Let him take care of you.'

'I don't need him. I don't need anyone…' Still I would punish myself.

'Alice…'

'Don't—just don't! If you're about to bless me, don't think of it!' I rubbed the sudden moisture from my cheeks with my sleeve. 'Your God will rejoice at my sufferings. Perhaps you should offer up an extra *Ave* and a *Deo Gratias* for my ultimate punishment.'

Tears were streaming down my face.

'You can't go like this…'

'What will you do? Put the record straight? Paint me as a virtuous woman? No one will believe you…I will always be the King's whore. And I was—I think I filled the role with superb competence.' I opened the door, looking back over my shoulder to the shine of gold and jewels on the bed beside Edward's hand. 'Do you think the boy will wear the crown as magnificently as *he* did?'

'No. No I don't think he will.'

'Goodbye, Wykeham.' I knew I might never see him again. 'He said I should take them, you know…'

'I expect he did.' Wykeham bowed low. 'Take care.'

I laid my hand on the latch, suddenly without the strength to lift it. I felt as empty as a husk. I knew there were things to do. Except that at that moment I had no very exact idea of what they were.

All I knew was that I wanted to be with Windsor.

The horrors of that day were not to be at an end. Could it get any worse? It could. It did. When all I wanted was to escape, from my own grief, from the unbridled excess I had indulged in to justify Wykeham's censure, there in the Great Hall stood two figures just arrived. One had a high piping voice, the other the mien of a public executioner.

The child king and his mother.

In a moment of sheer cowardice I considered disappearing through the maze of rooms and corridors before Joan could even notice me. She now had the power to draw my blood. In the aftermath of what had happened, I felt that I might bleed all too readily.

No! No! You will not retreat!

I had never avoided confrontation and I would not start now. Gathering my resources, I embraced my role with a hard-edged veneer of arrogance as if Edward had not just died in my arms. Thus I descended the staircase with a swish of my velvet skirts and swept a magnificent curtsey to the ten-year-old boy who now wore my lover's crown.

'Your Majesty.'

Richard, God help him, clearly did not know what to do or say. His forehead furrowed and he gave me a nervous smile. 'Mistress Perrers…' He looked up to his mother's face for some idea of what he should do next. Then he bowed to me with studied solemnity.

'There is no need to bow, Richard.' Joan's painted face was brittle. And unbearably calculating. 'So Edward is dead, is he?'

'He is, my lady.' How scrupulously polite I was.

'Mama...' The boy tugged on his mother's sleeve.

'You are King now, Richard,' she told him.

Still it meant nothing to him. He turned back to me, his pale face alive with anticipation. 'Will you take me to the royal mews, Mistress Perrers, to see the King's falcons?'

Your falcons!

The realisation nipped at my heart. 'No, Sire,' I replied gently, although my greatest wish was to be away from there, away from Joan and her son. 'It is too late tonight. Shall I send for refreshment, Majesty?'

'Yes. If you please. I'm hungry...' He almost danced on the spot with impatience. '*Then* can we go and see the hunting birds?'

Joan's hand descended on her son's shoulder like a metal lock. 'Mistress Perrers—or is it Lady de Windsor? How does one know? Mistress Perrers will not be staying, Richard.' And to me, her lips curled with vicious pleasure, her eyes suddenly hot with satisfaction: 'You have no role here. Your reign, Queen Alice, is over.' She had the upper hand at last and would revel in applying it. 'I will give orders for your chambers to be cleared forthwith. I expect you to be gone before—let me see, I suppose I can afford to be magnanimous—sunrise.' Smoothing her hand over the fair hair of her son, she smiled. 'You will ensure that you take nothing with you. If you do—' her teeth glinted '—you may be sure that I will demand recompense.'

So she would strip me of all my personal possessions—

not unexpected. Neither, I suppose, could I blame her after a lifetime of disappointment. But I would fight back.

'I will take nothing that is not mine, nothing that was not given to me,' I replied as I clutched the rings tightly in my hand so that the settings dug into my flesh.

'By an old and besotted man who could not see you for your true worth.'

'By a man who loved me.'

'A man you bewitched by who knows what evil means.'

'A man I respected above all others. Anything he gave me was of his own free will. I will take what is mine, my lady.'

So I curtseyed to her, a deep obeisance, as if she were herself Queen of England.

'Get out of my sight!'

I turned and walked away, the clear voice of the child carrying down the length of the hall. 'Can we go and see the falcons *now*? Why will Mistress Perrers not take me?'

It would be hard for him to be King. It would be impossible for him to step into Edward's shoes.

I left Sheen. It was in my mind that I would never return there, or to any of the royal palaces that had been my home. Joan was right, however malicious the intent behind her words. My reign, if that is what it was, was over. I didn't know how I felt. My emotions were as hard and cold as the gemstones I clutched in my hand.

Chapter Sixteen

Every living soul in London could claim to have rubbed up against the closing minutes of Edward's final journey to his burial on the fifth day of July in Westminster Abbey, close to Philippa's final resting place, just as he had promised her. Did the worthy citizens not crowd the streets to watch the passing of the wooden effigy with its startlingly lifelike death mask? Even the wooden mouth dragged to the right, memento of the spasm of muscles that had struck him down. Edward's people stood in dour silence, remembering his greatness.

This is what I was told.

Edward was clothed in silk, his own royal colours of white and red and cloth-of-gold gleaming, his coffin lined with red samite. He was accompanied to his tomb with bells and torches and enough black cloth, draped and swagged, to clothe every nun in Christendom. A feast celebrated his life, the food valued at over five hundred pounds—at the same time as the gutters were filled with the starving. Such wanton extravagance. But he had been a good man and the citizens of London would not begrudge the outward show. Why should their King's life not be celebrated? The isolation and failure of his last years—when had been the last time any of them had set eyes on him?—were pushed aside by those who bore witness to this final journey.

But what of me?

Should I not have been allowed to say my final farewell? So I think, but it was made clear to me that my presence was neither welcome nor appropriate. It was made more than clear by a courier from the mother of the new child-monarch who announced the news with set face as if he had learned the lines of rebuff by rote.

'You are not to attend, mistress.' The messenger at least dismounted and marched to where I waited for him. I had thought he might shout it from beyond the courtyard arch. 'It is unseemly for one who is not a member of the family to ac-company the coffin. His Majesty King Richard has ordered that you remain outside London during the ceremonies.'

'His Majesty?'

'Indeed, mistress.' Not a flicker of an eye, not a quiver of a muscle. But we both knew the truth.

'I will consider the request.'

The courier looked askance but presumably carried a more suitable response back to Westminster, while I called down curses on Joan's malevolent head. But she had the power now in the name of her son and I was banished. I must remain at Pallenswick, where I had been reunited with Windsor. I watched the courier gallop from my land, watched until his figure was swallowed up by distance. Then I leapt into action.

Ordering my barge and an escort to be made ready for the following day, I sped up the stairs to my chamber to search out suitable garments in which to mark Edward's passing.

But I had discarded no more than three gowns as too drab or too showy before Windsor lounged in the doorway.

'I didn't know you were here,' I said, engrossed in my indecision. 'I thought you were riding over to inspect the repair of the mill wheel.'

'To hell with the mill wheel. Don't do it,' he ordered, without preamble.

'Do what?'

'Don't play me for a fool, Alice. Don't go.'

So he had the measure of me. How could he read me so well? He was the only man who could. I kept my eyes on my busy hands, matching a fur-trimmed surcoat to an under-robe of black silk.

'Why should I not? Do I obey the directives of Joan?'

His stare was intimidating enough. 'I don't want to have to visit you tomorrow night in a dungeon in the Tower!'

'Then *don't* visit me. I won't expect you.' Crossly, furious at Joan and at my own weakness that I felt the hurt of it, I spread the garments on the bed, then began to search for shoes in a coffer.

'So you admit you might end up there?'

'I admit to nothing. I only know that I must go!'

'And you were never one to take good advice, were you?'

'I took yours, married you, and look where that got me! A whole fleet of enemies. And banished, forsooth!' Entirely unfair, of course, but I was not concerned with being dispassionate. I stood and looked at him, daring him to disagree, my hands planted on my hips.

And he did. Of course he did. 'I think you made the enemies well enough without me.'

I took a breath, accepting his deliberate provocation. 'True.' And I smiled faintly, the sore place beneath my heart easing a little just at the sight of him, strong and

assured, filling the doorway to my room. But I turned my
back against him. Suddenly I wanted him, to tell him how
much I loved him, but dared not.

'You loved him, didn't you?' he stated.

I looked up, startled, from my unwinding of a girdle
stitched in muted colours—I would pay my final respects
with commendable discretion. 'Yes. I did.' I thought about
what I wanted to say, and explained, as much to myself as
to Windsor. 'He was everything a man should be. Brave and
chivalrous, generous with his time and his affections. He
treated me as a woman who *mattered* to him.' My words
dried. 'You don't want to hear all that.'

'Quite a valediction.'

'If you like. Are you jealous?' Completely distracted now
from the embroidered belt in my hands, I tilted my head
and watched him. Without doubt, jealousy as green as emeralds in the ring I had refused spiked the air between us.
'I don't think you are necessarily either loyal or principled.
Only when it suits you.'

Now, there was a challenge. What would he say to that?

'God's Blood, Alice!' The bitterness in the tone shivered
over my skin.

'So you are jealous.'

He thought for a moment. 'Not if you lust after me more!'

Which made me laugh. 'Yes. You know I do.' Impossibly
forthright, Windsor always had the capacity to surprise me,
and to confess to lust was far easier than to admit to love.
The power would remain with me. 'I had a love—a deep
respect—for Edward, but I lust after you—just as you lust
after me. Does that make you feel any better?'

'It might. Prove it.'

Abandoning the garments, my mood softening under his

onslaught, I walked towards him and he took me in his arms. We understood each other very well, did we not?

'I want to be with no one but you, Will,' I said, and pressed my lips to his.

I hoped he would be satisfied, and although I thought he might push me, to my relief he did not. What was it that made me love him so much? What was there to bind me to him? We did not hunt together, as I had with Edward. We did not dance—Windsor, I suspected, was as wrong-footed at dancing as I. There was not a poetic bone of romance in his whole body to seduce me into love and longing. We did not even have the intricate and magical workings of a clock to bind us. What was it then, except for naked self-interest? Was that all it was? I did not think so, but I could not tally the length and breadth of it as I might assess a plot of land.

But I loved him. And pretended I did not.

'Glad to hear it.' He kissed my mouth, his desire evident. 'Do I come with you?'

'No. I'll go alone.'

'I still say you shouldn't be…'

I placed my fingers over his mouth. 'Will, don't…'

His teeth nipped at my fingertips. 'Do you want me to stay tonight?'

'Yes.'

So he did.

'I'll keep you safe, you know,' he murmured against my throat, his skin slick, his breath short, when I had proved to him that his jealousy had no grounds.

'I know,' I replied as I fought against the dread that threatened my contentment, that the powers ranged against his protection of me might be too great.

'I'll not let any harm you.'

'No.'

His arms held the black fears at bay and we enjoyed each other; my heart was lighter with the rising of the sun.

'Don't go!' he murmured.

And still the dangerous word *love* had not been uttered between us. I was forced to accept that it never would.

I ignored Windsor's advice and went to Westminster.

Anonymous in black and grey, nothing more than a well-to-do widow—I was not completely lacking in good sense. I took myself to Westminster, to the Abbey, with two stalwart servants to force a way through the crowds. I would be there. I would let the mysticism of the monastic voices raised in Edward's requiem mass sweep over me and thank God for Edward's escape from the horrors of his final days. I would not be kept out, not by Joan, not by the Devil himself. The crowds were predictably ferocious but no impediment to the elbows of a determined woman.

We approached the door. A few more yards, and then it would be possible to slip inside. I forced my way through the throng. Joan would never notice me.

A blast of trumpets brought everyone around me to a halt, apart from the usual haphazard pushing and jostling, until those at the front were thrust back by royal guards. I edged my way as close as I could, and there, walking towards the great door, was the new King, not yet crowned, pale and insubstantial in seemly black, his fair hair lifting in the wind. A poor little scrap of humanity, I thought. None of the robust presence of father or grandfather, neither, I suspected, would there ever be.

And at his side? My breath hissed between my teeth. At his side, protective, self-important, walked his mother. Joan the Fair, her sour features unable to restrain her final triumph. Stout and aged beyond her years, wrapped around in black velvet and sable fur, she resembled nothing less than one of the portly ravens that inhabited the Tower.

Damn you for standing in my path to Edward's side.

She was so close I could have touched her. I had to restrain myself from striking out, for in that moment of blinding awareness I resented her supremacy, her pre-eminence, the power that she had usurped that was once mine. A power against which I had no defences.

Did she sense my hostility? There was the slightest hesitation in Joan's footstep, as if my antagonism gave off a rank perfume of its own, and she turned her head when she had come level with me. Our eyes met, hers widened, her lips parted. Her features froze, and I was afraid of the threat I saw writ there. It was within her authority to bring down the law on my head, despite the solemnity of the occasion. My future might just rest in those plump, dimpled hands. What had possessed me, to risk this meeting? I wished with all my heart that I had heeded Windsor's caustic warnings.

Joan's mouth closed like a trap and her hesitation vanished. How sure she was! With a little smile she placed one hand firmly on her son's shoulder, all the time urging him forward into the Abbey. So much said in that one small gesture. And then they had moved past me, so the *frisson* of fear that had touched my nape eased. She would let me go.

But Joan stopped. She spun swiftly on her heel. The men at arms lining the route stood to attention, halberds raised, and fear returned tenfold, flooding my lungs so that I could not breathe. Would she? Our eyes were locked, hers in malice, mine in defiance, for that moment as immobile as the carved stone figures that stared out with blind eyes above our heads. Would she punish me for all I had stood for, all I had been to Edward? For this ultimate provocation in the face of her express orders?

Joan's smile widened, with an unfortunate display of rotted teeth. Yes, she would. I almost felt the grip of hard hands on my arms, dragging me away. But she surprised me.

'Close the door when we are entered. Let no one pass,' Joan ordered. 'The proceedings will begin now that the King is come.' And she turned away as if I were of no importance to her, yet at the end could not resist. 'Your day is over,' I heard her murmur, just loud enough so that I might hear. 'Why do I need to bother myself with such as you…?'

For the briefest of ill-considered moments, spurred by the brutal insolence, I considered following in the royal train, slipping through before the great door was slammed to take my rightful place beside my royal lover's tomb. Insisting on my right to be there.

Ah, no!

Sense returned. I had no rightful place. Sick at heart, I fought my way out of the crowds and back to my water transport, where I was not altogether surprised to find Windsor waiting for me. Neither was I displeased, although, furious with Joan but mostly with myself for my impaired prudence, in true woman's fashion I took my embittered mood out on him.

'So you've come to rescue me!' A nasty nip of temper.

'Someone had to.' Suitably brusque in the circumstances. 'Get in the barge.'

I sat in moody, glowering silence for the whole of the journey; I had been put in my place, more by Joan's final words than by anything else. And Windsor allowed me to wallow, making no attempt at conversation to discover what had disturbed me, simply watching, with a pensive gaze, the life on the river bank pass by.

Why do I need to bother myself with such as you…?

I had always known that the days of Edward's protection would end, had I not? There was a new order in England in which I had no part. I must accept this, until the day of my death.

My personal mourning for Edward was far more satisfying, to my mind, and what he would have wished me to do. On my return, I did what he had loved, what he had reminisced over even when he had barely been able to sit upright against his pillows. I took a horse, a raptor on my fist, Braveheart at my heels—older but no wiser—and hunted the rabbits in the pastures around Pallenswick. The hunting was good. When the falcon brought down a pigeon my cheeks were wet with tears. Edward would have relished every moment of it. And then, retired to my own chamber, I drank a cup of good Gascon wine—'dear Edward, you will live forever in my memory'—before I turned my back on the past and looked forward.

But to what? Isolation and boredom. But that was surely better than being hunted down by a bitter woman bent on vengeance, despite her words that I was nothing to her. I knew it was not in Joan's nature to abandon the chase. Thrusting myself under her nose had not been wise.

'I shouldn't have gone, should I?' Wrapped in a heavy mantle, unable to keep warm, I huddled over the open fire when the weather turned unseasonably wet and wild.

'I told you not to,' Windsor remarked, entirely without sympathy, except that his hands were astonishingly warm around my freezing ones.

'I know you did.' I was moody and out of sorts, much like the winds that buffeted us.

'Don't worry. Your banishment was rescinded by Gaunt himself.'

'Do you believe that she'll forget?' His optimism was unusual.

'No.' So much for optimism! He scowled down at his fingers encircling my wrists, with the cynicism I appreciated in a world of flattery and empty promises. 'How much did the King leave her in his will?'

I answered without inflection. 'A thousand marks. Not enough to crow about. And Richard gets Edward's bed with all the armorial hangings.'

Scowl vanishing, Windsor guffawed immoderately. 'Far better that *you* should have had the bed!'

'Joan will probably have it burnt to rid herself of the contamination of my presence. She'll not let the boy sleep in it.'

'Are you mentioned?' he asked.

'No.' I had no place in Edward's will. He had given me all that he could, all that he had wished to give.

'At least that should give her cause for rejoicing!'

'I doubt it. When I left Sheen I made sure I had Philippa's jewels packed in my saddle bags and Edward's rings safe in the bodice of my gown. Short of searching my body in full public view, she couldn't get her hands on them!'

Windsor laughed again, then sobered. 'Enough of Fair Joan. We can't spend the rest of our lives worried out of our minds, can we? So we won't.'

Which I had to admit was the best advice I could get.

Windsor released my wrists and raised his cup of ale in a toast.

'To the storms. Long may they last. May they flood the roads and river banks between London and Pallenswick until Joan forgets.'

I took his cup, finished the ale, and echoed the sentiment. 'To the storms.'

* * *

The rain and winds abating, the roads were soon open again and the Thames once more busy with river traffic, so we heard of events in London and elsewhere. Some encroached on my existence not at all. How strange that was.

The boy Richard, clad in white and gold, was crowned on the sixteenth day of July. A Thursday, forsooth! Unusual, but chosen as the auspicious Eve of St Kenelm, an undistinguished but martyred child king of the old kingdom of Mercia.

'Doubtless Fair Joan thought the lad needed all the happy auguries he could get,' Windsor growled.

It was a sound assessment. There were troubles afoot. In the absence of a strong English army with a King at its head, the French had seized the initiative with numerous incursions along the south coast of England, burning and pillaging all they came upon. The town of Rye became an inferno. Some French marauders even reached Lewes, but we felt safe enough.

How strange to have no association with it, to be entirely divorced from the King's planning to drive the French out. Who would take on the direction of foreign policy? Gaunt, I supposed. I closed my mind to it, for it no longer touched me.

But some events, through association, touched me closely.

Wykeham, my dear Wykeham, was formally pardoned, thus confirming the healing of the wounds between Edward and his former chancellor. At least I had been able to achieve that much for an old friend. Wykeham wrote.

I am restored to grace, but not to political office. I shall turn my mind to the matter of education at Oxford with the building of two new colleges. I know

that will appeal to you—although no woman will set
foot within their doors! I might owe you that—but we
must both accept that it cannot be done.

It made me smile. How difficult for a priest to acknowl-edge a debt to a sinful daughter of Eve, but he had done it and with such elegance. I wished him well. I thought we were unlikely to meet again.

Finally some unsettling news that made me laugh—and then frown. With the meeting of Parliament, Gaunt was invited to join a committee of the Lords to deal with the threats from across the Channel.

'So Gaunt's star is in the ascendant,' Windsor remarked, reading Wykeham's letter over my shoulder.

'To be expected,' I replied. 'He has the blood and the experience.'

'Unfortunately no reputation for success!'

Windsor's contempt did not disturb me. What would Gaunt's waxing power mean for me now? Our ambitions no longer ran in parallel courses. But Windsor was thought-ful, taking Wykeham's letter to reread at his leisure. It al-ways worried me when Windsor felt the need to brood over a cup of ale.

But I laughed when I read of Parliament's outrageously high-handed petition to young Richard. How predictable of them! In future, only Parliament should have the right to ap-point Richard's Chancellor, Treasurer and every other high office of state they could discover. Parliament would con-trol the King at every step. No one was ever to be allowed to do what *I* had done when Edward had been too ill to do it for himself. There would never be another Alice Perrers, ruling the royal roost.

Yes, I laughed, but there was not much humour in it.

* * *

I found nothing to laugh at afterwards. A heavy hammering on my door at Pallenswick, much like the thump of a mailed fist, brought me hot-foot from my receipts and estate records. Windsor, I knew, was engaged in the draining of water meadows over at Gaines. Neither would I expect him to knock on my door when he returned—we still led a strange peripatetic life, in no sense a united household, as if our marriage was still some unshaped business entity that sometimes demanded our intimacy and sometimes did not. No, Windsor would not knock. Rather he would fling the door open and stride inside, his voice raised to announce his arrival, filling the house with his formidable, restless presence. This was not Windsor. My heart tripped with a fast rebirth of the fear that always lurked deep within me, but I would not hide. I strode towards the repeated thud.

'A group of men, mistress.' My steward hovered uncertainly in the entrance hall. 'Do I open to them?'

No point in dithering. 'Do so.' If this was a threat, I would face it.

'Good day, mistress.'

Not a mailed fist, but a staff of office, and potentially just as forceful. The man at my door was clothed in the sober garments of an upper servant: a clerk or a gentleman's secretary. Or, a breath of warning whispered over my neck, a Court official. I did not know him. I did not like the look of him, despite his mild expression and his courteous bow, or of the body of a dozen men at his back. My courtyard was crowded with pack animals and two large wagons.

'Mistress Perrers?'

'I am. And who are you, sir?' I asked with careful good manners.

All had been quiet on the London front over the past

months, Richard getting used to the weight of the crown and Joan queening it over the Court. I had not stirred from my self-imposed exile.

'Keep your head down,' Windsor had advised after my previous flirting with danger. 'They've too many problems to be concerned about you. Defence of the realm has taken precedence over the old King's mistress. Another few months and you'll be forgotten.'

'I don't know if I like that thought.' Obscurity did not sit well with me. 'Do I want to be forgotten?'

'You do if you've any sense. Stay put, woman.'

So I had, and as the weeks passed with no further evidence of Joan's malevolence, my dread had abated. But if Windsor was well informed, as he usually was, what was this on my doorstep? It did not bode well. Mentally I cursed Windsor for his over-confidence, and for his absence. Why was a man never around when you needed him? And why should I need him anyway—could I not deal with this encroachment on my own property? I eyed my visitor. This man carried far too much authority for my liking in his black tunic and leather satchel. My throat dried as his flat stare moved over me from head to toe.

But they cannot arrest you. You have committed no crime. Gaunt stood for you! He rescinded the banishment!

I breathed a little more easily.

The official bowed again. At least he was polite, but his men had an avaricious gleam.

'I am Thomas Webster, mistress.' From the satchel, he took a scroll. 'I am sent by a Commission appointed by Parliament.' Soft-voiced, respectful despite those assessing eyes, he held out the document for me to take. I did so, unrolling it between fingers that I held steady as I scanned the contents. It was not difficult to absorb the gist of it within seconds.

My breathing was once more compromised. My hand crushed one of the red seals that spoke of its officialdom, and I pretended to read through it again whilst I forced a deep breath into my lungs. Then I stood solidly on my doorstep, as if it would be possible for me to block their entry.

'What's this? I don't understand.' But the words were black and clear before my eyes.

'I am given authority to take what I can of value, mistress.'

The beat of my heart in my throat threatened to choke me. 'And if I refuse?'

'I wouldn't, if I were you, mistress,' he said dryly. 'You've not the power to stop me. I have a list of the most pertinent items. Now, if you will allow me?'

So they came in with a heavy clump of boots, Webster unfolding his abomination of a list. It was an inventory of all I owned, everything that Pallenswick contained that belonged to me.

Panic built, roaring out of control.

'The house is mine!' I objected. 'It is not crown property. It was not a gift from the King—I bought it.'

'But bought with whose money, mistress? Where did that money come from?' He might have smirked. 'And whose are the contents? Did you buy those too?' He turned his back on me, beckoning to his minions to begin their task.

There was no answer I could give that would make any impression. I stood and watched as the order of Parliament's Commission was instigated. All my property hauled out before me into the courtyard and stowed in the wagons and on the pack animals. My linen, my furniture, even my bed.

Jewels, clothing, trinkets, and through it all Webster reading from his despicable list.

'A diadem of pearls. A gold chain set with rubies. A yard of scarlet silk ribbon. A pair of leather gloves, the gauntlets embroidered in silver and...'

'A yard of ribbon?' A cry touching on hysteria gathered in my throat.

'Every little bit helps, mistress. We have a war to fund,' he replied caustically. 'Those jewels will fetch by our reckoning close to five hundred pounds. Better a well-armed body of men to defend English soil than these pretty things round your neck!'

It was useless. I watched in silence as everything that was mine was carried out of my house. When I saw the robes clutched in the arms of a burly servant, a heap of fur and silk and damask in rich blue and silver, the robes that Edward had had made for me for a second great tournament at Smithfield, I choked back the tears. They had never been worn, that second tournament never held. The robes were cast on the wagon with all the rest.

And there I was, left to stand in the entrance hall of my own house that echoed with emptiness.

'Have you finished?'

'Yes, mistress. But I should warn you. Parliament has taken on the burden of your creditors. Any man with a claim against you is invited to put forward his demands.'

'My creditors?' It grew worse and worse.

'Indeed, mistress. Any man with a grievance for extortions or oppressions or injuries committed by yourself—' how he was enjoying this! '—can appeal to Parliament for redress.'

'Where—where did this order come from?' I demanded. Oh, I knew the answer!

'From Parliament, mistress.'

Inhaling slowly, I clenched my fists against the shriek of anger in my head. This was not from Parliament. I would wager the pearl diadem that had just disappeared into the pack on the back of a mule. I knew whose fingers were in this pie. So she was not content to allow me to live in obscurity! I knew from whence this campaign of retaliation had stemmed and it was vicious! I could see her rubbing her hands with the satisfaction of it.

God's Blood!

I forced myself to think coldly and logically. I had other property, well furnished. I would allow her this, however furious it made me.

And then I saw Webster removing yet another scroll from his satchel.

'Have you not taken everything you can?'

'This is not a reclamation order, mistress. It is for you to present yourself in London.'

I snatched it from him. Read it. I was to appear before the House of Lords.

'A trial?' I gasped. He stood unspeaking, stony-faced. What possible charges had they discovered now? 'Tell me!' I demanded. 'Is this a trial?'

'It is written there, mistress.' Webster indicated the document crumpled in my hand. I must appear before the House of Lords on the twenty-second day of December. And the charge against me? Fraud. Treason!

Treason? That was not possible!

But I knew that anything was possible. Fury was replaced by terror. This was to be no political slapping of my knuckles. This was a *trial* with legal consequences. How far would Joan go in her desire for revenge? The penalty for treason was death.

* * *

Windsor returned from a damp morning in the flooded meadows around Upminster to find me sitting mindlessly on the floor in the now-empty parlour. No furniture, no tapestry, even the log basket beside the fireplace had been taken... I was stunned, as if Joan had struck my face with the flat of her hand—as she had once so long ago. When I failed to register the echo of his boots on the polished boards, he knelt, lifting the document from my unresisting fingers. Skimming down it, he swore fluently, threw his gloves and sword onto the floor and sat down beside me.

'I see the vultures have been.'

'Yes.' His boots in close proximity to my skirts were filthy with mud and slime and the odd strand of duckweed. I did not care.

'Is every room as empty as this?'

Words failed me. I lifted my hands, let them drop. Misery engulfed me.

'What are you going to do?' He thrust the question into the silence.

'I think I'll sit here and wait for the axe to fall on my neck.'

'Really?' Windsor stood. He gripped my forearms and with a flex of muscles stood, lifting me with him. 'Stand up, Alice. You need to stand on your feet. You need to think!'

'I can't.'

'Is the woman I love so easily intimidated?'

I stood rigid in his embrace, unable to think, unable to respond. Into which black hole had all my courage vanished? I was full to the brim with self-pity, and because I no longer felt brave I wept for my own weakness, for all I had lost. That the gifts given to me by Edward out of love and gratitude should be snatched back in spitefulness, destroying the physical evidence of Edward's place in my life. And when honesty forced me to consider that I had not always been entirely without blame, I wept for that too. I had enjoyed my power as King's Concubine. I could not be completely absolved of using crown gold for my purchases, but I had always paid it back. Hadn't I? Well, for the most part I had paid my debts. And here was the day of reckoning. I wept into Windsor's shoulder.

'Is the woman I love so lacking in backbone that she will stand and weep rather than fight for what is rightfully hers?'

Harsh words, but he tightened his hold and propped his chin on top of my head until I began to relax and take my own weight. The solid beat of his heart had a reassurance all of its own. When I eventually rested my forehead against his chest and could breathe evenly again...

The word blazed in my mind. I looked up sharply, dislodging his chin, seeing myself reflected in his eyes.

'*What* did you just say?'

'Which bit of it? That you lacked backbone?'

I ran my tongue over dry lips, scrubbed at my face with a square of linen that Windsor obligingly offered me, and frowned. 'I think you said that I am the woman you love?'

'You are. Didn't you know? You don't look very pleased with the idea.'

My hands tightened on his sleeves. 'Say it again. As if you mean it.' In case he did not. Pray God he did!

'Dear Alice. I love you. You hold my sun and moon in your hands!'

'And that is poetic!'

I thought his answering smile was a little wry. I could not believe it! But I must, mustn't I? Windsor was not a man to say what he did not mean. An immeasurable joy rioted through me, as if to fill me with a shimmering light to disperse the shadows in my mind and heart. Until all the events of the morning flooded back...

I stared at him. 'Why did you have to tell me now?'

'When should I tell you?'

Windsor was humouring me, distracting me. I pushed his hands away so that I stood alone. 'Tomorrow. Last week. Any time but when my face is blotched with tears and my home stripped bare and my mind full of Joan's perfidy.'

'I thought you knew.'

'How could I? You have never said it before.' How could he be so obtuse? There he stood, solid and real and *difficult*! And infinitely loved. 'I want to enjoy it, not have it outweighed by the fact that I might be staring financial ruin in the face—even death if they prove treason against me. And I think you should know—' I did not even hesitate '—I love you too.'

Windsor grinned. 'There you are, then!'

I plastered my hands over my mouth. 'I didn't mean to say that!'

'I don't see why not.' He had captured my hands again, humour still lurking in the curve of his mouth. 'We'll celebrate our mutual love and worry about Venomous Joan together.'

His mouth was hot and sure on mine.

'Oh, Will...'

'I've just proclaimed my undying love for you. And you don't look very happy about it!'

I sighed. 'I'll come about.'

'Let me help.' And he kissed me again.

My thoughts were all adrift as I sank into that embrace. But not for long. This was no time for amorous sighs and pleasurable longings. I was not yet free to enjoy them, as Windsor well knew. Framing my face in his hands so I must attend, concentrate, Windsor began to speak in a low, controlled voice that belied the emotion that pulsed beneath his skin. 'Now, listen to me. You need to be strong, Alice. Listen!' With his hand beneath my chin he made me look at him. 'You will stand before the Lords and answer every question they put to you. There is no evidence against you of fraud. As for treason! They'll not make that stick.'

'You are so confident.' I frowned, not at all persuaded.

'God's Blood! No, I'm not! I am too realistic. But you need to show a confident face or they'll tear you apart.'

'Why would they do it? Now, when my days at Court are over?'

'You know why. They'll destroy you for the days when you held power and they did not.'

'Can we stop them?'

'I don't know. How can we know, until we know their evidence? But we'll have a damned good try.'

I took a deep breath, conscious at last of some of the despair sliding away, and I asked what I wanted most in the world.

'When I have to go—will you come with me?'

'The Devil himself wouldn't keep me away! Don't weep any more.' His gaze was fierce, his hands steady as he took the linen and finished mopping my tears with a thoroughness he might use to dry his horse after a rainstorm. 'Are you not my wife? Do I not love you? Be brave, Alice. You have been so all your life. We will go together to Westminster and brave the bloody scavengers in their den. As for now…I think we are owed some time of our own. In God's name, we haven't claimed much over the years.'

'To do what?' My thoughts were still wayward, seeing the malevolent, sneering faces of Edward's Court ranged against me.

With a huff of impatient breath, Windsor clasped my shoulders and shook me.

'Stop thinking! Come to bed—and I'll show your doubting mind that I truly do love you and it's not a figment of your imagination. On the other hand, we don't have a bed, do we?'

'No!' I felt ridiculous tears begin to well again, but managed a croak of a laugh.

'I swear it won't be a problem!'

In my bedchamber—our bedchamber—Windsor spread his cloak on the floor in a patch of sunshine, folding his tunic for my head. And in broad daylight he gave me a glimpse of what I had never known—a distilled essence of the magic of unencumbered love, freely given, freely received. I felt the chains of duty and expectation slip away, replaced with soft bonds of delight and passion and hot desire.

'Convinced?' he asked between kisses.

'Oh, Will…'

I could not string two words together, wrapped as I was in the moment. It was impossible not to admire his soldier's body, firm and well muscled, as he stripped off hose and boots. The sunshine softened the hard planes, highlighting the power of thigh and shoulder.

'Poitiers?' I murmured, pressing my lips to an old scar that ran along his ribs, angling from sternum to waist.

'Yes.' He stretched, lifting me with him, enquiring, 'Are you intending to kiss all my scars?'

'That would take far too long.' He loosed my shift and I stood naked, exposed. 'I am in lust and desire, Will. My knees are weak with longing…'

'And with love?' His own lust and desire was as evident as the liquid heat between my own thighs.

'Yes, and love.'

The floor was hard, no goosedown, no linen, no lavender-scented coverings. It mattered not. I let him take me as he wished. Or perhaps I did not exactly allow it at all. He was not a man to ask permission, and I would have it no other way. My mind was wiped free of everything but the two of us, there together in an empty house, the sun gilding breast and thigh. Two private people entirely absorbed in each other, attracting no interest from the outside world.

'Why do we love one another, Will?' I asked.

'No idea. Don't worry about it. Some things are granted simply to be enjoyed...'

His enjoyment of me was like balm to my soul, his weight solid, his possession thorough. I held onto him, when every muscle and nerve shivered in response to his attentions, as I had never needed to hold onto any man before. My heart was so full of joy, so much that I might weep again. But I did not. It was a time for rejoicing and Windsor's clever hands pushed back the shadows.

But not for ever.

When he slept, hair mussed, face buried in his tunic folds, I lay awake. A trial? Unknown evidence? I held Windsor's love for me close, a talisman to ward off the fear.

'Did they get Philippa's jewels, then?' Windsor asked when it became necessary for us to dress.

I fear my expression bordered on the smug. 'What do you think?'

'God's Blood!' His laughter echoed strangely in the unfurnished room. 'Tell me, then.'

'It pays to be prepared and vigilant. But they will require a little polishing.'

With some forward planning against the day when this might happen—had I not always been chary of just such an eventuality?—as Thomas Webster had begun to issue his orders, my steward had hidden them, together with Edward's rings, in a sack half-full of weevil-ridden flour. Webster, thank God, had considered the confiscation of the detritus of my cellars beneath his dignity.

Windsor was making headway with the laces of his tunic. 'By the by, I have this for you… I was distracted.' He delved into inner lining. 'I don't think I've ever given you a gift before.'

He took out a silver looking glass. It shone enticingly in the soft light, its engraved stems and leaves skilfully intertwining around the rim like the arms of lovers.

I frowned. 'No!' I said, stonily, ungraciously.

Windsor stared at the glass, and then at me with solemn astonishment, as if my female mental processes were beyond his understanding. 'Alice, my love! I haven't stolen it! I came by it by fair means—and show me a woman who does not use a glass.'

'She sits before you.'

'But why? Why will you not?'

'I don't like what I see.' This was veracity, not me seeking compliments.

'Which bits?'

Was this the time for humour, when I still sat, dishevelled, in my shift? 'All of them… I'm not… Oh, Windsor!' Infuriated, for it was a pretty thing, I clasped my hands in my lap.

'At what age does a woman begin not to care about her appearance? I think she must be on her death bed.'

He fell to his knees beside me on his much-creased cloak, held the glass up, and with his free hand traced the line of one of my too-dark brows.

'I see no ugliness,' he said softly, 'for you are lovely in

my eyes. I want you to see *Alice*. I want you to see the face of my wife and the woman I love.'

Which took every word of refusal out of my mind. How could I not accept the gift without unforgiveable churlishness? And my image was not as bad as I had feared. The face that looked back at me was no beauty, but the lack of symmetry was striking in itself. Even the brows were supportable. I tilted my chin and smiled, and my reflection did likewise: perhaps this unexpected happiness had given me a softening of feature. So I became an owner of a looking glass when I vowed I would not, and was not displeased when Windsor kissed every bit of my reflected face.

We moved to Gaines where we had a bed—so far at least. I knew exactly the impression I wished to make at my appearance before the Lords. I had thought I would be edgy, apprehensive of the outcome; terrified, in fact, my mouth dry, heart thudding so that I must swallow against nausea. And I was, all of those, but more than that I was defiant! Since the visit of the deplorably efficient Webster, Joan, with the backing of the courts, had been encroaching step by poisonous step. My beloved manor near Wendover, Edward's gift, had been taken from me, my people turned out, my furnishings impounded, without me even being there to give my yea or nay. As I was informed, my ownership of it was not legal. It had reverted to the crown, and was now the property of King Richard. Not that he had much use or pleasure from it. On his mother's advice he granted it to his half brother, Thomas Holland. Joan's son by one of her earlier, dubious, probably bigamous marriages.

I'm sure it gave her inordinate pleasure!

I seethed with my powerlessness.

Disconcertingly, Gaunt too made much of my inability to

fight back. My house on the banks of the Thames hopped easily from my hand to his. All my London property along the Ropery was added to the total of the royal duke's own wealth in London. Two of my choicest manors dropped neatly into the pocket of Gaunt's son-in-law. I was truly dispensable in Gaunt's eyes. He had no further use for me, and I learned a hard lesson. Never trust a man who puts power before loyalty. Holy Virgin!

I tried to contact Greseley at the Tabard but without success. He had gone to ground like a hunted fox. I might rant at his invisibility but must accept the wisdom of it. It would be far too easy for the slime of my guilt to coat my agent from head to toe, rendering him easy meat for arrest.

So, to attend my so-called trial, I dressed not with circumspection but in a blaze of rebellion. I still had one fine robe left to me.

'There!' I smoothed my hands down my bodice before fastening a loop of gold and opals around my wrist to match the collar lying snugly against my collarbone, addressing Jane, who sat on the floor of my bedchamber to watch the transformation from country wife to Court lady. Not all my garments were stored at Pallenswick. 'I'll show them I don't fear them!' I announced, and marched down to the parlour where Windsor awaited me. For a long moment he remained slouched in a chair and looked me over.

'By the Rood, Alice!' His voice was more belligerent than his slouch.

'Is that good or bad? I thought I looked very well for my summons to kneel before the over-mighty Lords.'

Lips tight pressed, without a word, Windsor marched me back to my chamber, picking Jane up off the floor where she still sat and depositing her in the middle of my bed with an absent-minded ruffle of her curls.

I clenched my hands into fists. 'I don't like your high-handedness!'

'And I despair of your lack of perspicacity!' He faced me, his manner annoyingly imperious, his voice cracking like a whiplash. Neither did I appreciate his choice of words. 'Are you stupid? You are on trial, Alice. Fraud and treason. How difficult do you want to make it for yourself? Do you really want to antagonise the misbegotten titled scum who'll sit in judgement over you before the first word is uttered?'

I felt my face flush with heat. 'They are already antagonised! What does it matter what I wear?'

'Oh, it matters! You look like a concubine!'

'I was a concubine!'

'I know. We all know. But there's no need to slap them in their high-blooded faces with it. Look at yourself, in all honesty!'

He spread his arms to take in my appearance, and I forced myself to see myself through his eyes. Through the eyes of the Lords. It was, I suppose, on the edge of regally treasonable. As if I had usurped the power of the monarchy for myself. Not quite with the flamboyance I had worn as Lady of the Sun but with enough éclat to take the eye, for I wore the same violet silk and gold cotehardie that had driven Isabella to wrath.

'You're fighting for your freedom here—perhaps even…'

'My life?' I snapped back, the flush fading to ice pallor.

'Don't be melodramatic.' He barely hesitated. 'I can't say I see you on a scaffold, but you can't argue against it—there'll be more than one of those ranged against you who'll call for your death.'

He pushed his hand through his hair and groaned. 'You need to be careful, don't you understand? If they choose to resurrect witchcraft against you…' I saw the worry in him. 'You need to wear something less…challenging.'

'If you say so.' I knew he was right. Of course he was. I sighed and began to strip off the splendidly offending garments. 'It's difficult when the mother of the King is sharpening her nails, isn't it?'

He did not reply. As I stood with my outer robe crushed in my hands, I admitted, because I needed his help and his fire in my belly: 'I am afraid. Oh, Will, I am afraid.'

And Windsor's voice gentled at last. 'I know.' He took the garment from me, laying it on the bed, smoothing its folds with care. 'But we know well how to manage hostile forces, do we not?'

'Oh, we do.' The under-robe, unlaced by Windsor's nimble fingers, fell around my feet. I sighed again. 'I'm sorry. I let my emotions run away with me.'

'Of course you did. You're a woman. And a very dear one to me. I won't let them harm you, you know.'

'I think you might not have a voice in the matter!'

'How little faith you have in me.' He thrust a pair of plain leather shoes into my hands. 'Don't stand there thinking about it. If you're late they'll sneer even more down their aristocratic noses. But remember. I will be with you. I'll not let you suffer alone.'

I dressed rapidly and circumspectly, going to my trial in sobriety and seemliness. No jewels! To wear even one of Philippa's jewels would put a flame to dry kindling laid ready for the fire.

Thus I returned to London for the first time since Edward's funeral. It seemed to me a much longer stretch of time than the actual weeks it had been since I had fled from the door of the Abbey with Joan's triumphant prediction resounding in my ears. Momentarily my spirits leapt at the familiar noise and bustle, the sight of wealthy merchants and their wives in as much finery as Edward's sumptuary laws would allow. The glimpse of the Thames between warehouses, opaque like grey glass in the winter air, drew me. I was not a natural country dweller and never would be— then recalled with a cold squeeze of a hand around my heart that I was not here for the pleasures that London could offer.

I touched Windsor's arm for reassurance, grateful when he covered my hand with his own. If affairs went badly for me I might spend my days in a dungeon or banished from the realm. Or worse… Trying to reply to some bland comment made by Windsor as we wove a path between beggars and whores and the dregs of the London gutters that milled by the waterside, I swallowed against a knot of pure terror.

Dismounting at the Palace of Westminster, Windsor took charge of our horses and I questioned one of the officials. Where were the Lords intending to meet? I was directed to a chamber that Edward had sometimes used for formal audiences such as the visit of the three Kings so many years ago. So this too was to be very formal. But then there was no time to think of anything. Windsor was pulling at my mantle and we walked briskly towards my fate. Guards barred our way at the door. The lords were not yet assembled. Impatiently I turned away to see a man sitting on one of the benches usually occupied by petitioners, waiting for us.

'Wykeham.' Windsor nodded briefly.

'Windsor.' Wykeham reciprocated.

The two men eyed each other with little warmth. That would never change.

'I thought that you of all people would have kept clear of this place!' I said to hide my astonishment that the bishop should be here. 'It's not politic for a sensible man to be seen in my company.'

'You forget.' His grimace as he kissed my fingers was a praiseworthy attempt at a smile. 'I'm a free man, pardoned and reinstated. I shine with honest rectitude. Parliament in its wisdom has turned its smiling face on me, so nothing can touch me.'

I had never heard him so cynical. 'I hope I can say the same for myself after today—but I am not confident.'

'I expect you can talk them round!' His mordant humour had an edge. Warmed by his attempt to reassure me, however much an empty gesture it proved to be, I asked what I had never asked before.

'Pray for me, Wykeham.'

'I will. Even though I'm not sure it matters to you. You spoke for me when I needed it.' He pressed my fingers before releasing them. 'I'll do what I can, lady. The lords might listen if I speak for you…'

And they might not. The unusual term of respect almost brought me to tears.

'You have some strange friends, my love,' Windsor observed when Wykeham was gone. 'Priest or not, the man is enamoured of you. God help him!'

'Nonsense! I helped to get him dismissed.'

'And you reunited him with Edward. You are too hard on yourself.' He folded my hands in his and kissed my lips, my cheeks. 'Remember what I told you,' he whispered against my temple.

And then I was on my own.

Without any fuss or fanfare, I was shown into the chamber. There was no chair placed for me this time: I was expected to stand throughout. Before me and beside me, on three sides, the ranks of hostile faces stared their enmity, just as I had imagined. And in the end Windsor could not keep his promise to be with me—he was barred at the door. He did not bother to argue when faced with the points of the guards' halberds. I could imagine him pacing the chamber outside to no avail.

I looked around, at those I knew and those I did not. Would there be justice? I thought not.

Be calm. Be reasoned. Be aware. Don't allow yourself to be tricked into any admission that can be used against you. Tell the truth as much as you can. Use the intelligence God gave you. And don't speak out of turn or with misplaced arrogance.

Windsor had been brutal in his advice.

But I was so alone. Even his love could not still the rapid trip of my heart.

'Mistress Perrers.'

I looked up sharply. Their spokesman, a sheaf of pages in his hand, was Henry Percy, Earl of Northumberland, Marshall of England. A close associate of Gaunt. I did not like this. I did not like it at all, but I clung to my resolve and I inclined my head.

'My lord.'

'You are summoned here to answer to charges of a most serious nature. Do you understand?'

So that was how it would be. Formal and legal, entirely impersonal. I still did not know what the charges were.

'Yes, my lord. I understand.'

'We require you to answer questions concerning your past conduct. There are outstanding charges against you of fraud and treason. How do you plead?'

'Innocent,' I replied instantly. 'To both. And I question the validity of any evidence against me.' I might be circumspect in my replies but I would not be a fool. I knew what they were about, concocting some spurious occasion on which I had committed treason. Even fraud was a matter for debate.

'They are serious charges, mistress.'

'In what manner have I ever committed fraud?' I kept my voice clear and strong and confident, my spine straight as a halberd staff. 'I have never used dishonest deception or trickery to benefit myself. I have never used false representations. If you are questioning my holding of royal manors, they were freely given to me by King Edward, gifts of his generosity, out of his affection for me.' Let them accept that statement! 'Those I purchased in my own name were done so openly and legally, through the offices of my agent. I utterly deny the charge of fraud, my lords.'

My breathing, with great effort, was slow and controlled, my voice even and commanding. What evidence could they possibly have?

'But in the matter of treason, mistress…'

'Treason? On which occasion did I violate my sworn allegiance to my King?' I was on firm ground here. Not even this august body could find evidence of my bringing the state of the King into danger. 'I challenge you to find any evidence of my being a danger either to the King's health or to the security of the realm.' Perhaps not wise, but fear compelled me to state my case so bluntly. I appraised the faces turned towards me. Some met my gaze, some looked anywhere but at me. 'Well, my lords? Where is your evidence?'

The Lords moved uneasily on their benches, whispered together. Earl Henry shuffled his documents.

'We must deliberate, mistress. If you would wait in the antechamber?'

I stalked out.

'What's happening?' Windsor was immediately there, drawing me to sit on the bench recently vacated by Wykeham.

'They are deliberating.'

'What, in God's name? You were barely in there for five minutes!'

'I don't know.' I could not sit but prowled across the width of the room and back.

'I presume it's not going well?'

'Nothing is going well. They charged me but refused to produce any evidence against me. What do I make of that? If they have no evidence, why call me here? I am afraid, Will. I'm afraid, of what I don't know.'

'I wish I could be there with you.' He rose to prowl with me.

'I know.' I leaned into him. 'But I don't think it would do any good. Even the Archangel Gabriel himself could not keep the Lords from tearing out my throat.'

Within the half-hour I was called back.

'Mistress Perrers.' Earl Henry, with a self-satisfied air. 'The Lords have debated the evidence against you. That you did wantonly and deliberately disobey the orders issued by the Good Parliament.'

What was this? A completely new direction? Fraud and treason had suddenly been abandoned, unless it was treason to disobey Parliament. In that moment I realised that the Lords had known from the beginning that these charges were untenable. But what was the implication here? I felt the ground shift under my feet. This was far more dangerous, a presentiment of it shivering along my spine. How I wished for Windsor's strength beside me, but I must fight my own cause.

'Which orders?' I asked genuinely puzzled. Had I not

obeyed them to the letter? Surely this could not be witch-craft again? Nausea gripped my belly.

'The orders that banished you from the person of the King and from living anywhere in the vicinity of the royal Court...'

But had I not done what they asked of me, to the letter?

'I reject that accusation.'

'Do you?' A complacent curve of Earl Henry's mouth at-tested to his certainty that my denial would hold no weight. 'You were banished—and yet you returned to be with His late Majesty in the weeks before his death...'

Be calm! They cannot prove your guilt on this...

'I observed the orders,' I stated, choosing my words with care, whilst my heart galloped like a panicked horse. 'I lived in retirement. I did not return to Court until my lord of Gaunt had the orders against me rescinded. I state this, a fact that must be well known to all here present, as proof of my innocence.'

'This Chamber knows nothing of that. It believes that you are guilty of breaking the terms of your banishment by Parliament. A most heinous crime.'

'No! I did not! I was informed by the hand of my lord of Gaunt himself that I was free to return.'

'And you have proof of this?'

'No. But the pardon must exist.'

The letter. What had happened to it? My thoughts skit-tered like rats in a trap. There must be proof...

'Furthermore,' Earl Henry continued as if I had not spo-ken, 'you are charged that you used your malign influ-ence on His Majesty King Edward, in the final days of his weakness, to achieve the pardon of Richard Lyons, whom Parliament had condemned for his dire culpability in matters of finance. By your instigation Lyons was released from the Tower.'

It was simply not true. I considered the accusation, my mind racing over the facts. There was no evidence of my involvement. There was *none*! My spirits rose, and yet I was puzzled at this accusation.

'Lyons was pardoned on the authority of my lord of Gaunt, in King Edward's name, when the decisions of the Parliament were reversed,' I replied, once more sure of my ground. 'He and my lord Latimer were both released. It is no secret. It must have been known to your lordships.'

Earl Henry denied it. 'This Chamber holds that you are guilty of effecting the pardon of this man, a man considered to be a threat to the realm.'

'No!'

'The scale of his embezzlement was an outrage. To grant him a pardon was an act against the authority of Parliament...'

'There must be Court officials who know the truth. Gaunt himself...'

Earl Henry's eyes met mine, horrifyingly bright with his supremacy over me. 'We are aware of none. Not one has come forward in your defence.'

'I can find them.' How amazingly composed I sounded, yet the palms of my hands were slick with sweat. 'The lawyers involved with the case will speak for my lack of involvement. I had nothing to do with Lyons's pardon. It must be on record that my lord of Gaunt had the legal papers drawn up.'

Silence. Not even the habitual scuffling of my aristocratic judges. I found that my hands had curled into fists, nails digging into soft flesh. Then Earl Henry gave a curt nod.

'It must not be said that this Chamber is guilty of trampling justice underfoot. We will allow you time to find your witnesses, mistress. We will hear them and assess their evidence.'

'How long?' I asked. 'How long will you give me?'

'One afternoon and one night, mistress.' A smile, a smirk, if I was not mistaken.

'But that's impossible…'

'A committee appointed by us will meet tomorrow at ten of the clock to hear your evidence.'

'I beg for longer, my lords…' I looked round the faces, but knew that my plea fell on wilfully deaf ears.

'That is the best we can do.'

I walked from the room, shoulders straight, head high. They knew I would lose.

'One afternoon and one night? By God! They're sure of themselves. And I don't like having a door slammed in my face!' Windsor struck his fist against the wall, then became fiercely practical. 'So where do we start?'

'It was Gaunt's doing, he ordered Lyon's release. The evidence must exist,' I fretted. 'All I need is someone to unearth it from wherever it's filed away and stand beside me to put it before the Lords' Committee.'

'Who? Who would know?'

We were walking rapidly through the corridors to the wing of the vast palace given over to Court business, a rabbit warren of clerks and lawyers.

'I don't know. One of the Court's legal men. There are enough of them.'

'But will they?'

'Will they what?' My mind was already leaping ahead. Who could I pin down?

'Find the evidence. Present it before the Committee. Who

can you find to stand before the Lords and challenge their rulings?'

I stopped in my tracks. 'Why would they not?'

'If there's an interest to keep the evidence hidden...' He raised his hand as I opened my mouth to deny such an outcome. '*If*, I say...then retribution against any man who spoke in your defence could be sharp and swift. It could keep mouths firmly closed. Even if the evidence still exists...and I have my doubts!'

I blinked to hear it spoken so brutally. For was it not what I feared? The assurance of Earl Henry had stirred my fear to hot flames.

'I can't do *nothing*! I can't just *accept*!' I retaliated.

'No. And our time is slipping past.' Windsor had redoubled his pace. 'Let's see who we can track down to their legal lair. Who was the man who took all your property from Pallenswick? He might consider that he owes you at least the truth.'

'Why is it, Will,' I grumbled, 'that you always think along the lines of debts that can be called in and gifts that need to be reciprocated?'

'Because I've spent my life calling them in or repaying them!' He strode on, pulling me with him. 'Do you remember his name?'

'Thomas Webster.'

'Go and talk to him.' He pushed me through a door that would take me into the legal rabbit run. 'I'll see if any of Edward's servants manage to have a memory that I can prick. With a dagger if I have to.'

I tracked Thomas Webster down to a small shabby room where he was surrounded by vellum, ribbons and seals and the smell of ink and elderly documents. How evocative that smell was, with memories of past times. Safer times. Master

Webster looked up impatiently as I entered, then, seeing me, instantly dismissed his clerk. Not, I decided, a good sign.

'Master Thomas Webster!' I stood before his desk, arms at my sides, as he came slowly to his feet.

'Mistress Perrers…'

'Do they exist?'

He knew why I was here in his den. His eyes shifted beneath mine, and slid down to where one hand toyed with an inky quill. He knew exactly my meaning: the documents to prove that Gaunt had had the pardons drawn up.

'I am sure they do, mistress.'

'Will you find them for me? Will you stand as witness for me?'

'No, mistress.'

'Why not?'

Now he looked at me. 'You know the reason. It's more than my position is worth to help you.'

'Will you not even help me to prove that my banishment from Court was revoked by my lord of Gaunt?'

He did not even bother to answer.

'Then who will?' I demanded. 'Who will help me?'

His face as bland as a baked custard tart, he cast the quill with its ruined nib onto the desk. He did not need to reply. As I discovered in further fruitless search for the whole of that afternoon, no one would help me. The Court lawyers became invisible. They vanished into the stonework and panelled walls like cockroaches at the approach of a candle. Those who I cornered claimed astonishing loss of recall.

'It's hopeless!' I met up with Windsor, who was looking unusually harassed, in the Great Hall.

'So Webster is intransigent?'

'Webster is a self-serving bastard!'

'Edward's servants are also less than cooperative,' he

remarked. 'But there is one who might just come up to the mark…'

'How much did you pay him?'

'Best not to ask! I wouldn't wager on him appearing in the final shake-up, but at least he did not refuse outright.'

I had little hope. If a lawyer would not stand for the truth, with all the legal documents to prove his case, how could I expect a page or servant to put himself forward against the will of Parliament?

'Don't give up hope, Alice.' Windsor's face was grim. 'Not until the final judgement is given. There's always hope.'

'I'm not so sanguine.'

'Neither am I! But we can't both give up before we begin!'

I balked at the unexpected harshness, but he drew my hand through his arm and led me toward the screened door at the end.

'What do we do now?' I asked.

'We stir up the kitchens to find us ale and something that passes for food. Then we keep my wavering witness under surveillance.' His grin had a not altogether pleasant edge. 'If he changes his mind, we do all we can to change it back!'

We had little sleep that night.

Ten o'clock. Edward's beloved clock at Havering would be marking the hour. The Committee appointed to examine my evidence occupied a smaller, more intimate chamber: just large enough to hold a half dozen of their number and the accused. And a witness, if one were brave enough. Or sufficiently foolhardy…

I entered. I curtseyed to the chosen lords seated before me behind a table, a solid barrier between accusers and accused. I looked from face to face to see who would determine my future.

The temperature in the room dropped to ice.

Seated in the centre of my judges, presiding over the case against me, was Gaunt himself. My erstwhile supporter, my ally, who had striven to win my allegiance, who had annulled my banishment to allow me to return to Edward.

Sitting in judgement?

I inhaled slowly, deeply, trying to calm the terror that flared anew. Why had he chosen to do this? What effect would his weighty presence have on the judgement for or against me? I did not even need to ask the question. It was as plain as the flamboyant black and red damask of his tunic. I looked directly at him. He looked at me. If I had hoped to find a friend amongst the Lords, I had been woefully mistaken, but then, I had never trusted him, had I? I had been right not to. Gaunt's presence, I knew full well, would destroy the one solitary hope I had clung to, however hopelessly, through that endless night, that he might once again come to my rescue. He was here to punish me. He was here to destroy any evidence that we had worked together in the past by making an example of me. He was hunting, his eyes as hard and cold as granite, and I was the quarry. I would find no rescue here.

'Mistress Perrers…'

My attention was dragged back, my interrogator once more Earl Henry. Not that it mattered. Gaunt might not personally undertake the examination of my evidence, but his authority coloured the whole proceedings. The outcome was, I feared, his to direct.

'Mistress Perrers—we will weigh your evidence to support your innocence. Have you discovered any lawyer who will speak of the origin of Lyon's pardon? Have you discovered the documents?'

'No, my lords. I have not.'

'Then the evidence against you still stands and you must be presumed guilty.' How gentle his voice. How venomous!

'I have found one who will speak for me,' I stated.

'Indeed?' The disbelief in that single word was impressive. Chilling to the depths of my soul.

'I would call John Beverley to give evidence,' I said.

'And he is?'

'An attendant in Kind Edward's retinue. A personal body servant. A man the King—the late King—trusted implicitly.'

'Then we will hear him.'

The door at my back was opened. I prayed, I prayed as hard as I could that John Beverley had not fled.

'Keep him here, whatever you do!' I had told Windsor that morning. 'And stop scowling at him.' John Beverley, Edward's body servant, the only man Windsor and I could locate who had a smidgeon of courage and respect for the truth. Whatever it had taken from Windsor, we had got him at least as far as the door to the chamber. I thought perhaps the means employed by my determined husband had been physical: Beverley was nervous. Beverley, I feared, was untrustworthy. But what choice had I but to put my freedom into his hands? All I could do was pray that his past loyalties would hold true. He entered, thinning hair untidy as if he had dragged his hands through it, his gaze flickering over the committee. When they rested on Gaunt, the nerves changed to horror. The skin of his face became grey, and my heart fell.

'John Beverley.' Earl Henry addressed him.

'Yes, my lord.' His hands were gripped ferociously, his broad features anxious.

'You were body servant to King Edward?'

'Yes, my lord.'

'We are here to ascertain the truth of the pardoning of Richard Lyons. You recall the matter to which I allude? To your knowledge, did Mistress Perrers persuade His late Majesty to grant Lyons a pardon?'

'Not to my knowledge, my lord.'

'Are you sure about that?'

'Yes, my lord.'

I sighed. Beverley was a man of few words, his eyes those of a terrified deer, facing the hounds. Pray God he would use those words on my behalf.

'How is that? How can you be so sure?'

'I was in attendance on his Majesty constantly in those last days, my lord.' A few petals of hope began to unfurl beneath my heart. Beverley's voice grew stronger as his confidence grew. Here was something he could speak of with authority. 'I never heard the matter of a pardon mentioned by the King or by Mistress Perrers.'

'So neither of them talked of it.'

'No, my lord. Neither King Edward nor his...nor Mistress Perrers. I swear the King never gave the order for a pardon for the man.'

A dangerous statement, all in all. If the pardon had not come from Edward, it had been on Gaunt's own initiative. Thus Gaunt usurping a royal power that was not the Prince's right to use. I held my breath as the tension in the room tightened. There was a shifting of bodies, the slide of silk against damask. A scrape of boots against the floor. And on Gaunt's brow a storm cloud gathered. If Beverley did not notice it, he was a fool. Would he stand by his word, or would he play the coward? Windsor's intimidation or monetary inducement suddenly weighted little against Gaunt's unspoken ire.

'You will swear to that? You will take an oath to that effect?' asked Earl Henry. 'That Mistress Perrers did at no time persuade the late King to issue a pardon for Richard Lyons.'

'Well…yes, my lord.'

'It would, you understand, be dangerous to swear to something of which you are to any degree uncertain…'

'Ah…' And as I watched him, Beverley's eyes skipped from Earl Henry to Gaunt.

'Do you claim, Master Beverley, that Mistress Perrers had *no* influence on the King's decisions? You say that you were with the late King constantly.'

'Yes, my lord.'

'But were there not times when Mistress Perrers was alone with the King, without your presence?'

'Of course, my lord.'

'And during those times, could she perhaps have raised the question of Lyons and his pardon?'

'Well…she could, my lord.' Beverley gulped.

'If that is so, are you free to say that Mistress Perrers did not undertake the pardon of Richard Lyons?'

I heard him swallow again, seeing the pit before his feet, a dark morass of claim and counterclaim, that he had dug for himself. I too saw it, but forced myself to stand perfectly still, watching Gaunt's face.

'No, my lord. I suppose I am not.'

'Then, by my reckoning, you cannot support Mistress Perrers with your testimony. Can you?'

'No, sir. By my conscience, I cannot.' I thought Beverley sounded relieved at having the decision made for him.'

'Thank you. We appreciate your honesty. You are free to go.'

Gaunt's face was blandly tranquil, satisfied with a job

well done as he looked at me. It was as if we were alone in the room and I knew that I would be judged without mercy.

The Committee conferred in low voices.

John Beverley left the chamber with not one look in my direction, keen to dissociate himself from any suspicion of connivance between us. I could hardly blame him. Not all men were like Windsor, who I knew would stand by me to the death. Standing alone before Gaunt's hand-picked lordly minions, I knew that I needed him as I had never needed anyone before. Since Philippa's intervention in my life I had struggled and manoeuvred to keep my feet in the fast-flowing stream of Court politics. I had striven to make my future and that of my children safe. I was even proud of my success. All now brought to nothing. Here I stood, helpless and vulnerable, without friends.

Except for William de Windsor.

The strange sense of relief that I was not completely alone, whatever happened, was my only glimmer of hope in this moment of dread.

'Mistress Perrers!' There was Earl Henry, demanding my attention. Gaunt's expression was carved in stone. Earl Henry stepped forward. 'We have made our decision. This is our judgement...'

And how little time it took to undermine all I had made of my life.

'We consider you to be guilty of obtaining the pardon for Richard Lyons.'

Guilty!

'Therefore this Committee, in the name of the Lords of the Realm of England, confirms the original sentence delivered by the Good Parliament. The sentence of banishment...'

Banishment...! Again! The word beat heavily against my mind.

But Earl Henry had not yet finished twisting the knife in my heart's wound.

'Also we command the forfeiture of all your remaining lands and possessions obtained by fraud and deceit.'

The enormity of it shook me. The illegality of my actions was simply presumed without any need to show proof. My own purchase of land and property was presumed to be through deceit, and so I was to be stripped of everything, whether illegal or not. I was *presumed* guilty, not proven to be so. So much for the balance of the law. How they must hate me. But had that not always been the case?

'Do you understand our decisions, Mistress Perrers?'

I stood unmoving, aware of all those eyes. Some condemning, some sanctimonious, some merely curious to see how I would react. Gaunt's eyes glittered with triumph and avarice. My estates were open to his picking. From ally to enemy in that one sentence. I could barely comprehend it. And when I did, I despised him for it.

'I understand perfectly, my lords,' I remarked. 'Am I free to go?'

'We are finished here.'

I curtseyed deeply and walked from the room.

Am I free to go? I had asked. But where would I go?

Before my mind could fully grasp what had been done, I was standing in the antechamber. The judgement had been passed; I was not restrained, yet banishment, a black cloud, pressed down on me. Blindly I looked for Windsor, waiting for me by the window. I think I must have staggered, for in three strides he was beside me, holding my arm.

'Beverley played the rabbit, I presume! He scuttled out before I could get my hands around his scrawny little neck.'

I blinked, unable to string two thoughts together or find words to explain what had been done to me.

'Alice?'

I shook my head. 'I need to…'

One close look at my bleak expression was enough for him. 'Don't try to speak. Come with me.'

He lost no time but led me out into the icy air. I shivered but was glad of the cold wind on my face. In the courtyard horses were waiting with Windsor's servants. As if from a distance, I realised that he had feared this, and made provision even as he had encouraged me to believe that justice would smile in my favour.

'Thank you,' I whispered. How dear he was to me. How much I had begun to lean on his good sense, his cynical streak of practicality.

He raised the palm of my hand to his lips, then, realising how cold I was, stripped off his own gloves and drew them onto my hands, wrapping his own mantle around my shoulders. The warmth was intense, welcome, despite the cruel tingling of my fingers.

'You are very…kind to me.'

'Kind, by God! Do I not love you, foolish one?' He peered into my frozen face. 'I suppose you still don't believe me. But this is neither the time nor the place to beat you about the head with it. Just accept that it's true and that I won't desert you. Feel that?' He pressed my gloved palm to his chest. 'It beats in unison with yours. Is that poetic enough for you? Perhaps not but it's the best you'll get at this juncture.' His kiss on my mouth was firm. 'Now, up with you. Before the vermin change their mind. I'll take you home.'

'But where is home now?'

'Home is with me.'

What a strange place and time for such an assurance. Beneath the harsh exterior was a level of sensitivity that always had the power to move me. His intuitiveness was a thing of wonder. And he must have known: I needed those exact words to bite through the paralysing horror. Neither did he wait for any reciprocal response from me. Blasted by rampant shock and fear, I could not tell him what had occurred. By now I was shivering constantly, a reaction that had nothing to do with the whip of the wind off the river. I gripped the reins that he forced between my fingers but sat there, unable to make the simplest of decisions, until he leaned from his own mount and grasped my bridle. With an impatient grunt he pulled my horse after him into a stumbling trot.

It jerked me back into my senses and I pushed my mount alongside his.

'Will they enforce the banishment this time?' I asked, even as I knew the answer.

'So that's what they did. I wondered what had reduced you to silence.'

I could not smile at the heavy humour. 'Yes, and worse.'

'Who was it?'

'Gaunt. He was there. He sat in judgement on me.' All I could see was his hard face. His furious desire to wash his hands clean of his association with me.

'Then we'll not wait around to find out.' He urged our mounts on into a faster trot, our escort keeping pace.

'Where are we going?'

'To Gaines. Do you agree?'

Why not? Would I be safe anywhere? 'Yes. To Gaines. It is our own. They cannot question my ownership of Gaines since it is in your name too.' I saw his quizzical look. Of course, he didn't know. 'Oh, Will! They're going to take away all my property, my land…'

He showed no surprise.

'Then I'll take you to one of my own manors, if you prefer. You and the girls…'

I thought about it, the cold in my belly beginning to melt. He would take care of me, whatever happened. Yet I decided that I needed the comfort of familiar surroundings. 'No. Take me to Gaines. And, Will…?' He looked across. Face vivid and alive, strong enough to face any danger. 'I know you love me. And I love you too.'

'I know you do. Now, get on, woman. The sooner we're out of London the better, before they find another crime to hang around your neck.'

Chapter Seventeen

It was not my neck the Lords had their eye on. It was Windsor's. The Lords launched their new assault against Windsor, not against me, with a charge breathtaking in its audacity, its low cunning: the most obvious of charges that it would be impossible for him to deny. Windsor was accused of harbouring a woman who was under sentence of banishment. He was ordered to London to appear before the Lords.

'How dare they?' I raged. Anger could most assuredly take the chill from terror. 'How dare they transfer my guilt onto you?'

'They dare with no compunction whatsoever,' Windsor remarked with astonishing nonchalance. 'It's a perfectly pragmatic decision by Gaunt, or Princess Joan, to make life unpleasant for you.' Infuriatingly, unlike me, he seemed to have no concerns, admitting his guilt openly to the official who brought the summons, with me standing at his side, my hand clamped by his to his arm, as if to prove his culpability for all to see.

'I can hardly deny it, can I?' he remarked mildly, offering

the courier a cup of ale before his return journey. 'We've been sharing a roof and a bed, to the knowledge of everyone who cared to take an interest in our doings. It's no secret that we're married, is it, Lady de Windsor?' He bowed to me and smiled placidly at the startled official. Since when did the accused ever admit to guilt?

I growled my disapproval.

Windsor went to London to face his accusers.

'Look for me within the month. If not, I'm in the Tower. Send me a parcel of food and wine!' His mouth warm but fleeting on mine, his mind already racing ahead. 'Don't worry! And for your safety don't leave Gaines—or they'll have you clad in a white shift and crucifix before you can sneeze. We don't want that, do we?' I caught the spark in his eye. 'What do I know about bringing up young girls? They need their mother here. So stay put!'

What sort of advice was that? My nerves were raw with worry. All I could do was sit at home and harry the servants as the days lumbered past, all my old fears surfacing, my body cold, my mind frightened, and unbearably lonely. As the weeks crawled, it was driven home to me how much had been stripped from me. All I had strived to acquire, all the social pre-eminence I had enjoyed was destroyed. All my much-valued independence was gone, every morsel of bread that passed my lips, every garment on my back, rested on the goodwill of Windsor, who was even now fighting for his freedom before the Lords. What would I do if they clapped him behind bars? How would I live?

How could I tolerate his loss in my heart?

My mind was in torment.

Why was it that time allows us to ponder our gravest fears rather than our brightest hopes? Once I had been certain that Windsor would stand by me, certain that I would never be alone again. I had been so sure. But now the doubts crept in. What if I was wrong? Would he betray me under Parliament's intimidation? Would he abandon me and leave me to Joan's mercies? Would he promise never to see me again, if that was what they demanded from him in return for his own freedom? No one could ever deny that Windsor had a streak of self-interest as wide as the seas between England and France.

The days were endless and I felt increasingly bereft.

Thank God! Thank God! Four long weeks and Windsor returned.

'What did they say?' I demanded, standing at his horse's shoulder, looking up into his face and making no attempt to hide the anxiety that had raged since the day of his departure. I had not even waited until he dismounted but had run out into the courtyard from my bedchamber without veil or shoes, and now gripped his bridle so fiercely that his horse sidled and tossed its head. I held on, wincing at the stones beneath my feet.

'And good day to you too, my lady!' he replied as the animal snorted, sidestepping.

'Don't play with me, Windsor.'

'Wouldn't dream of it. If you'll allow me to dismount…'

I stepped back. 'Well?' He swung to the ground in a cloud of dust, beating it from his tunic and the folds of his mantle. 'Now will you tell me? Why keep me waiting?' Fear was a hard knot in my throat and my blood was laced with lead.

His stare was speculative. 'They've dropped the charge against me.'

As simple as that? 'I don't believe you!'

'I can't think why not. I told you not to worry!'

'So you did.' I grimaced at his easy confidence, a confidence I might once have had. 'I'm so pleased, Will…but I still can't quite believe…'

'There's more!'

I sighed. So there was more. Of course there was. The knot that had momentarily slackened tightened again and my blood seemed to drain to my feet. 'Tell me. What terms did they demand?'

'The members of Parliament in their wisdom have changed their collectively narrow minds on the little matter of your banishment.'

'Changed their minds…?'

'You are, as of yesterday, free. And so am I, from the charge of wilfully consorting with a banished woman.'

Still unsure, I watched Windsor's expression for any reaction, for confirmation, but there was none. It might have been chipped out of stone. He neither expanded on his news nor did he move to touch me. There was something between us, much like one of Wykeham's formidable walls of stone blocks. So there was something more that he was not telling me.

'There's a fly in this bowl of pottage,' I said, hating to have to ask, fearing the answer. 'What is it?'

'How do you know there is one?'

'I can tell by your face.'

'And there was I thinking I was being inscrutable!'

I punched his arm, not playfully. 'There is always a price to be paid by someone.' I frowned. 'Joan would never want the banishment lifted.' I was certain of it. So what had prompted this turn of fortune in my favour?

'Pour me a cup of ale, my love, to rid my mouth of the poison of Court negotiations—' Windsor tossed his reins to a waiting groom and wound an arm around my waist in his habitual comforting greeting '—and I might just tell you all. It's been a long few weeks. I feel in need of some home comforts.'

He kept me waiting while he ate his way through a plate of beef and a flat loaf, by which time I was all but hopping with frustration, but I knew him well enough to keep my mouth closed and my impatience to myself. I sat opposite him, eyes fixed on his every move, every damned mouthful of bread and meat, and waited.

He drained the cup.

'Another cup of ale?' I enquired sweetly.

'I might...'

I stretched for the pottery jug, then held onto it and did not pour. 'A slab of cheese perhaps? A collop of mutton?'

'Well, I might be persuaded...'

'And I might empty this over your head!'

He laughed. 'You won't provoke me!'

'But *you* provoke *me!*'

'I'll do it no more.' The lines of his face grew stern. 'Accept the lifting of the banishment for what it is, Alice.'

'Because I won't like what they demand in recompense.'

'No. You won't. There are strings well and truly attached.'

Well, there would be. My voice caught. 'You said they had changed their minds...' Surely he would not hide an even worse outcome from me? No, no. He would not have sat through a meal without telling me. He had said I was free, that we both were. But what had that woman done? How far would Joan's vengeance stretch?

'God's Blood, Will!'

His hands, now unoccupied with knife and bread, took mine. 'No, no. Do you think me so cruel? You are free, Alice, as I said. No banishment. You don't get your manors back—you can't expect miracles—but there's no further punishment. But here's the rub.' And there was the gleam of friendly mischief back in his eyes. 'You are free as long as you live with me, as my wife, and I am willing to keep you and stand surety for your good behaviour.'

I inhaled sharply. 'A prisoner!'

'I thought you might see it in that light.'

'So I have to live within your governance.'

When he handed me his cup, I gulped the ale inelegantly.

'As would any wife with her husband. And Parliament in its wisdom has decided to leave the penalty of banishment intact, to hang over your head, undeserving as you are of their compassion. To ensure your future good behaviour.' His teeth showed in a cold smile.

'So I am not pardoned.'

'Not completely.' His expression warmed. 'And you have of necessity to please me, so that I don't cast you off.'

'We cannot live without arguing,' I retorted.

'Oh, I think we can.' He stretched his hands across the board again, to pin my restless fingers flat beneath his. 'Don't you trust me? After all we've been through? And I thought you liked living with me.'

'Of course I do. But, oh, Will!' The words were there before I could stop them. 'When you didn't come back, I was afraid that you would betray me,' I admitted. 'I thought you would agree never to see me again, and I would be alone…'

'Foolish girl!' He was completely unmoved by my lack of faith. By now he knew my buried fears well enough. 'I will only abandon you and drive you from my door if you are very bad and argue over every juncture.'

Turning my hands so that they could grip his, I sighed softly, letting myself respond appropriately to his dry wit. 'Then I must be good. I'd better start now!' I reached for the jug again and refilled his cup, one question still remaining. 'Why did they do it, Will?'

'That's simple, my love. The situation in France is deteriorating and they need able men.'

I stared at him as his implication opened up, like a foul, bottomless pit at my feet.

No! Oh, no!

A cold wind shivered down my spine and it took my breath. Of course it would happen. Had I tried to delude myself that it would not? Perhaps I had, clinging to the hope that his alienation from the Court would play into my hands and keep him close. But this *volte face* on the part of the new government made perfect sense if I were capable of assessing the creeping horror of it in cold blood. They would find him a post because he was a man of talent, and he would take it because he was, and always would be, a man of supreme ambition. He would leave me. He might love me, but he would leave me. Had I not always feared it? My heart leapt violently against the cage of my ribs as I struggled for words.

'And they need *you*,' I managed to say equably.

'Me, as you say. I think they have in mind a position for me. So they're keeping me…sweet.'

'You bargained with them.'

'I did. They've too many other troubles, not least a child king, to spend time on you and me.'

'What did Joan say? Did you see her?' I asked, trying to deflect my mind from the one thought that filled it to capacity and beyond.

'Briefly.' His mouth twisted with distaste but there was a flash of enjoyment after all. 'Joan kept her opinions to herself in the presence of the young King's counsellors. She managed to refrain from cursing you—but from the look in her eye I expect she has set fire to Richard's inherited bed. But for once she made the right decision. She put the good of the realm—my expert offices—before her personal vendetta—you, my love. She needs me.'

Windsor yawned widely. How could he sit there, oblivious to the fear that swamped me like a winter deluge? And then he surprised me, as he often did, sliding his hands across the table to take hold of mine.

'It's not worth a candle for you to worry, you know. Now, since you're legally bound to be an amenable wife, in case I cast you from my door for your reluctance in wifely matters, come and help me remove these boots. I will not leave you today or even tomorrow… Come and be with me, Alice.'

I laughed. No, he was not oblivious at all. Burying my fears—there would be time enough to wallow in despair—I removed more than his boots. Neither was I reluctant.

It was good to have him home.

The days passed. A week and then a second. No news from Court. Perhaps Windsor had misread the signals and he was still in disfavour. He seemed entirely unconcerned, picking up the reins of estate matters as if he had never been away, while I allowed myself to hope a little, the fretful anxiety that I strove so hard to hide gradually beginning to release its hold.

'You're looking remarkably content—for you—Alice,' he said as we rode out together in a moment of companionship snatched from the demands of a busy day at the end of the second week. 'Now, why is that?'

'No reason.' I would not confess to my own weakness, would I?

'They will give me an appointment, you know,' he said sombrely. 'It will come.'

Sometimes I wished he did not know me better than I knew myself. Still, I hoped that he would be proved wrong.

But Windsor, damn the man, was right. What an uncanny nose he had for political intrigue. As the moon began to wax, he was offered the eminent position of Governor of the newly acquired port of Cherbourg. His eyes positively gleamed at this new venture, and in them I read that he could not refuse. Neither should he, politician that he was, through blood and bone and sinew.

Loneliness loomed, beckoned for me. Long hours when he would be so far from my reach that… Furious, I stamped down hard on its grinning face.

'You'll take it,' I said, a statement rather than a question. Even as my whole being cried out to him to refuse it, I managed a smile.

'I think I will.' He slid me a quizzical glance over the official request, heavy with its ink and red seals. 'But they'll not get me cheaply. I'll make them pay for my loyalty.'

'With what?'

'Aha! Nosy!'

'Tell me!'

'Not I. Or at least not until I'm sure of my ground.'

Not for the first time, his confidence, his damned superiority, rattled me. 'Are you so sure you'll find the right bait to hook Parliament?'

'Certainly I am. There are few with my expertise in handling difficult provinces or squeezing money out of a reluctant populace.'

He spent the next few days in the parlour, his lawyer and clerk in attendance, the door firmly closed against me, emerging, so it seemed to me, only to eat and sleep. The work was long and laborious if the number of ruined quills was anything to go by.

Then without a word of explanation we were packed and off to London.

'Why won't you tell me?'

'It would risk ill luck to air it at this stage. It's the Lords I need to convince.' He was morose and preoccupied, staring between his horse's ears. Perhaps he was not as confident as he would like me to believe, which made me shiver. Then suddenly he grinned. 'But they will have no answer to make against my arguments, so there's no reason for you to be concerned.'

Westminster. The memories it stirred up tiptoed unpleasantly over the skin of my arms, making me uneasy enough to look over my shoulder. How was it that dread embedded itself, even when the reason for it was gone, easily reawakened. When *I* had appeared before the Lords, Windsor had been refused admission. Would I be forced to wait out the time in an anteroom with pages and servants whilst he put some questionable bargain before the lordships that they could not refuse? I hated the thought of my powerlessness in the whole proceedings.

I was not even sure why he had insisted that I accompany him.

'Why am I here, Will?' I asked in the end as we stood in that same ill-fated antechamber that had seen my mind freeze at the thought of banishment.

'Are you afraid?' He looked surprised. 'Alice, my love. Would I have brought you back here if I had thought you in any danger at all?' He raised my hand to his lips in an unexpected grave and formal salute. 'You are here as Lady de Windsor, my excellent wife, under my protection. The law can't hurt you…'

'No, it's not that,' I admitted. 'I'm just not sure why you need me…'

'Because you are essential to me. Do you think you can manage an air of outraged innocence for the next hour?'

I stared at him.

'Perhaps not. Just don't speak unless spoken to. Keep your eyes down in a wifely, respectful manner. And follow my lead. And here…'

Rummaging in the leather purse at his belt, he removed an object that glinted gold. Seizing my left hand, he pushed the ring onto my finger. It was a tight fit. With a grunt of irritation as if it were my fault, he forced it over my knuckle.

'And make sure it's obvious to every one of them!'

Before I could ask more, Windsor was ushering me into the chamber and I was left to take in the atmosphere. The Lords were expecting an undemanding session to confirm Windsor's promotion. Self-congratulation sat comfortably on them; until I entered at Windsor's side, with Windsor brushing aside any objection, addressing the Lords with impressive authority. A little bubble of laughter swelled in my breast. The expression on their collective faces—one of fury—was a blessing to me. Windsor ignored it.

'My lords.' His voice and stance captured their attention. 'The lady, known to you all, is here at my invitation. She is my wife, my lords. Lady de Windsor. The matter is pertinent to her and so the law makes provision for her attendance. She should not be required to stand. A seat for her, if you please.'

An attendant scurried forward with a stool. Windsor led me to it, ignoring the rumble of comment. I sat. I tried for the outraged innocence, my blood humming in expectation as I turned the gold circle with its ruby stone around my finger. It did not turn easily. What in heaven's name was he about? Gaunt, to my relief, was not present, but I did not think it would have mattered one way or another to Windsor.

Windsor bowed to me then to the assembled gathering and began without preamble. 'I am honoured by your offer of the post of Governor of Cherbourg, my lords.'

'We value your experience, Sir William.' I watched with pleasure Earl Henry's uncertainty.

Windsor bowed again, impressively austere in his courtesy. 'I am gratified. However, I find my acceptance of the honour is compromised—and I am undecided. A small matter that you alone can rectify, my lords.'

'We will do all we can...'

'It is the status of my wife, my lords.'

It was as if every man there held his breath. So did I.

'Indeed, sir?' Earl Henry had no documents to help him now. I did not smile. I sat demurely with eyes downcast.

'I request, my lords, a reversal and annulment of all your judgements against her.' Windsor's voice filled the chamber. The air was as thick as smoke.

What are you doing, Windsor? They'll never do it.

'The law demands that a man—or woman—be tried in the weighty matters of fraud and treason before the Court of the King's Bench. When my wife was summoned by your august selves, she was given judgement by a commission.' He allowed his eyes to roam thoughtfully over the startled faces. 'My wife was not given due process before the King's Bench, which is her right. Thus I hold the judgement against her—of banishment from the realm, and most pertinently the confiscation of her property—to be illegal.'

'I-it was a time of great uncertainty, Sir William,' Earl Henry stammered.

'It was a time when the law should have been upheld, my lord, as you and I both know.' Windsor drove on the attack. 'Furthermore, my wife was not permitted to be present during the whole of the deliberations concerning her guilt or innocence. She was asked to leave the chamber. I know because I was cognisant to the whole series of events during your deliberations. This is not lawful, my lords. Do I continue? For I regret that there was yet another serious discrepancy between your conduct and the law of the land.'

'Ah…! I am not aware…'

'My wife, my lords, was not given adequate time to locate witnesses and prepare her case.'

'But… Sir William…'

Oh, how he made them squirm. Oh, how I rejoiced!

'One afternoon and one night, my lords. I know it for a fact since I was present with my wife at the search for those who might stand for her. It was not sufficient. It was not *legal*.'

There was no response. Earl Henry studied the knots in the floor at his feet.

'And finally, my lords. My wife was tried as *femme sole*, a woman alone, and in her own unwed name.' How uncompromising his stance before the assembled lords. He did not speak loudly and yet it seemed to me that his voice rang from the stone arches. Yet the thud of my heart in my ears almost drowned it out.

'That should not have happened, my lords, as you are aware. You chose to take advantage of a woman alone. But Alice de Windsor is my wife and thus not without protection. By law her property is mine. Whatever the judgement against her, Parliament had no right to confiscate her property since, to put it simply, my lords, it was no longer hers to be confiscated.' I could taste the disdain in his condemnation. 'The property is mine, my lords, and I demand its return. Immediately. As I demand a pardon for a judgement against Lady de Windsor that should never have been given.'

Oh, it was masterly. But would they bend before such

erudition? I saw Windsor's hands tighten infinitesimally on the folds of the hat he held.

'If you will give my arguments due consideration, my lords, and uphold the rights of my wife in this case, I will consider the post you offer me. Otherwise...'

The pause lengthened. Windsor made no attempt to fill it. The covert threat hung in the air.

We were asked to wait without as they deliberated. Whilst I fretted and fussed, Windsor sat, in silent contemplation of some distant scene, his shoulders against the wall, his booted ankles crossed. Only when we were re-summoned did he take my hand and squeeze it hard.

And he led me in.

Neither of us sat. Their conclusion was stated within the time it took for the sun's rays to crawl, snail-like, the width of a fingernail across the floor The Lords, cowards that they were but with ludicrous dignity, deferred any decision on their trampling of the legal niceties of my case until the meeting of the next Parliament. I felt my courage draining away again.

You've lost, Will. It's a hopeless cause to get them to recognise my innocence. I admire you for it. I love you for it. But you should never have taken them on. You'll lose your chance of promotion... Oh, Will! Why did you risk it?

'But you do admit to the validity of my arguments,' Windsor pressed them, unaware of my premonition of disaster.

'We think that the new Parliament will consider the force of your argument, Sir William,' Lord Henry intoned.

'Excellent. Then I will *consider* the post of Governor of Cherbourg.'

'Ah—we trust you will do more than consider, Sir William.'

'That, Earl Henry, might all depend.'

They understood each other very well.

The audience was at an end.

Windsor waved my doubts away. 'I'll get it. And you'll get your pardon.'

'They'll keep the banishment hanging over me until the day I take my last breath…'

'They won't.'

'And my manors are lost to me for ever, mostly, I suspect, in Gaunt's devious hands.'

'I'll be the new Governor of Cherbourg before the month's out. Just for once, Alice, accept that you're wrong.'

'Do you want this back?' I asked crossly, wishing he did not sound quite so pleased at the prospect, trying all the time to work the ring over my knuckle without success. 'Now that there's no further need for me to keep it! If I can get it off! You might have to take a sword blade to it.'

'Keep it!' he watched my efforts with amusement, until he closed a hand on mine to stop me. 'You played your wifely part magnificently. Besides…' he kissed my palm, and then my much-abused finger joint '…I should have given you this years ago. It's of no great value. It was my mother's. I don't think she would have approved of you, but still.'

'I'm not good enough for you, I suppose.' I scowled to hide my pleasure at the simple little ring. It was of inestimable value to me.

'No. She would have labelled you a self-serving harlot of the first order.' He saw my brows snap together. 'Not to worry. She didn't have a very high opinion of me either…'

Was he never serious? I hissed my irritation. Windsor kissed me until I stopped. And he was right, of course.

'Will you really reject the preferment?' I asked. 'If you

don't get your own way?' Who could know what this complex, enigmatic man might do?

His face was fierce with his achievement. 'They'll never
know. And neither will you.'

Epilogue

Windsor went off to Cherbourg, looking every inch the puissant Governor with his weapons polished, his horse's coat gleaming, and a new tunic and boots to mark the pre-eminence of the position. A port and fortified town, Cherbourg had been obtained by England on excellent terms from Charles of Navarre, and now promised to be a lucrative as well as prestigious post for its new official. As I watched his wagons and pack animals plod steadily into the distance, I knew that he would enjoy the challenge of bringing it firmly under English dominion, and of raising the revenues from the merchants there. In past days he had positively shimmered with energy. Life had been tedious for him since the end of his Irish sojourn. Windsor was meant for rural isolation as little as I.

As for domestic bliss together, living into our dotage with love embracing us?

Never. The love was true. My heart was healed by it. But we were both too independent to rest entirely on the other.

'Come with me!' he urged, even at the eleventh hour

when the horses were stamping and sidling at the delay. 'Pack your bags and come to Cherbourg.'

His stare urged me, his tone was imperative. His hands were strong around my wrists. By the Virgin, I was tempted. But…

'And do what? Sit in my parlour and stitch altar cloths whilst you play the great man?'

'You could entertain the merchants and their wives, seducing them to toss gold into English coffers.'

I raised my brows.

'You could buy up property in and around Cherbourg.'

I shook my head.

'You could dress in silk and emeralds and play Lady de Windsor to your heart's content.'

'I have already dressed in silk and emeralds. In another life.'

'Other women find it satisfying.' Impatient though he was, his lips, pressed hard against my temple, my mouth, almost seduced me.

'I am not other women.'

'No, you are not.' His smile was a little twisted. 'And I love you for that alone. Then stay and hold my manors for me.' He kissed me again, then scooped up Jane and held her high above his head. 'Look after your lady mother for me. Don't allow her to become too combative if her position as lady of the manor is undermined.'

Jane laughed and squirmed, uncomprehending. Joan hung back, suddenly shy, behind my skirts. Braveheart joined her.

'Farewell, my Alice.'

'Farewell, Will. Keep safe.'

And then he was gone.

* * *

I wept. In the privacy of my chamber. In the far reaches of the great barn where no one would hear me. I missed him. Oh, how I missed him. You should have gone with him, I told myself again and again as those tears blinded my eyes. This is all your fault—there would be no hindrance to you living across the Channel. My banishment might still exist before the law to be enforced at any time—the new Parliament had not met to find its way to reconsider it— but Windsor was certain of it, and as long as I lived under Windsor's roof no harm would come to me. So what if I had little to do other than order the household and ply a needle and gossip with merchants' wives? I would be with Windsor.

He has gone! He has left me! How can I live my life without him? Who will comfort me? What will I do if he forgets me...?

'What a miserable excuse for a sensible woman you are!' I snarled.

How will it be if one day I cannot remember his face, the fall of his hair?

You survived his absence well enough when he was in Ireland. Stop whining!

And so I set myself to work, a time-honoured distraction. I had made my decision. Much as I enjoyed Windsor's company, much as he had become essential to my happiness, life as the Governor's wife in Cherbourg held no attractions for me and the pull of my beleaguered property, still under confiscation, was strong. So I remained at Gaines with my two growing girls and Braveheart—grey-muzzled now but still prepared to chase the coneys from the orchard—and wrote Windsor long, informative letters. And sometimes, when he had the time, he wrote back.

And I invariably wept again.

His visits home were sweet with reconciliation. It was not so difficult a journey for him, but they were rarely frequent enough for me.

'Alice!' Exuberant as ever. 'Come and welcome your lord and master.'

'I see no lord and master.' I looked askance at him, much as I did when we had first met, this time from my superior position on horseback. My heart was thudding so hard I could have fallen at his feet. 'Do I know you?'

His growl of laughter stirred my belly to hot desire.

I had ridden home to Gaines from settling a dispute boundary between two of Windsor's recalcitrant tenants to find the usual chaos of arrival. There in the midst of all, directing horses and baggage, was Windsor, now striding towards me. His face was alight with the same saturnine smile that had piqued my curiosity about this man so long ago at Edward's court.

'I hear you've been wielding a heavy stick for me against my tenants.' He held out his arms as I slid down from my horse. 'My love, my dear, my impossibly belligerent one.'

Not caring that we had an interested audience, I simply walked into his embrace. He had returned. His clasp was all-encompassing, his lips warm and gratifyingly familiar on mine. All the nagging, futile emptiness in my chest dissolved as his arms tightened around me. As if he would never let me go, even though I knew he would when the time came.

'How long, Will?' The only thing that mattered. I clung to him, my forehead pressed hard against his shoulder, mindless in my pleasure.

'I can manage a few weeks at least. Cherbourg is well in hand.' He released me to search in one of his saddle bags. 'First things first. I have this for you.'

I found I was smiling foolishly. It was good to see him. I did not greatly care what the gift was—a jewel, a pair of gloves, presumably something small enough to be packed into so confined a space. But it was neither. With a flourish, Windsor produced a letter, presenting it to me with a courtly bow.

'This is yours, Lady de Windsor. A meagre piece of parchment, and much travelled—but of immeasurable value.'

He was sombre as I opened the sheet, smoothing out the creases. I glanced up at his stern face, then back down to the directive with its heraldic emblem and red seal.

'They've done it, Will!' I gasped. 'They've done it at last!'

There it was: beyond all my hopes. My banishment formally, officially, legally, revoked. A pardon granted to me for my breaking of Parliament's command—the crime that I had never committed.

'Did you doubt it?' Windsor asked, his smile like a shaft of sunlight to pierce my heart.

'Yes. Oh, yes. I doubted it,' I replied, light-headed with the joy of it.

'I didn't,' he responded with the arrogance I had come to accept. 'I'm too valuable to antagonise. They knew I could always rescind my decision, leaving them in the lurch to find a new Governor. Now, don't weep over it!' He took the parchment from me, sliding it into his belt. 'It's far too valuable to be blurred by unnecessary tears! You lost Gaunt's original letter—we'll not lose this one.'

I covered my face with my hands, my relief beyond

words, and the tears continued to flow. Windsor took my wrists in a gentle grip and drew my hands down.

'Does that give your restless soul some contentment?'

'Some.' I managed a little laugh. 'My thanks, Will.'

'And that's not all.' He paused until he had my attention. 'You'll get your property back, legally acknowledged as yours.'

'All of it?' Now, that I could not believe.

He shook his head. 'Not the manors in Edward's gift. They'll not do that. But all the lands legally purchased by you and Greseley—they will be restored.'

'That's enough.' I could barely utter the words. 'It's wonderful! I'll have Pallenswick again...'

'But they are not quite yours...' He was leading me into the house.

I stopped.

'What?'

'They will be restored to *me*—as your husband.' His shout of laughter at my shocked expression disturbed the doves roosting on the roof of the stables, sending them up into a white-winged cloud.

'God damn them to hell! I don't agree with that...'

'Did I think you would?'

'But I—'

'It's the best you can get, Alice. You know how the law stands. Your possessions are mine. But I'm a very generous husband.' He was solemn again, holding my hands strongly, palm to palm with his, to prevent my possible retaliation. He still read the fire in my eye. 'I make you free of your manors. And the moneys from them is yours to use for yourself and your children.'

'How generous!'

'Exceedingly! Does it not satisfy you, Alice?'

I sighed a little as I allowed my thoughts to settle. I had never thought it to be in my heart and mind, in my very soul, to be satisfied. It was not in my nature. Had I not always been restless, striving for the unreachable, driven to make a life that was safe and secure, for my children, for me? I had never accepted my place in life. Being Philippa's damsel had never been enough and my need for land had become, some would say, an obsession. I would say it was fighting for my survival in a world that could condemn and destroy just as swiftly as it could build up and aggrandise. I had experienced both highs and the lows and, looking back, I regretted none of it.

Narrowing my eyes against the sun, I took in the scope of my home. It was not the royal court but its walls were substantial and its land productive. I had had more than my entitlement, had I not? I had experienced the ultimate power. Now, here before me, was bitter reality, and I must be honest enough to acknowledge that I would never wield power again. I shrugged my acceptance, even of the fact that my land now existed only in my husband's name. A woman was dependent on a man however much she might like to deny it, and if I would choose to be dependent on any man, it would be William de Windsor.

There he stood, the sun silvering his hair at the temples, the courtyard brimful of his presence, the haunting smile that remained a constant companion even in his absence. Who'd have thought that the infamous Windsor would have a haunting smile? But he did for me. Suddenly all my old yearning for what could never be mine was stripped away. At least for that day.

'Well?' he asked with a gesture towards the sun-warmed

walls. 'I could do no more for you than this, ungrateful hussy.'

'I know. And I am very grateful,' I replied. I took his arm and we stepped together inside our home. I smiled. 'I am satisfied.'

* * * * *

ACKNOWLEDGEMENTS

All my thanks:

To my agent Jane Judd who appreciated the
possibility of Alice Perrers as an unconventional
heroine. Her advice and support, as always,
are beyond price.

To Jenny Hutton and the MIRA team at Paradise Road.
Their guidance and commitment were
invaluable in enabling Alice Perrers to
emerge from infamy.

To Helen Bowden and all at Orphans Press who come to my
rescue and continue to create
masterpieces out of my genealogy and maps.

To Phia McBarnet who patiently introduced me
to the benefits of social media and set my foot
on the steep learning curve.

AUTHOR NOTE

Alice Perrers is a shadowy character whose origins and life are difficult to penetrate. Despite recent research her ancestry is uncertain and there is no record of her birth. If she knew her family, she never made claims on them or promoted them when she came to power. We know nothing of her education except that she was clearly able to read and write and deal with numbers, quite an achievement for a girl of no apparent social standing. It seems that she was married briefly to Janyn Perrers, a Lombardy money-lender living in London, and it was during this period that she obtained her first piece of property.

From these obscure origins Alice rose to be one of Queen Philippa's damsels and ultimately the King's mistress in Edward III's later years. How she achieved such pre-eminence has also gone unrecorded. All we know is that Alice ruled the royal roost and was generally detested for doing so. We know that her downfall was plotted by the Good Parliament but she survived it and remained at Court until Edward's death in 1377. And then the vindictive courtiers sharpened their knives…

I have made use of the outline of Alice's life as far as we know it. As for what we do not know, I have used some 'historical imagination' and make no excuses for doing so. Alice was accused by contemporaries of being a greedy, rapacious and wanton woman, wheeling and dealing to achieve a fortune in land and jewels for herself. If even half of this is true, she must have been a remarkable woman.

INSPIRATION

I was inspired to write the story of Alice Perrers because, despite her rise to complete pre-eminence in the court of Edward III, we know so little about her. And what history has recorded of her—from the mouths of clerics and courtiers—has been a tale of notoriety. She is definitely Alice the Bad.

So how did she achieve her pre-eminence? How did she come to the attention of the Queen to become her damsel and to the notice of the King to become his mistress? How did she come to Court at all if she was, as rumour suggested, the illegitimate abandoned child of a common labourer and a tavern whore? This is the role of the historical novelist, to place Alice in her historical period and fill in the gaps in a seemly fashion.

It is noticeable that the accusations laid against Alice came from men—powerful men in church and state who resented the power that Alice was able to wield. Not once do we hear Alice's voice raised in her own defence. I thought that she deserved to have her voice restored to her. She is not a conventional heroine, but I believe there is more to her than Alice the grasping, greedy royal mistress. Perhaps Alice the quintessential business- woman is more apt, for she showed a remarkable ability to acquire land and administer it. Much of what she achieved would, if she had been a man, have been forgiven, or at least tolerated: royal favourites were obviously in receipt of titles and wealth. Because Alice stepped be-yond what was acceptable for a woman of the fourteenth century she became an object of infamy.

In the light of this I decided that Alice deserved a re-evaluation. She was a smart woman and quite definitely a survivor. I hope I have done her justice in writing *The King's Concubine*, restoring Alice to her place in history and allowing us to see the woman behind the façade.

AND ALICE AT THE END OF HER DAYS...

The recording of events in Alice's life is more secure in her later years.

In 1381, after the end of *The King's Concubine*, her husband William de Windsor was recalled from his position as Governor of Cherbourg and lived with Alice at Upminster, was created a baron and so sat in the House of Lords from 1381 to 1384. He died at Greyrigg in Westmoreland, his family home, in September 1394, leaving his land, interestingly, to his three sisters, not to Alice.

Much litigation followed, of course. Alice, in typical combative mood, was determined to get what she considered to be hers, but without success. She lived on, alone, at Upminster and died there in the summer of 1400, leaving her lands and houses to her two daughters, as well as some bequests to the church, the poor and the upkeep of local roads.

She was buried in the church in Upminster.

As for Alice's children:

John was recognised as Edward's son and knighted by the King. There is some debate over Jane, Joan and Nicholas. Even their actual birth dates are uncertain. I considered it more likely that they were all Edward's children rather than Windsor's, given their ages and since Windsor never claimed them as his and left no property to them. Nor is there evidence that Alice had an intimate relationship with any other man. None of her children were fathered by Janyn Perrers.

We know a little of their history.

John de Southeray was born in 1364. He was knighted in April 1377 and died some time after 1383. He married Matilda Percy, a daughter of the powerful Percy family in the north.

Nicholas Lytlington died in 1386. He was Abbot of Westminster Abbey and made a name for himself collecting books and manuscripts.

Joan married Robert Skerne. Jane married Richard Northland. Both of them disappeared into respectability. Nothing like their infamous mother.

FURTHER READING ABOUT ALICE PERRERS...

There is astonishingly little, simply because the evidence for her life is lacking.

Lady of the Sun: the Life and Times of Alice Perrers by F. George Kay is a historical biography, but deals more with 'the times' than with Alice herself.

Recent historical novels about Alice Perrers:

The King's Mistress by Emma Campion.
The People's Queen by Vanora Bennett

Loved this book?

Visit Anne O'Brien's fantastic website
at **www.anneobrienbooks.com** for
information about Anne, her latest books,
news, interviews, offers, competitions,
reading group extras and much more…

Follow Anne on Twitter **@anne_obrien**

www.anneobrienbooks.com

London, 1938.
Meet Daisy Driscoll, the
working class orphan whose
luck may be about to change…

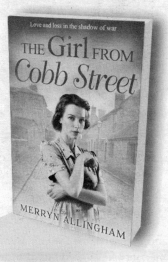

The war has just begun when Daisy meets and falls
madly in love with Gerald Mortimer. But when
Gerald returns to serve in India as a cavalry subaltern,
Daisy is left alone once more and, unbeknownst
to Gerald, pregnant with his child…

Wed by duty, Daisy struggles to adjust to life with her
new husband and soon discovers that Gerald is
in debt, and tragedy is about to strike…

www.mirabooks.co.uk

COMING SOON

**A dramatic new tale of desire and devotion
in book three of the new Cynster trilogy by**

Stephanie
LAURENS

A Match For Marcus Cynster

Marcus Cynster is waiting for Fate to come
calling. He knows his destiny lies near his home
in Scotland, but what will it be? Who is his fated
bride? One fact seems certain: his future won't lie
with Niniver Carrick, a young lady who attracts
him mightily and whom he feels compelled
to protect—even from himself.

www.mirabooks.co.uk

A freak accident reveals a secret that 13-year-old Ava has been terrified to share

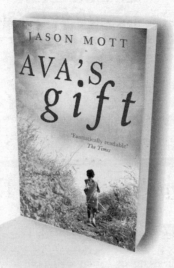

Ava has a unique gift: she can heal others of their physical ailments. Now the whole world knows and people from all over the globe want to glimpse the wonder of a miracle.

But Ava's ability comes at a cost and, as she grows weaker with each healing, she finds herself having to decide just how much she's willing to sacrifice in order to save the ones she loves most.

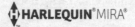

DI Richard Poole returns in this brand-new murder mystery from the creator of BBC One series *Death in Paradise*

Aslan Kennedy has an idyllic life: leader of a spiritual retreat for wealthy holidaymakers on one of the Caribbean's most unspoilt islands, Saint-Marie.

Until he's murdered, that is.

While the case appears to be open and shut, Detective Inspector Richard Poole is convinced that the evidence he's presented with doesn't quite stack up. In fact, he's certain that the person who's just confessed to the murder is the one person who couldn't have done it…

www.mirabooks.co.uk